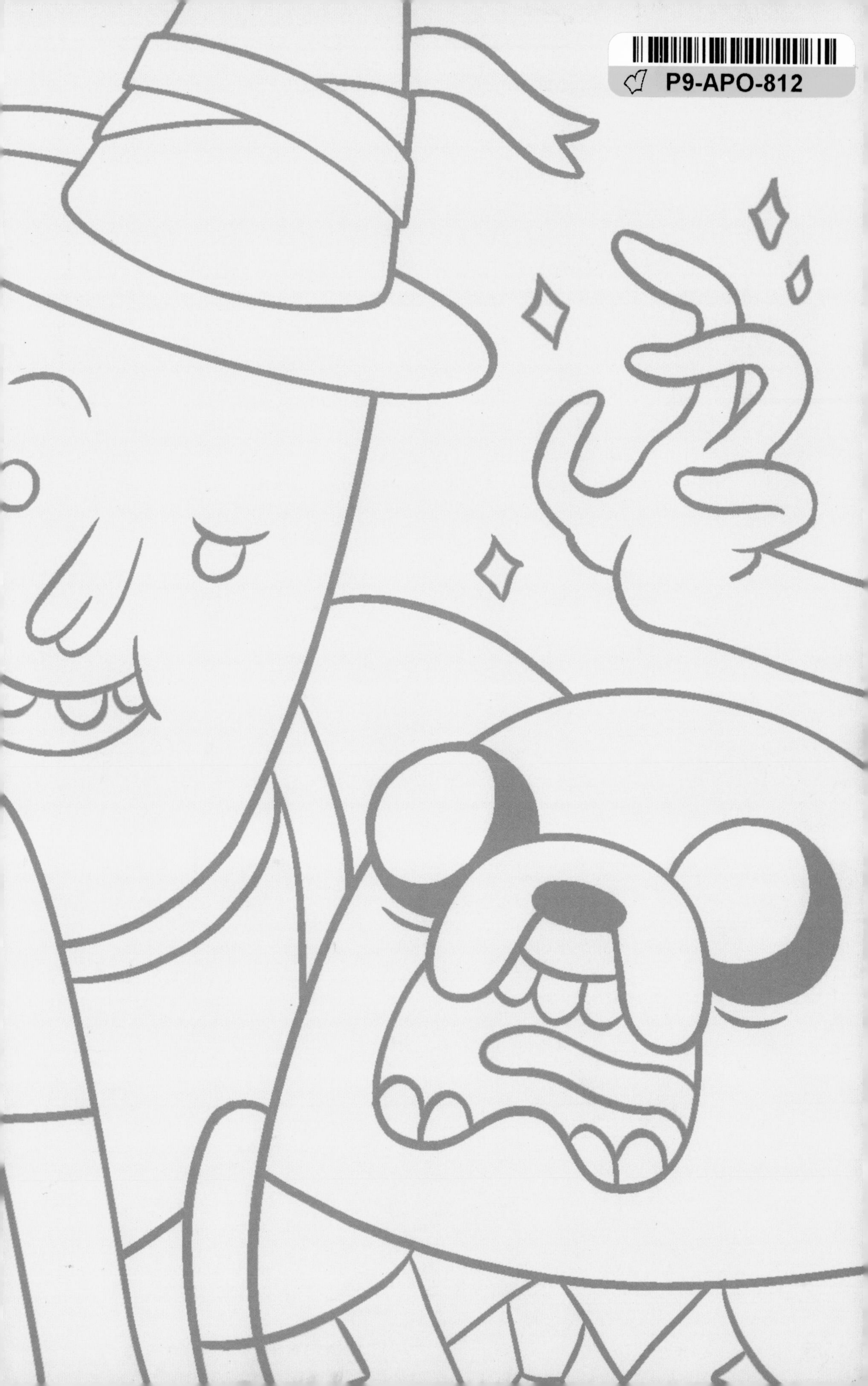

Published by
KaBOOM!

Ross Richie CEO & Founder
Matt Gagnon Editor-In-Chief
Filip Sablik President of Publishing & Marketing
Stephen Christy President of Development
Lance Kreiter VP of Licensing & Merchandising
Phil Barbaro VP of Finance
Arune Singh VP of Marketing
Bryce Carlson Managing Editor
Mel Caylo Marketing Manager
Scott Newman Production Design Manager
Kate Henning Operations Manager
Sierra Hahn Senior Editor
Dafna Pleban Editor, Talent Development
Shannon Watters Editor
Eric Harburn Editor
Whitney Leopard Editor
Jasmine Amiri Editor
Chris Rosa Associate Editor
Alex Galer Associate Editor
Cameron Chittock Associate Editor
Matthew Levine Assistant Editor
Sophie Philips-Roberts Assistant Editor
Jillian Crab Production Designer
Michelle Ankley Production Designer
Kara Leopard Production Designer
Grace Park Production Design Assistant
Elizabeth Loughridge Accounting Coordinator
Stephanie Hocutt Social Media Coordinator
José Meza Event Coordinator
James Arriola Mailroom Assistant
Holly Aitchison Operations Assistant
Megan Christopher Operations Assistant
Morgan Perry Direct Market Representative

ADVENTURE TIME™

MATHEMATICAL EDITION
Volume Nine

kaboom!™
CARTOON NETWORK. FREDERATOR

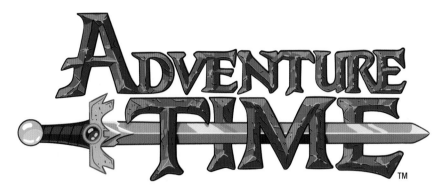

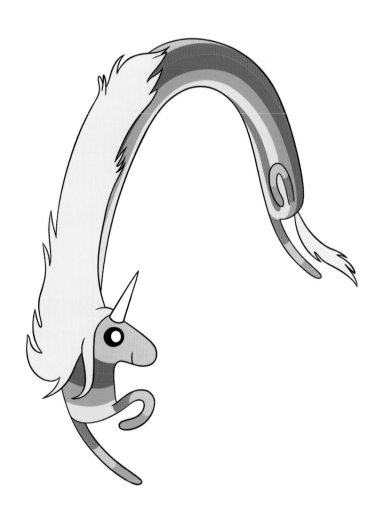

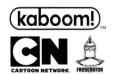

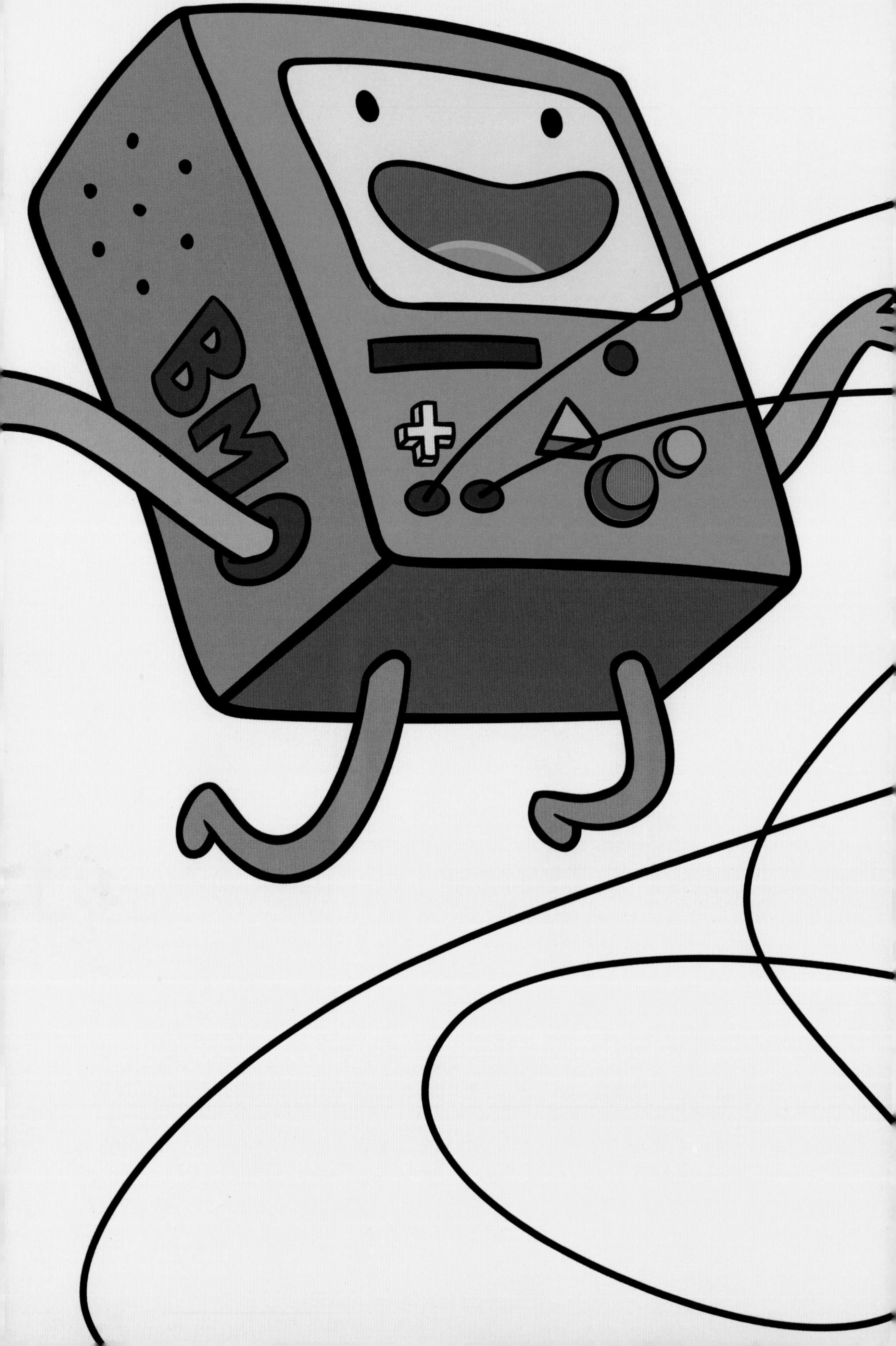
BMO

CREATED BY
Pendleton Ward

WRITTEN BY
Christopher Hastings

CHAPTERS ONE THROUGH THREE & CHAPTER FIVE ILLUSTRATED BY
Zachary Sterling
WITH INKS BY PHIL MURPHY ON CHAPTERS THREE & FIVE

CHAPTER FOUR ILLUSTRATED BY
Phil Murphy

COLORS BY
Maarta Laiho

CHAPTERS ONE & CHAPTER THREE THROUGH FIVE LETTERS BY
Steve Wands

CHAPTER TWO LETTERS BY
Warren Montgomery

COLLECTION AND COVER DESIGN
Chelsea Roberts
Scott Newman

ASSOCIATE EDITOR
Alex Galer

EDITOR
Whitney Leopard

With Special Thanks to Marisa Marionakis, Janet No, Curtis Lelash, Conrad Montgomery, Meghan Bradley, Kelly Crews, Scott Malchus, Adam Muto and the wonderful folks at Cartoon Network.

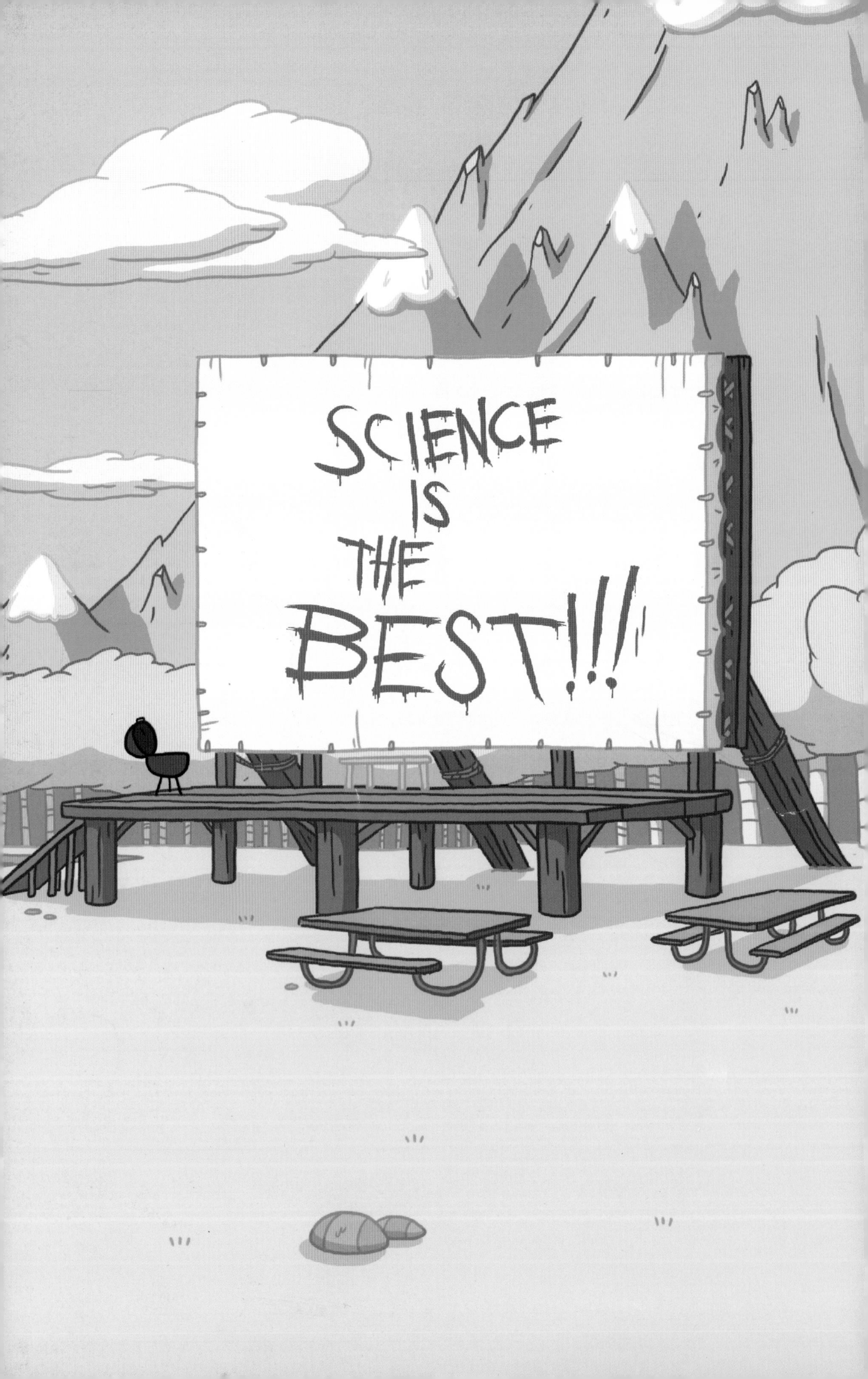
SCIENCE
IS
THE
BEST!!!

CHAPTER ONE

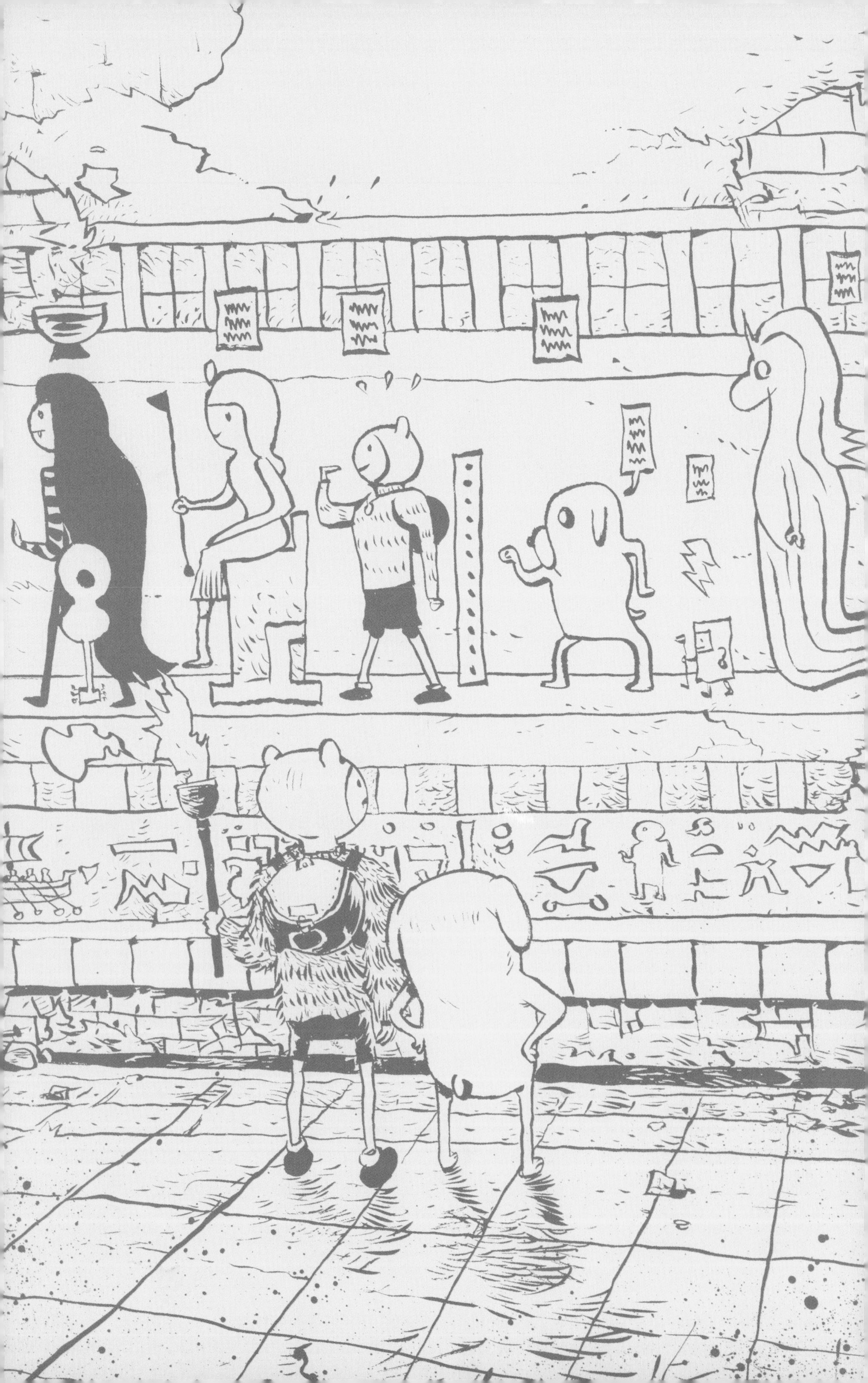

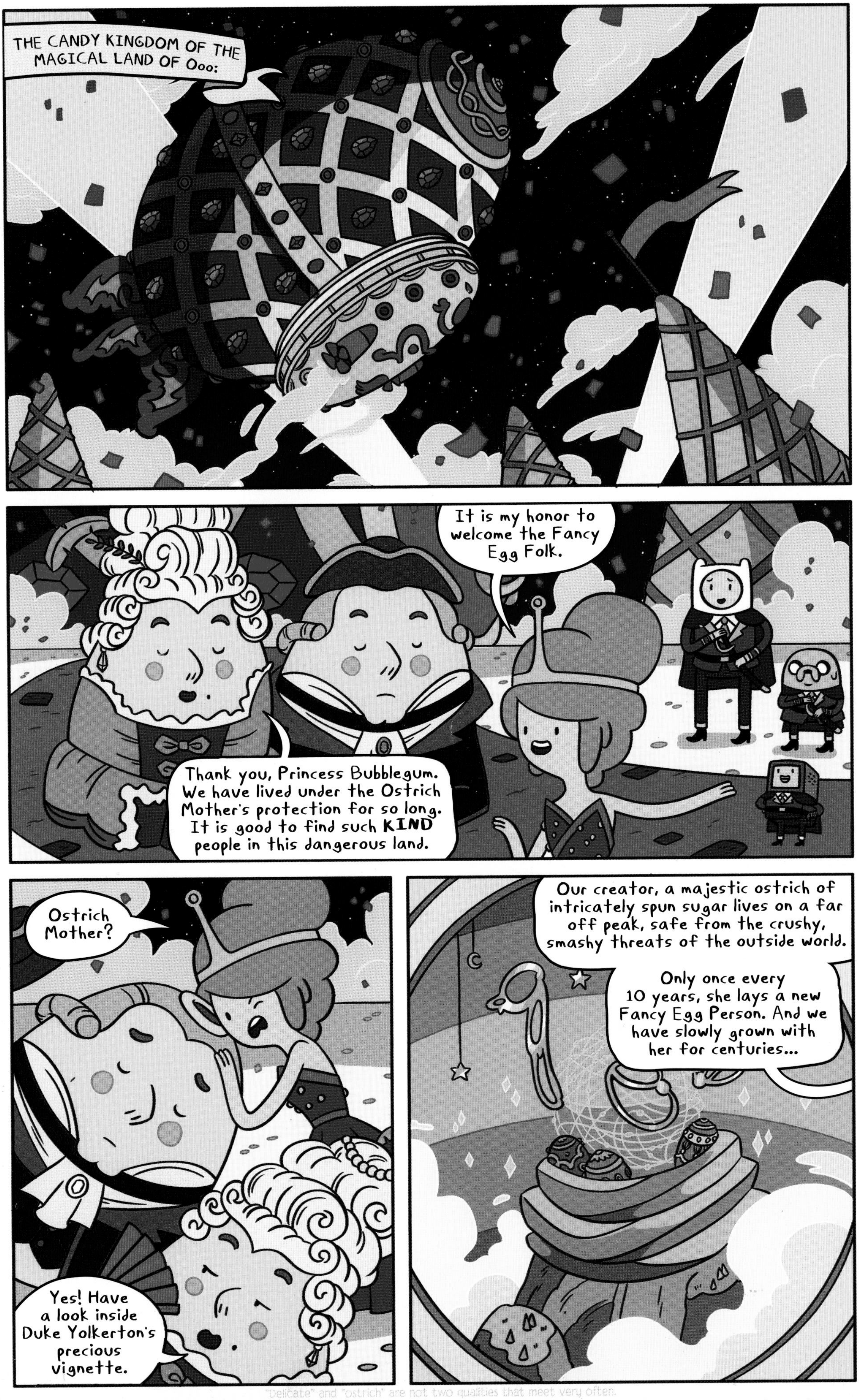
THE CANDY KINGDOM OF THE MAGICAL LAND OF Ooo:
It is my honor to welcome the Fancy Egg Folk.
Thank you, Princess Bubblegum. We have lived under the Ostrich Mother's protection for so long. It is good to find such KIND people in this dangerous land.
Ostrich Mother?
Yes! Have a look inside Duke Yolkerton's precious vignette.
Our creator, a majestic ostrich of intricately spun sugar lives on a far off peak, safe from the crushy, smashy threats of the outside world.
Only once every 10 years, she lays a new Fancy Egg Person. And we have slowly grown with her for centuries...

"Delicate" and "ostrich" are not two qualities that meet very often.

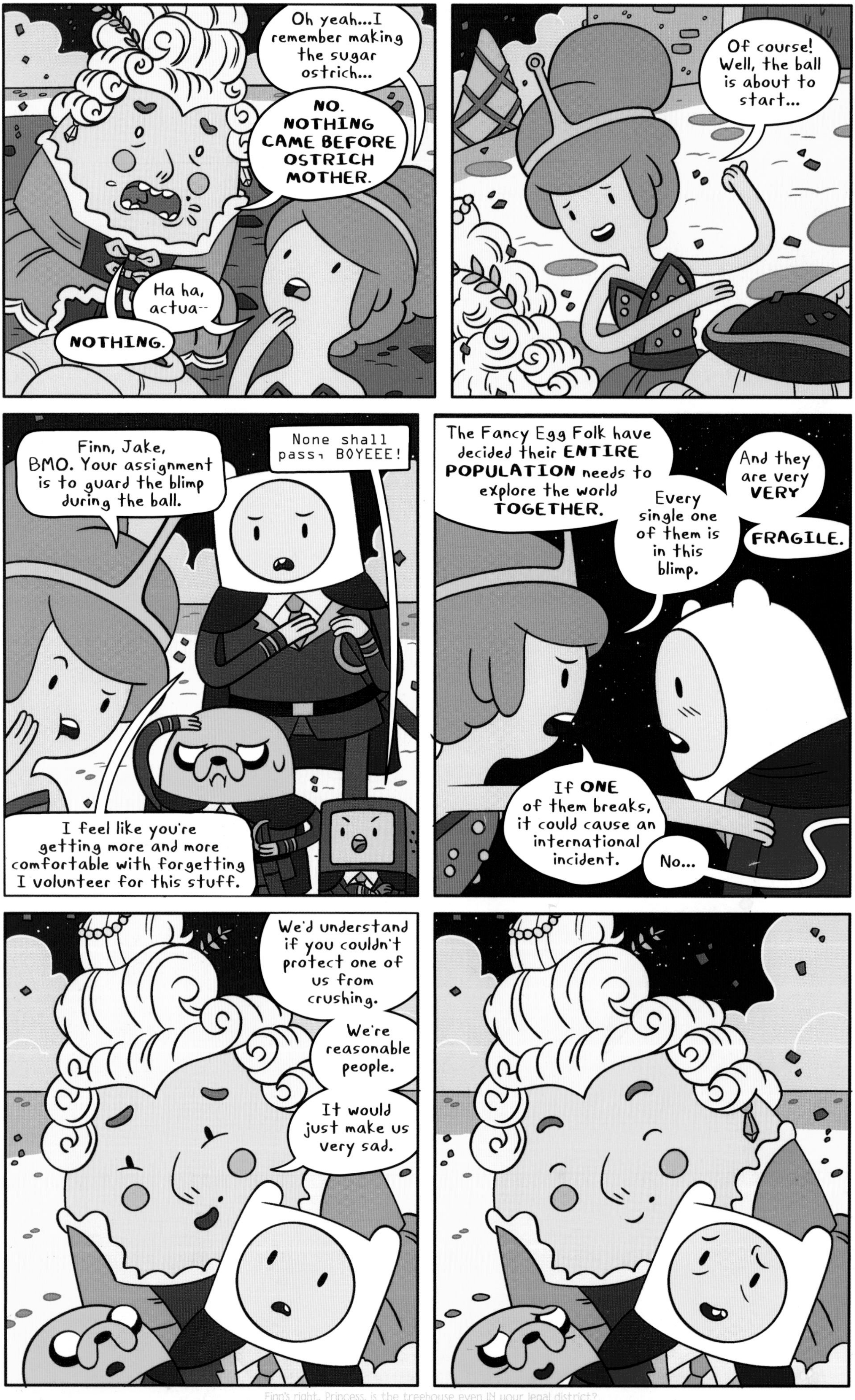
Oh yeah...I remember making the sugar ostrich...
NO. NOTHING CAME BEFORE OSTRICH MOTHER.
Ha ha, actua--
NOTHING.
Of course! Well, the ball is about to start...
Finn, Jake, BMO. Your assignment is to guard the blimp during the ball.
None shall pass, BOYEEE!
I feel like you're getting more and more comfortable with forgetting I volunteer for this stuff.
The Fancy Egg Folk have decided their ENTIRE POPULATION needs to explore the world TOGETHER.
Every single one of them is in this blimp.
And they are very VERY
FRAGILE.
If ONE of them breaks, it could cause an international incident.
No...
We'd understand if you couldn't protect one of us from crushing.
We're reasonable people.
It would just make us very sad.

Finn's right. Princess, is the treehouse even IN your legal district?

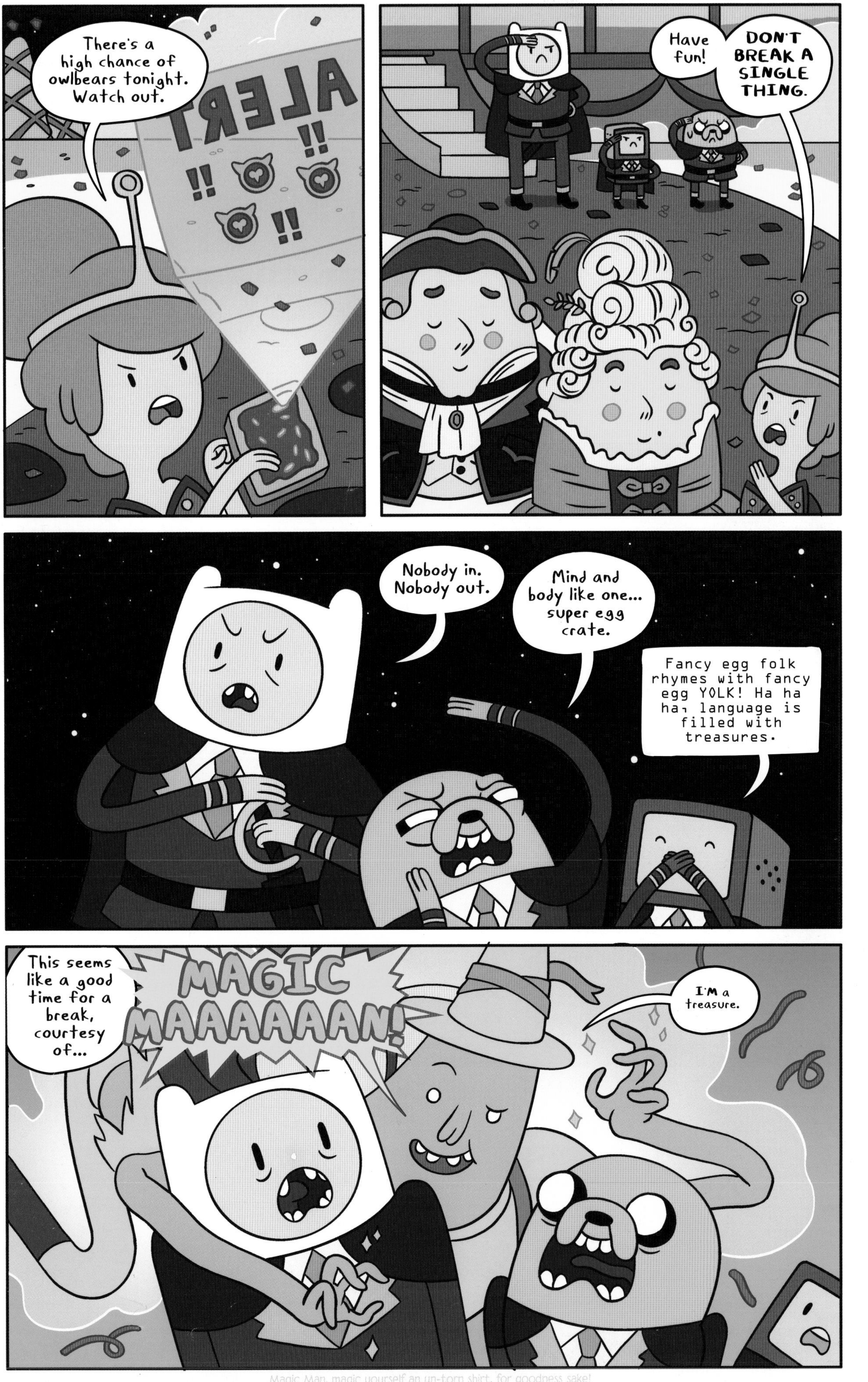
There's a high chance of owlbears tonight. Watch out.
ALERT
Have fun!
DON'T BREAK A SINGLE THING.
Nobody in. Nobody out.
Mind and body like one... super egg crate.
Fancy egg folk rhymes with fancy egg YOLK! Ha ha ha, language is filled with treasures.
This seems like a good time for a break, courtesy of...
MAGIC MAAAAAAN!
I'M a treasure.

Magic Man, magic yourself an un-torn shirt, for goodness sake!

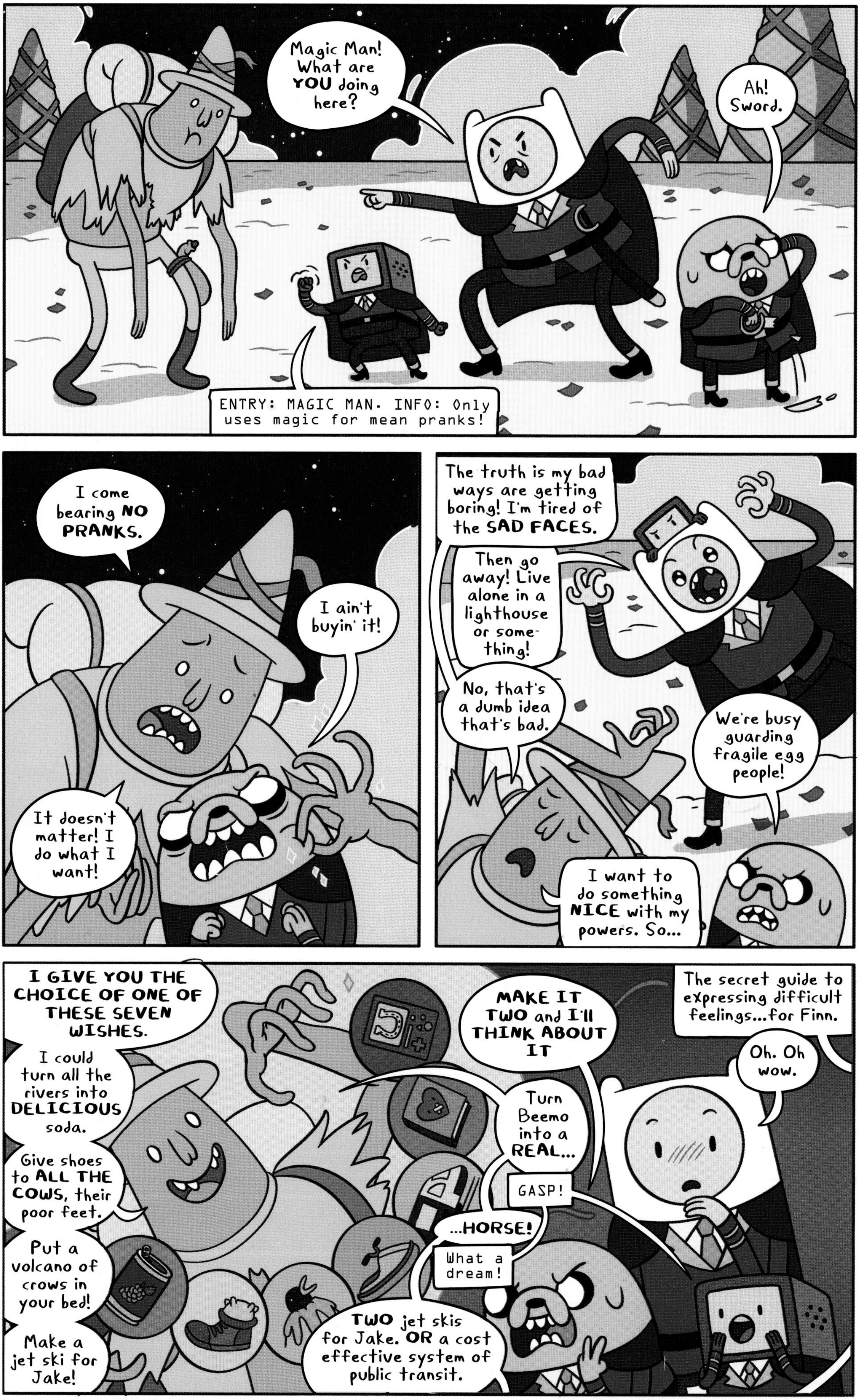
Magic Man! What are YOU doing here?
Ah! Sword.
ENTRY: MAGIC MAN. INFO: Only uses magic for mean pranks!
I come bearing NO PRANKS.
I ain't buyin' it!
It doesn't matter! I do what I want!
The truth is my bad ways are getting boring! I'm tired of the SAD FACES.
Then go away! Live alone in a lighthouse or some-thing!
No, that's a dumb idea that's bad.
We're busy guarding fragile egg people!
I want to do something NICE with my powers. So...
I GIVE YOU THE CHOICE OF ONE OF THESE SEVEN WISHES.
I could turn all the rivers into DELICIOUS soda.
Give shoes to ALL THE COWS, their poor feet.
Put a volcano of crows in your bed!
Make a jet ski for Jake!
MAKE IT TWO and I'll THINK ABOUT IT
Turn Beemo into a REAL...
GASP!
...HORSE!
What a dream!
TWO jet skis for Jake. OR a cost effective system of public transit.
The secret guide to expressing difficult feelings...for Finn.
Oh. Oh wow.

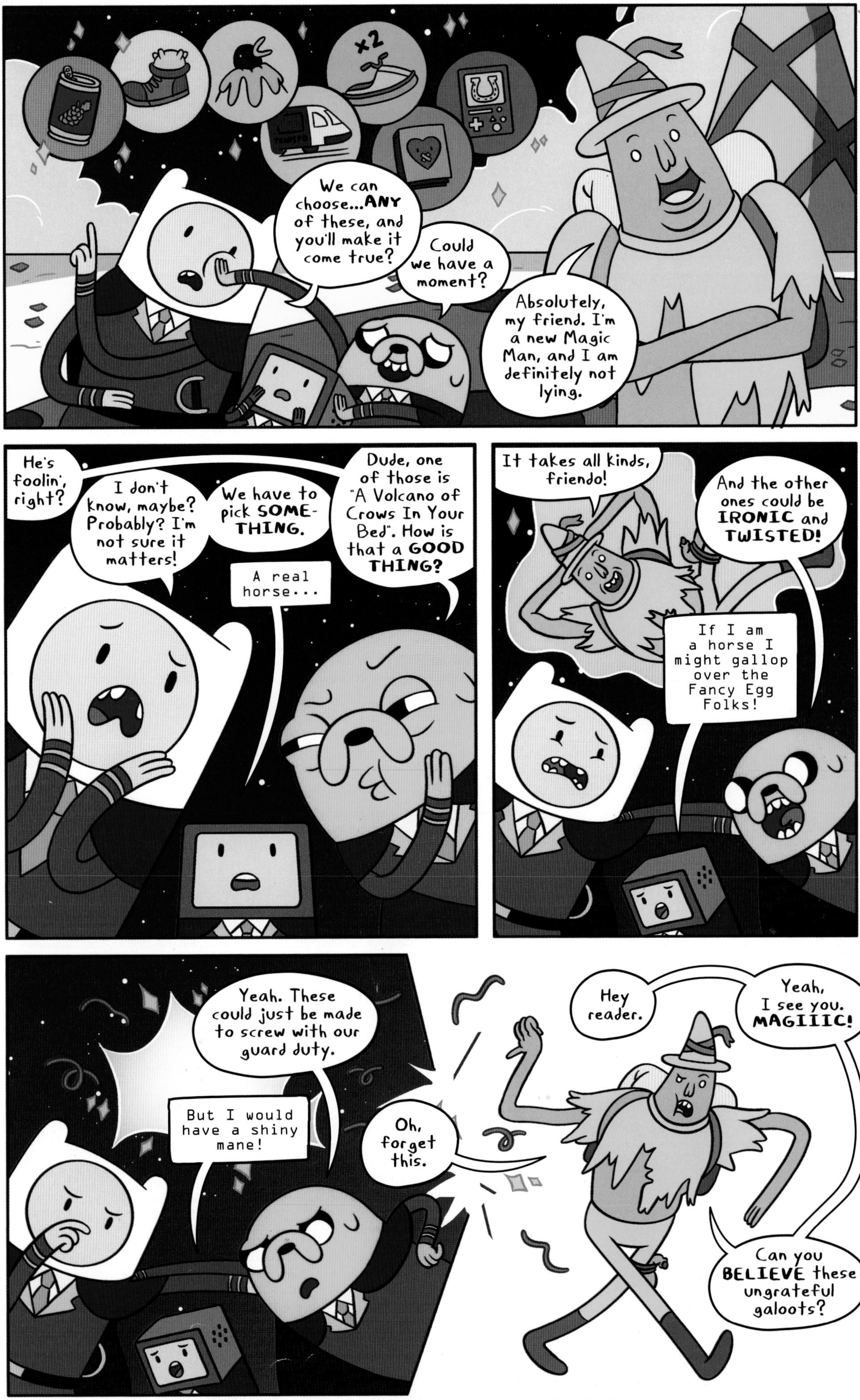

We can choose...ANY of these, and you'll make it come true?
Could we have a moment?
Absolutely, my friend. I'm a new Magic Man, and I am definitely not lying.
He's foolin', right?
I don't know, maybe? Probably? I'm not sure it matters!
We have to pick SOME-THING.
Dude, one of those is "A Volcano of Crows In Your Bed". How is that a GOOD THING?
A real horse...
It takes all kinds, friendo!
And the other ones could be IRONIC and TWISTED!
If I am a horse I might gallop over the Fancy Egg Folks!
Yeah. These could just be made to screw with our guard duty.
But I would have a shiny mane!
Oh, forget this.
Hey reader.
Yeah, I see you. MAGIIIC!
Can you BELIEVE these ungrateful galoots?

HEY! I'M the only one allowed to direct the audience around here!

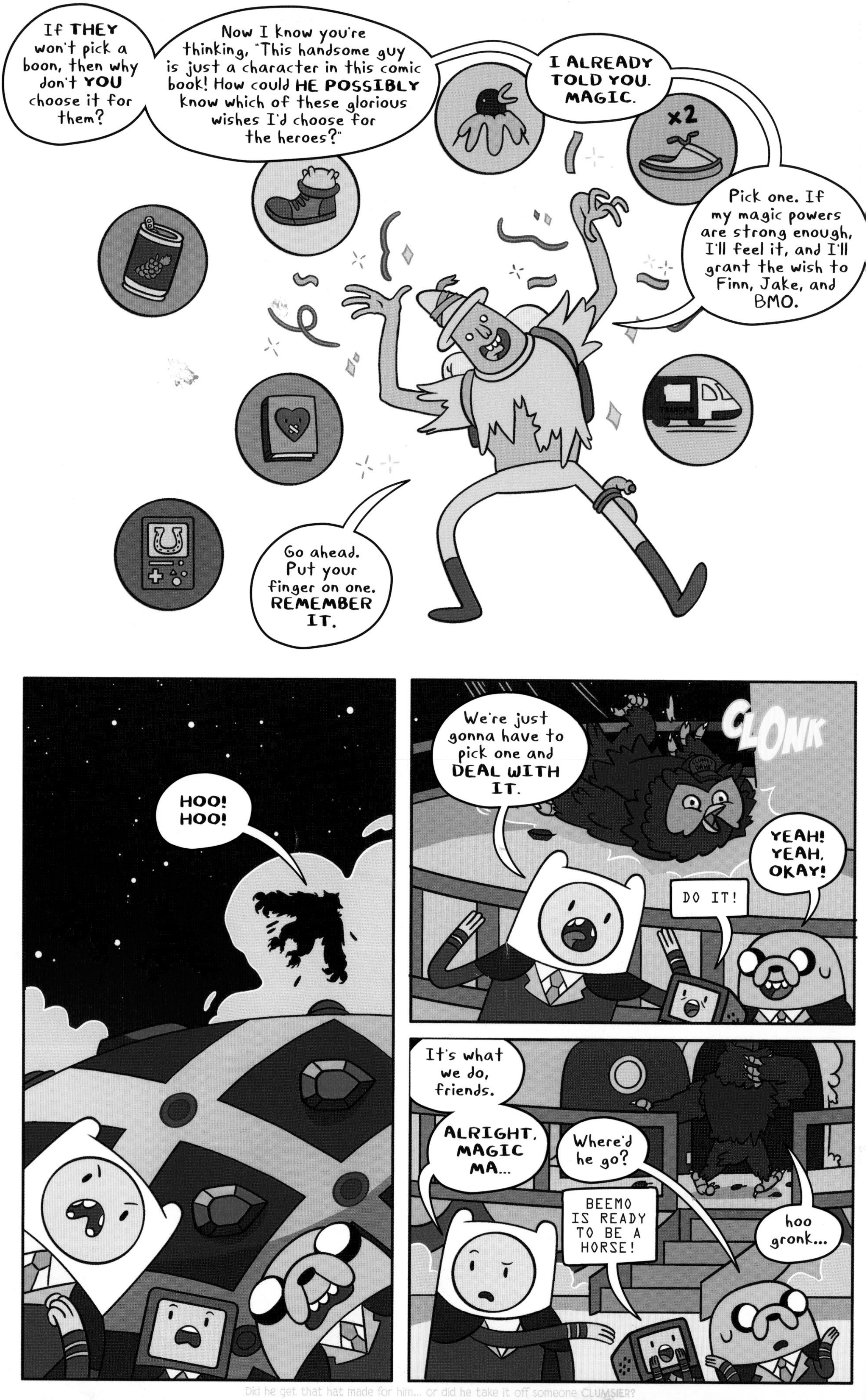

If THEY won't pick a boon, then why don't YOU choose it for them?
Now I know you're thinking, "This handsome guy is just a character in this comic book! How could HE POSSIBLY know which of these glorious wishes I'd choose for the heroes?"
I ALREADY TOLD YOU. MAGIC.
x2
Pick one. If my magic powers are strong enough, I'll feel it, and I'll grant the wish to Finn, Jake, and BMO.
TRANSPO
Go ahead. Put your finger on one. REMEMBER IT.
HOO! HOO!
We're just gonna have to pick one and DEAL WITH IT.
CLONK
CLUMSY DAVE
YEAH! YEAH, OKAY!
DO IT!
It's what we do, friends.
ALRIGHT, MAGIC MA...
Where'd he go?
BEEMO IS READY TO BE A HORSE!
hoo gronk...

Did he get that hat made for him... or did he take it off someone CLUMSIER?

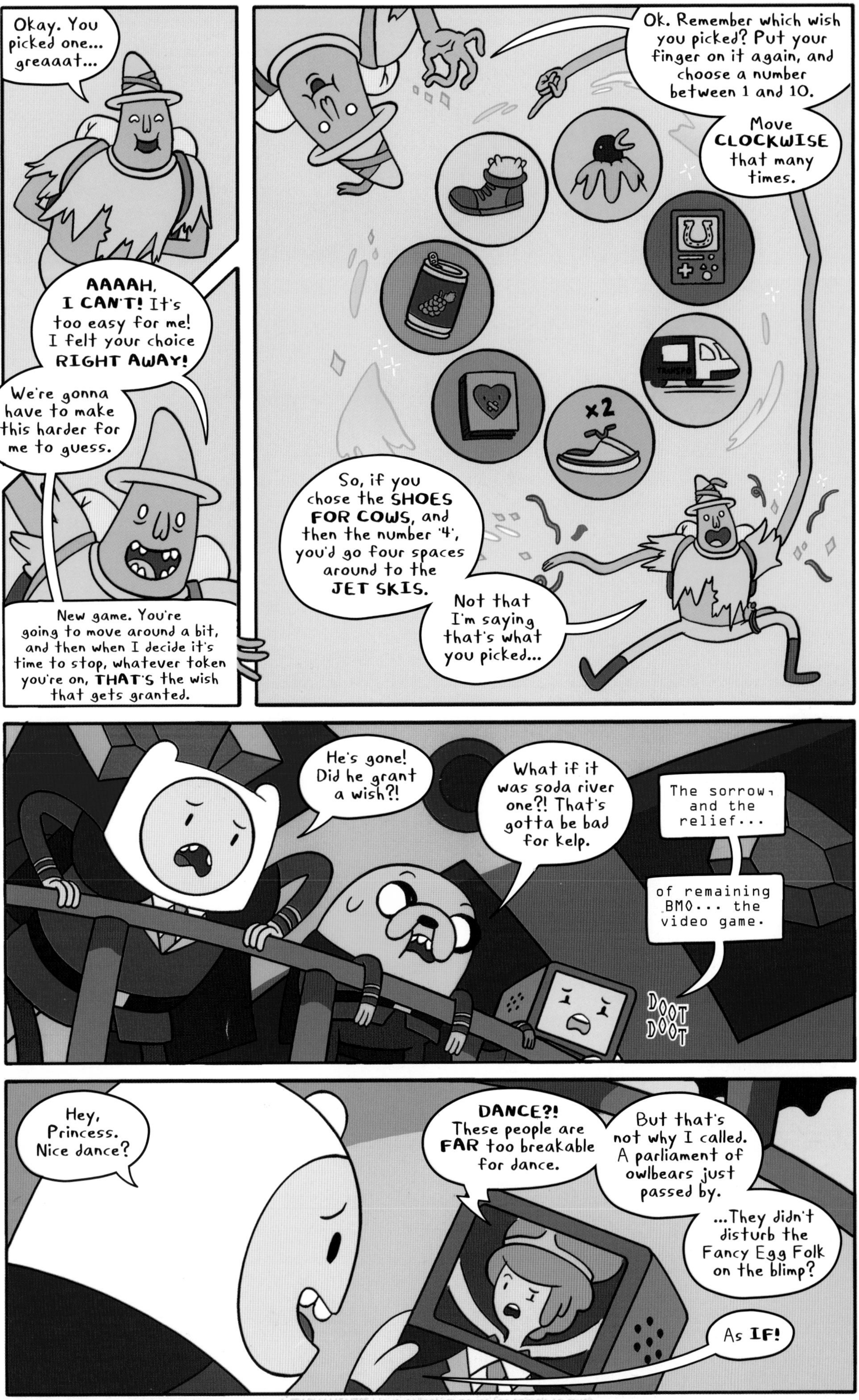
Okay. You picked one... greaaat...
Ok. Remember which wish you picked? Put your finger on it again, and choose a number between 1 and 10.
Move CLOCKWISE that many times.
AAAAH, I CAN'T! It's too easy for me! I felt your choice RIGHT AWAY!
We're gonna have to make this harder for me to guess.
New game. You're going to move around a bit, and then when I decide it's time to stop, whatever token you're on, THAT'S the wish that gets granted.
x2
So, if you chose the SHOES FOR COWS, and then the number '4', you'd go four spaces around to the JET SKIS.
Not that I'm saying that's what you picked...
He's gone! Did he grant a wish?!
What if it was soda river one?! That's gotta be bad for kelp.
The sorrow, and the relief...
of remaining BMO... the video game.
DOOT DOOT
Hey, Princess. Nice dance?
DANCE?! These people are FAR too breakable for dance.
But that's not why I called. A parliament of owlbears just passed by.
...They didn't disturb the Fancy Egg Folk on the blimp?
As IF!

A "PARLIAMENT?" I love collective nouns for animals so much.

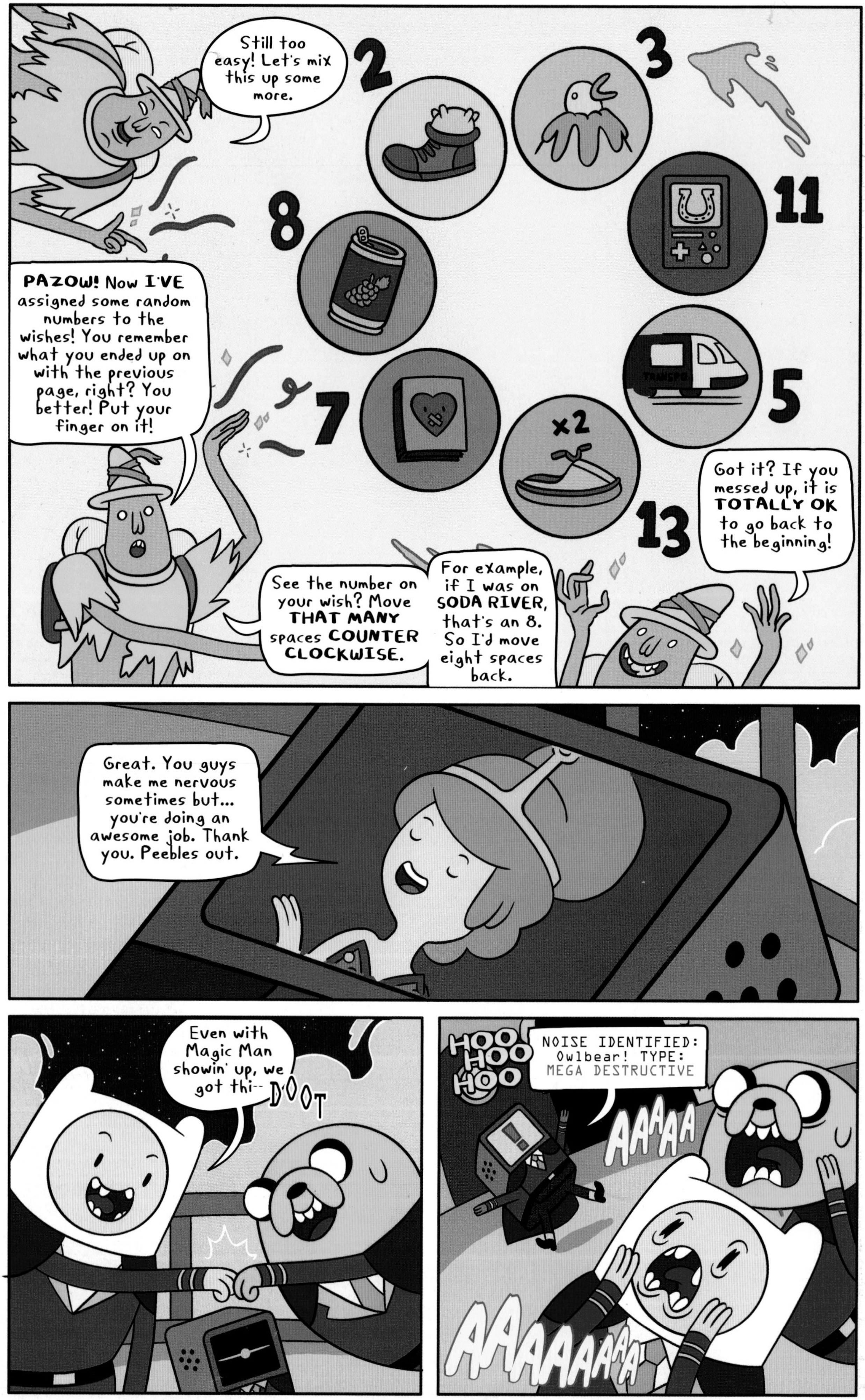

Still too easy! Let's mix this up some more.
2
3
11
8
PAZOW! Now I'VE assigned some random numbers to the wishes! You remember what you ended up on with the previous page, right? You better! Put your finger on it!
7
5
×2
13
Got it? If you messed up, it is TOTALLY OK to go back to the beginning!
See the number on your wish? Move THAT MANY spaces COUNTER CLOCKWISE.
For example, if I was on SODA RIVER, that's an 8. So I'd move eight spaces back.
Great. You guys make me nervous sometimes but... you're doing an awesome job. Thank you. Peebles out.
Even with Magic Man showin' up, we got thi--
DOOT
HOO HOO HOO
NOISE IDENTIFIED: Owlbear! TYPE: MEGA DESTRUCTIVE
AAAAA
AAAAAAAAA

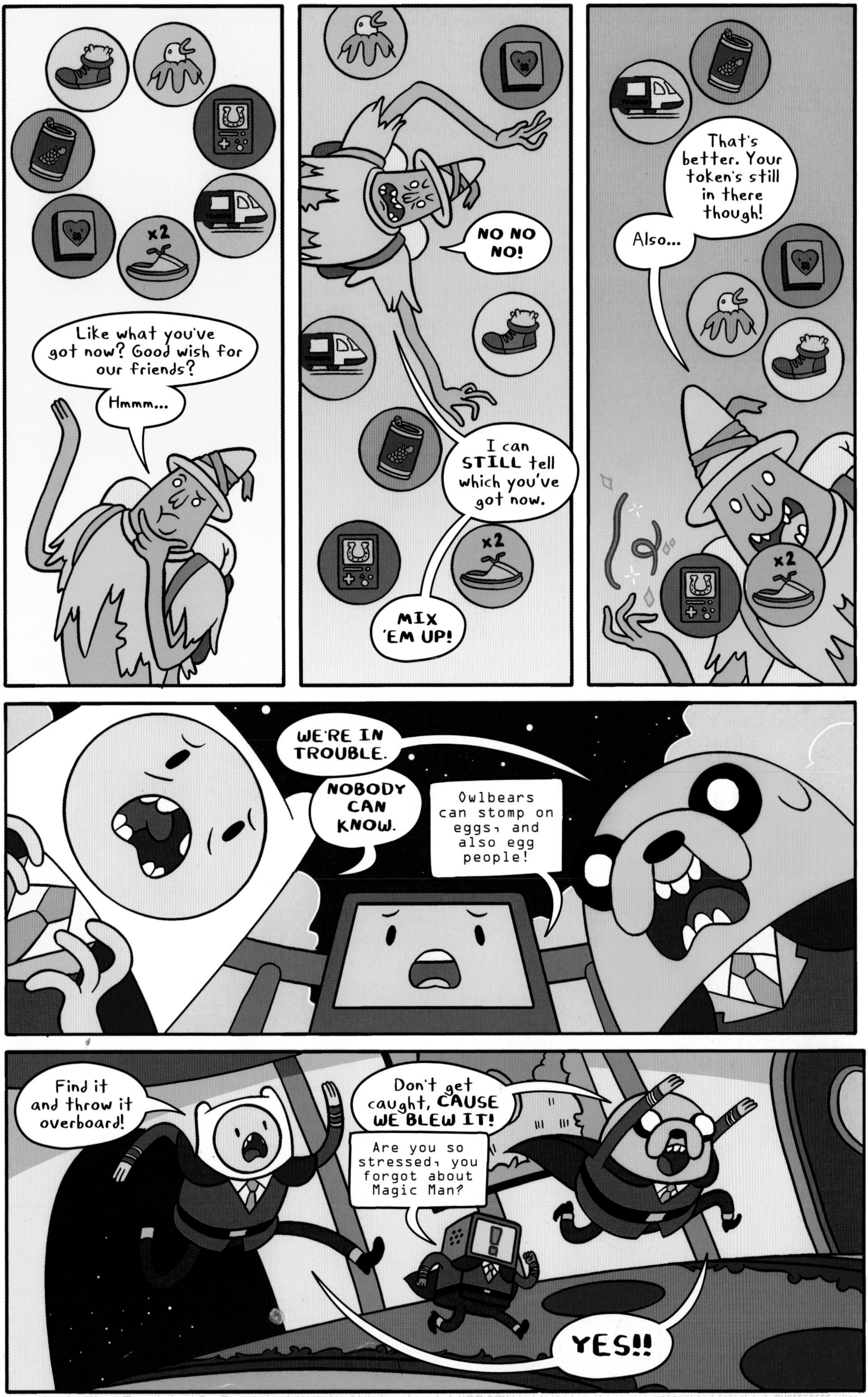
Like what you've got now? Good wish for our friends?
Hmmm...
NO NO NO!
I can STILL tell which you've got now.
MIX 'EM UP!
That's better. Your token's still in there though!
Also...
WE'RE IN TROUBLE.
NOBODY CAN KNOW.
Owlbears can stomp on eggs, and also egg people!
Find it and throw it overboard!
Don't get caught, CAUSE WE BLEW IT!
Are you so stressed, you forgot about Magic Man?
YES!!

I considered writing a "Forgot about Dre/Forgot about Magic Man" bit down here, but **HOO BOY** I just looked up the source material and talk about **CUSSESSSSS** yikes.

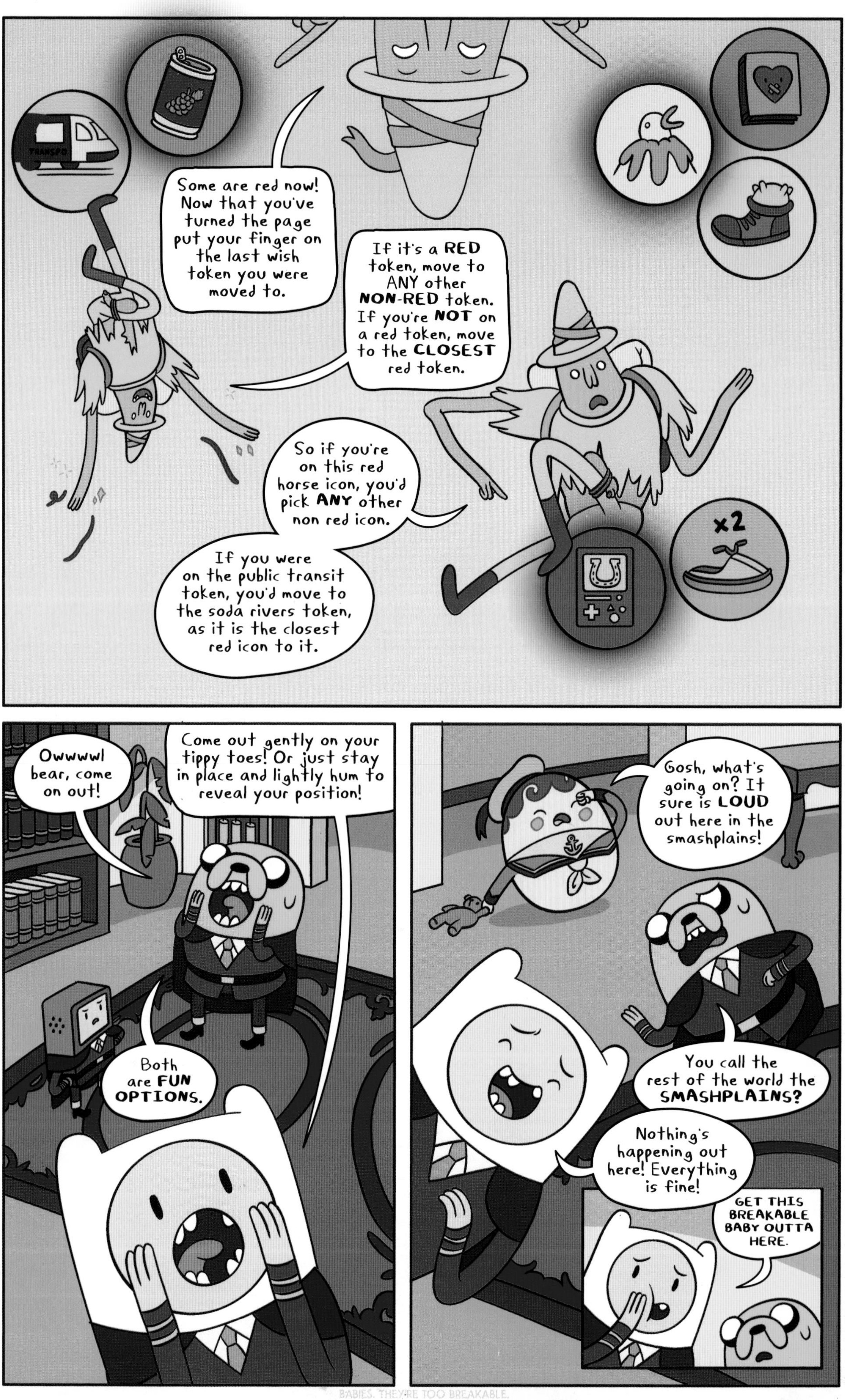
TRANSPO
Some are red now! Now that you've turned the page put your finger on the last wish token you were moved to.
If it's a RED token, move to ANY other NON-RED token. If you're NOT on a red token, move to the CLOSEST red token.
So if you're on this red horse icon, you'd pick ANY other non red icon.
If you were on the public transit token, you'd move to the soda rivers token, as it is the closest red icon to it.
x2
Owwwwl bear, come on out!
Come out gently on your tippy toes! Or just stay in place and lightly hum to reveal your position!
Both are FUN OPTIONS.
Gosh, what's going on? It sure is LOUD out here in the smashplains!
You call the rest of the world the SMASHPLAINS?
Nothing's happening out here! Everything is fine!
GET THIS BREAKABLE BABY OUTTA HERE.

BABIES. THEY'RE TOO BREAKABLE.

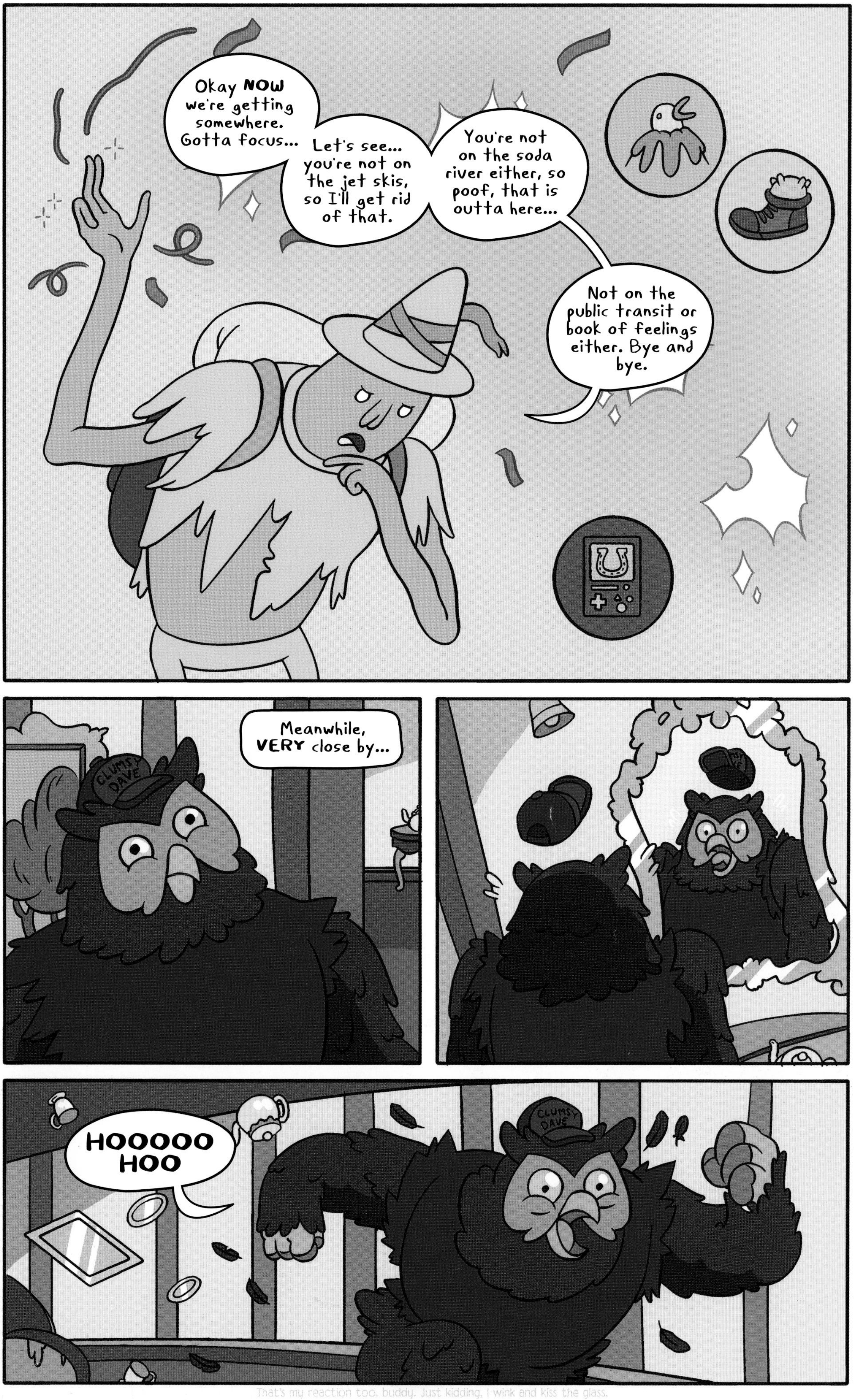
Okay **NOW** we're getting somewhere. Gotta focus...
Let's see... you're not on the jet skis, so I'll get rid of that.
You're not on the soda river either, so poof, that is outta here...
Not on the public transit or book of feelings either. Bye and bye.
Meanwhile, **VERY** close by...
CLUMSY DAVE
HOOOOO HOO

That's my reaction too, buddy. Just kidding. I wink and kiss the glass.

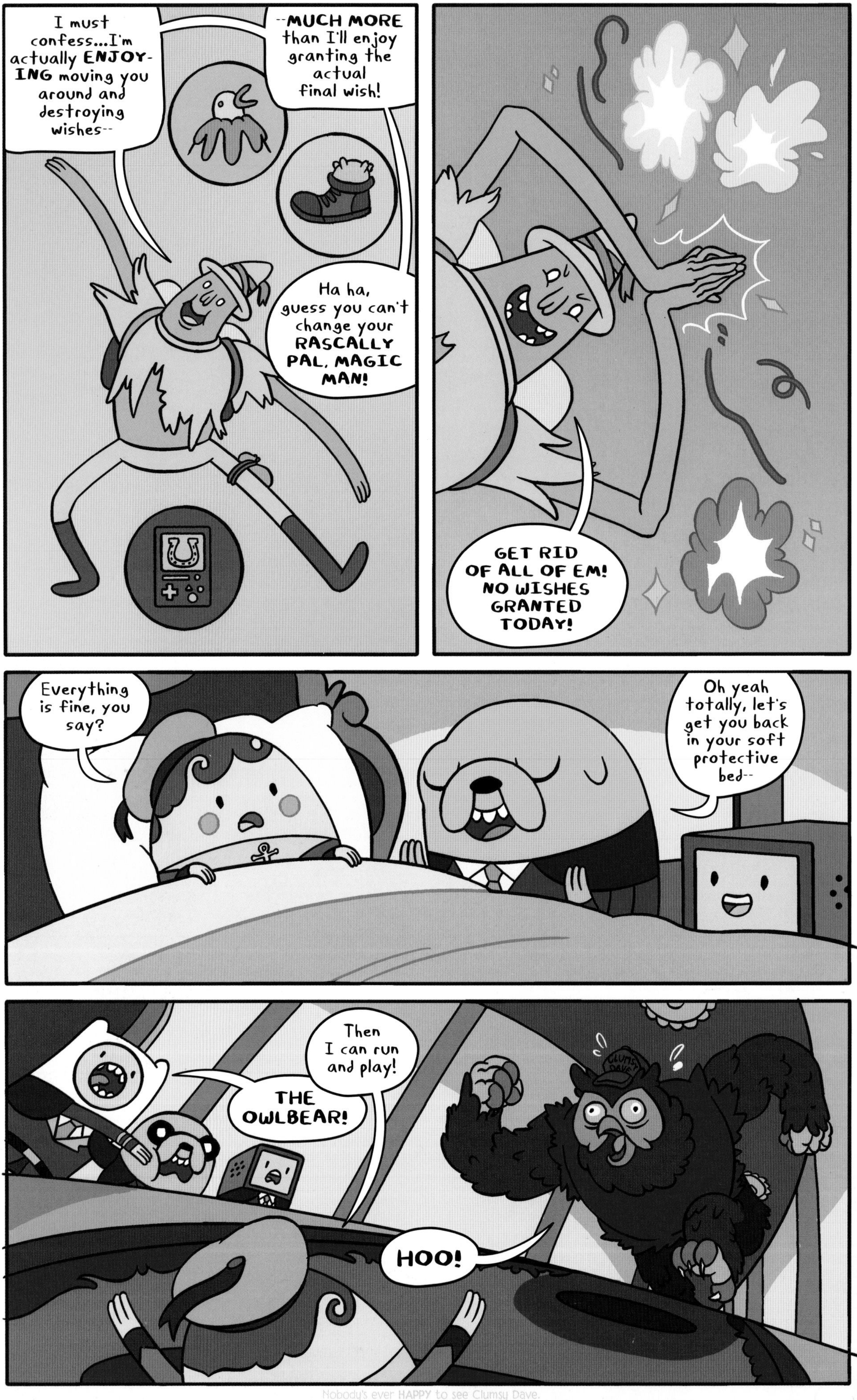
I must confess...I'm actually **ENJOYING** moving you around and destroying wishes--
--**MUCH MORE** than I'll enjoy granting the actual final wish!
Ha ha, guess you can't change your **RASCALLY PAL, MAGIC MAN!**
GET RID OF ALL OF EM! NO WISHES GRANTED TODAY!
Everything is fine, you say?
Oh yeah totally, let's get you back in your soft protective bed--
Then I can run and play!
THE OWLBEAR!
CLUMSY DAVE
HOO!

Nobody's ever HAPPY to see Clumsy Dave.

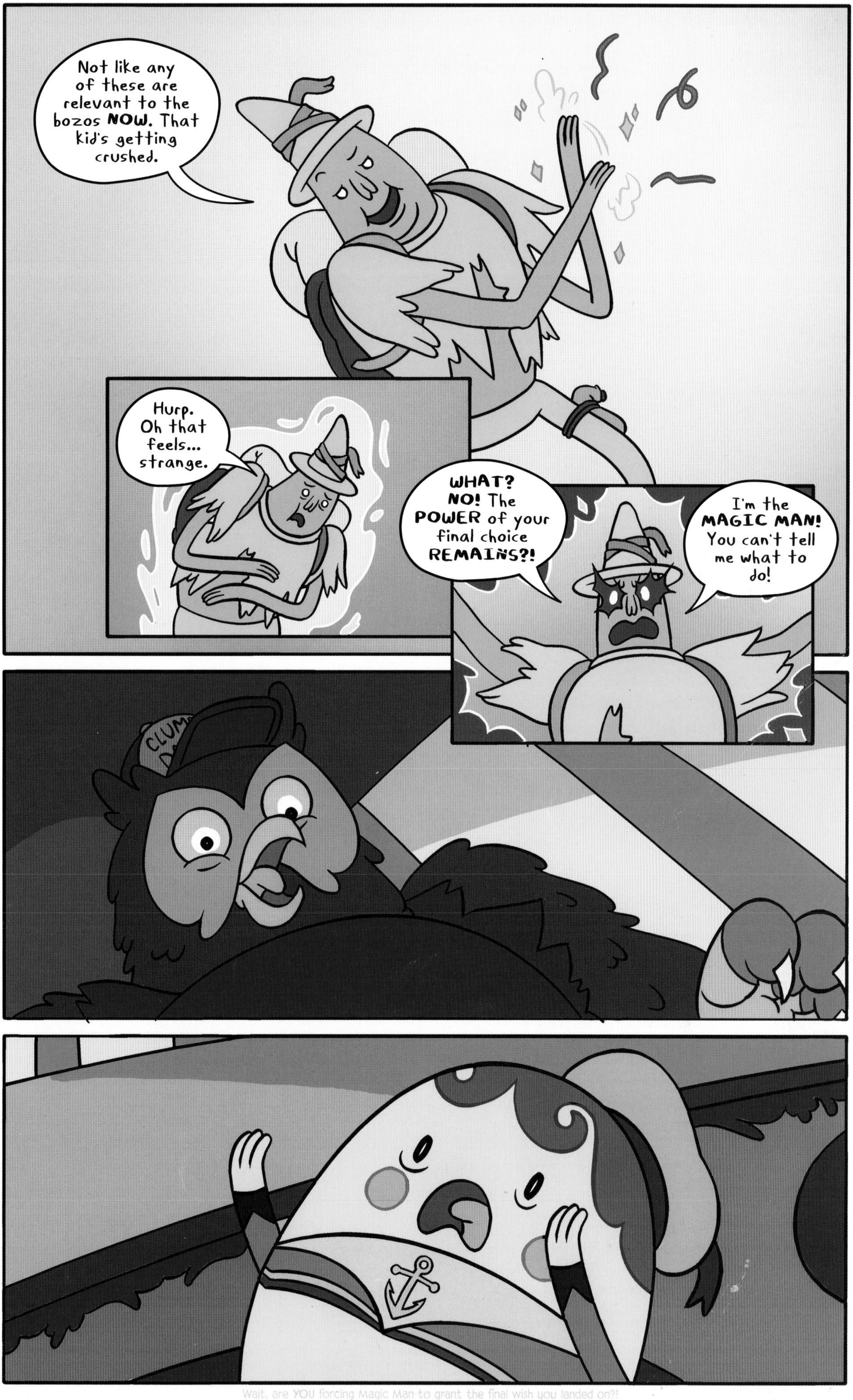
Not like any of these are relevant to the bozos NOW. That kid's getting crushed.
Hurp. Oh that feels... strange.
WHAT? NO! The POWER of your final choice REMAINS?!
I'm the MAGIC MAN! You can't tell me what to do!

Wait, are YOU forcing Magic Man to grant the final wish you landed on?!

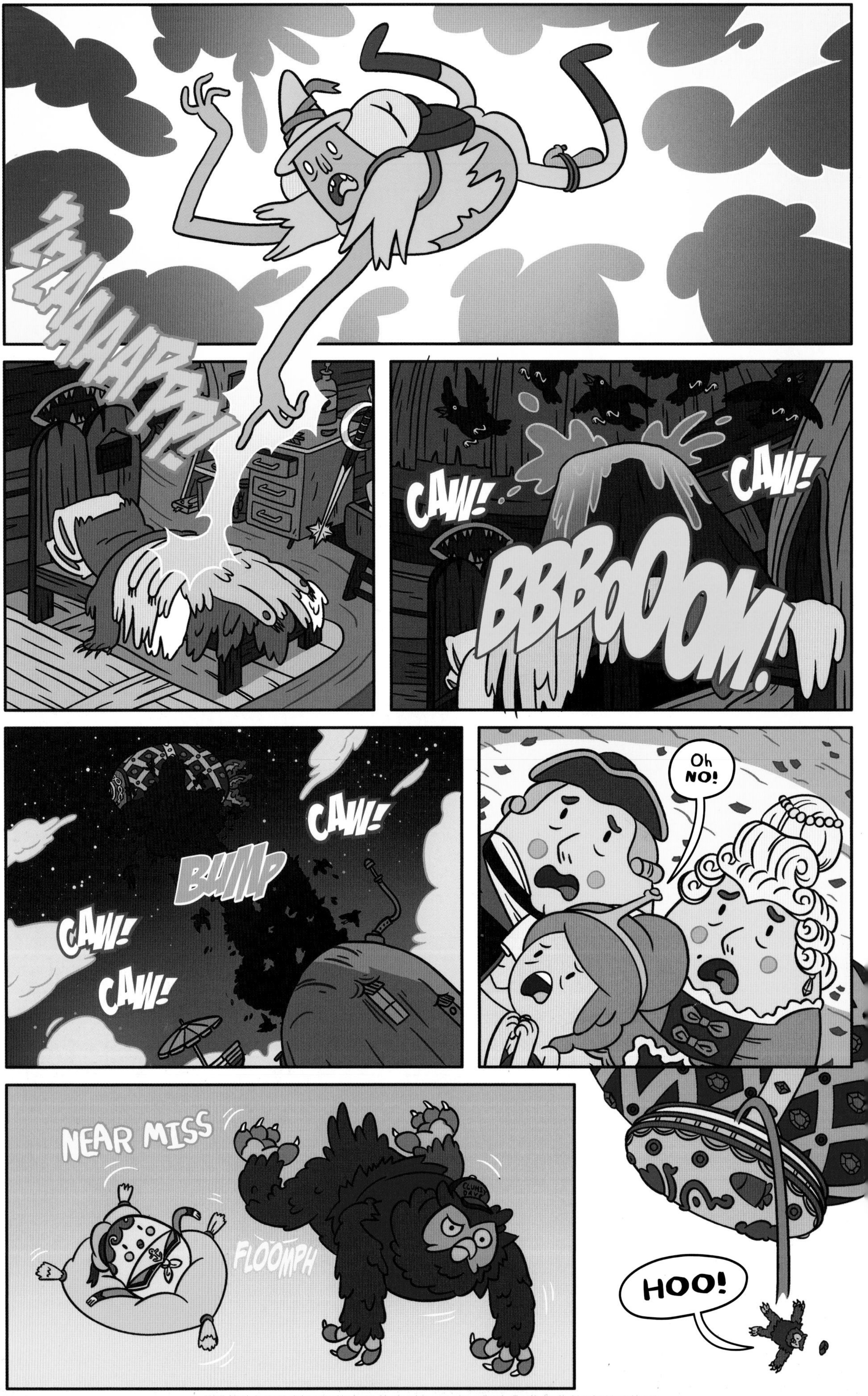
ZZAAAAPP!
CAW!
CAW!
BBBOOOM!
CAW!
BUMP
CAW!
CAW!
Oh NO!
NEAR MISS
FLOOMPH
HOO!

·Well that is certainly exactly how that wish was described. Can't fault Magic Man there.

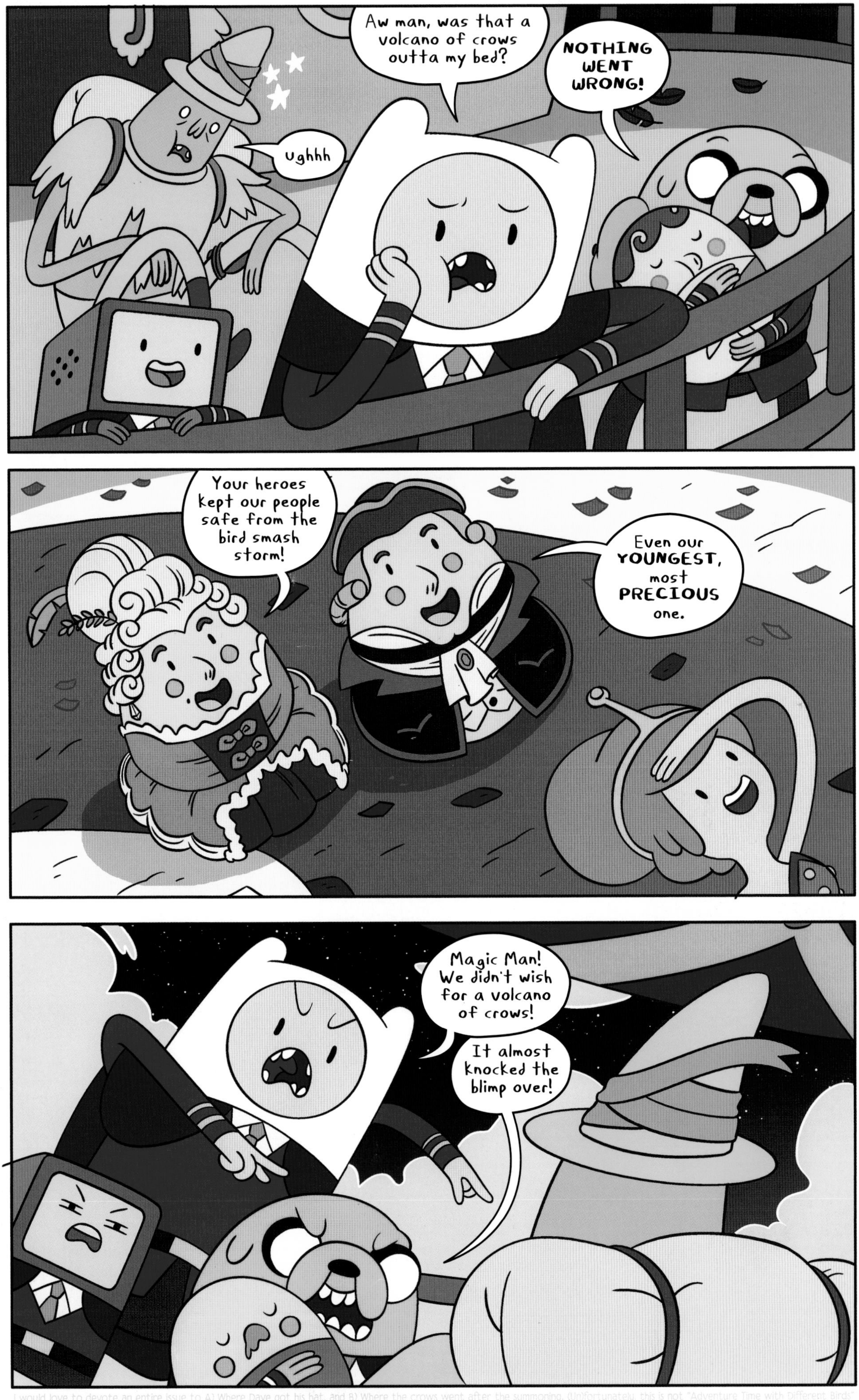

Aw man, was that a volcano of crows outta my bed?
NOTHING WENT WRONG!
ughhh
Your heroes kept our people safe from the bird smash storm!
Even our YOUNGEST, most PRECIOUS one.
Magic Man! We didn't wish for a volcano of crows!
It almost knocked the blimp over!

I would love to devote an entire issue to A) Where Dave got his hat. and B) Where the crows went after the summoning. (Un)fortunately, this is not "Adventure Time with Different Birds"

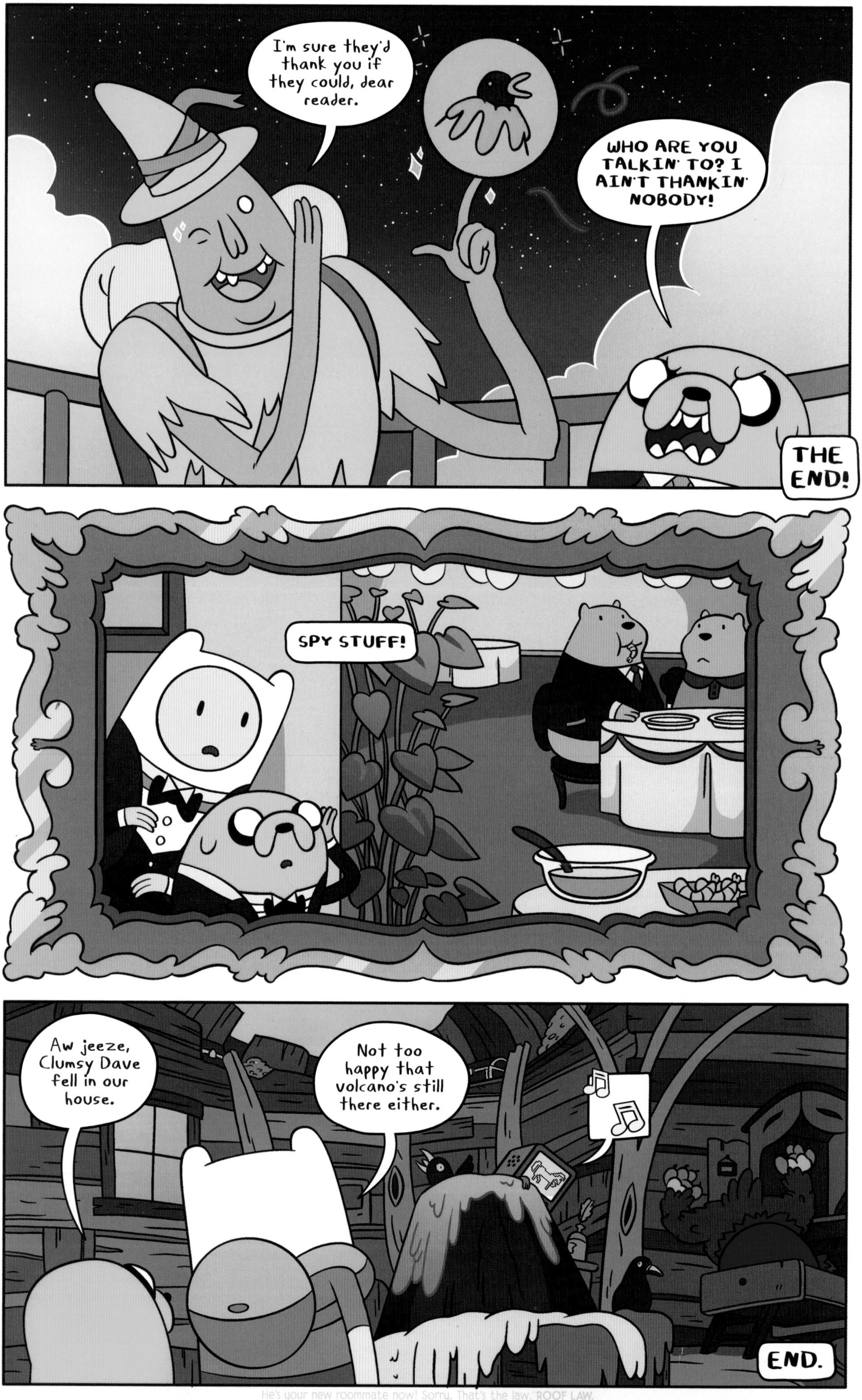
I'm sure they'd thank you if they could, dear reader.
WHO ARE YOU TALKIN' TO? I AIN'T THANKIN' NOBODY!
THE END!
SPY STUFF!
Aw jeeze, Clumsy Dave fell in our house.
Not too happy that volcano's still there either.
END.

He's your new roommate now! Sorry. That's the law. ROOF LAW.

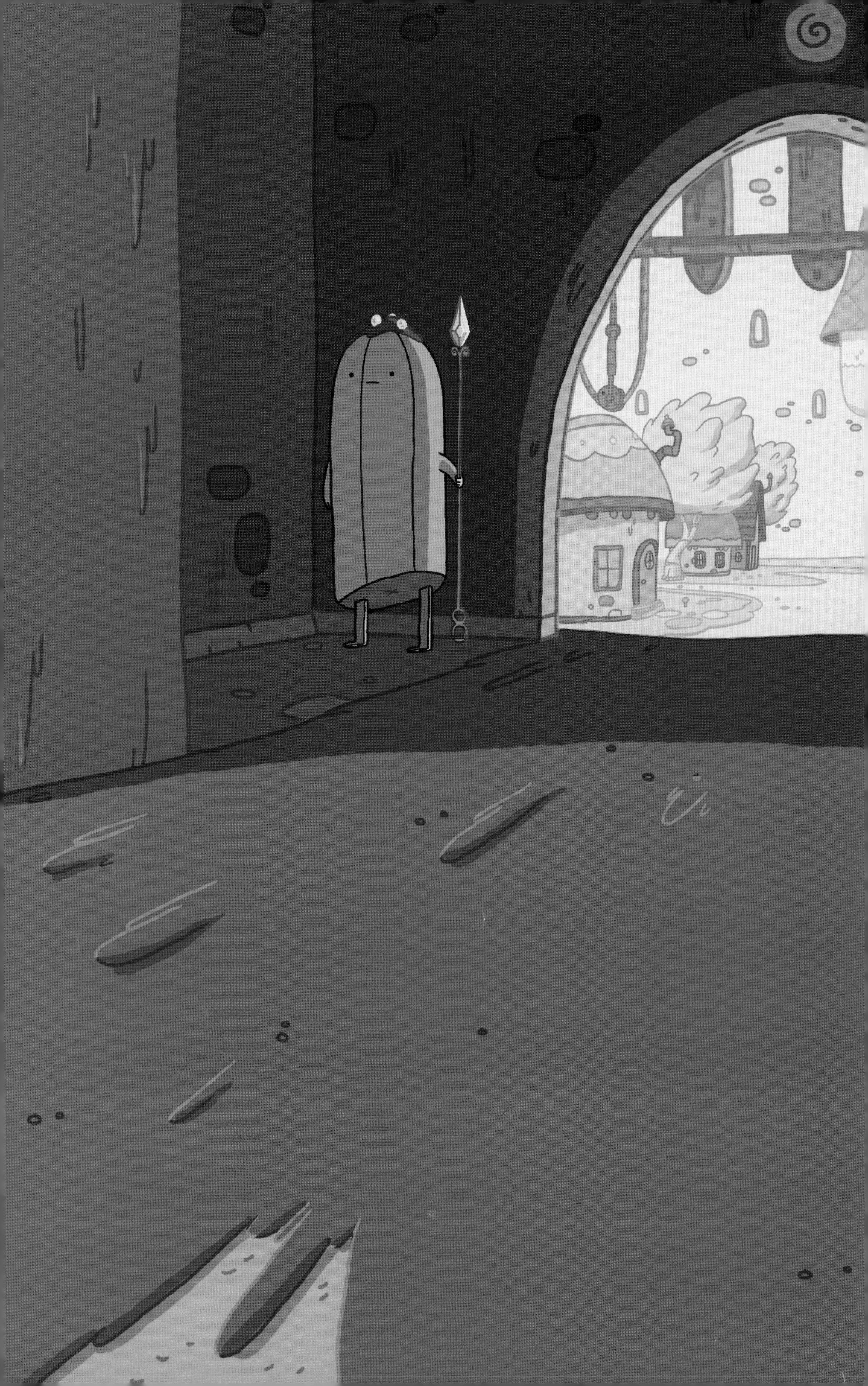

CHAPTER TWO

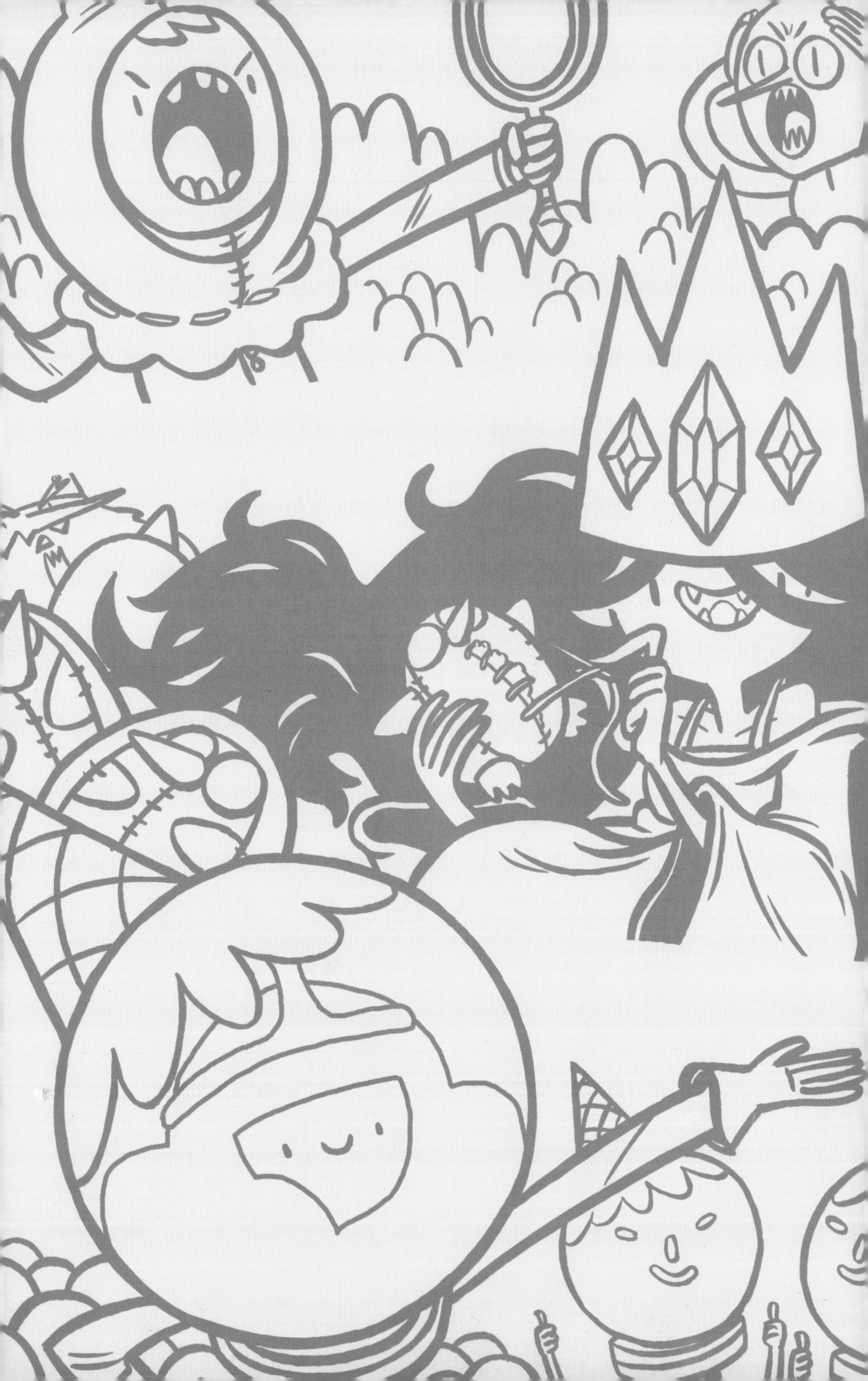

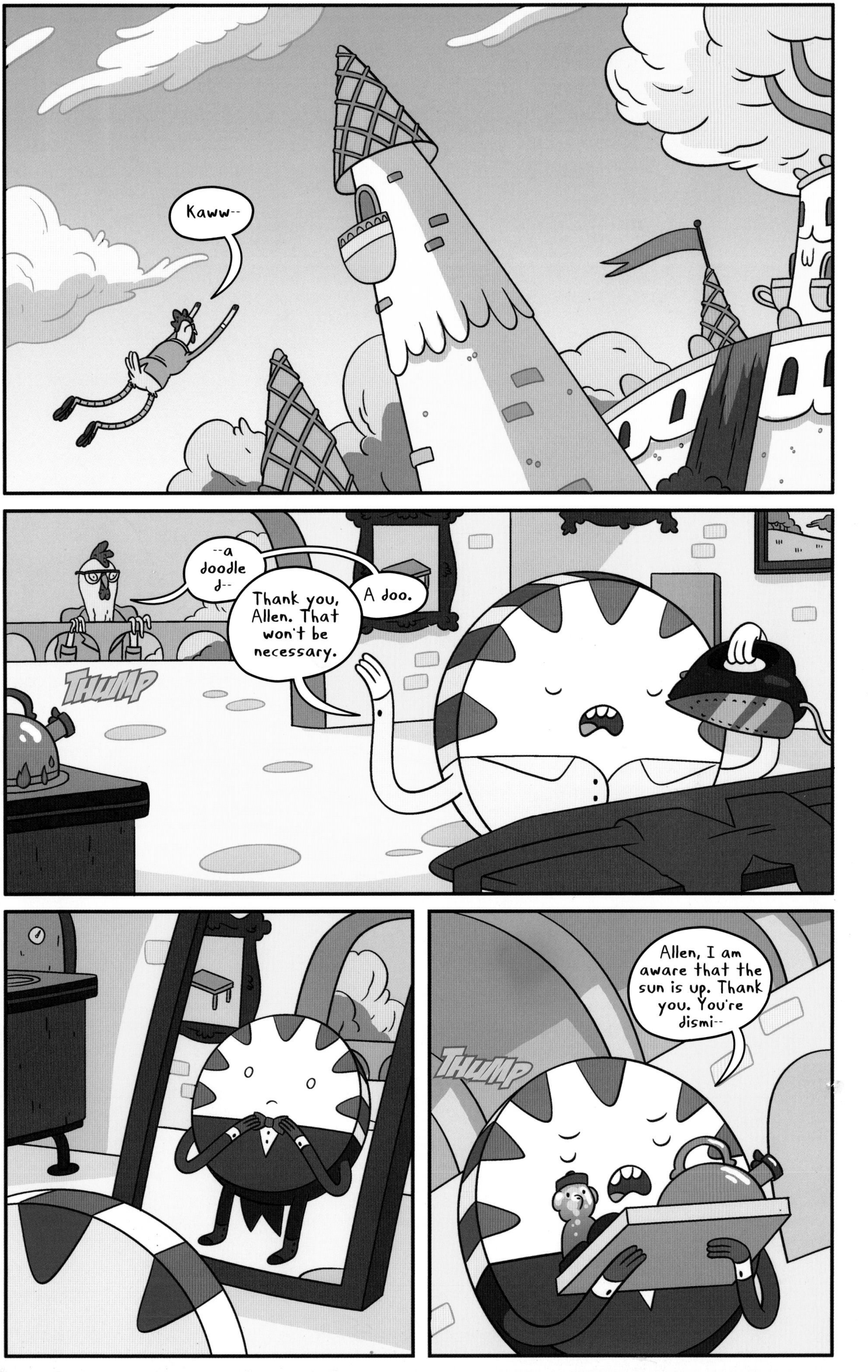
Kaww--
--a doodle d--
A doo.
Thank you, Allen. That won't be necessary.
THUMP
Allen, I am aware that the sun is up. Thank you. You're dismi--
THUMP

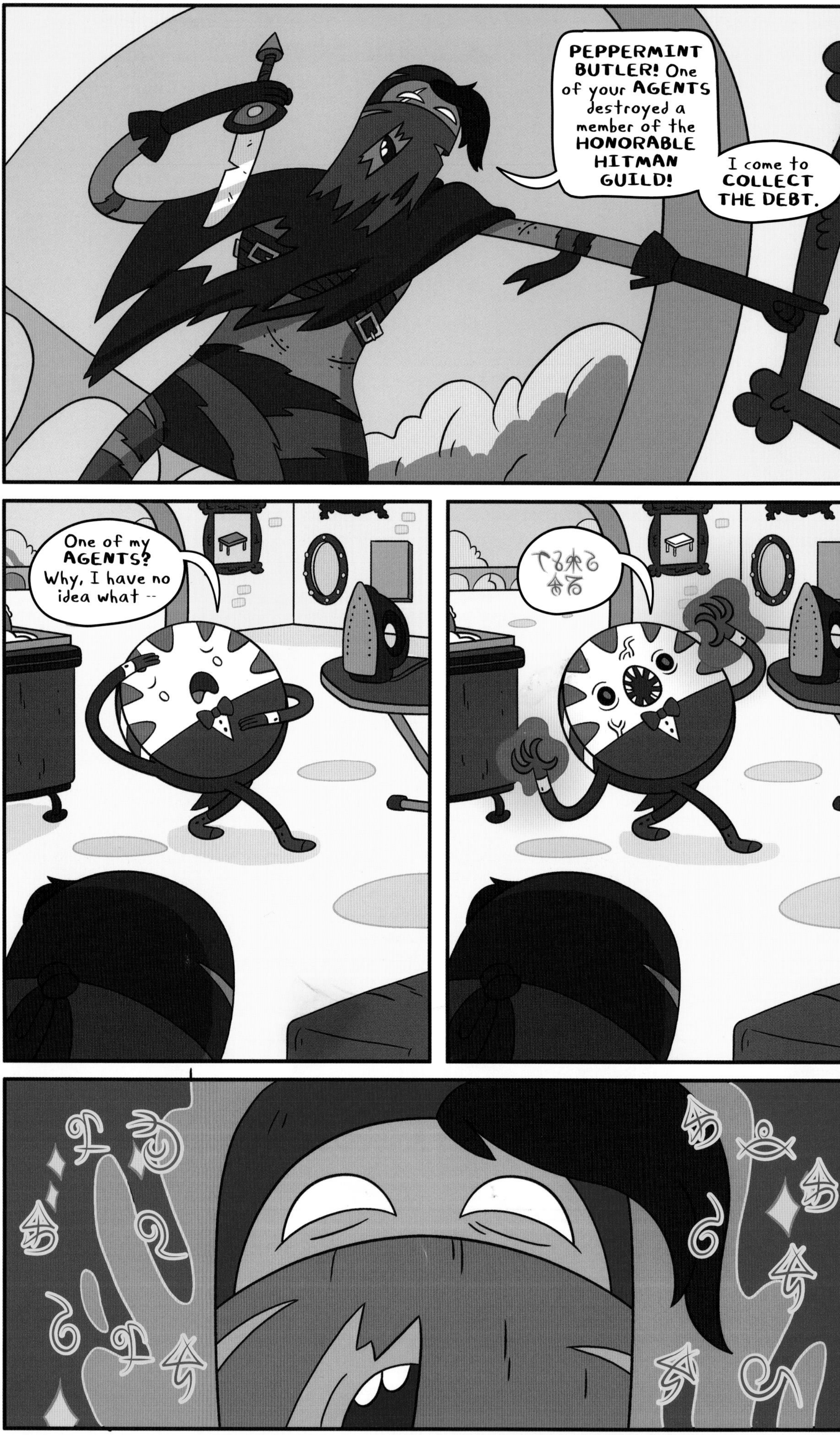
PEPPERMINT BUTLER! One of your AGENTS destroyed a member of the HONORABLE HITMAN GUILD!
I come to COLLECT THE DEBT.
One of my AGENTS? Why, I have no idea what --

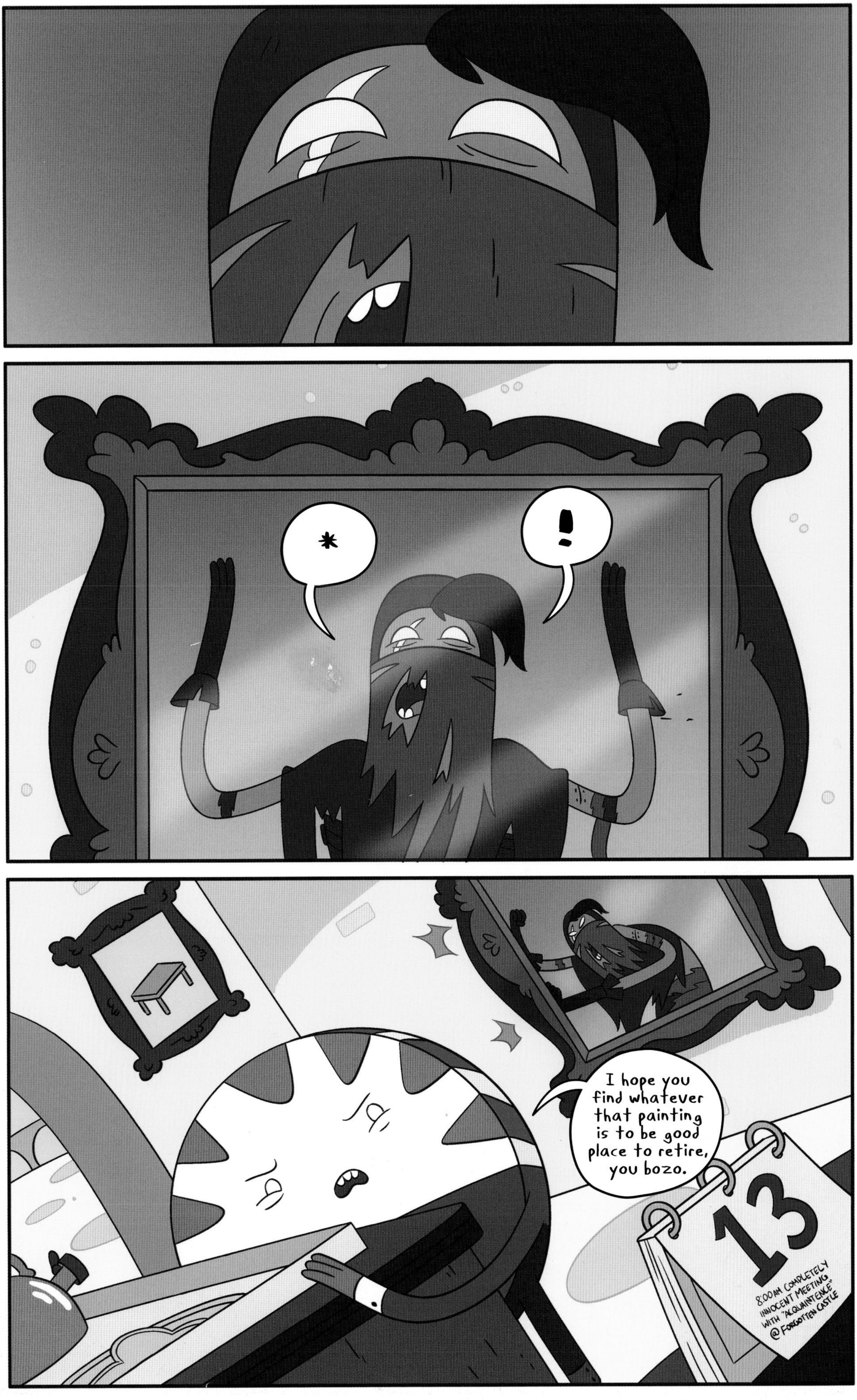
*
!
I hope you find whatever that painting is to be good place to retire, you bozo.
13
8:00AM COMPLETELY INNOCENT MEETING WITH "ACQUAINTENCE" @ FORGOTTEN CASTLE

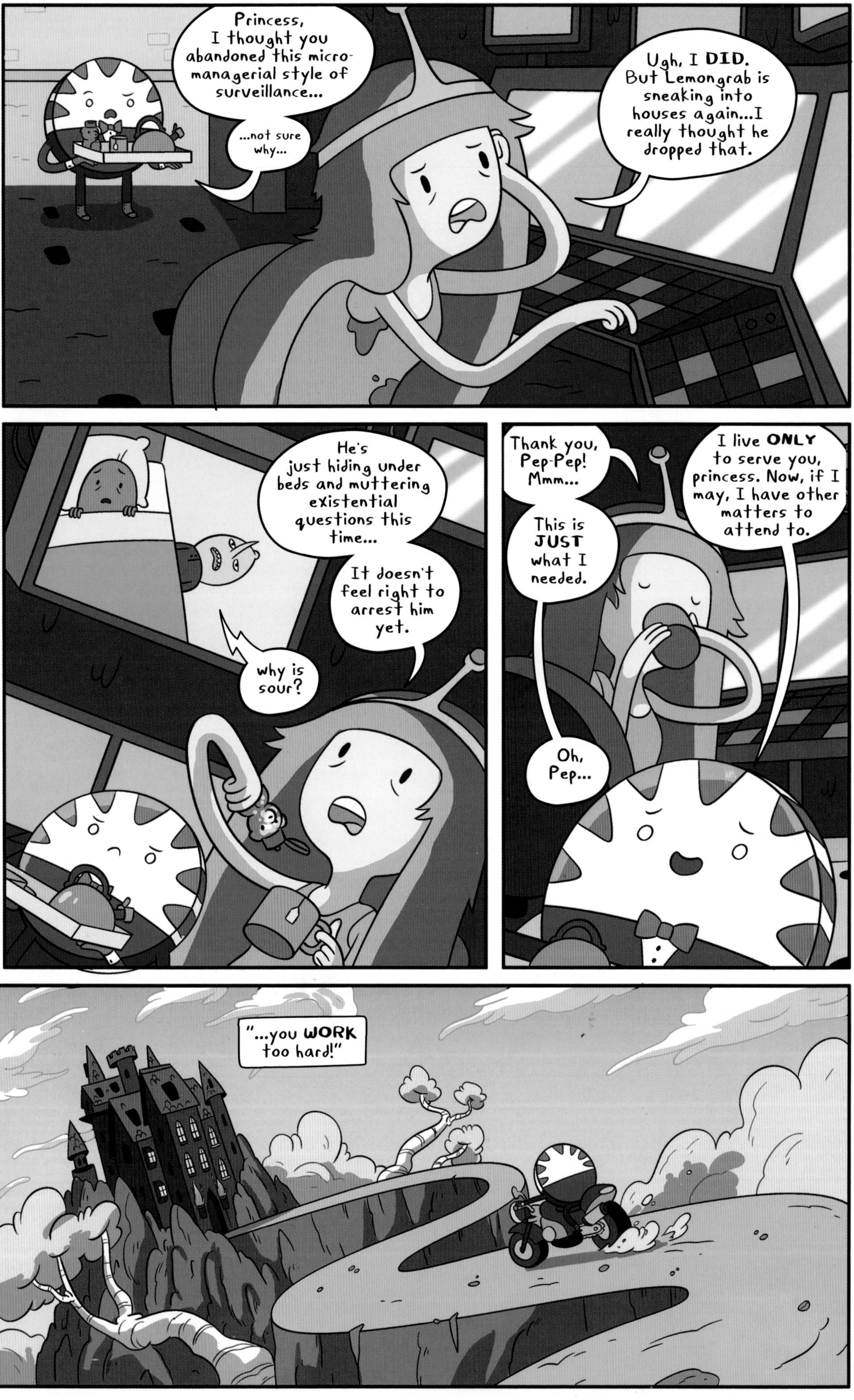
Princess, I thought you abandoned this micro-managerial style of surveillance...
...not sure why...
Ugh, I DID. But Lemongrab is sneaking into houses again...I really thought he dropped that.
He's just hiding under beds and muttering existential questions this time...
It doesn't feel right to arrest him yet.
why is sour?
Thank you, Pep-Pep! Mmm...
This is JUST what I needed.
I live ONLY to serve you, princess. Now, if I may, I have other matters to attend to.
Oh, Pep...
"...you WORK too hard!"

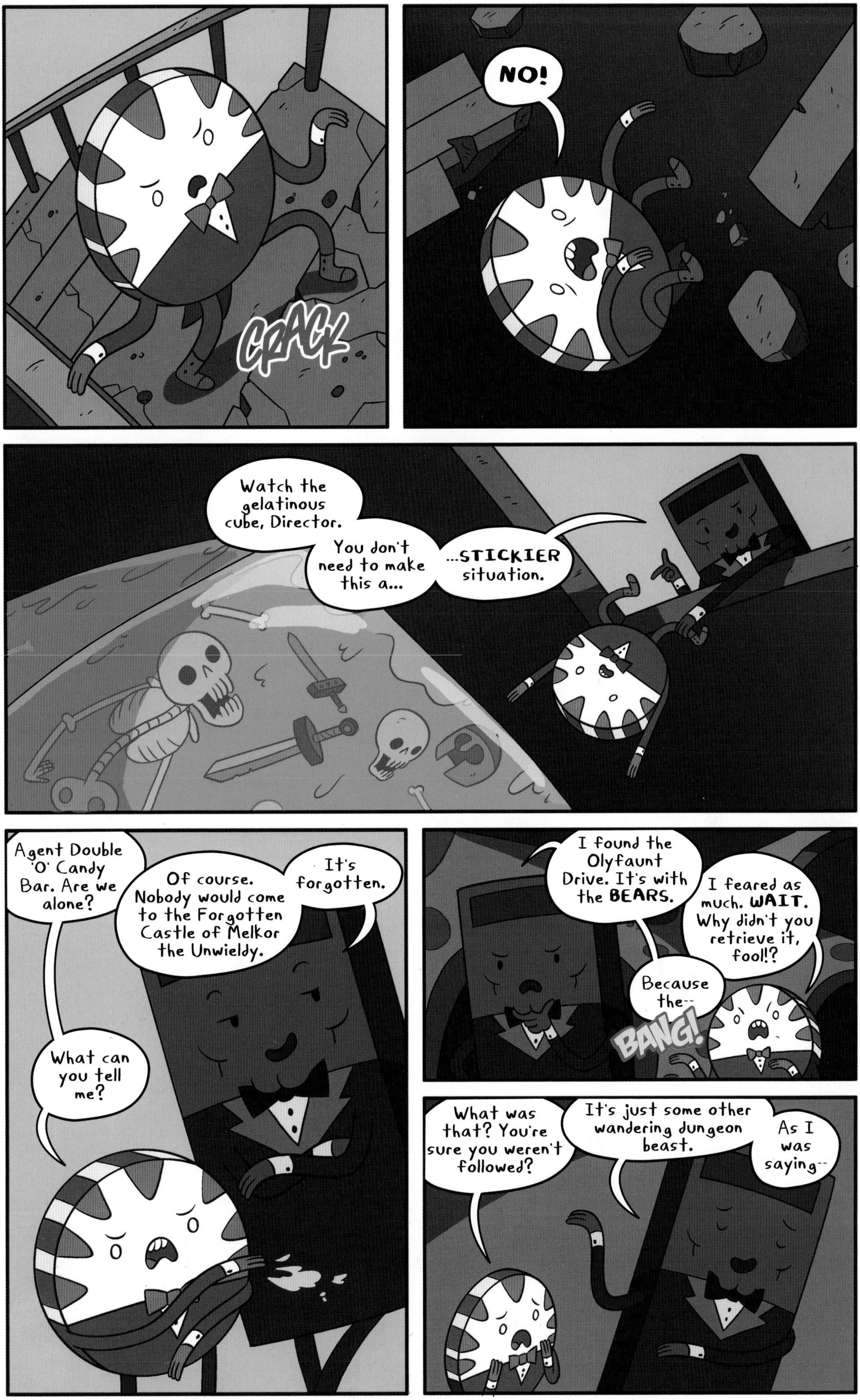
CRACK
NO!
Watch the gelatinous cube, Director.
You don't need to make this a...
...STICKIER situation.
Agent Double 'O' Candy Bar. Are we alone?
Of course. Nobody would come to the Forgotten Castle of Melkor the Unwieldy.
It's forgotten.
What can you tell me?
I found the Olyfaunt Drive. It's with the BEARS.
I feared as much. WAIT. Why didn't you retrieve it, fool!?
Because the--
BANG!
What was that? You're sure you weren't followed?
It's just some other wandering dungeon beast.
As I was saying--

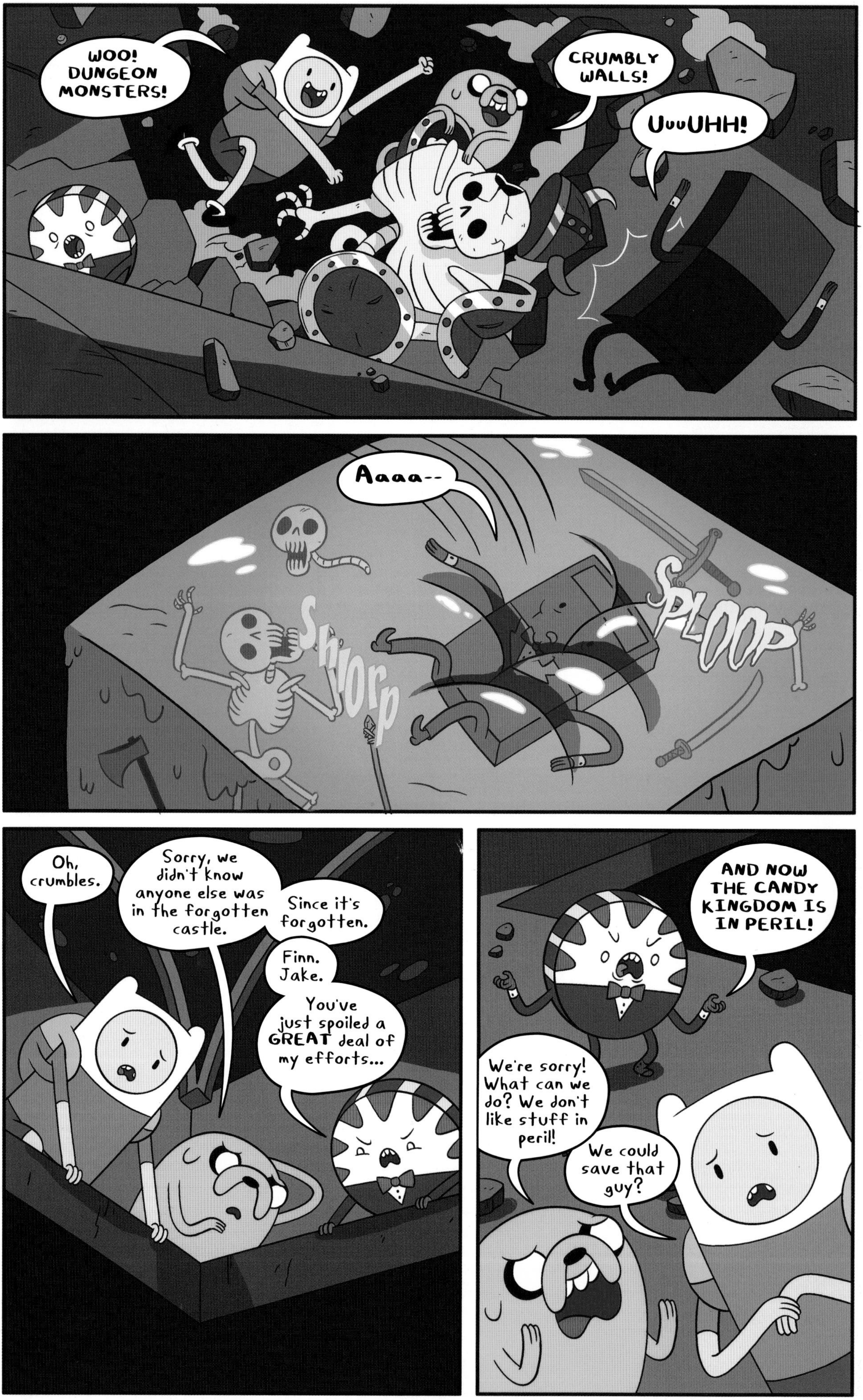

WOO! DUNGEON MONSTERS!
CRUMBLY WALLS!
UuuUHH!
Aaaa--
SHLORP
SPLOOP
Oh, crumbles.
Sorry, we didn't know anyone else was in the forgotten castle.
Since it's forgotten.
Finn. Jake.
You've just spoiled a GREAT deal of my efforts...
AND NOW THE CANDY KINGDOM IS IN PERIL!
We're sorry! What can we do? We don't like stuff in peril!
We could save that guy?

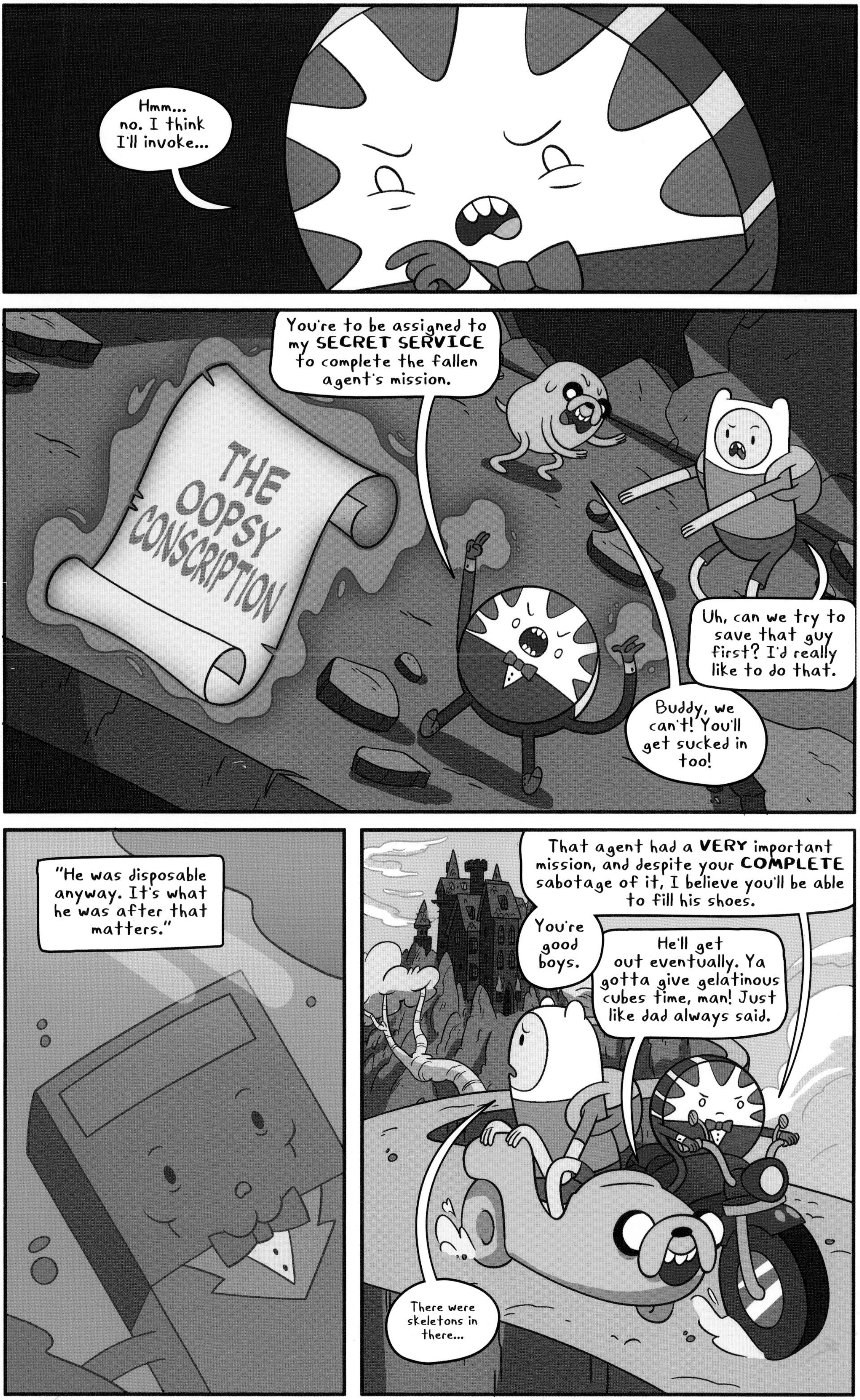

Hmm... no. I think I'll invoke...
THE OOPSY CONSCRIPTION
You're to be assigned to my SECRET SERVICE to complete the fallen agent's mission.
Uh, can we try to save that guy first? I'd really like to do that.
Buddy, we can't! You'll get sucked in too!
"He was disposable anyway. It's what he was after that matters."
That agent had a VERY important mission, and despite your COMPLETE sabotage of it, I believe you'll be able to fill his shoes.
You're good boys.
He'll get out eventually. Ya gotta give gelatinous cubes time, man! Just like dad always said.
There were skeletons in there...

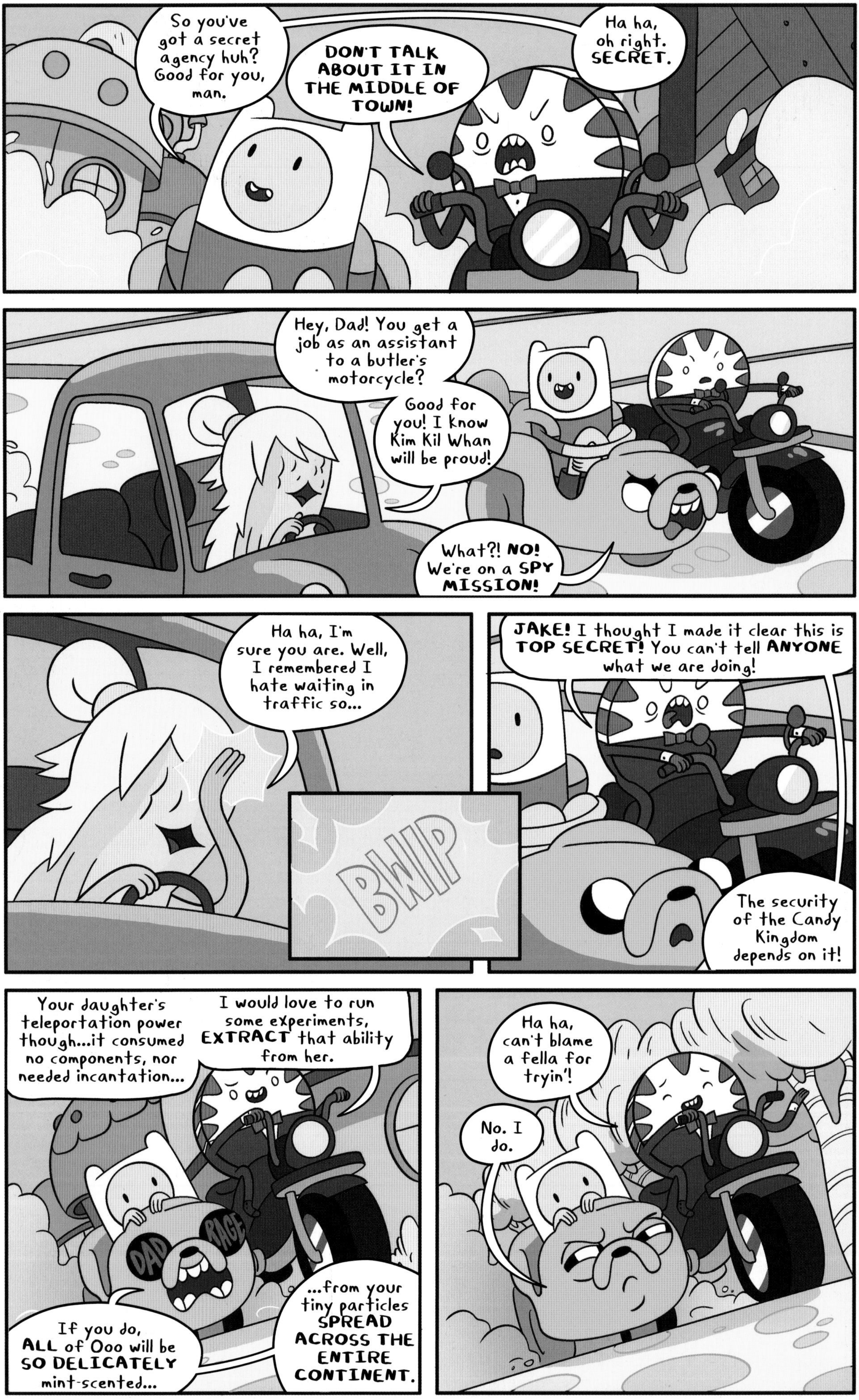

So you've got a secret agency huh? Good for you, man.
DON'T TALK ABOUT IT IN THE MIDDLE OF TOWN!
Ha ha, oh right. SECRET.
Hey, Dad! You get a job as an assistant to a butler's motorcycle?
Good for you! I know Kim Kil Whan will be proud!
What?! NO! We're on a SPY MISSION!
Ha ha, I'm sure you are. Well, I remembered I hate waiting in traffic so...
BWIP
JAKE! I thought I made it clear this is TOP SECRET! You can't tell ANYONE what we are doing!
The security of the Candy Kingdom depends on it!
Your daughter's teleportation power though...it consumed no components, nor needed incantation...
I would love to run some experiments, EXTRACT that ability from her.
DAD RAGE
If you do, ALL of Ooo will be SO DELICATELY mint-scented...
...from your tiny particles SPREAD ACROSS THE ENTIRE CONTINENT.
Ha ha, can't blame a fella for tryin'!
No. I do.

LATER:

Welcome! Get ready boys!

For what, for reading?

Hm?

BORING:
An Unremarkable
Exercise in Banality
By Dr. Yawn

Critics Agree!
"Don't read this book."

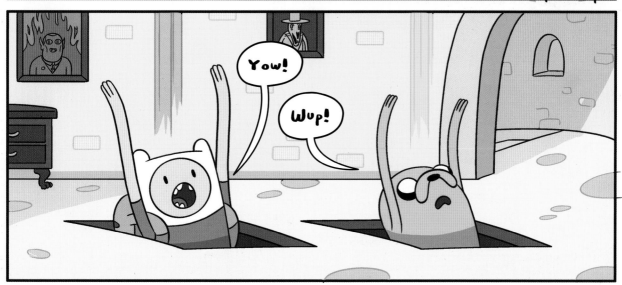

Yow!

Wup!

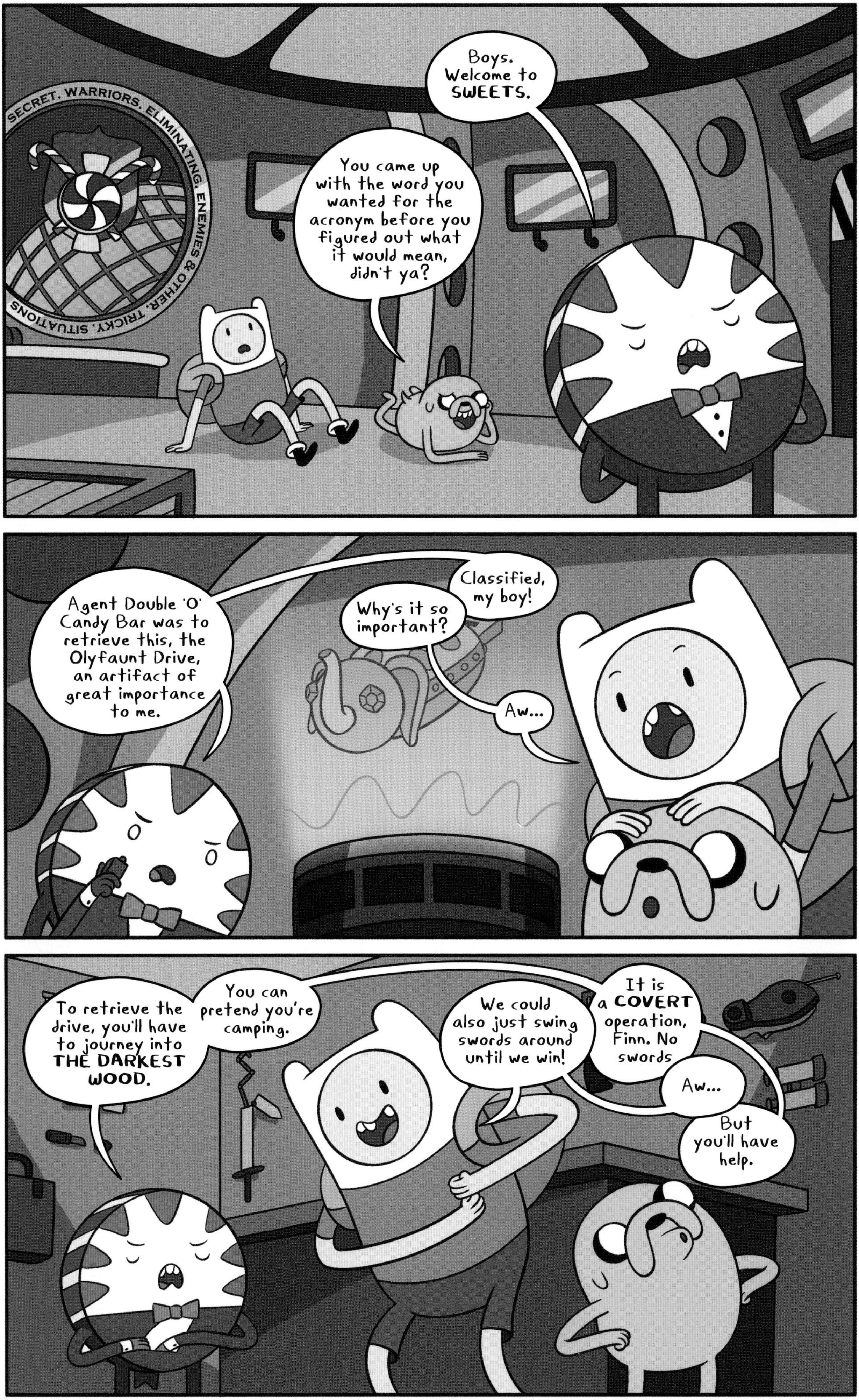
SECRET. WARRIORS. ELIMINATING. ENEMIES & OTHER. TRICKY. SITUATIONS
Boys. Welcome to **SWEETS.**
You came up with the word you wanted for the acronym before you figured out what it would mean, didn't ya?
Agent Double 'O' Candy Bar was to retrieve this, the Olyfaunt Drive, an artifact of great importance to me.
Why's it so important?
Classified, my boy!
Aw...
To retrieve the drive, you'll have to journey into **THE DARKEST WOOD.**
You can pretend you're camping.
We could also just swing swords around until we win!
It is a **COVERT** operation, Finn. No swords
Aw...
But you'll have help.

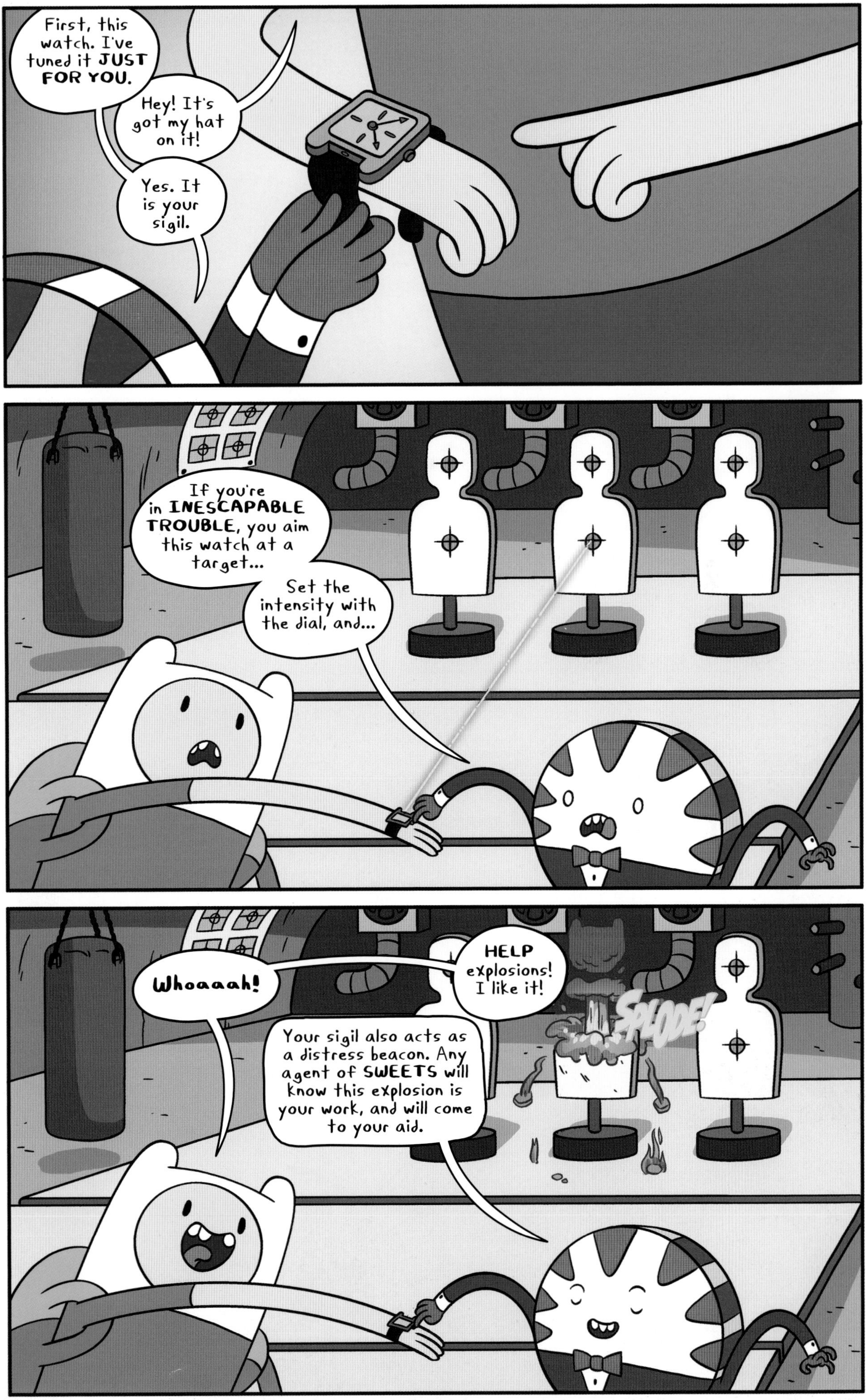
First, this watch. I've tuned it JUST FOR YOU.
Hey! It's got my hat on it!
Yes. It is your sigil.
If you're in INESCAPABLE TROUBLE, you aim this watch at a target...
Set the intensity with the dial, and...
Whoaaah!
HELP explosions! I like it!
SPLODE!
Your sigil also acts as a distress beacon. Any agent of SWEETS will know this explosion is your work, and will come to your aid.

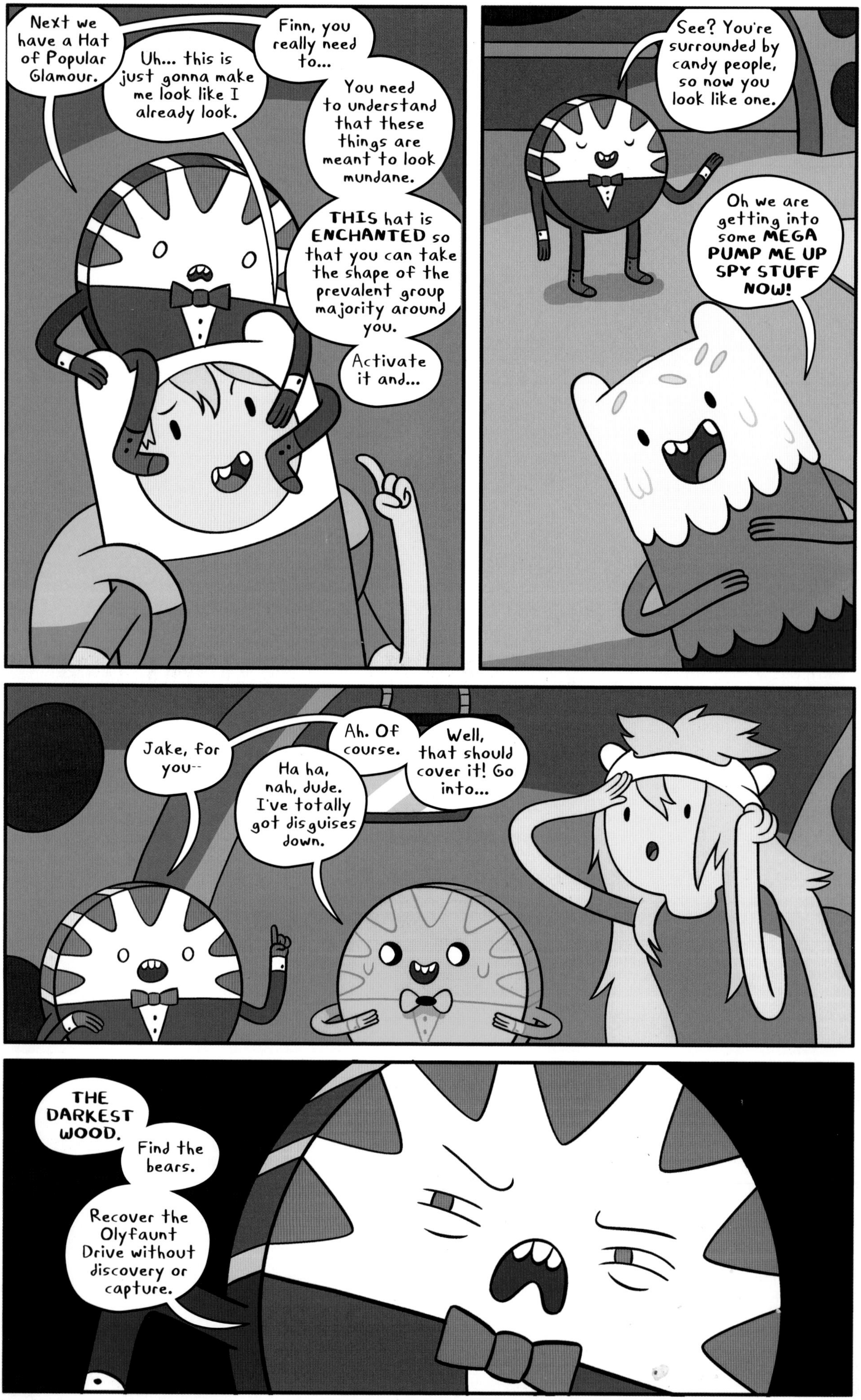
Next we have a Hat of Popular Glamour.
Uh... this is just gonna make me look like I already look.
Finn, you really need to...
You need to understand that these things are meant to look mundane.
THIS hat is ENCHANTED so that you can take the shape of the prevalent group majority around you.
Activate it and...
See? You're surrounded by candy people, so now you look like one.
Oh we are getting into some MEGA PUMP ME UP SPY STUFF NOW!
Jake, for you--
Ah. Of course.
Ha ha, nah, dude. I've totally got disguises down.
Well, that should cover it! Go into...
THE DARKEST WOOD.
Find the bears.
Recover the Olyfaunt Drive without discovery or capture.

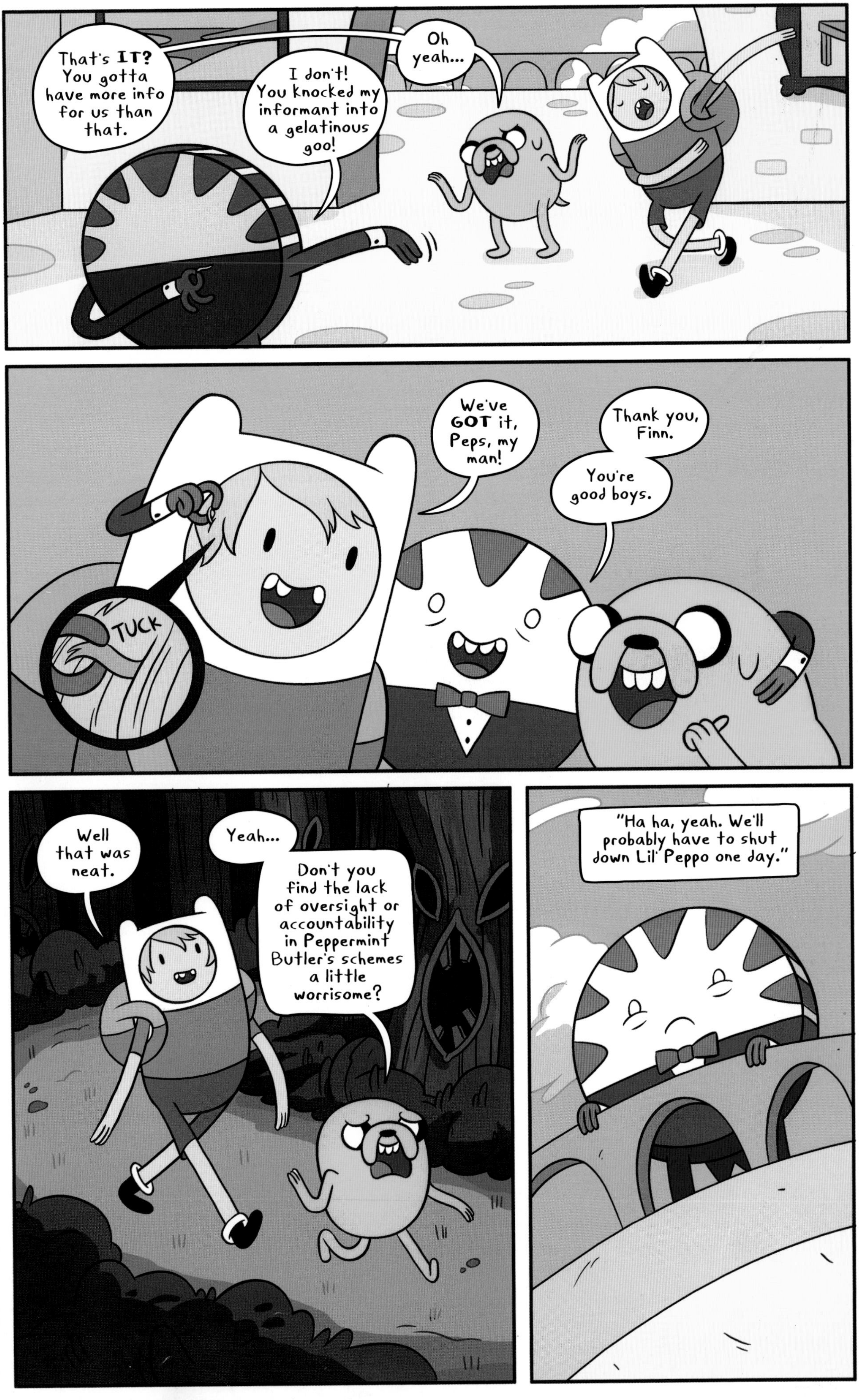

That's IT? You gotta have more info for us than that.
I don't! You knocked my informant into a gelatinous goo!
Oh yeah...
We've GOT it, Peps, my man!
TUCK
Thank you, Finn.
You're good boys.
Well that was neat.
Yeah...
Don't you find the lack of oversight or accountability in Peppermint Butler's schemes a little worrisome?
"Ha ha, yeah. We'll probably have to shut down Lil' Peppo one day."

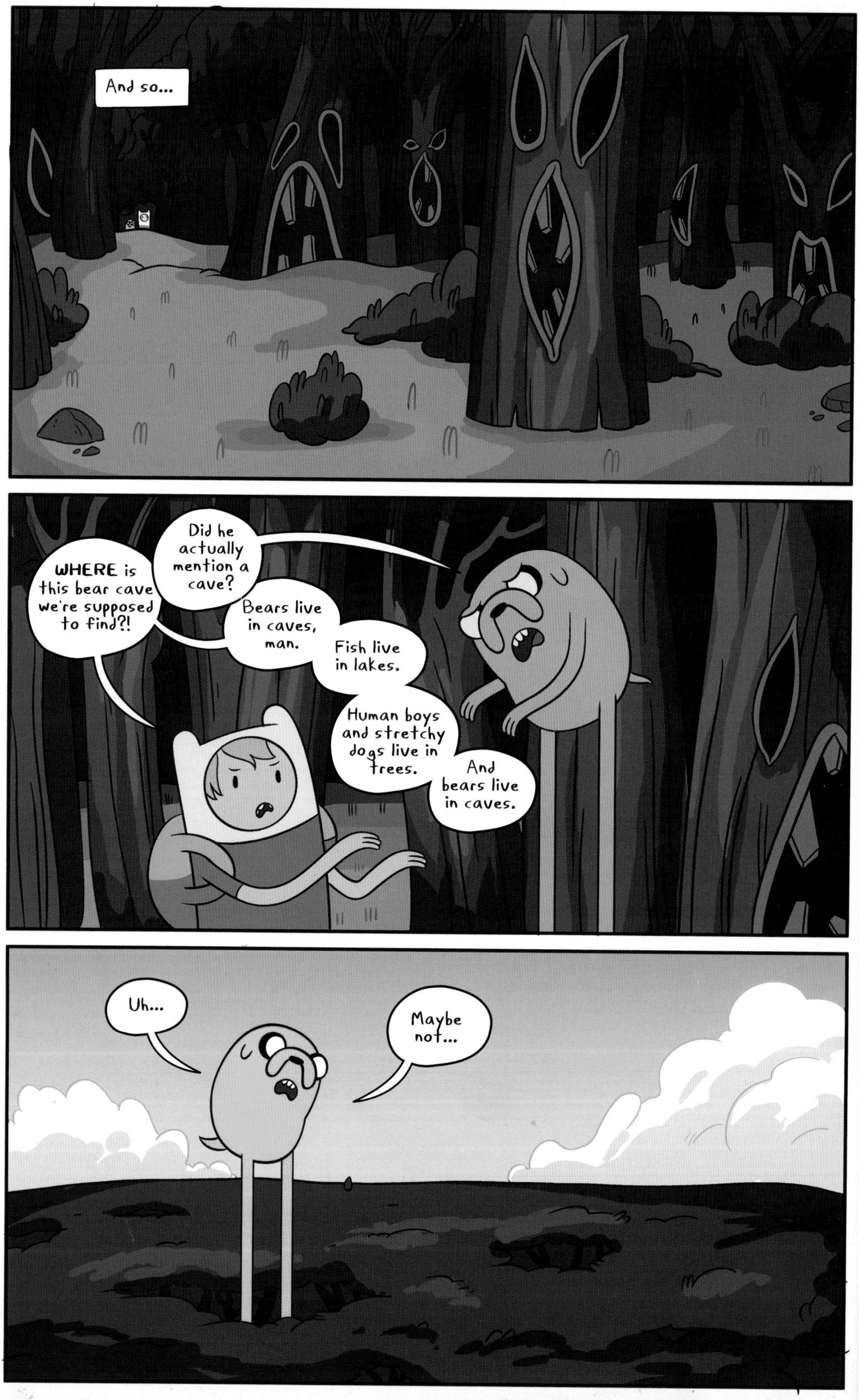
And so...
WHERE is this bear cave we're supposed to find?!
Did he actually mention a cave?
Bears live in caves, man.
Fish live in lakes.
Human boys and stretchy dogs live in trees.
And bears live in caves.
Uh...
Maybe not...

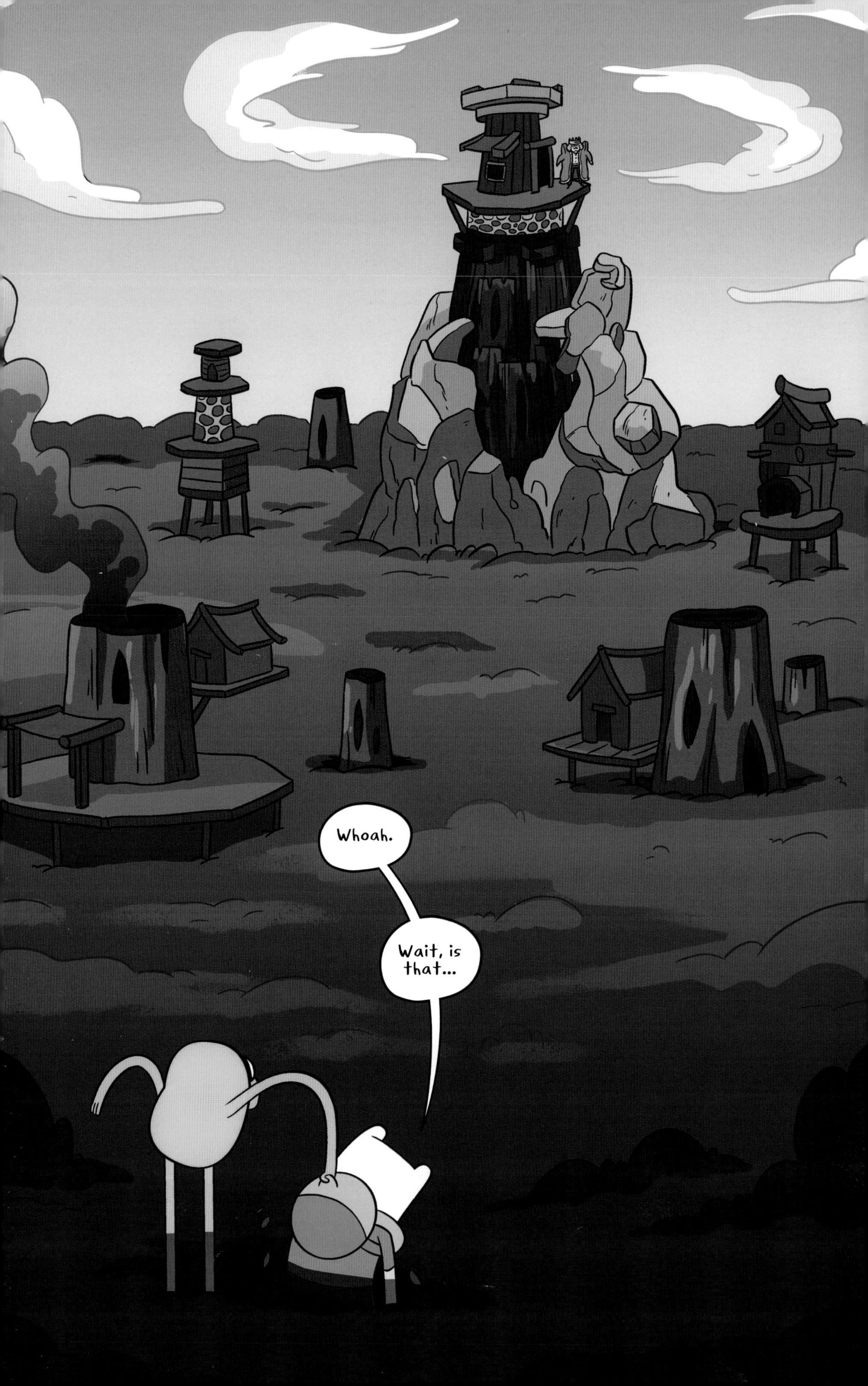
Whoah.
Wait, is that...

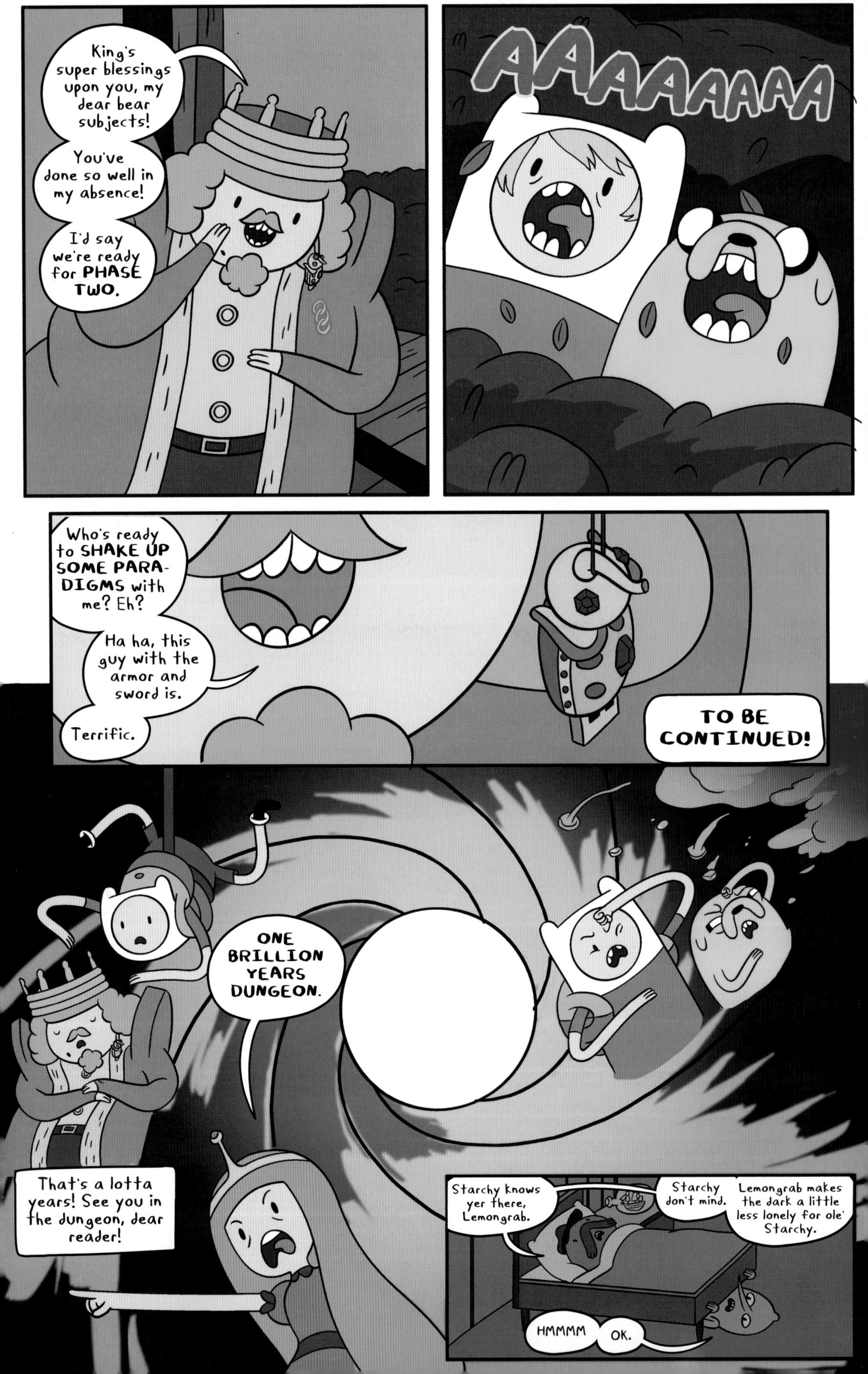
King's super blessings upon you, my dear bear subjects!
You've done so well in my absence!
I'd say we're ready for PHASE TWO.
AAAAAAAAAA
Who's ready to SHAKE UP SOME PARADIGMS with me? Eh?
Ha ha, this guy with the armor and sword is.
Terrific.
TO BE CONTINUED!
ONE BRILLION YEARS DUNGEON.
That's a lotta years! See you in the dungeon, dear reader!
Starchy knows yer there, Lemongrab.
Starchy don't mind.
Lemongrab makes the dark a little less lonely for ole' Starchy.
HMMMM
OK.

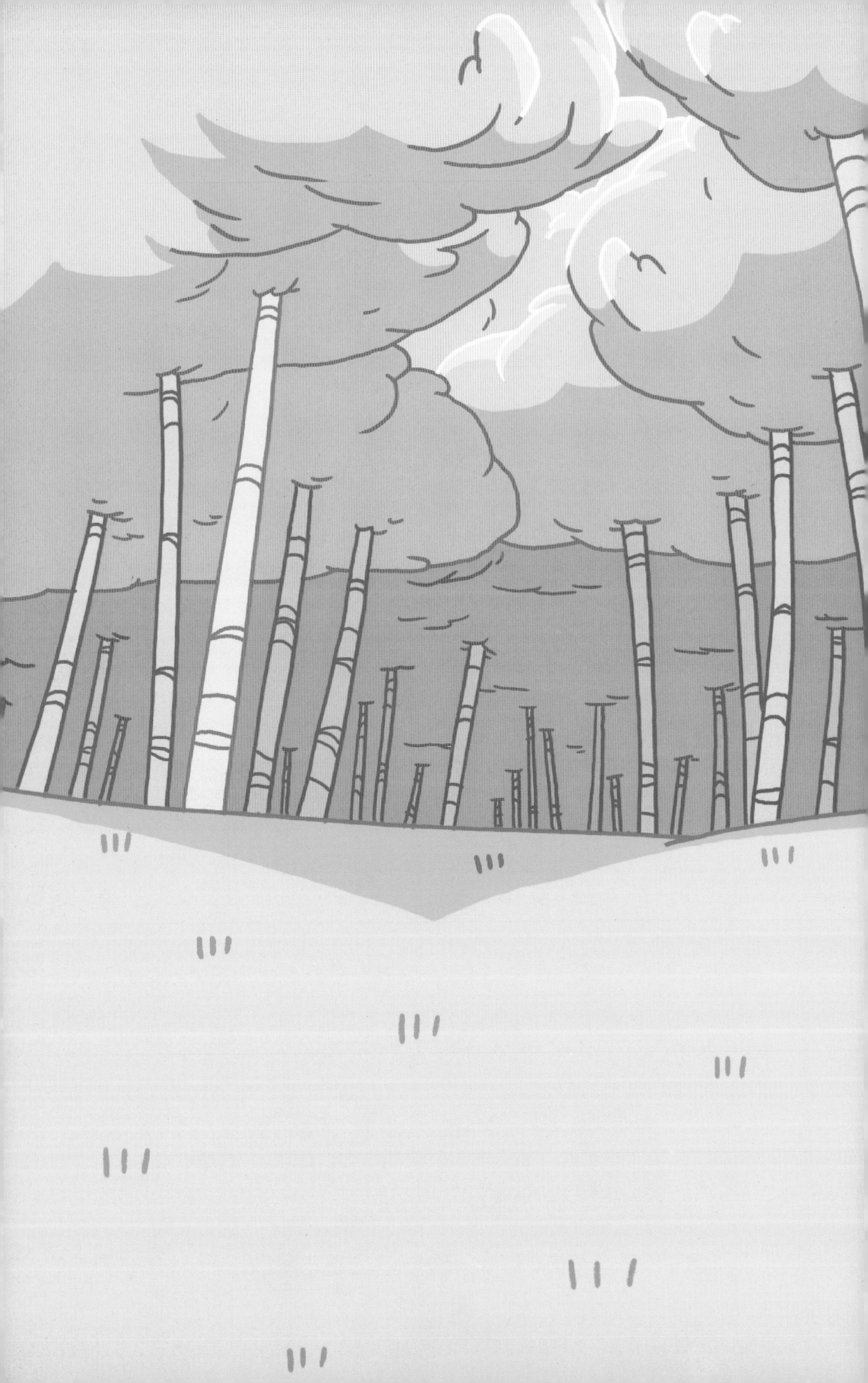

CHAPTER THREE

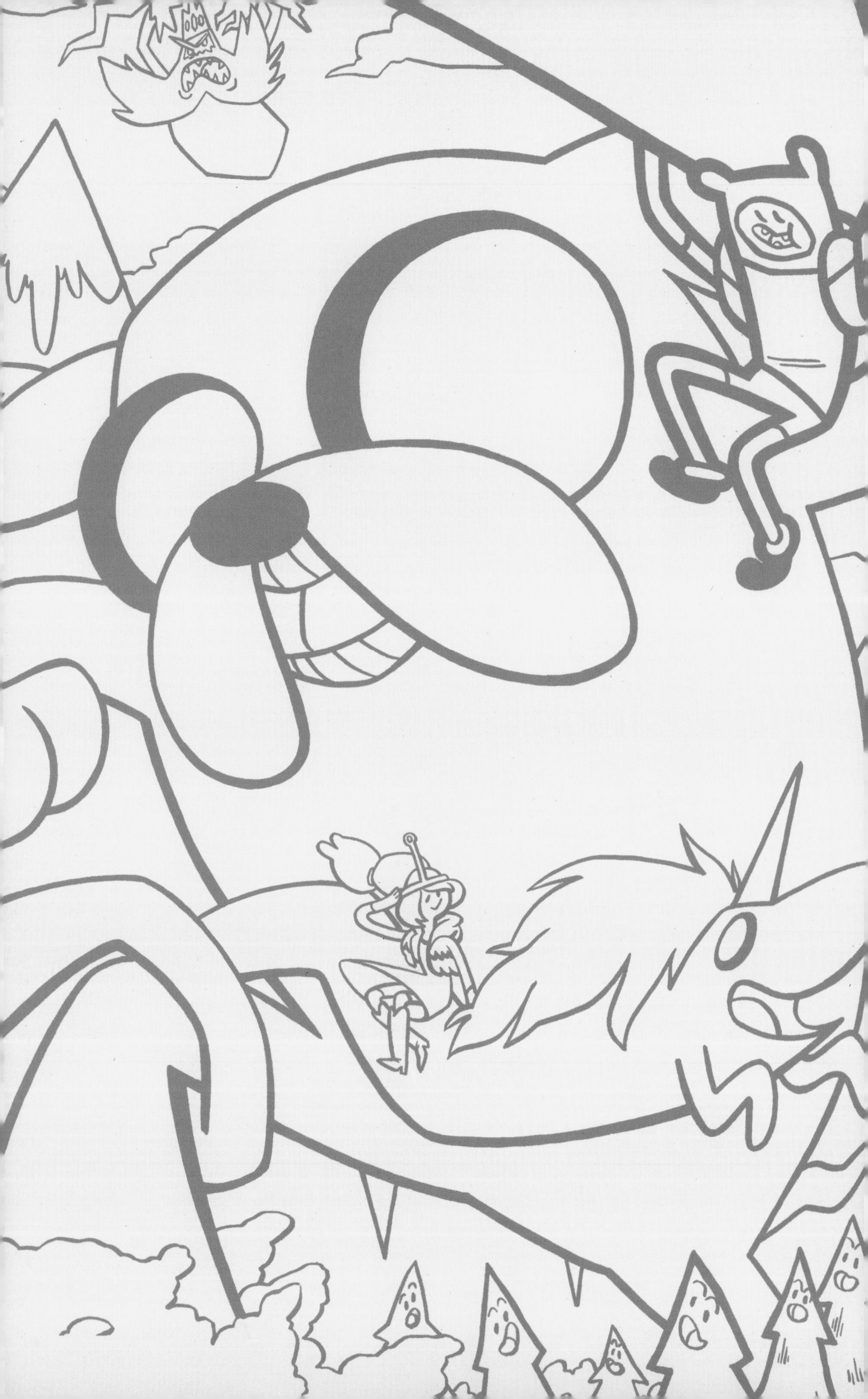

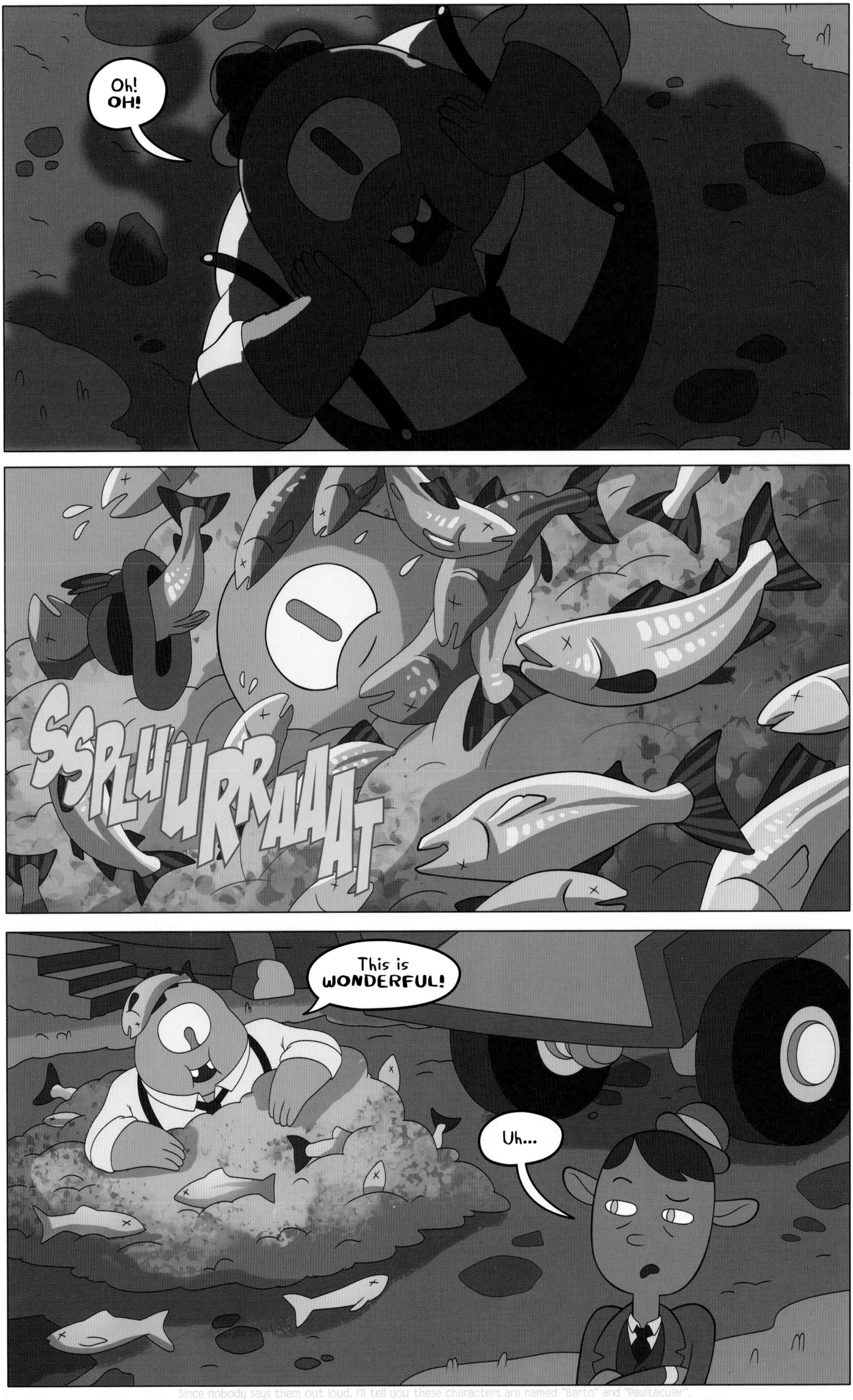
Oh! OH!
SSPLUURRAAAT
This is WONDERFUL!
Uh...

Since nobody says them out loud, I'll tell you these characters are named "Berto" and "Paultacular".

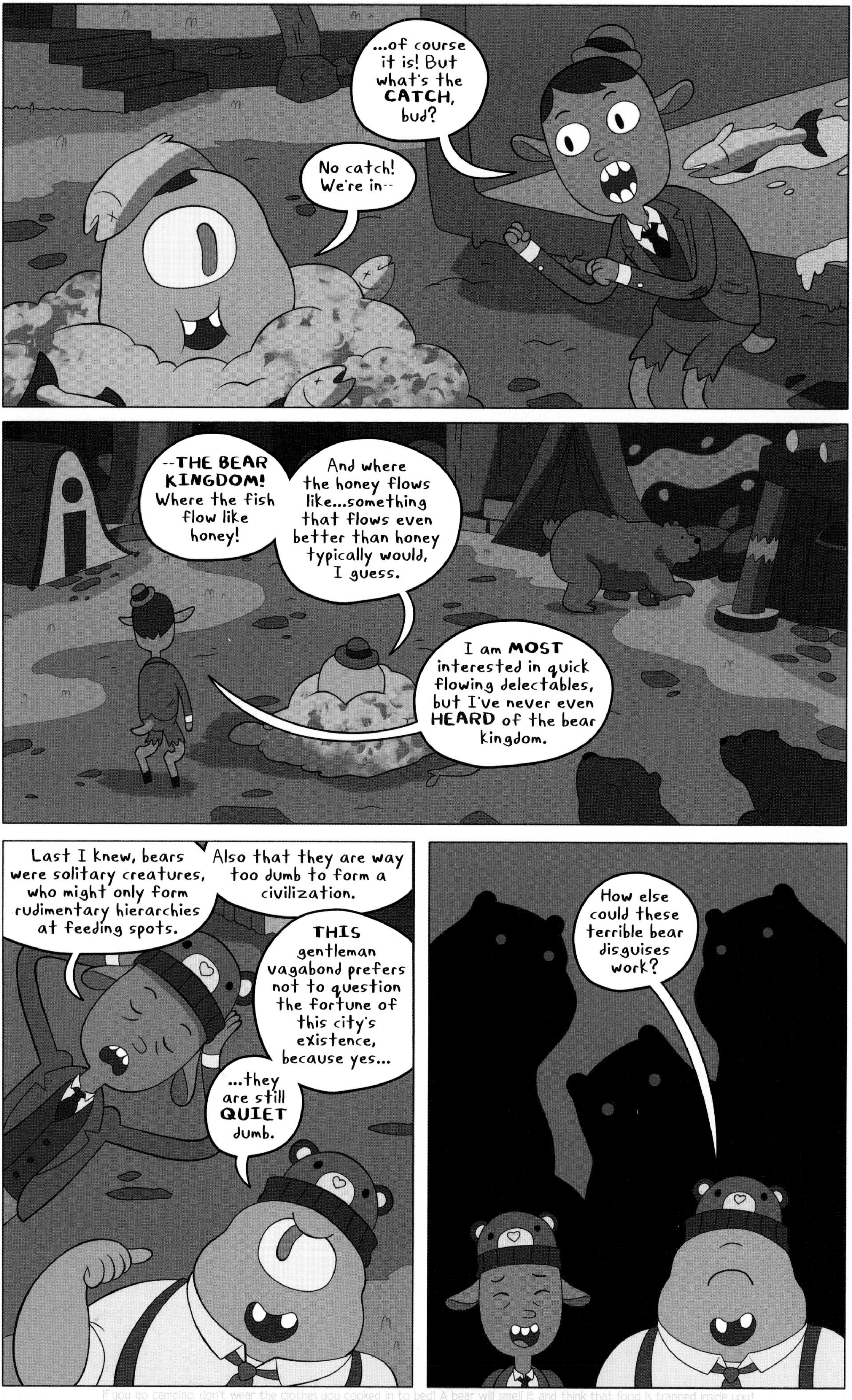
...of course it is! But what's the CATCH, bud?
No catch! We're in--
--THE BEAR KINGDOM! Where the fish flow like honey!
And where the honey flows like...something that flows even better than honey typically would, I guess.
I am MOST interested in quick flowing delectables, but I've never even HEARD of the bear kingdom.
Last I knew, bears were solitary creatures, who might only form rudimentary hierarchies at feeding spots.
Also that they are way too dumb to form a civilization.
THIS gentleman vagabond prefers not to question the fortune of this city's existence, because yes...
...they are still QUIET dumb.
How else could these terrible bear disguises work?

If you go camping, don't wear the clothes you cooked in to bed! A bear will smell it and think that food is trapped inside you!

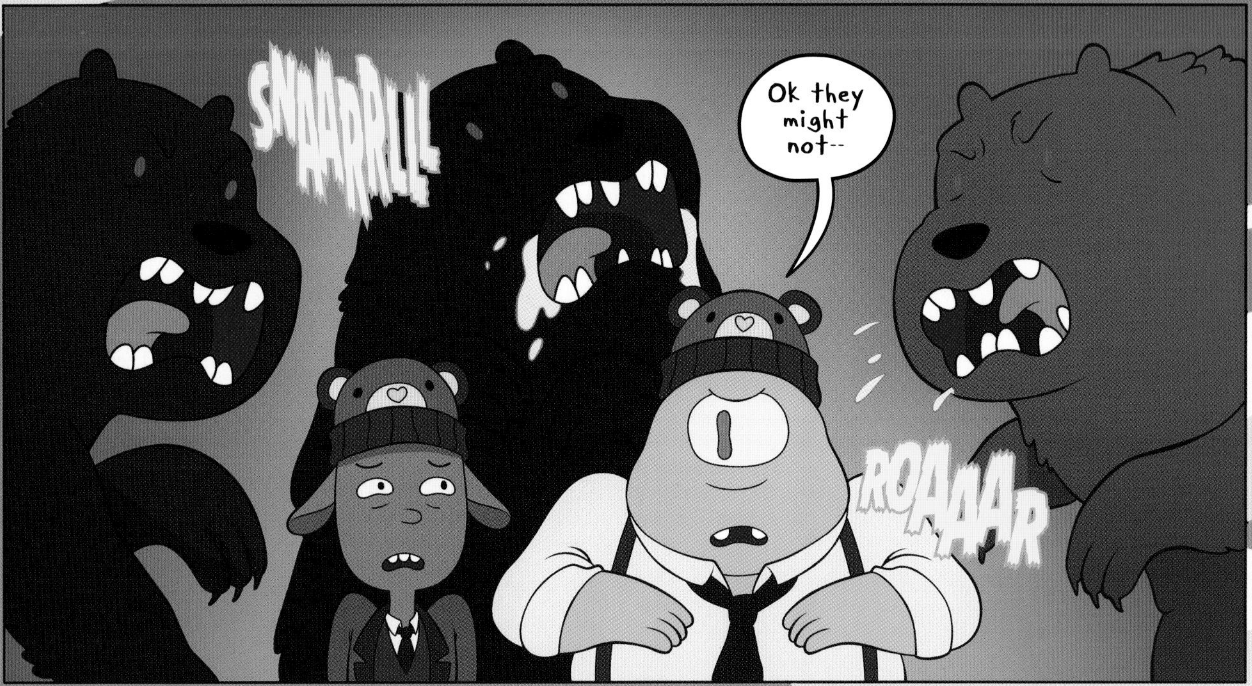
SNAARRLLL
Ok they might not--
ROAAAR

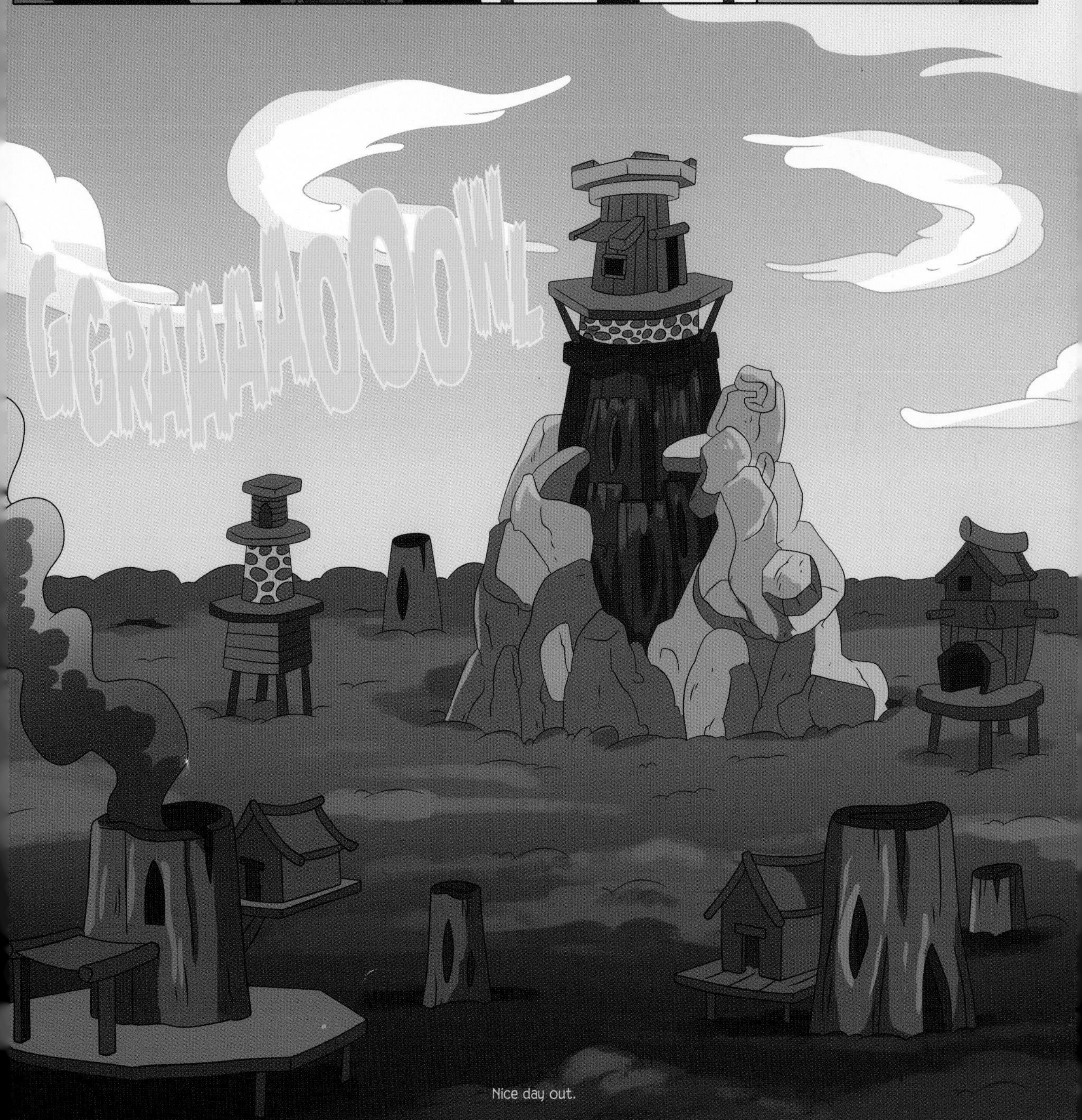
GGRAAAOOOWL

Nice day out.

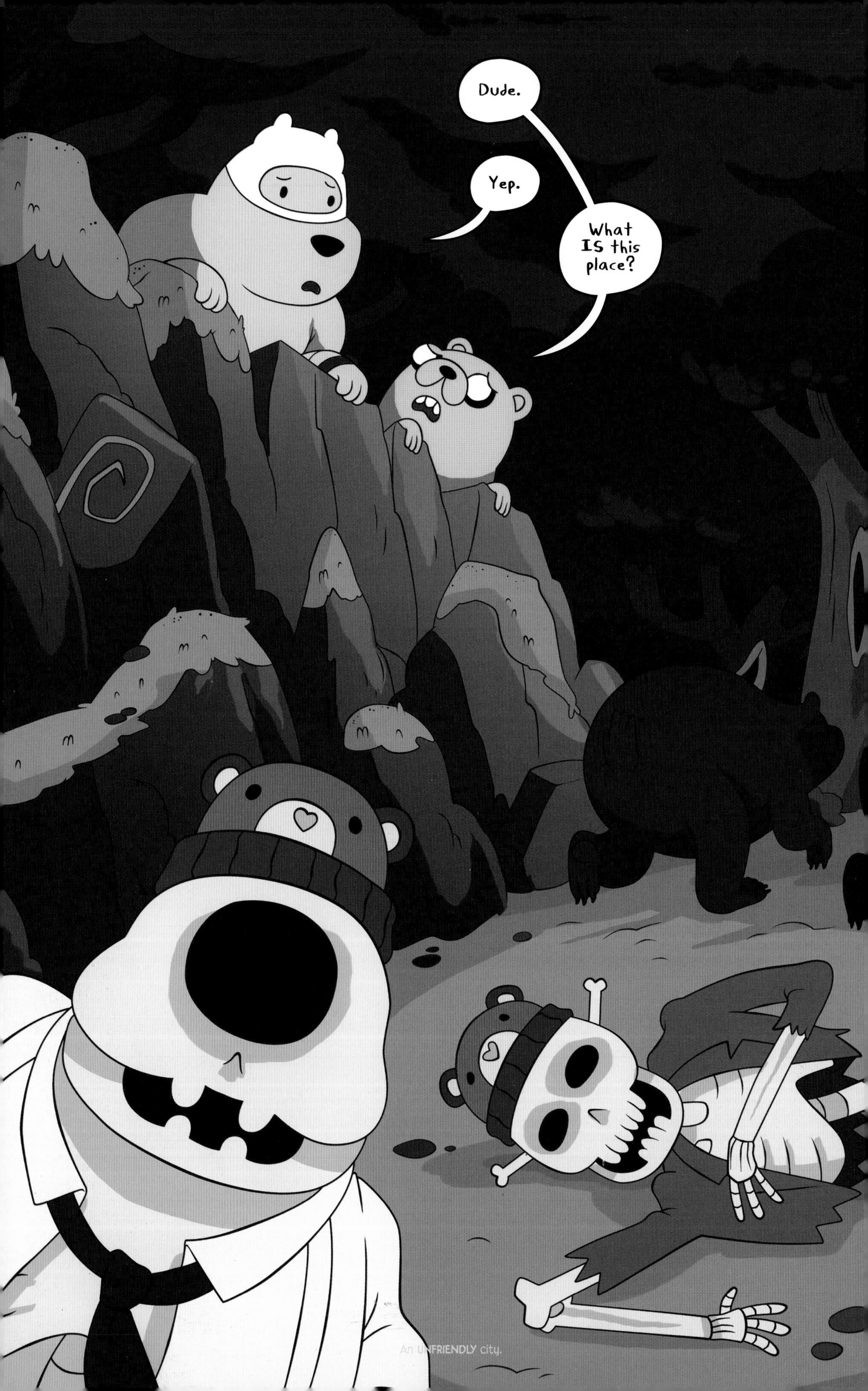
Dude.
Yep.
What IS this place?
An UNFRIENDLY city.

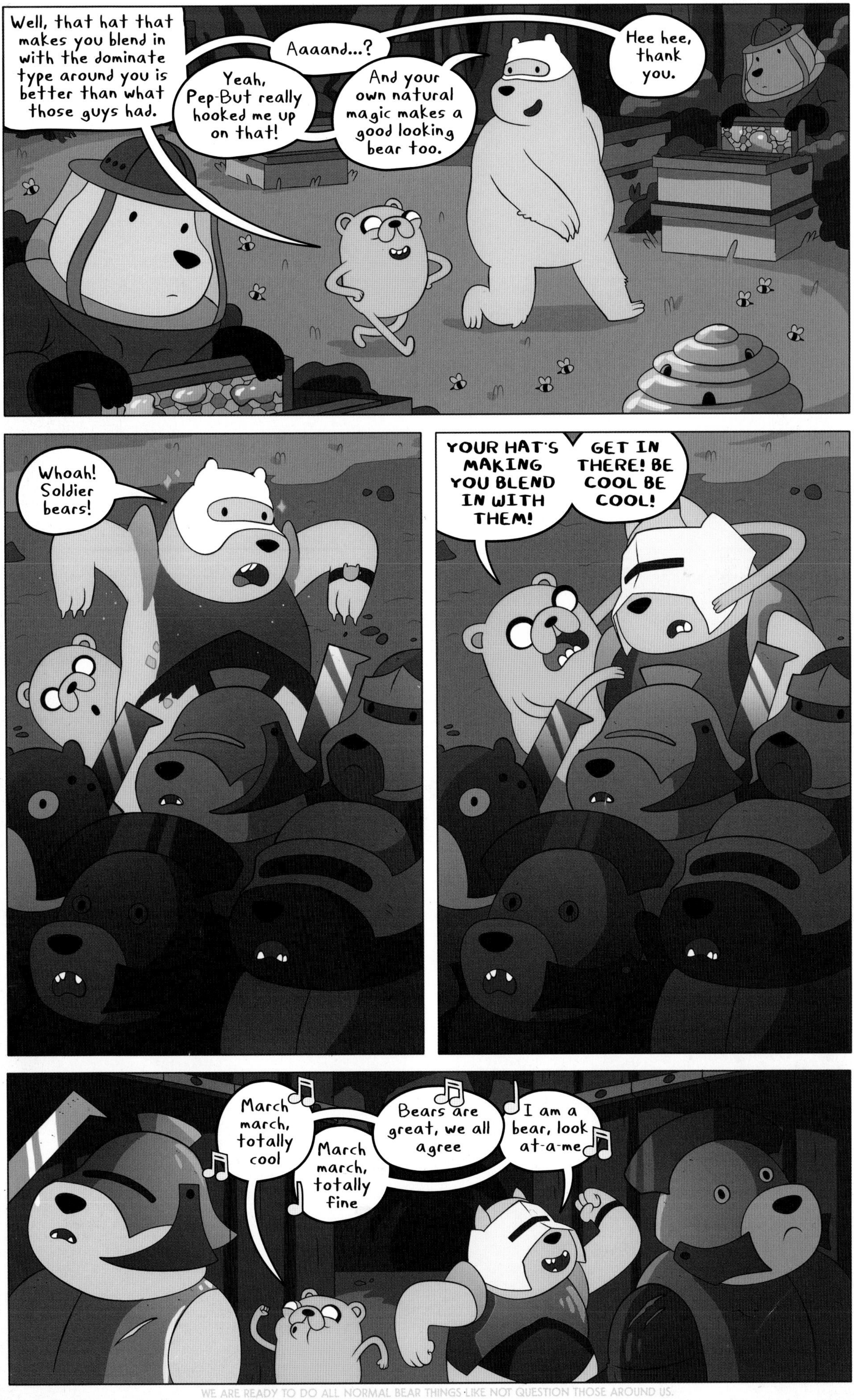
Well, that hat that makes you blend in with the dominate type around you is better than what those guys had.
Yeah, Pep-But really hooked me up on that!
Aaaand...?
And your own natural magic makes a good looking bear too.
Hee hee, thank you.
Whoah! Soldier bears!
YOUR HAT'S MAKING YOU BLEND IN WITH THEM!
GET IN THERE! BE COOL BE COOL!
March march, totally cool
March march, totally fine
Bears are great, we all agree
I am a bear, look at-a-me

WE ARE READY TO DO ALL NORMAL BEAR THINGS LIKE NOT QUESTION THOSE AROUND US.

Oh math.

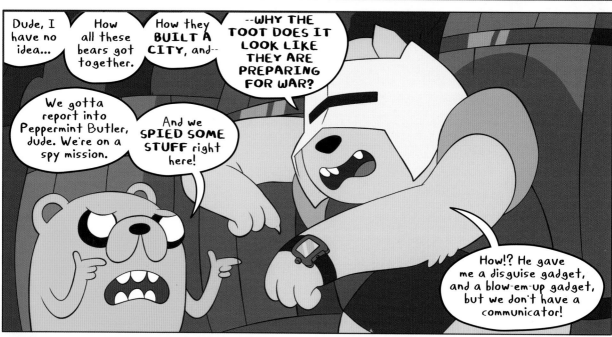

Dude, I have no idea...

How all these bears got together.

How they BUILT A CITY, and--

--WHY THE TOOT DOES IT LOOK LIKE THEY ARE PREPARING FOR WAR?

We gotta report into Peppermint Butler, dude. We're on a spy mission.

And we SPIED SOME STUFF right here!

How!? He gave me a disguise gadget, and a blow-em-up gadget, but we don't have a communicator!

Hmmm...

I got this.

Maybe just blow em all up. Get a pizza. Call it a day? No? Okay I'm a terrible spy.

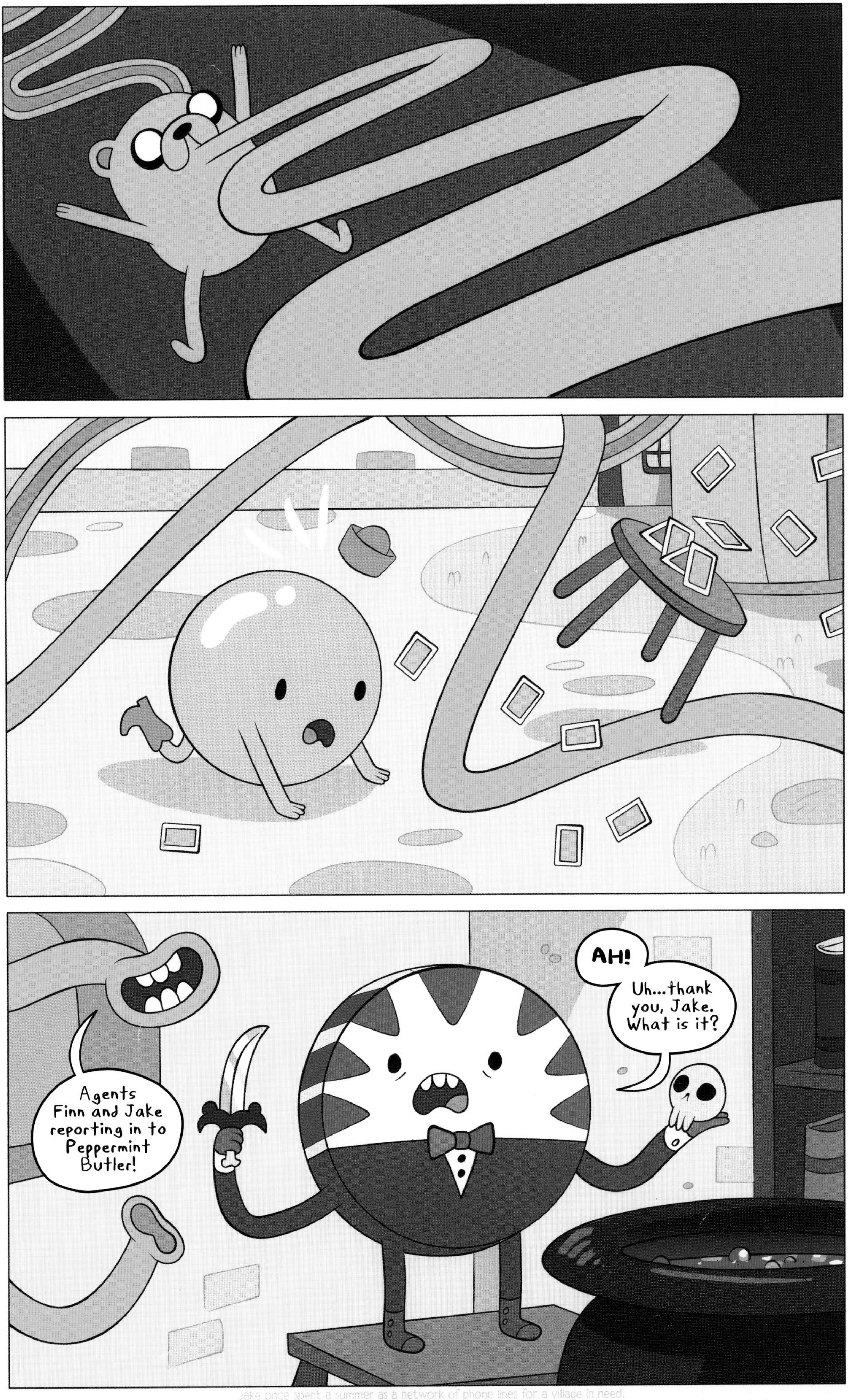

Agents Finn and Jake reporting in to Peppermint Butler!
AH!
Uh...thank you, Jake. What is it?

Jake once spent a summer as a network of phone lines for a village in need.

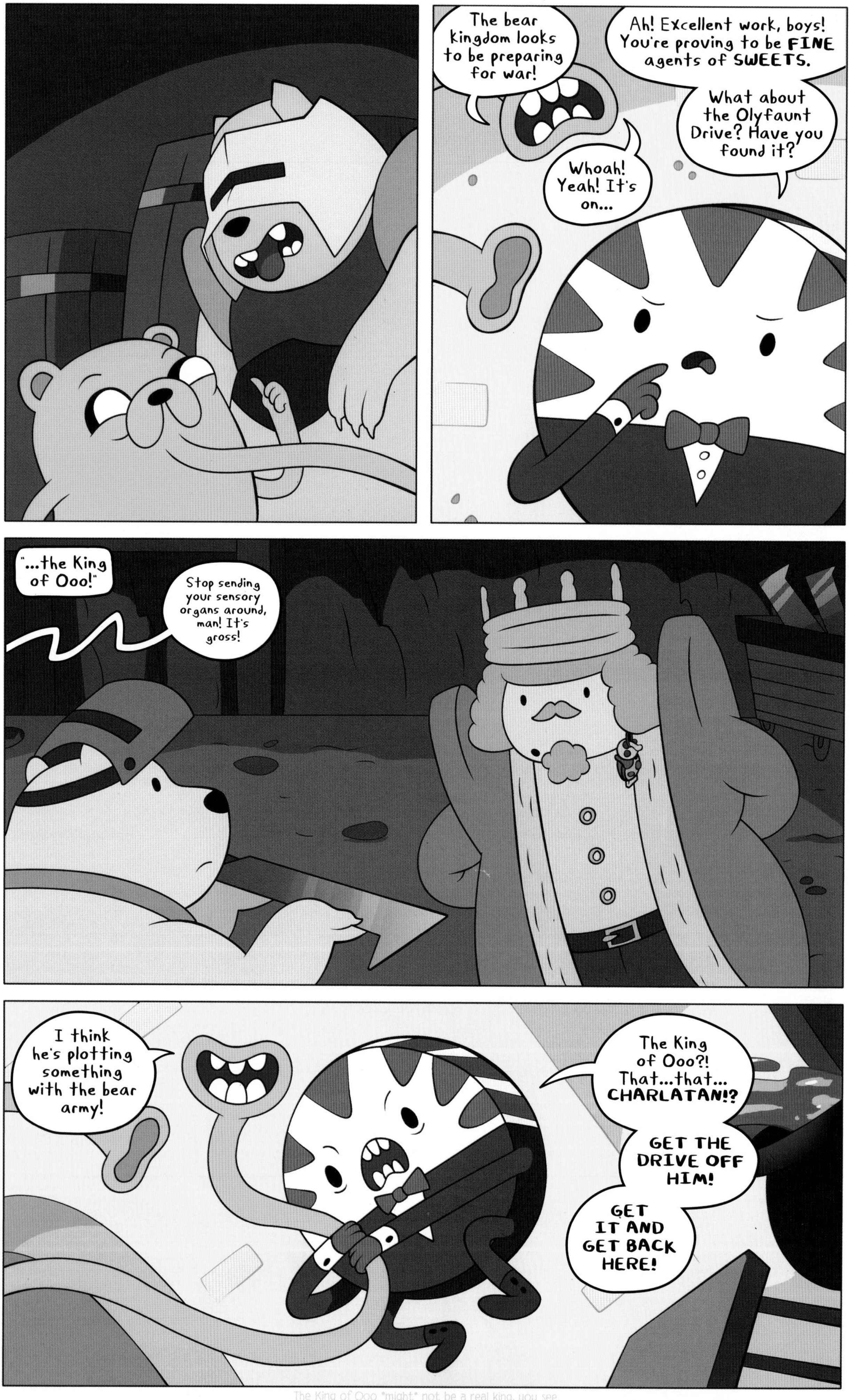
The bear kingdom looks to be preparing for war!
Ah! Excellent work, boys! You're proving to be FINE agents of SWEETS.
What about the Olyfaunt Drive? Have you found it?
Whoah! Yeah! It's on...
"...the King of Ooo!"
Stop sending your sensory organs around, man! It's gross!
I think he's plotting something with the bear army!
The King of Ooo?! That...that... CHARLATAN!?
GET THE DRIVE OFF HIM!
GET IT AND GET BACK HERE!

The King of Ooo *might* not be a real king, you see.

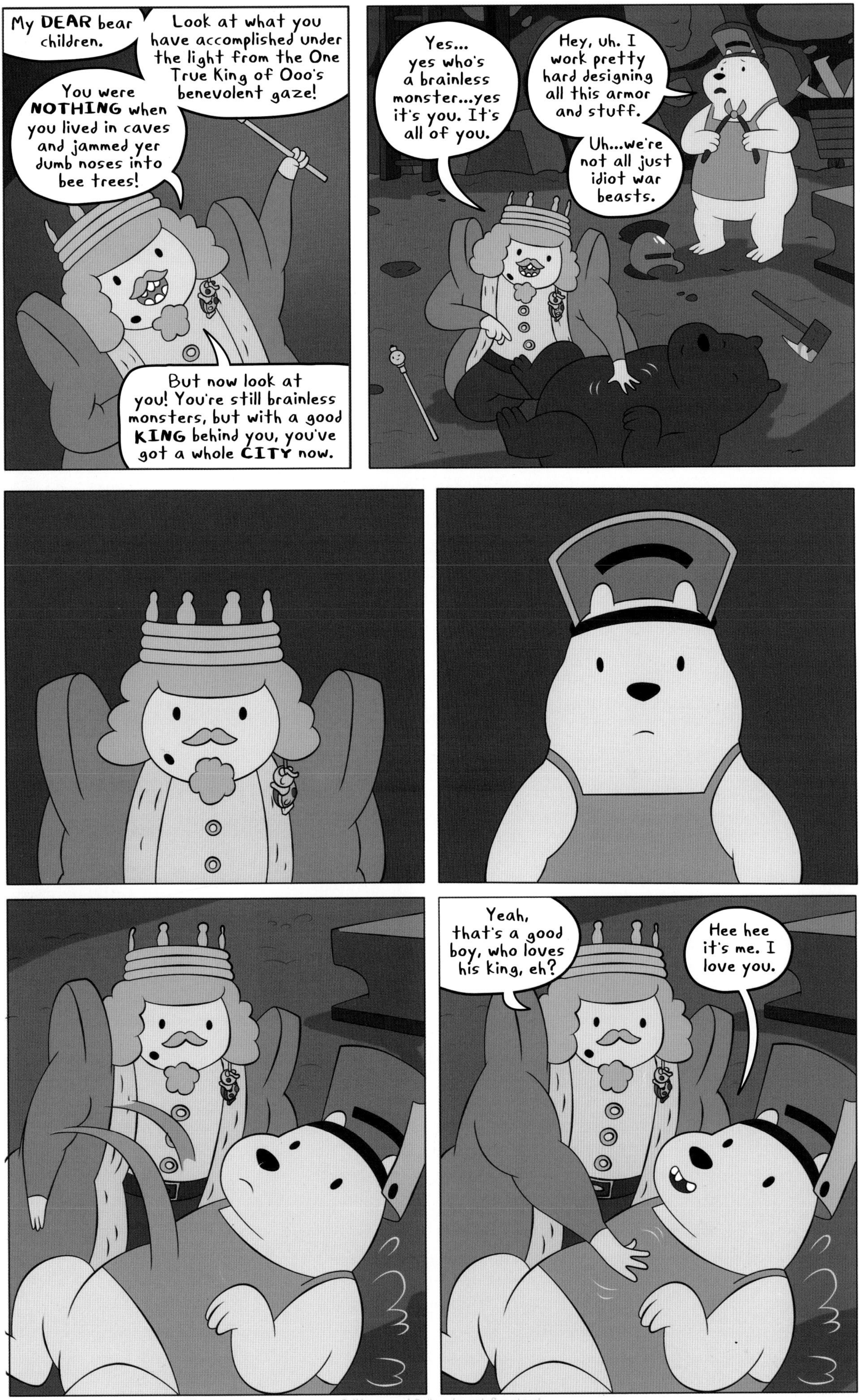

My DEAR bear children.
Look at what you have accomplished under the light from the One True King of Ooo's benevolent gaze!
You were NOTHING when you lived in caves and jammed yer dumb noses into bee trees!
But now look at you! You're still brainless monsters, but with a good KING behind you, you've got a whole CITY now.
Yes... yes who's a brainless monster...yes it's you. It's all of you.
Hey, uh. I work pretty hard designing all this armor and stuff.
Uh...we're not all just idiot war beasts.
Yeah, that's a good boy, who loves his king, eh?
Hee hee it's me. I love you.

Critics agree! Belly rubs get five stars!

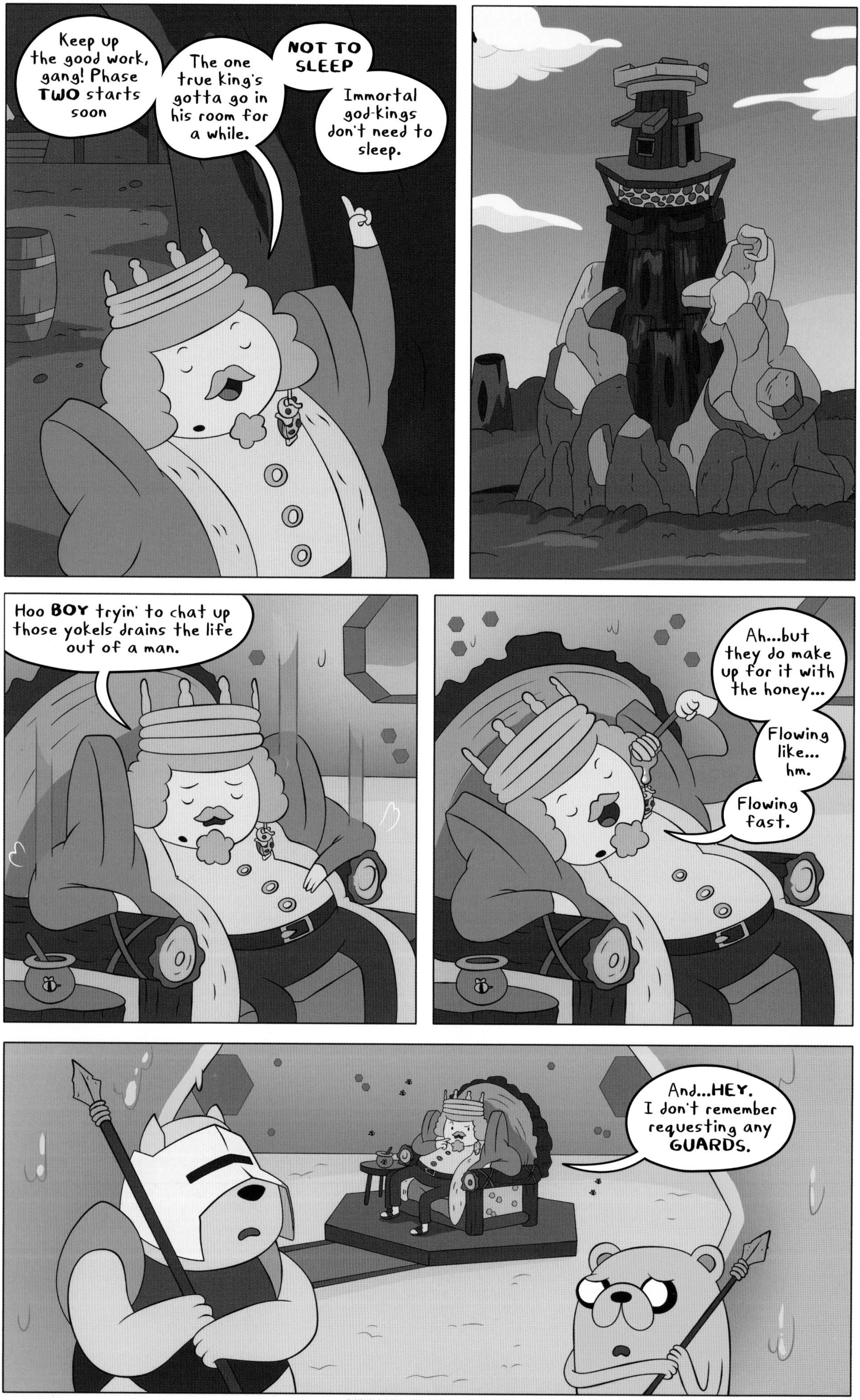

Keep up the good work, gang! Phase **TWO** starts soon
The one true king's gotta go in his room for a while.
NOT TO SLEEP
Immortal god-kings don't need to sleep.
Hoo **BOY** tryin' to chat up those yokels drains the life out of a man.
Ah...but they do make up for it with the honey...
Flowing like... hm.
Flowing fast.
And...**HEY.** I don't remember requesting any **GUARDS.**

"I THINK THAT'S FINN AND JAKE!

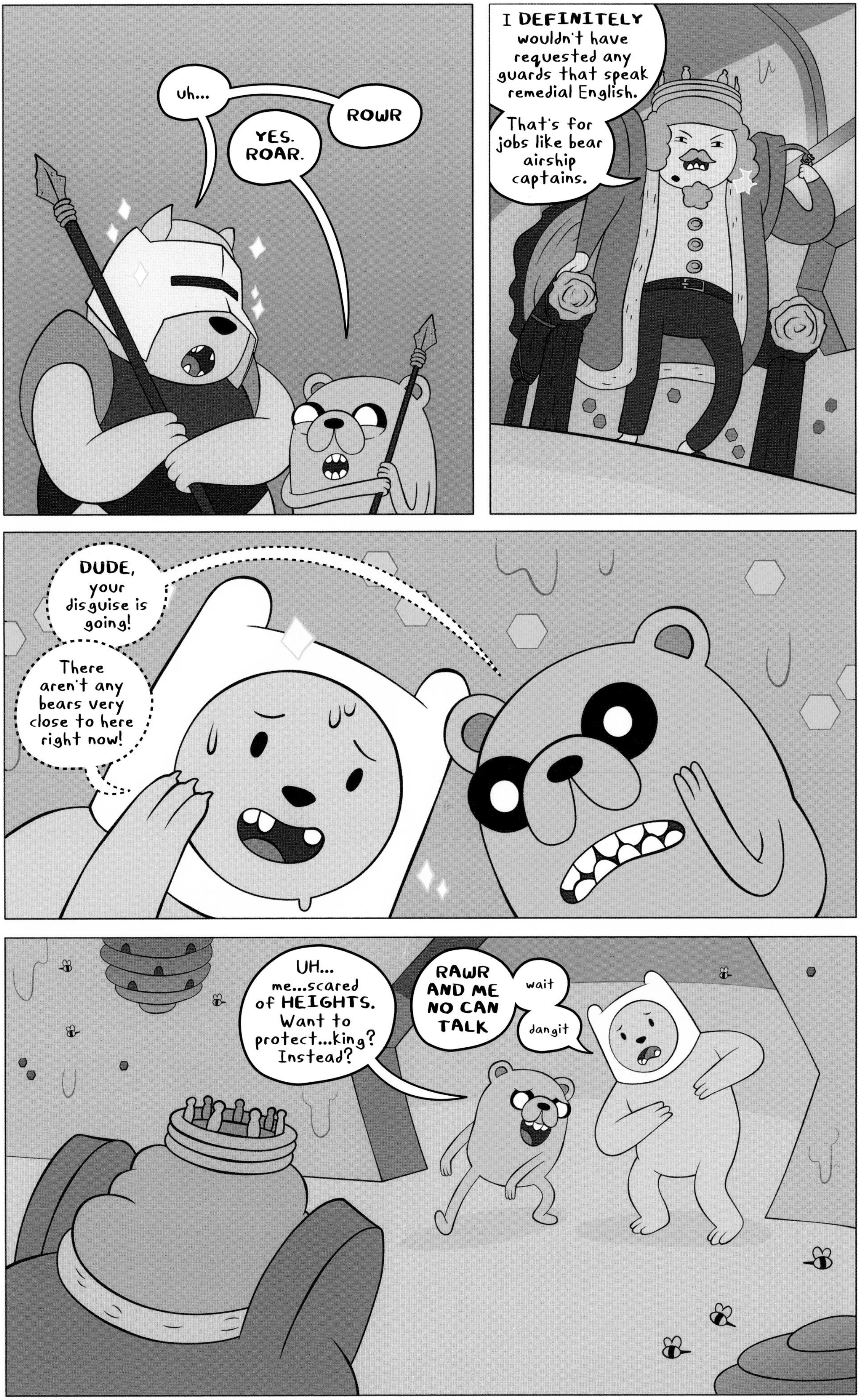

uh...
ROWR
YES. ROAR.
I DEFINITELY wouldn't have requested any guards that speak remedial English.
That's for jobs like bear airship captains.
DUDE, your disguise is going!
There aren't any bears very close to here right now!
UH... me...scared of HEIGHTS. Want to protect...king? Instead?
RAWR AND ME NO CAN TALK
wait
dangit

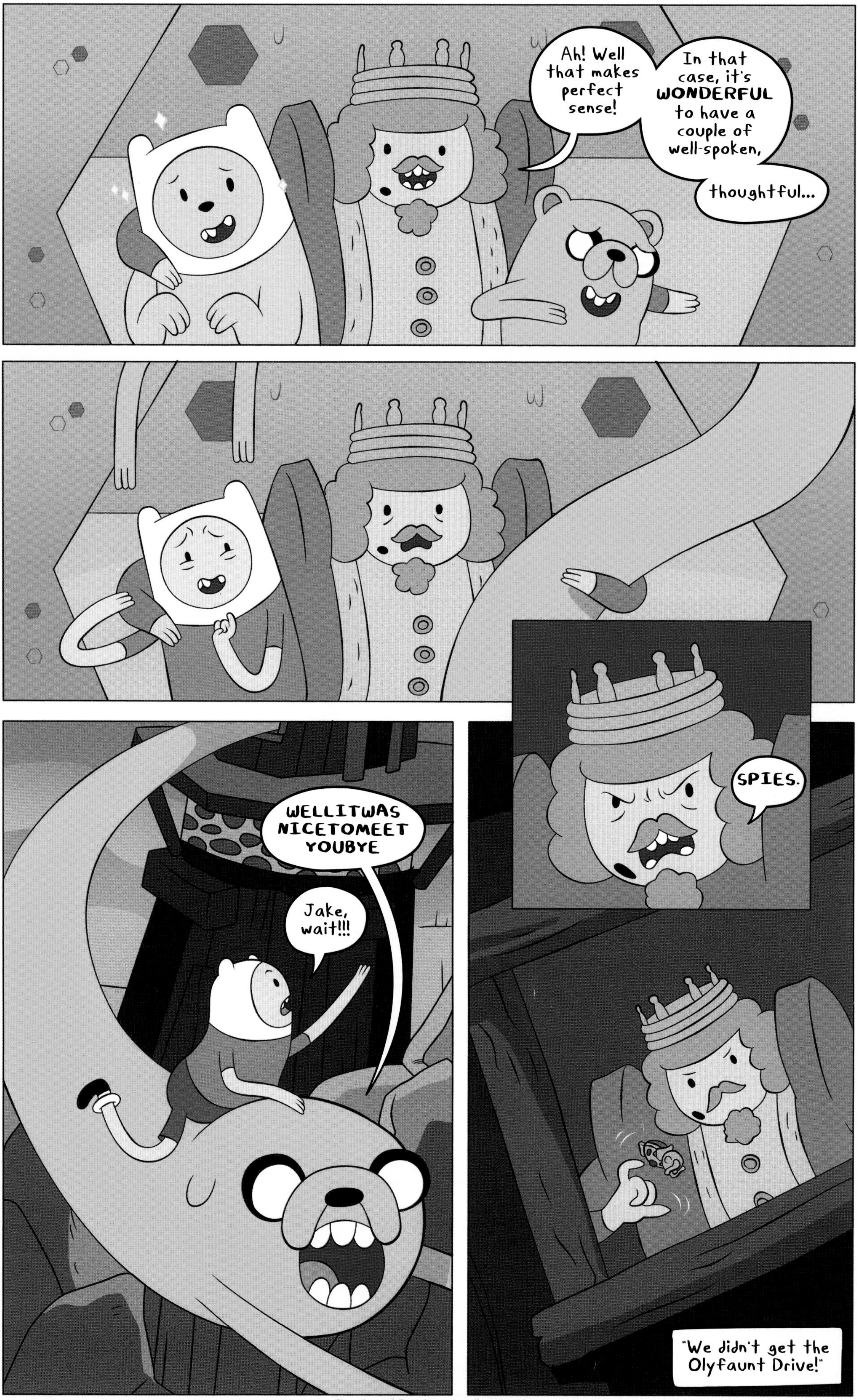
Ah! Well that makes perfect sense!
In that case, it's WONDERFUL to have a couple of well-spoken,
thoughtful...
SPIES.
WELLITWAS NICETOMEET YOUBYE
Jake, wait!!!
"We didn't get the Olyfaunt Drive!"

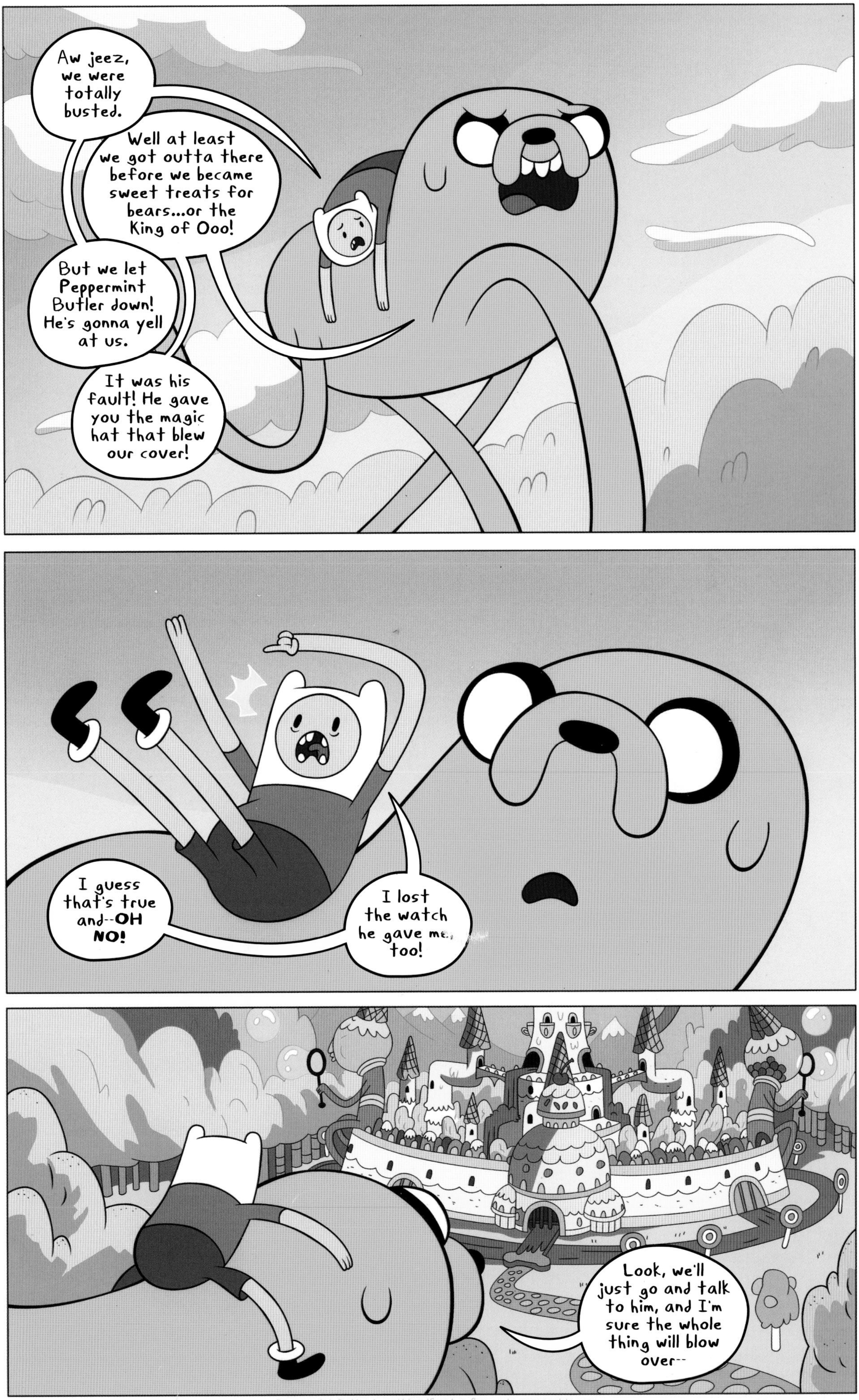
Aw jeez, we were totally busted.
Well at least we got outta there before we became sweet treats for bears...or the King of Ooo!
But we let Peppermint Butler down! He's gonna yell at us.
It was his fault! He gave you the magic hat that blew our cover!
I guess that's true and--OH NO!
I lost the watch he gave me, too!
Look, we'll just go and talk to him, and I'm sure the whole thing will blow over--

Peppermint Butler is nothing if not a famously reasonable man.

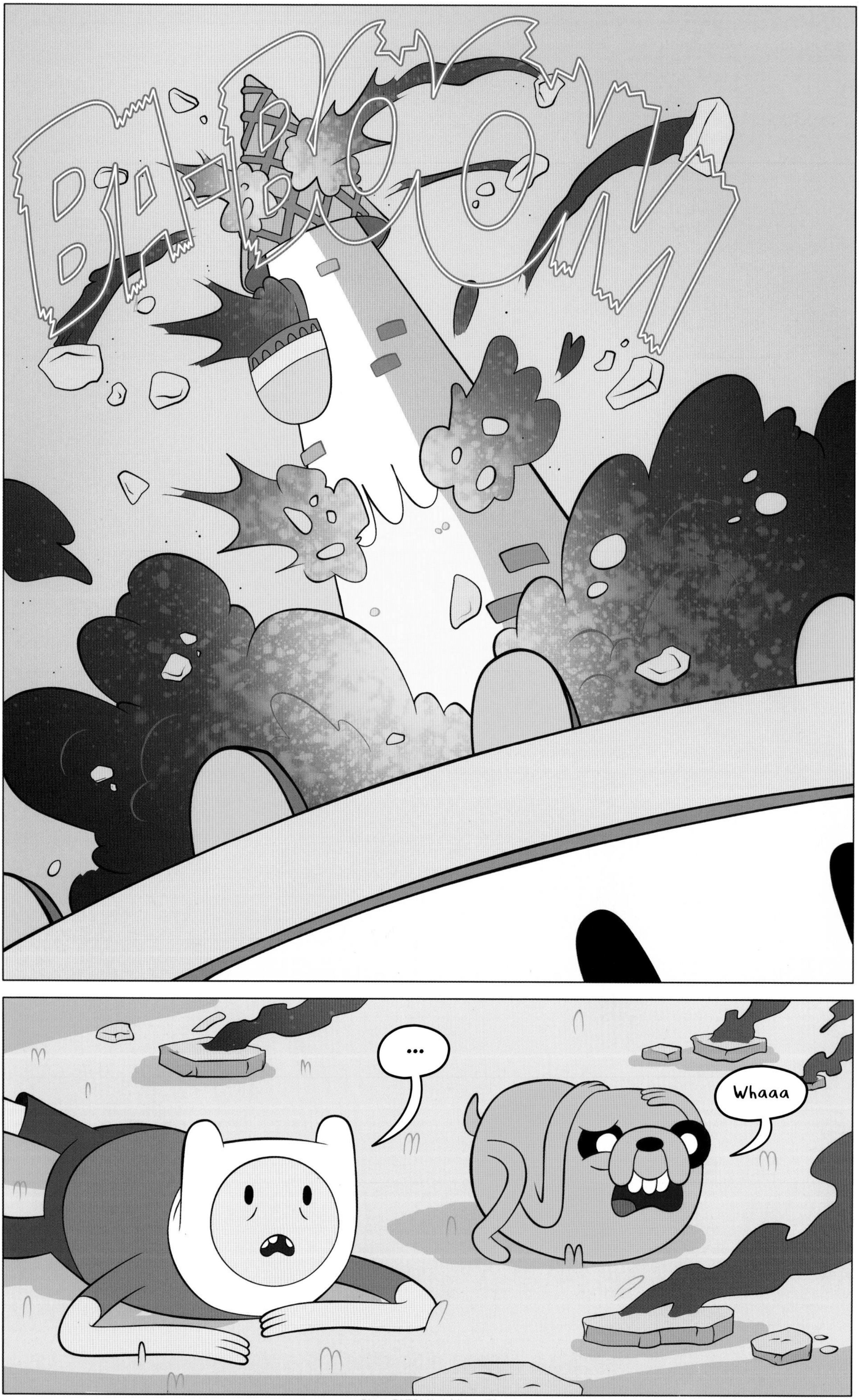
...
Whaaa

Blow OVER! Not blow UP!

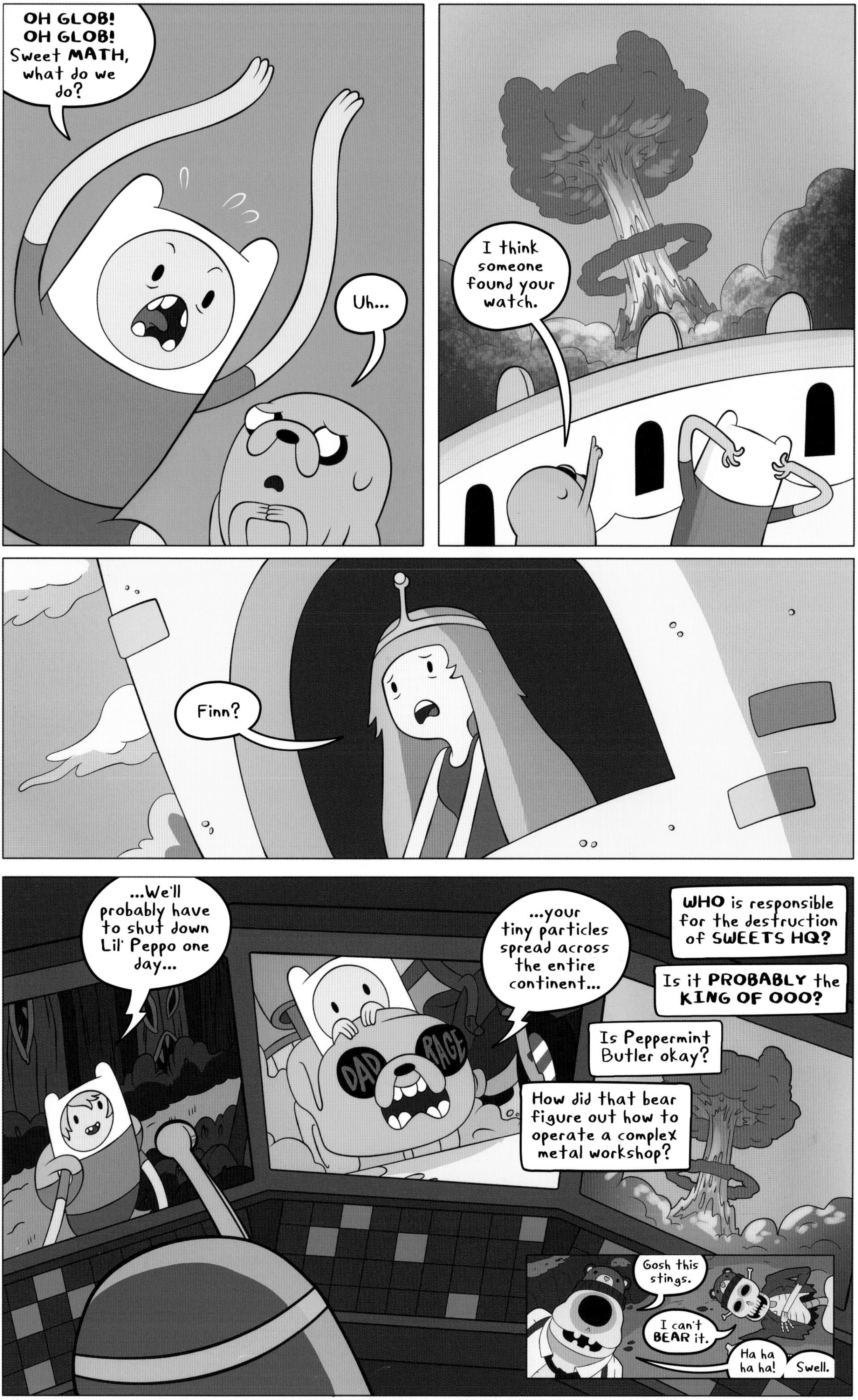

OH GLOB! OH GLOB! Sweet MATH, what do we do?
Uh...
I think someone found your watch.
Finn?
...We'll probably have to shut down Lil' Peppo one day...
...your tiny particles spread across the entire continent...
DAD RAGE
WHO is responsible for the destruction of SWEETS HQ?
Is it PROBABLY the KING OF OOO?
Is Peppermint Butler okay?
How did that bear figure out how to operate a complex metal workshop?
Gosh this stings.
I can't BEAR it.
Ha ha ha ha!
Swell.

No BONES ABOUT IT. Hard to get the BEAR NECESSITIES. Etc.

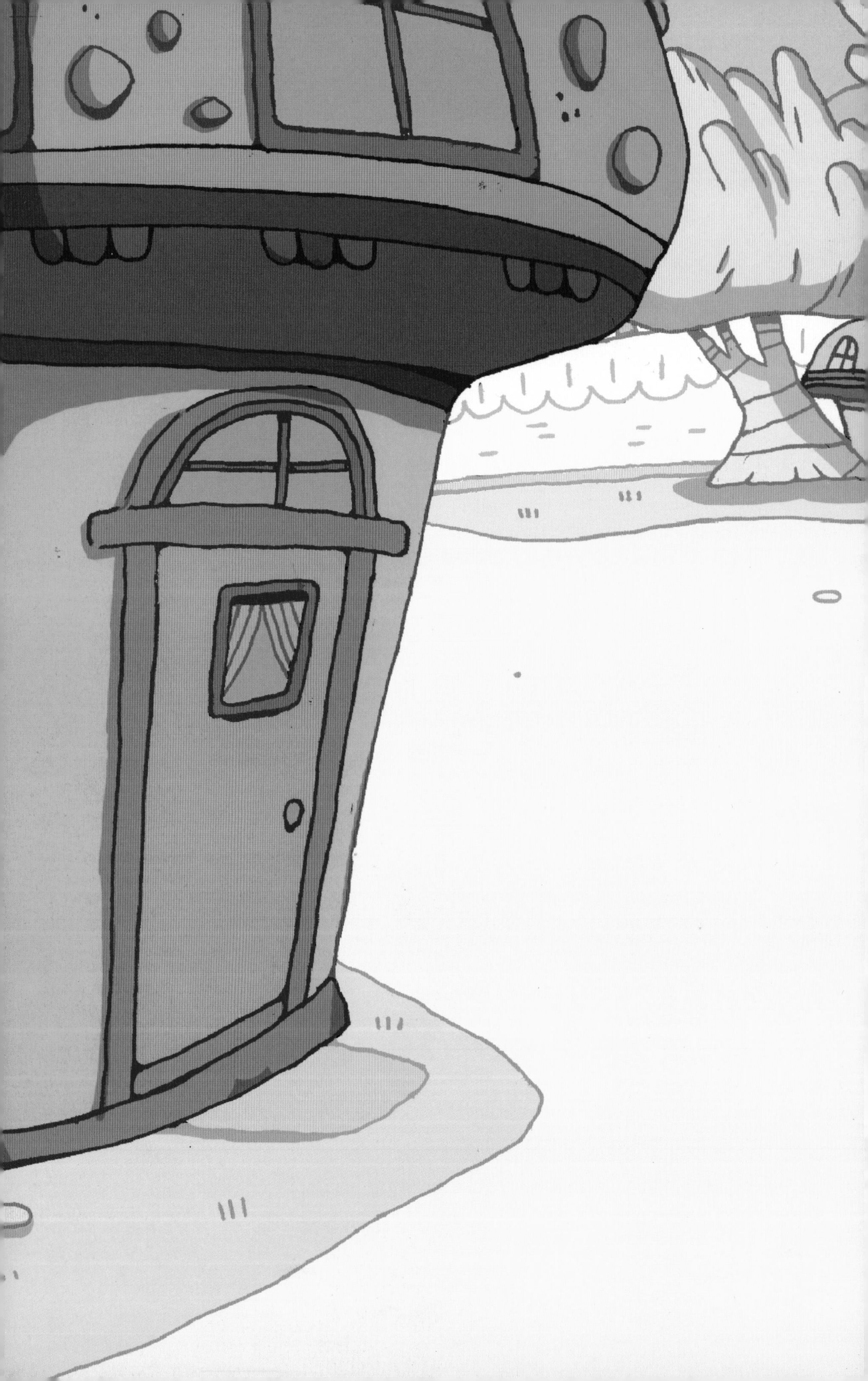

CHAPTER FOUR

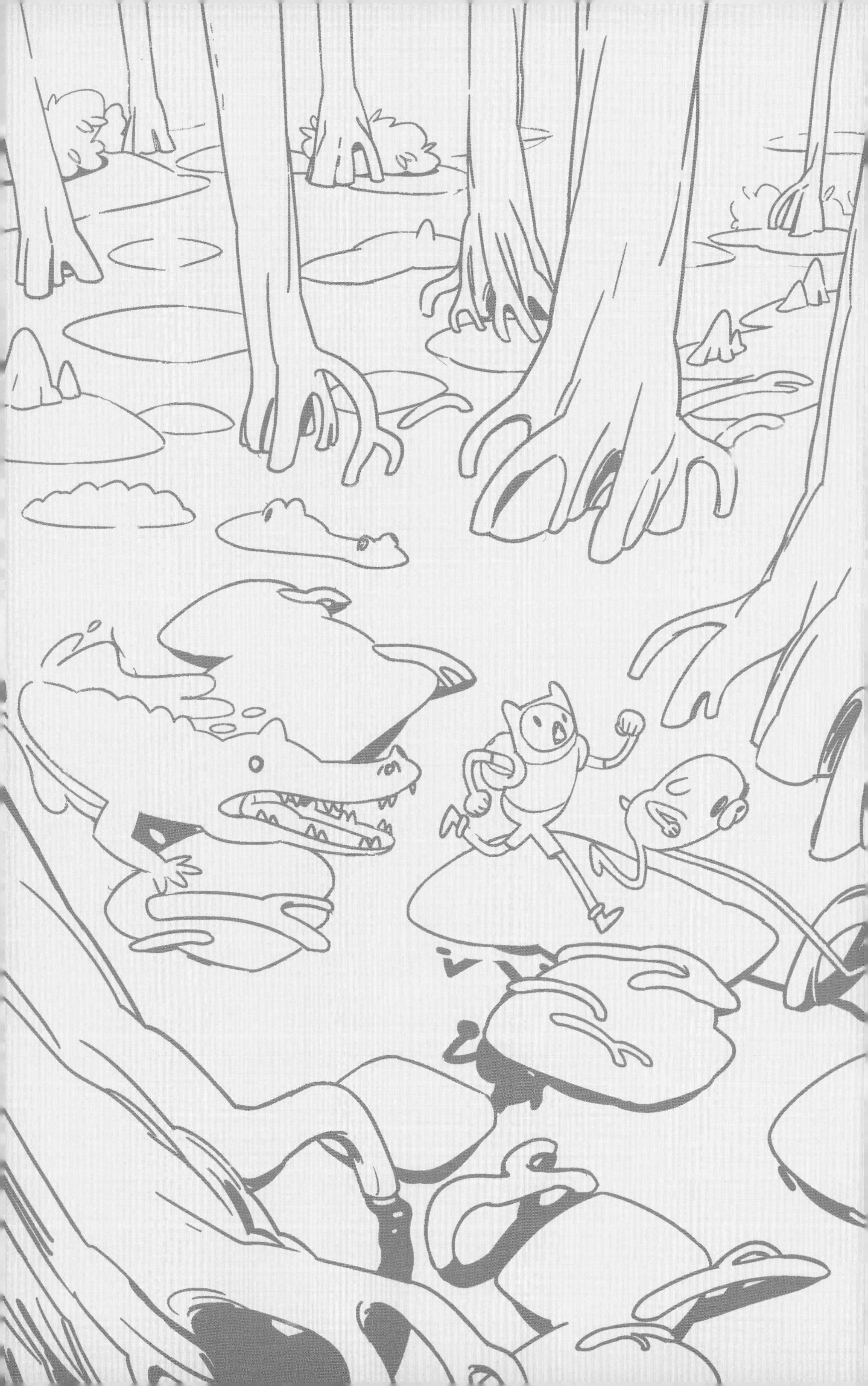

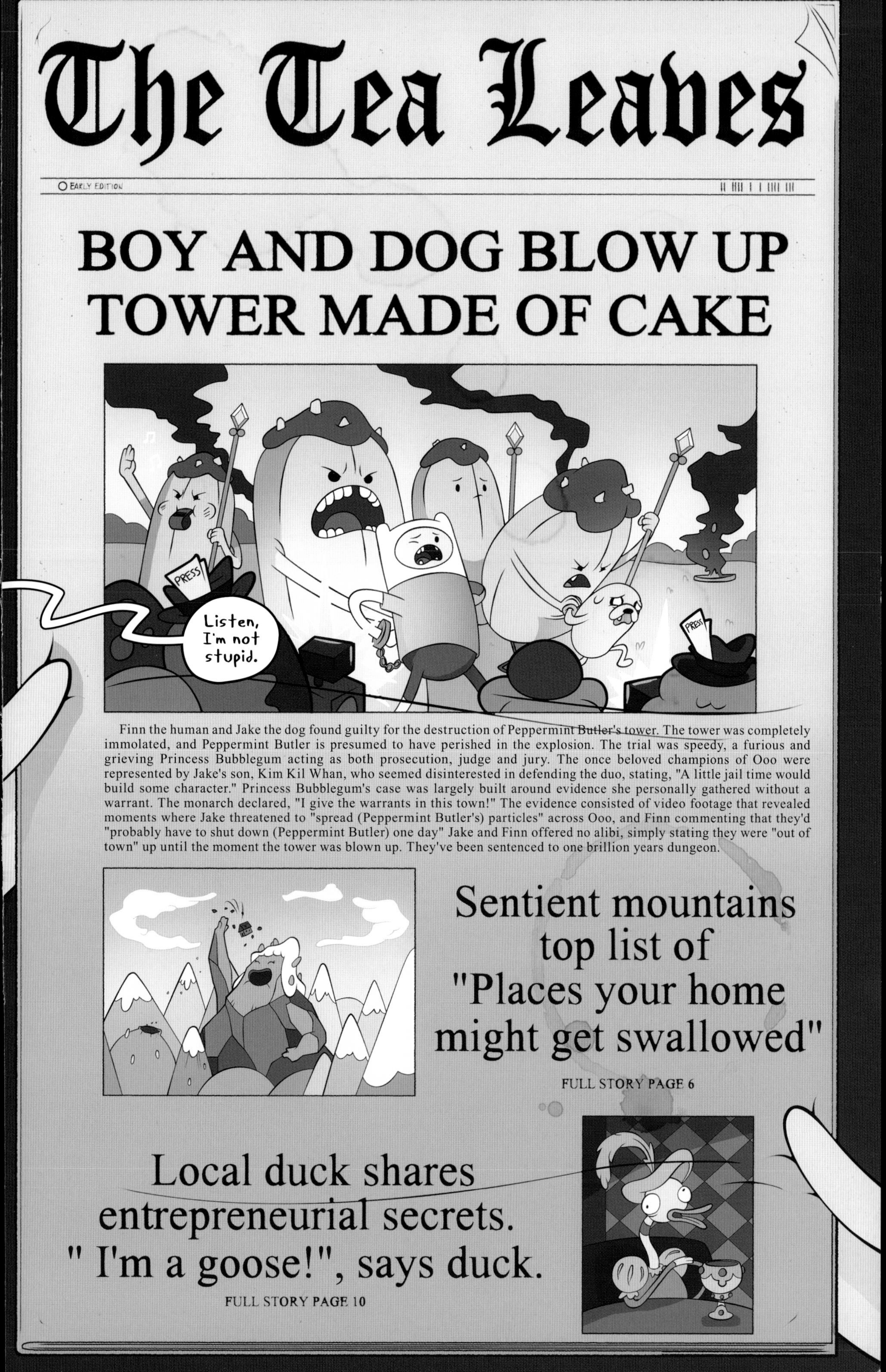

The Tea Leaves

EARLY EDITION

BOY AND DOG BLOW UP TOWER MADE OF CAKE

Finn the human and Jake the dog found guilty for the destruction of Peppermint Butler's tower. The tower was completely immolated, and Peppermint Butler is presumed to have perished in the explosion. The trial was speedy, a furious and grieving Princess Bubblegum acting as both prosecution, judge and jury. The once beloved champions of Ooo were represented by Jake's son, Kim Kil Whan, who seemed disinterested in defending the duo, stating, "A little jail time would build some character." Princess Bubblegum's case was largely built around evidence she personally gathered without a warrant. The monarch declared, "I give the warrants in this town!" The evidence consisted of video footage that revealed moments where Jake threatened to "spread (Peppermint Butler's) particles" across Ooo, and Finn commenting that they'd "probably have to shut down (Peppermint Butler) one day" Jake and Finn offered no alibi, simply stating they were "out of town" up until the moment the tower was blown up. They've been sentenced to one brillion years dungeon.

Sentient mountains top list of "Places your home might get swallowed"

FULL STORY PAGE 6

Local duck shares entrepreneurial secrets. " I'm a goose!", says duck.

FULL STORY PAGE 10

PRESS
Listen, I'm not stupid.
PRESS

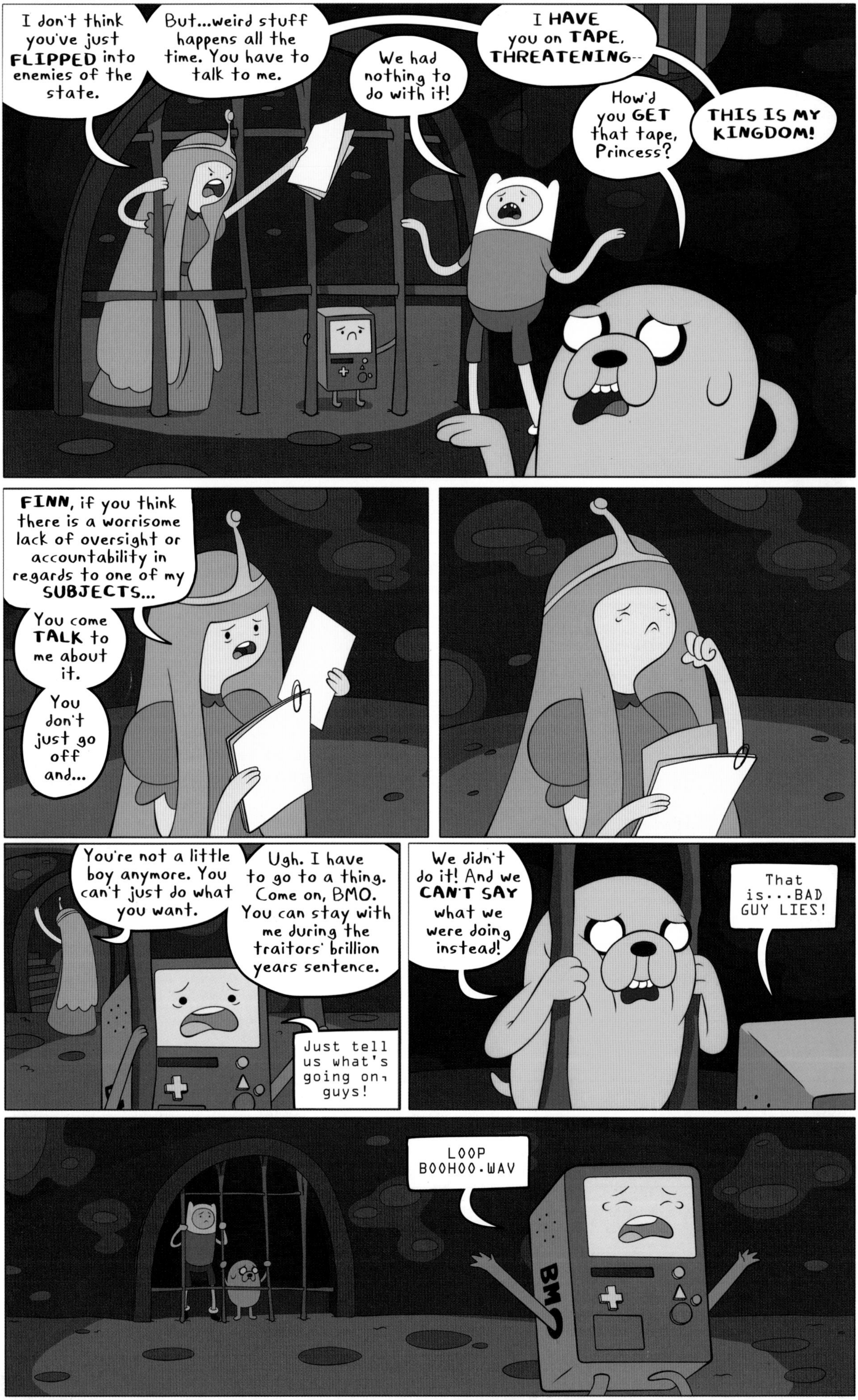
I don't think you've just FLIPPED into enemies of the state.
But...weird stuff happens all the time. You have to talk to me.
We had nothing to do with it!
I HAVE you on TAPE, THREATENING--
How'd you GET that tape, Princess?
THIS IS MY KINGDOM!
FINN, if you think there is a worrisome lack of oversight or accountability in regards to one of my SUBJECTS...
You come TALK to me about it.
You don't just go off and...
You're not a little boy anymore. You can't just do what you want.
Ugh. I have to go to a thing. Come on, BMO. You can stay with me during the traitors' brillion years sentence.
Just tell us what's going on, guys!
We didn't do it! And we CAN'T SAY what we were doing instead!
That is...BAD GUY LIES!
LOOP BOOHOO.WAV
BMO

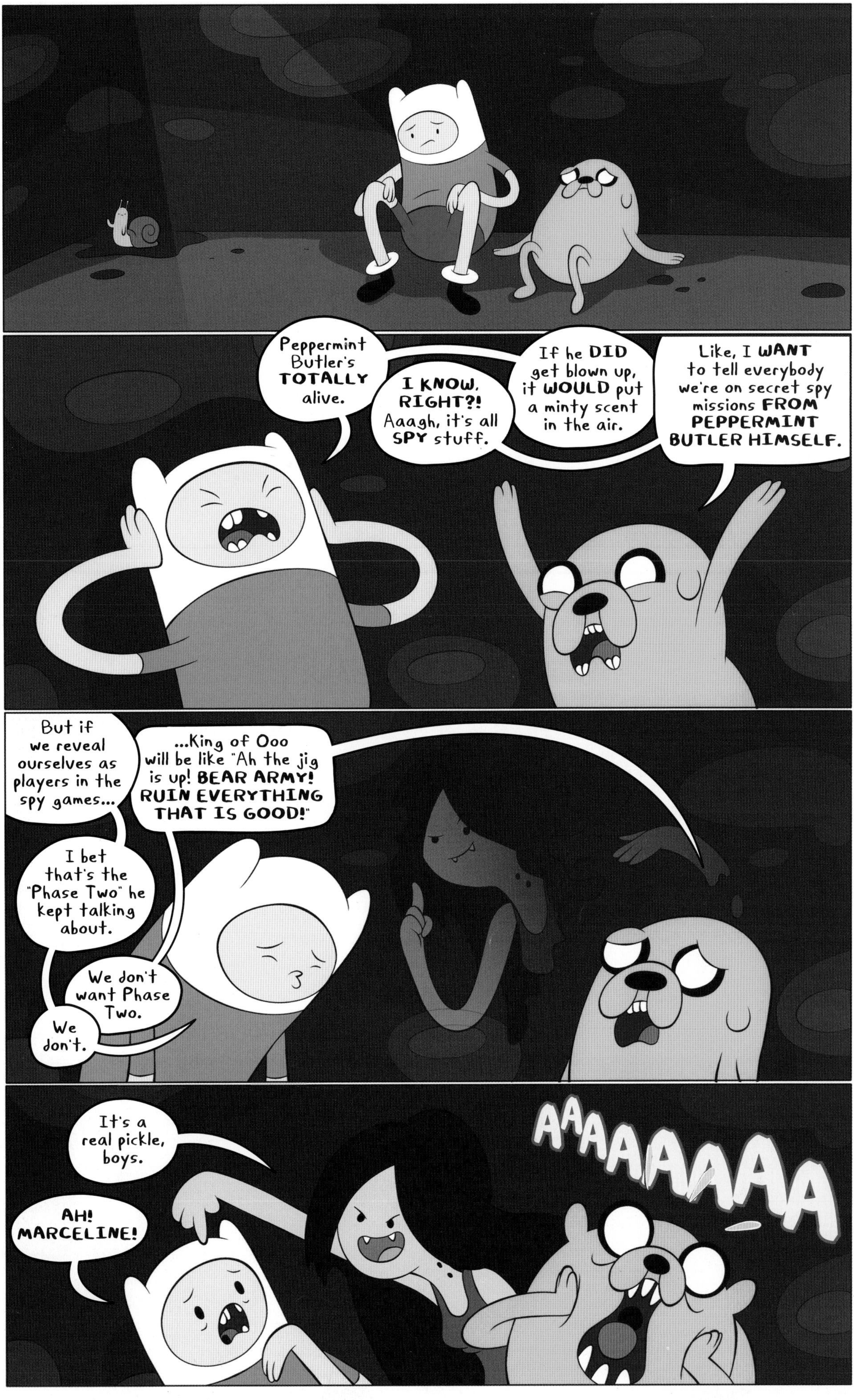
Peppermint Butler's TOTALLY alive.
I KNOW, RIGHT?! Aaagh, it's all SPY stuff.
If he DID get blown up, it WOULD put a minty scent in the air.
Like, I WANT to tell everybody we're on secret spy missions FROM PEPPERMINT BUTLER HIMSELF.
But if we reveal ourselves as players in the spy games...
...King of Ooo will be like "Ah the jig is up! BEAR ARMY! RUIN EVERYTHING THAT IS GOOD!"
I bet that's the "Phase Two" he kept talking about.
We don't want Phase Two.
We don't.
It's a real pickle, boys.
AH! MARCELINE!
AAAAAAAAA

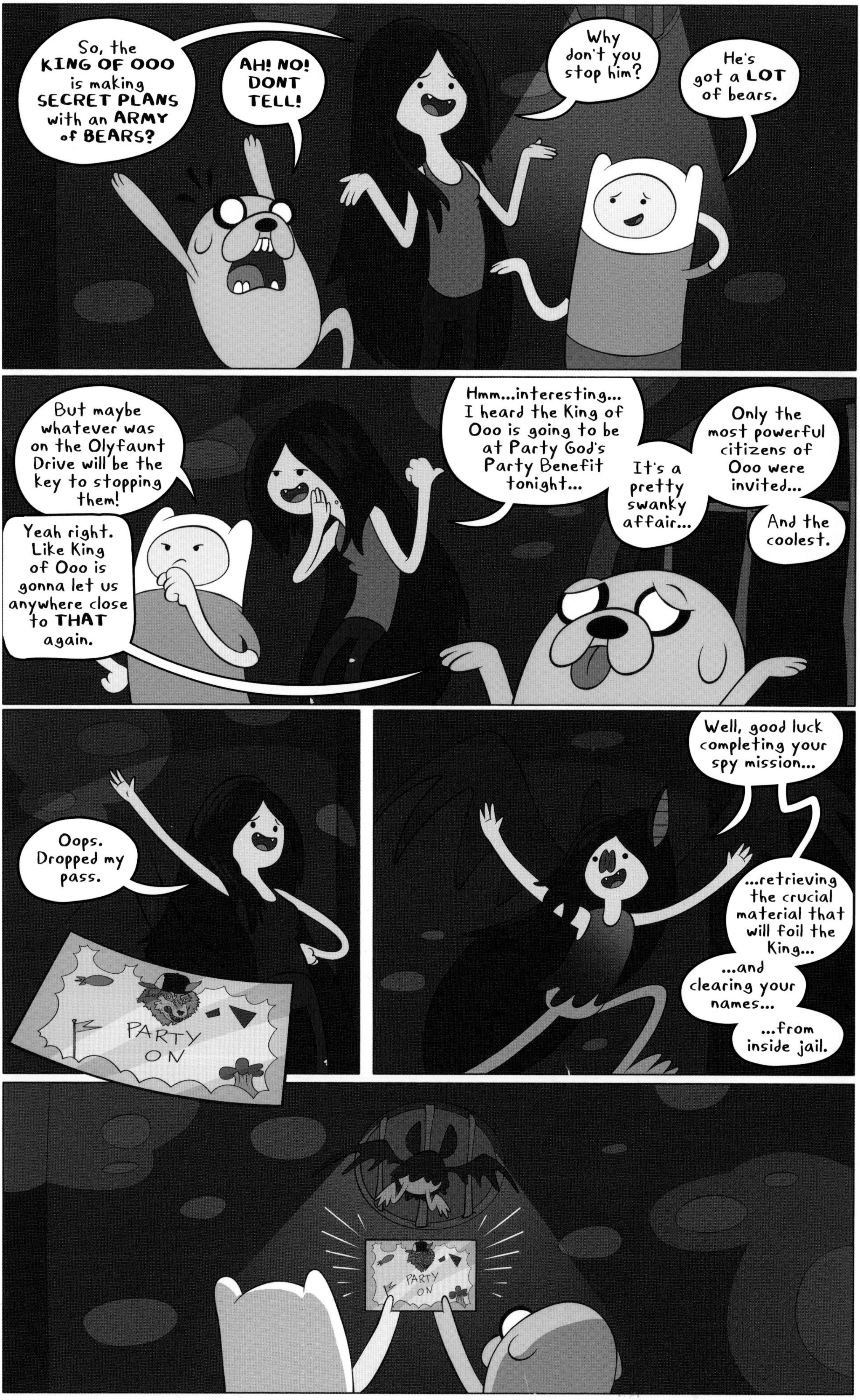
So, the KING OF OOO is making SECRET PLANS with an ARMY of BEARS?
AH! NO! DONT TELL!
Why don't you stop him?
He's got a LOT of bears.
But maybe whatever was on the Olyfaunt Drive will be the key to stopping them!
Yeah right. Like King of Ooo is gonna let us anywhere close to THAT again.
Hmm...interesting... I heard the King of Ooo is going to be at Party God's Party Benefit tonight...
It's a pretty swanky affair...
Only the most powerful citizens of Ooo were invited...
And the coolest.
Oops. Dropped my pass.
PARTY ON
Well, good luck completing your spy mission...
...retrieving the crucial material that will foil the King...
...and clearing your names...
...from inside jail.
PARTY ON

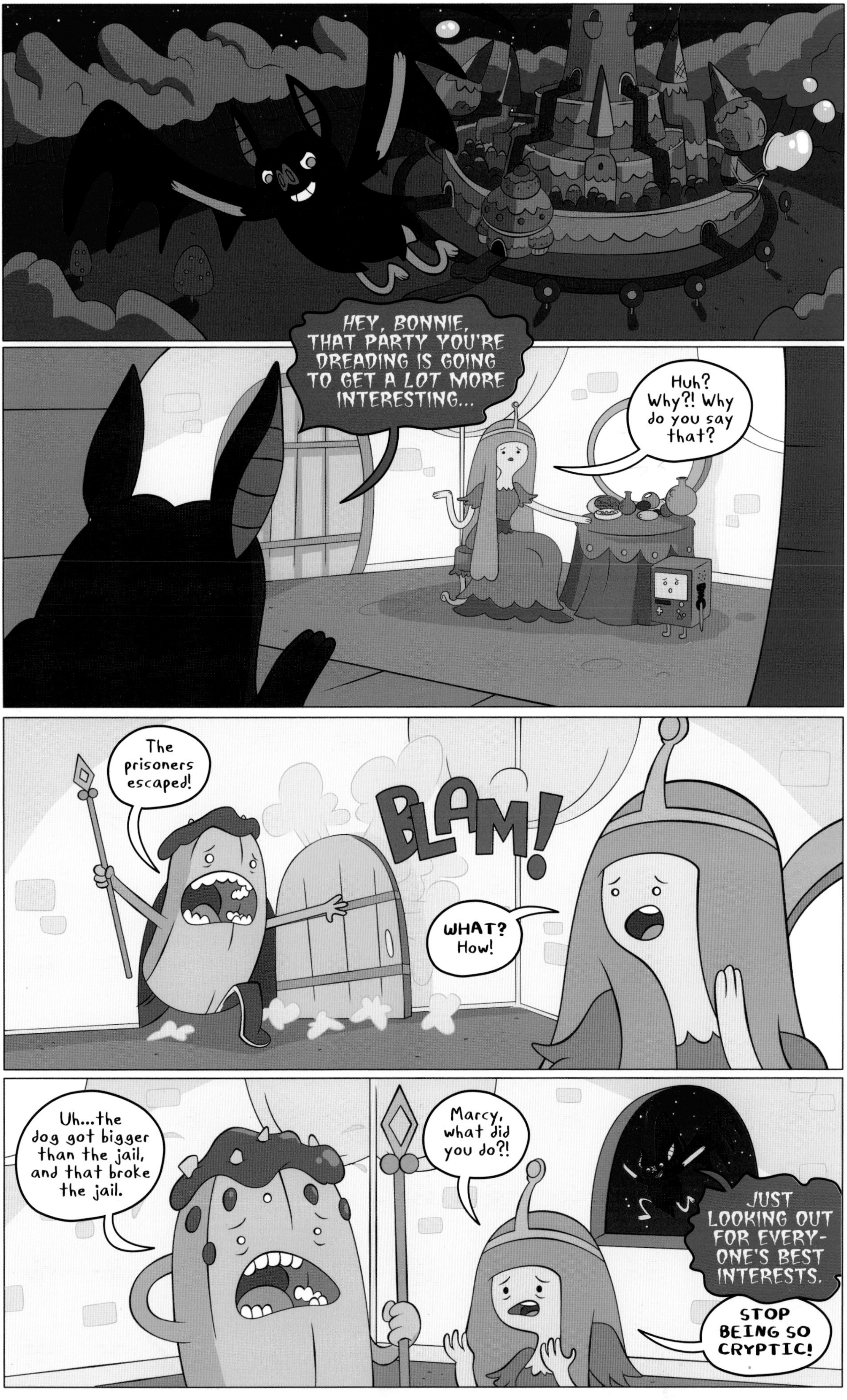
HEY, BONNIE, THAT PARTY YOU'RE DREADING IS GOING TO GET A LOT MORE INTERESTING...
Huh? Why?! Why do you say that?
The prisoners escaped!
BLAM!
WHAT? How!
Uh...the dog got bigger than the jail, and that broke the jail.
Marcy, what did you do?!
JUST LOOKING OUT FOR EVERY-ONE'S BEST INTERESTS.
STOP BEING SO CRYPTIC!

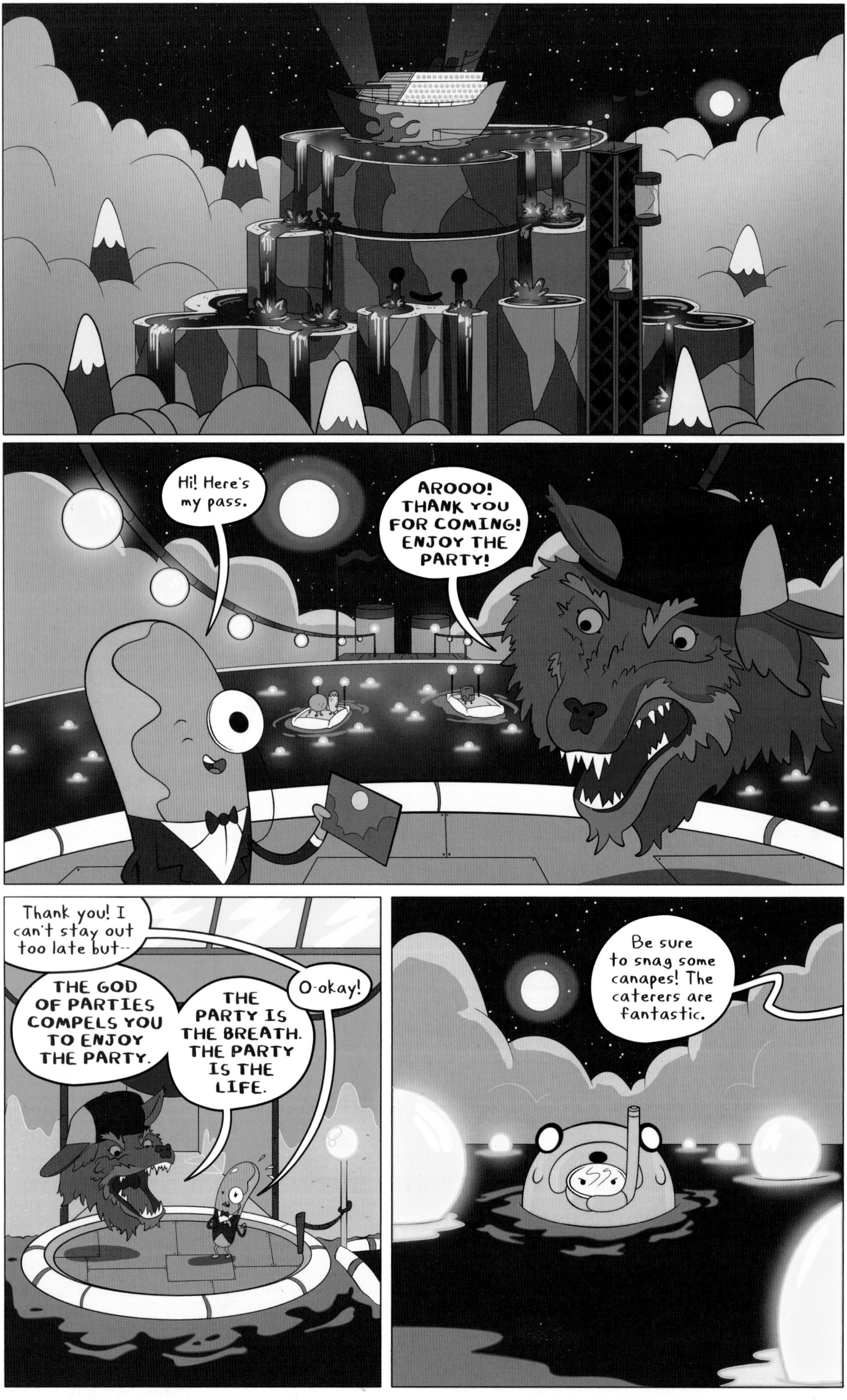
Hi! Here's my pass.
AROOO! THANK YOU FOR COMING! ENJOY THE PARTY!
Thank you! I can't stay out too late but--
THE GOD OF PARTIES COMPELS YOU TO ENJOY THE PARTY.
THE PARTY IS THE BREATH. THE PARTY IS THE LIFE.
O-okay!
Be sure to snag some canapes! The caterers are fantastic.

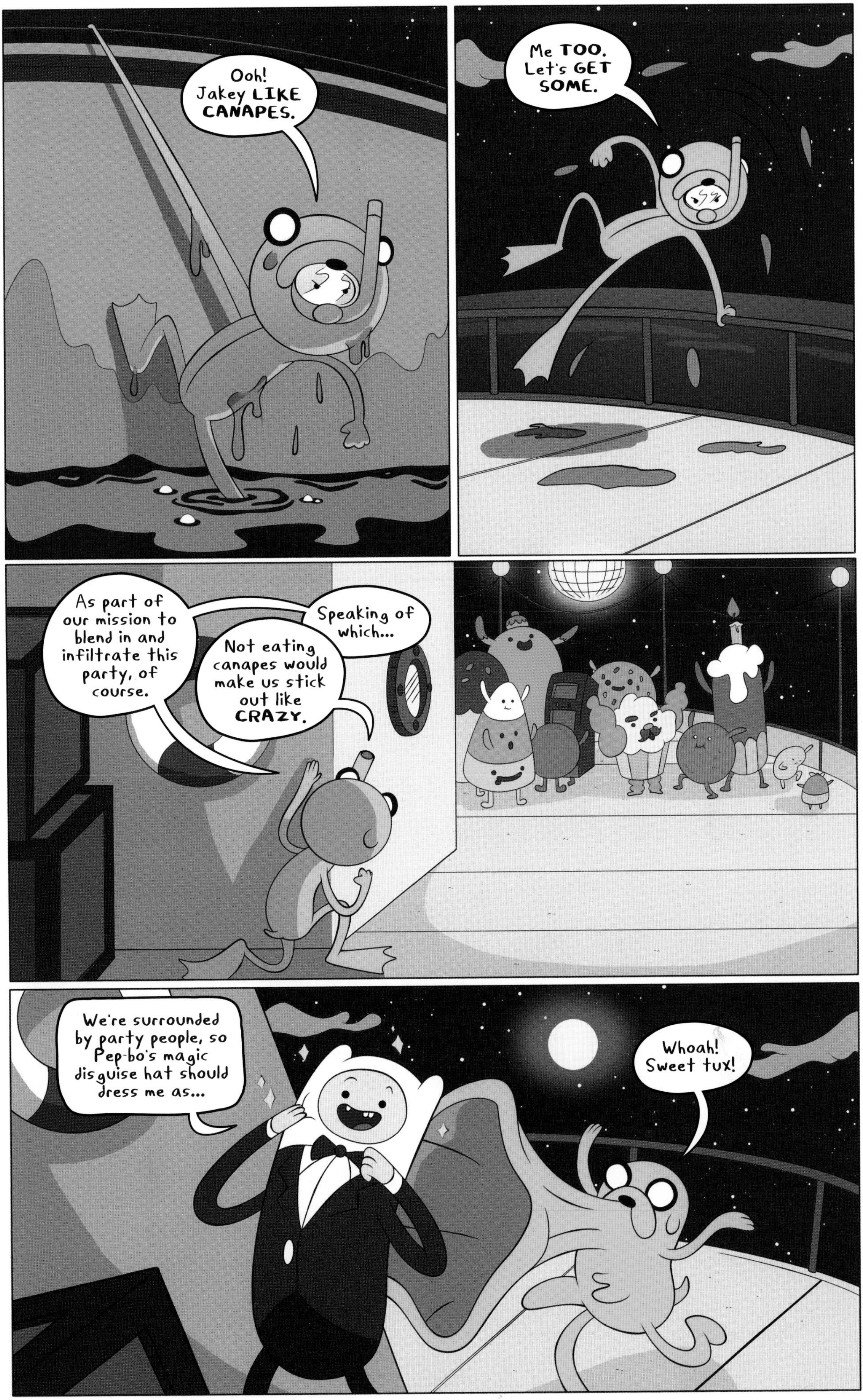
Ooh! Jakey LIKE CANAPES.
Me TOO. Let's GET SOME.
As part of our mission to blend in and infiltrate this party, of course.
Not eating canapes would make us stick out like CRAZY.
Speaking of which...
We're surrounded by party people, so Pep-bo's magic disguise hat should dress me as...
Whoah! Sweet tux!

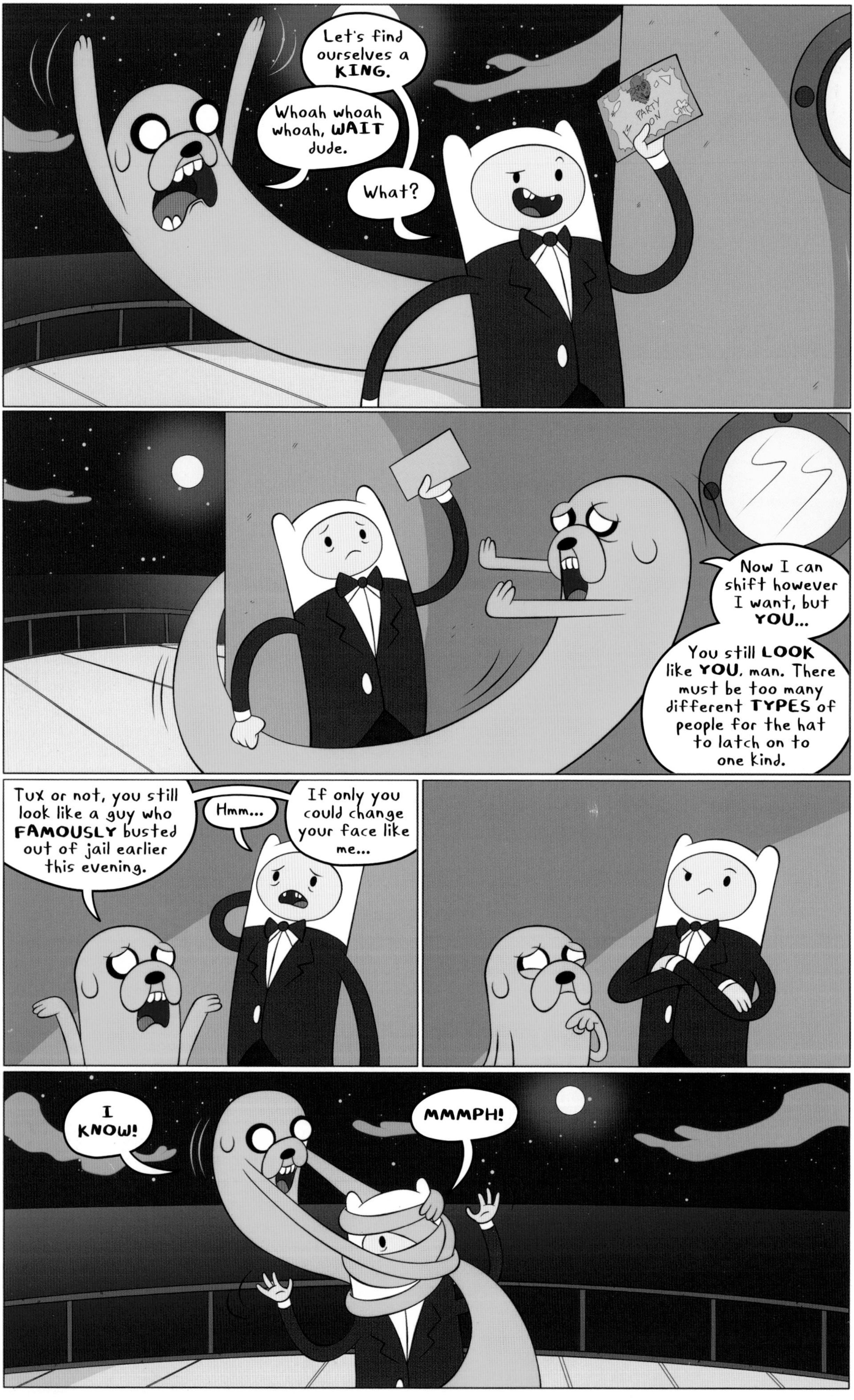

Let's find ourselves a KING.
Whoah whoah whoah, WAIT dude.
What?
PARTY ON
Now I can shift however I want, but YOU...
You still LOOK like YOU, man. There must be too many different TYPES of people for the hat to latch on to one kind.
Tux or not, you still look like a guy who FAMOUSLY busted out of jail earlier this evening.
Hmm...
If only you could change your face like me...
I KNOW!
MMMPH!

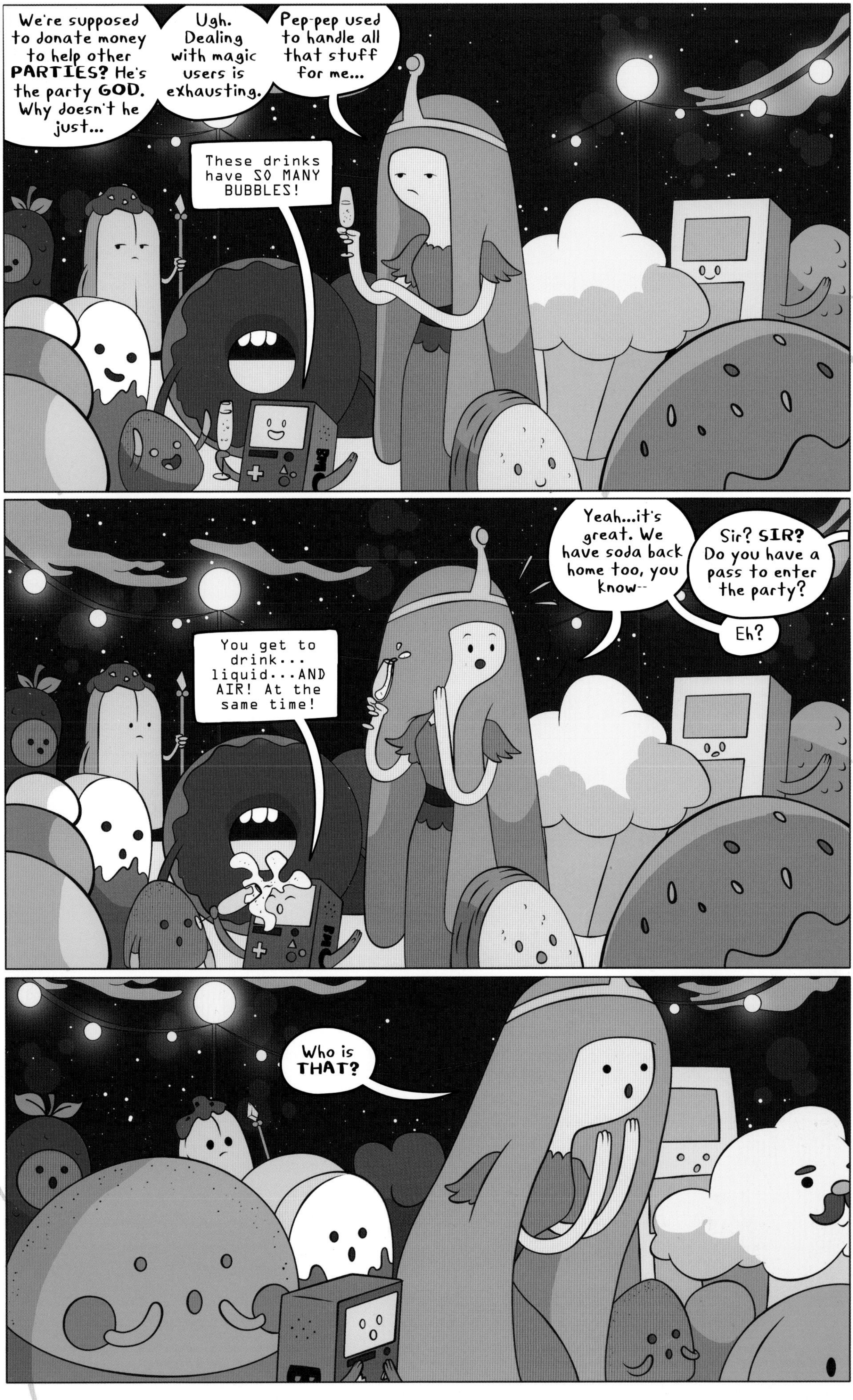
We're supposed to donate money to help other PARTIES? He's the party GOD. Why doesn't he just...
Ugh. Dealing with magic users is exhausting.
Pep-pep used to handle all that stuff for me...
These drinks have SO MANY BUBBLES!
Yeah...it's great. We have soda back home too, you know--
Sir? SIR? Do you have a pass to enter the party?
Eh?
You get to drink... liquid...AND AIR! At the same time!
Who is THAT?

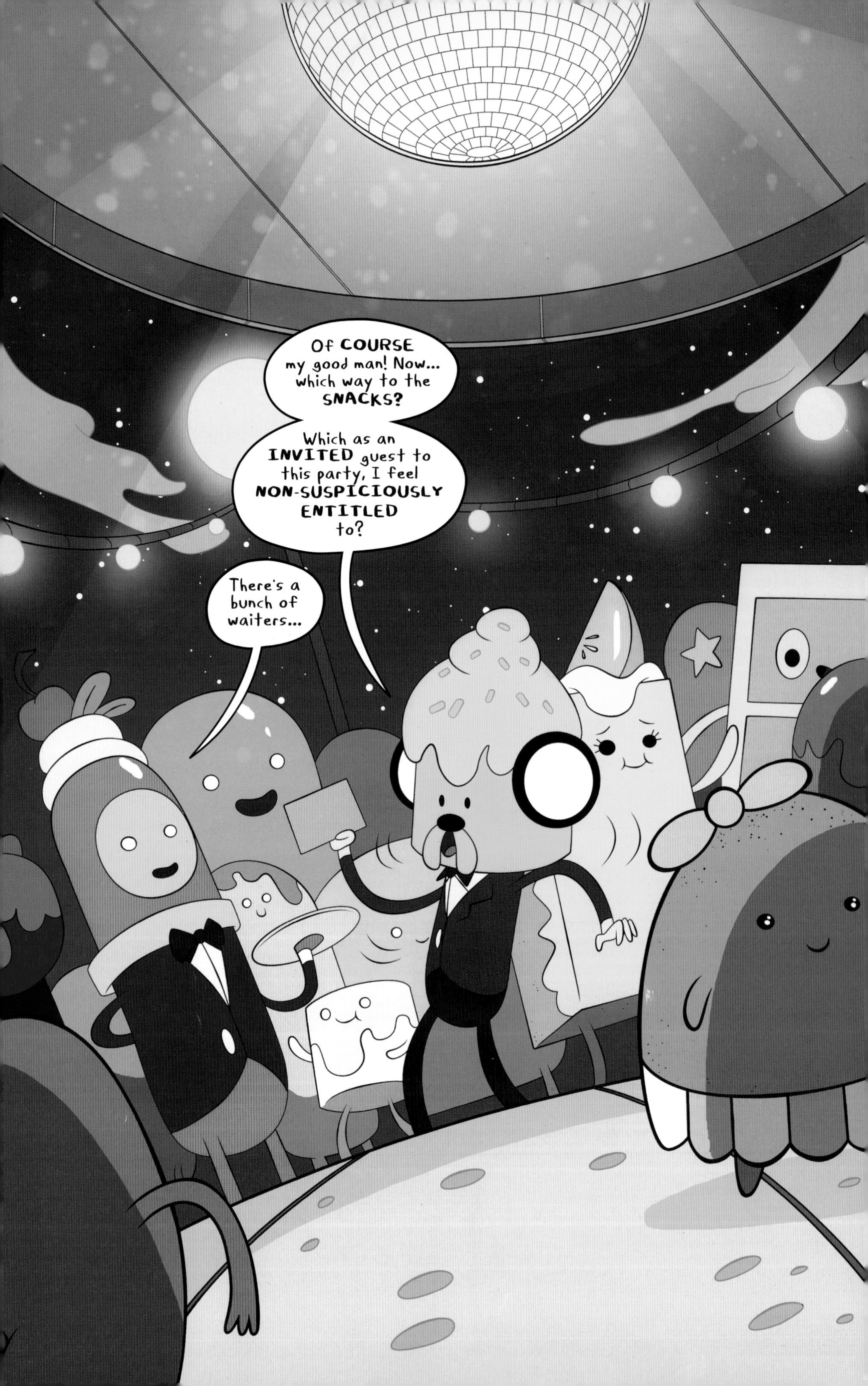

Of COURSE my good man! Now... which way to the SNACKS?
Which as an INVITED guest to this party, I feel NON-SUSPICIOUSLY ENTITLED to?
There's a bunch of waiters...

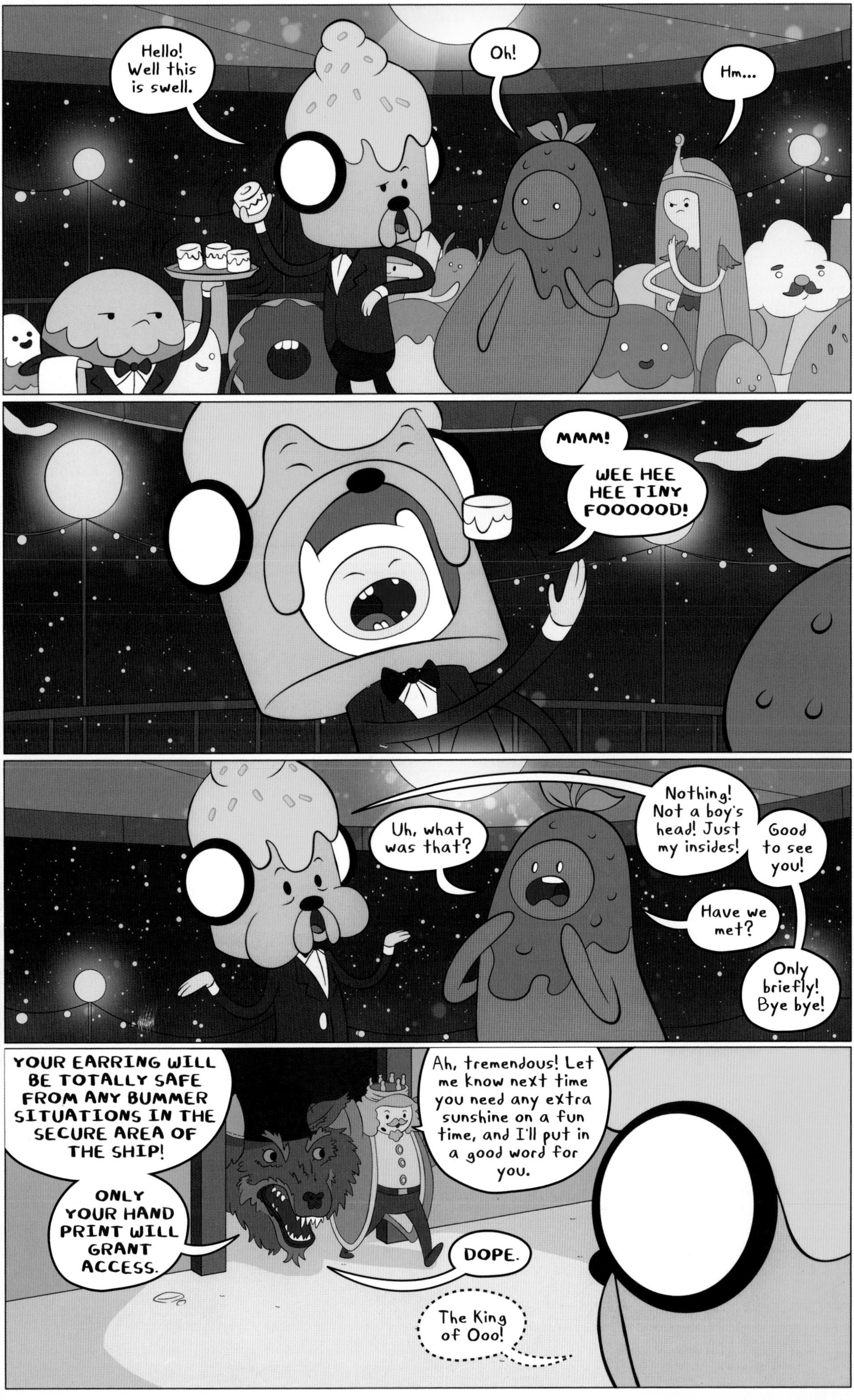

Hello! Well this is swell.
Oh!
Hm...
MMM!
WEE HEE HEE TINY FOOOOOD!
Uh, what was that?
Nothing! Not a boy's head! Just my insides!
Good to see you!
Have we met?
Only briefly! Bye bye!
YOUR EARRING WILL BE TOTALLY SAFE FROM ANY BUMMER SITUATIONS IN THE SECURE AREA OF THE SHIP!
ONLY YOUR HAND PRINT WILL GRANT ACCESS.
Ah, tremendous! Let me know next time you need any extra sunshine on a fun time, and I'll put in a good word for you.
DOPE.
The King of Ooo!

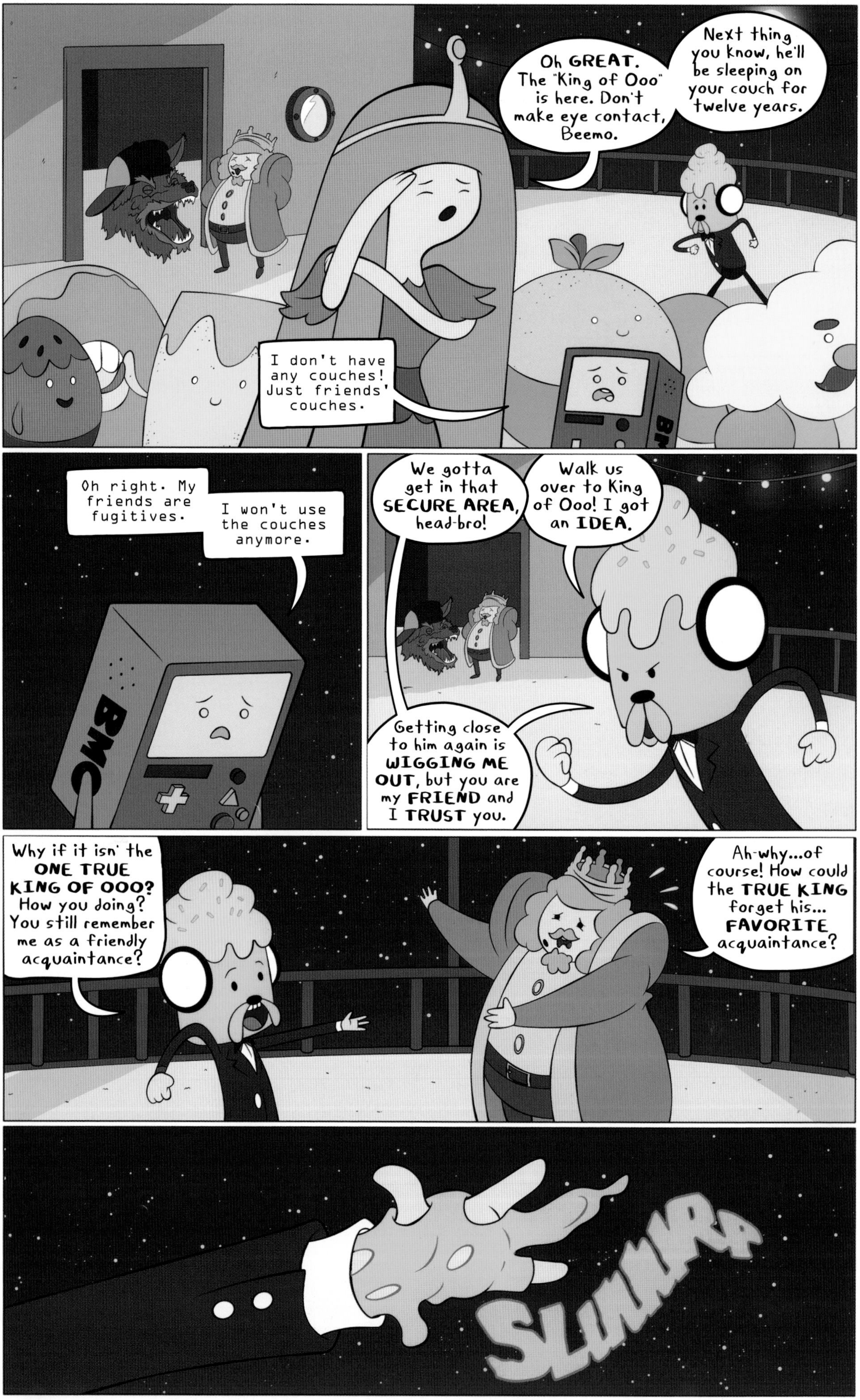
Oh GREAT. The "King of Ooo" is here. Don't make eye contact, Beemo.
Next thing you know, he'll be sleeping on your couch for twelve years.
I don't have any couches! Just friends' couches.
Oh right. My friends are fugitives.
I won't use the couches anymore.
BMO
We gotta get in that SECURE AREA, head-bro!
Walk us over to King of Ooo! I got an IDEA.
Getting close to him again is WIGGING ME OUT, but you are my FRIEND and I TRUST you.
Why if it isn' the ONE TRUE KING OF OOO? How you doing? You still remember me as a friendly acquaintance?
Ah-why...of course! How could the TRUE KING forget his... FAVORITE acquaintance?
SLUURP

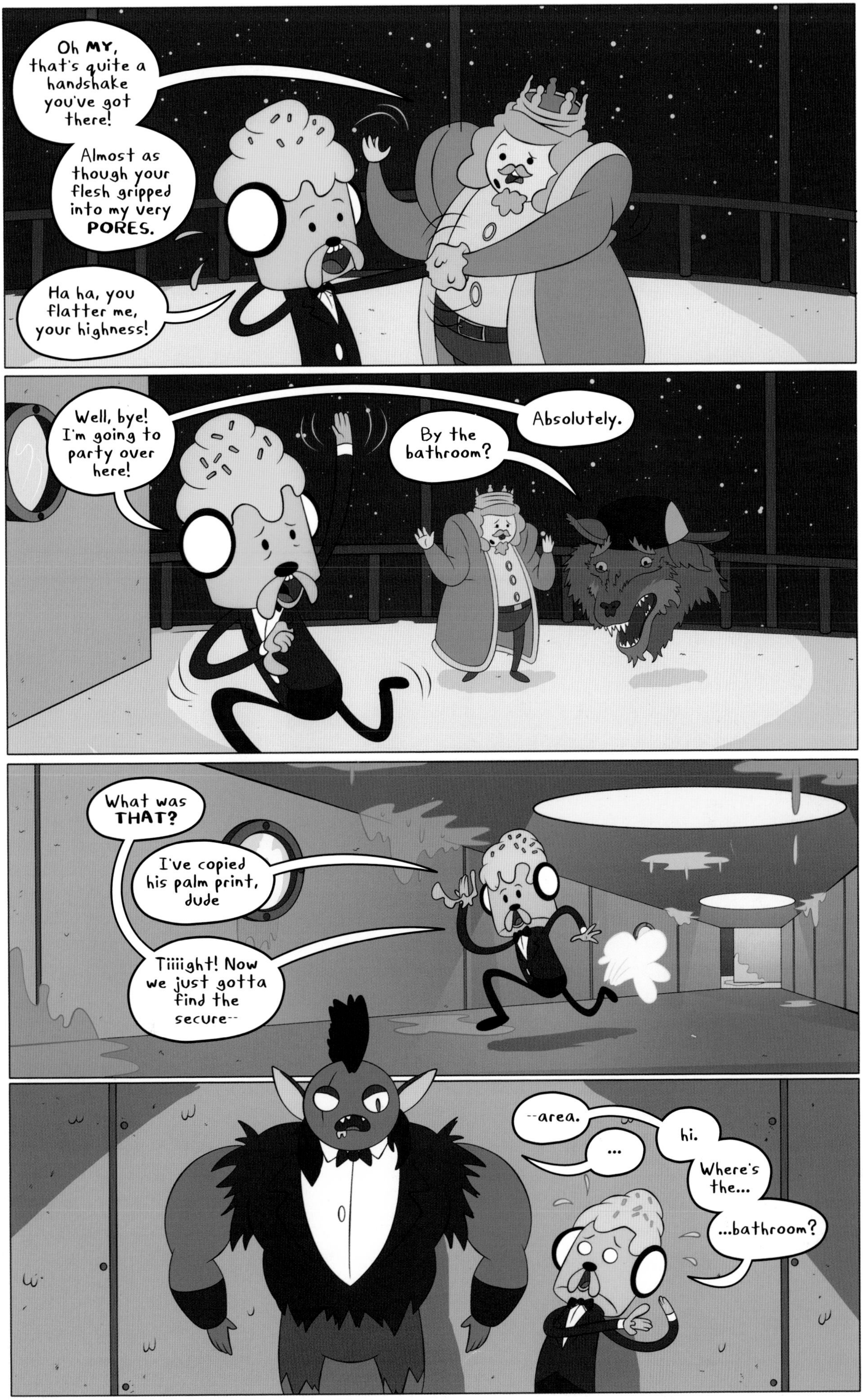

Oh MY, that's quite a handshake you've got there!
Almost as though your flesh gripped into my very PORES.
Ha ha, you flatter me, your highness!
Well, bye! I'm going to party over here!
Absolutely.
By the bathroom?
What was THAT?
I've copied his palm print, dude
Tiiiight! Now we just gotta find the secure--
--area.
hi.
...
Where's the...
...bathroom?

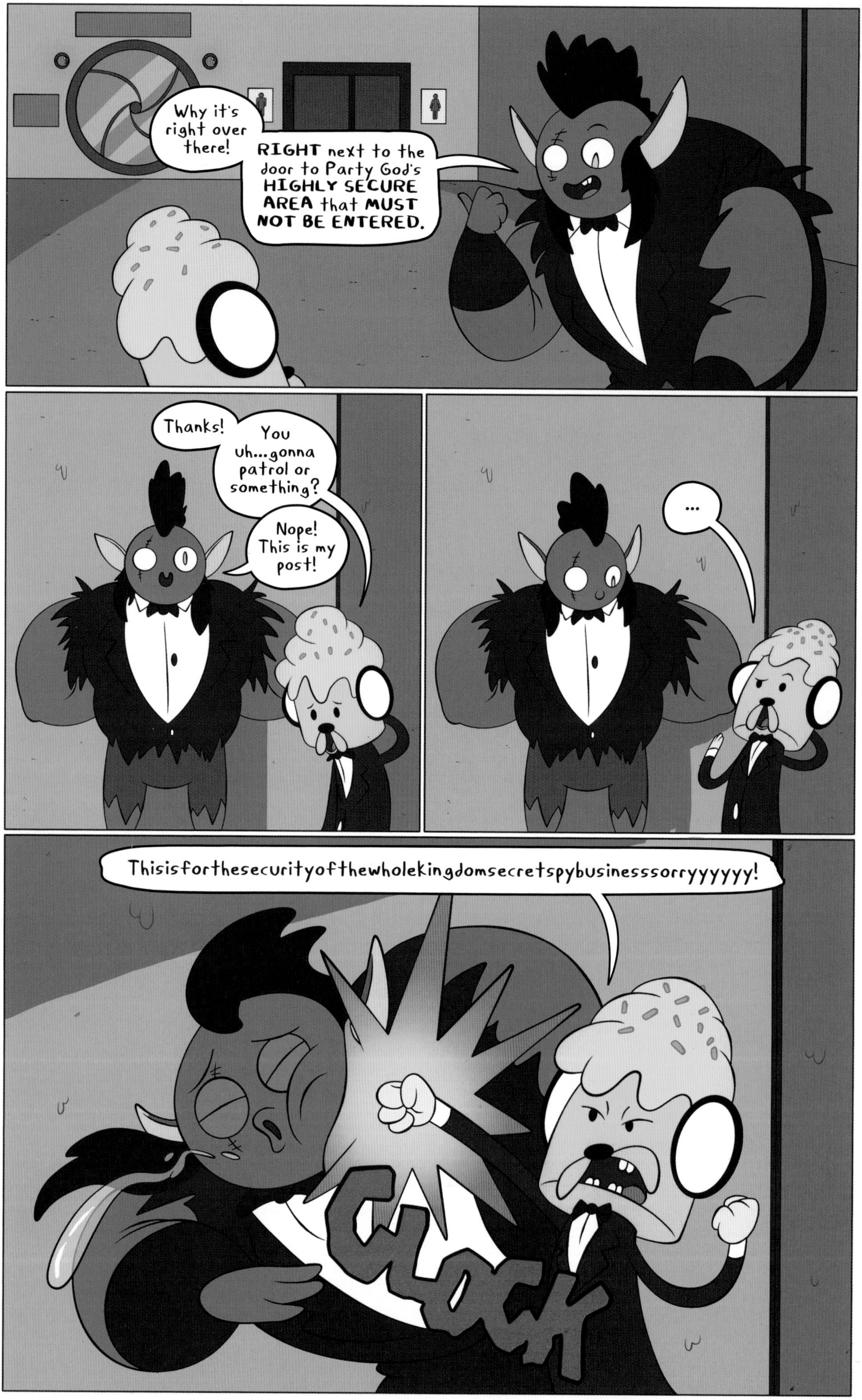
Why it's right over there!
RIGHT next to the door to Party God's **HIGHLY SECURE AREA** that **MUST NOT BE ENTERED.**
Thanks!
You uh...gonna patrol or something?
Nope! This is my post!
...
Thisisforthesecurityofthewholekingdomsecretspybusinesssorryyyyyy!
CLOCK

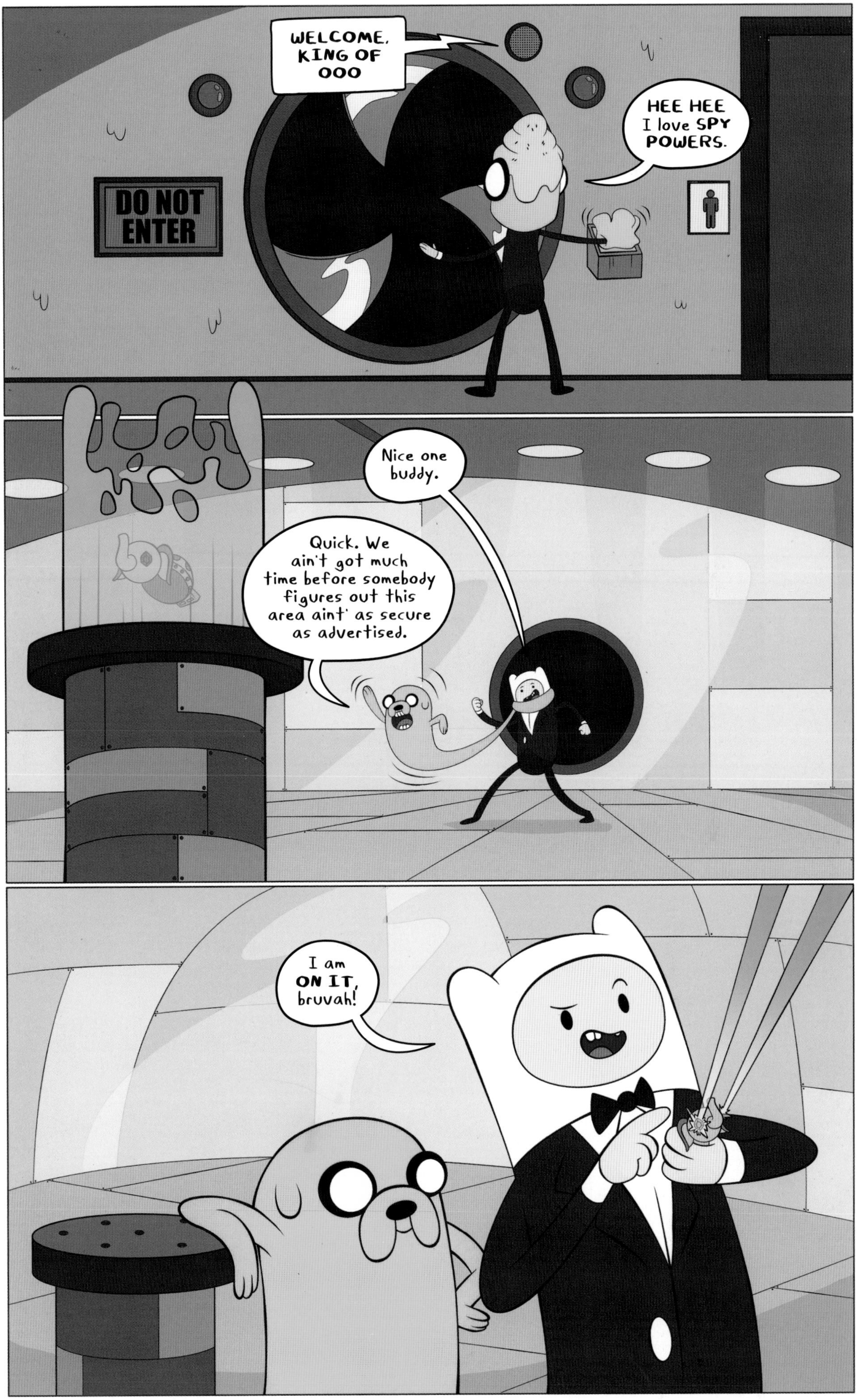
WELCOME, KING OF OOO
DO NOT ENTER
HEE HEE I love SPY POWERS.
Nice one buddy.
Quick. We ain't got much time before somebody figures out this area aint' as secure as advertised.
I am ON IT, bruvah!

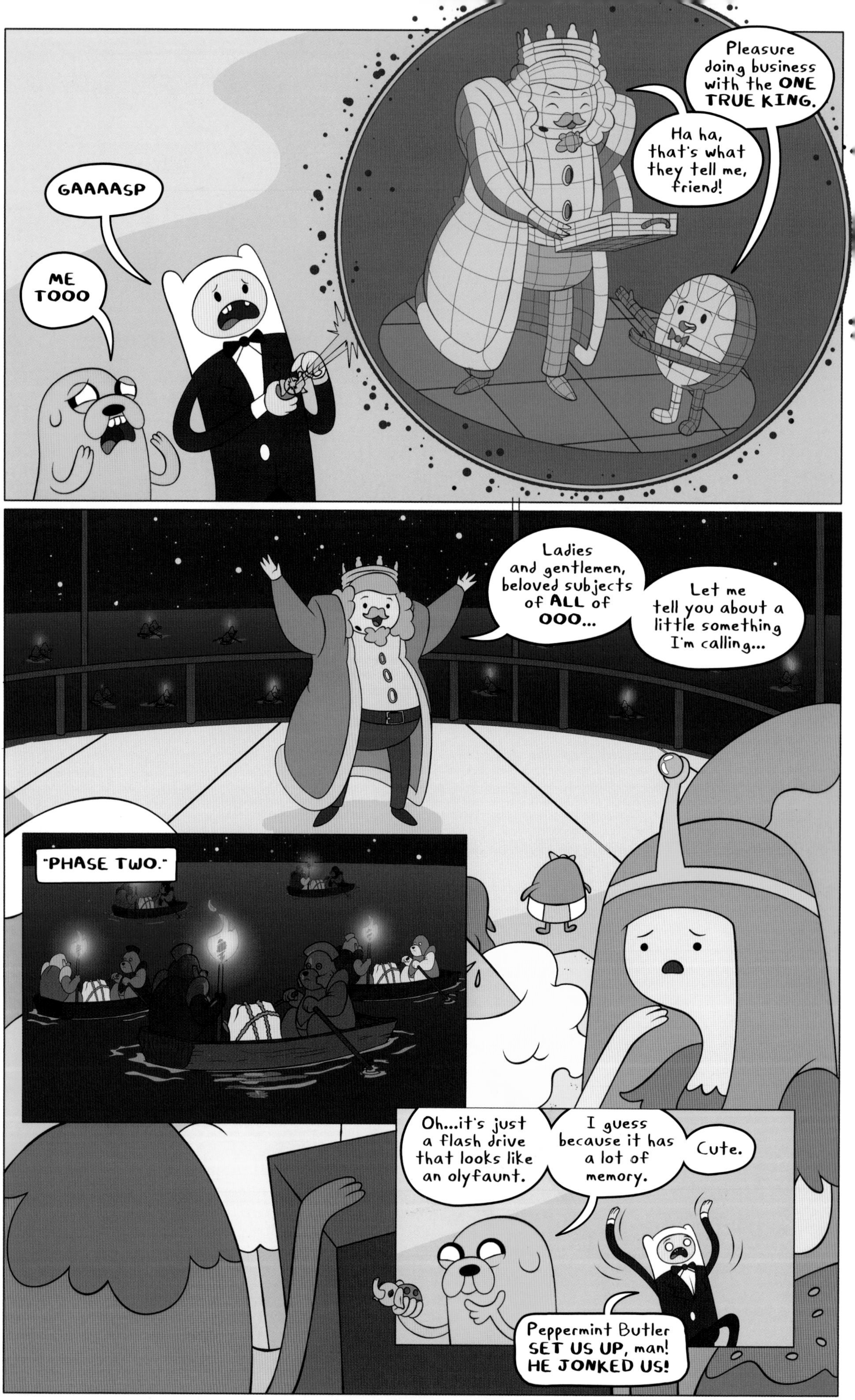
GAAAASP
ME TOOO
Pleasure doing business with the ONE TRUE KING.
Ha ha, that's what they tell me, friend!
Ladies and gentlemen, beloved subjects of ALL of OOO...
Let me tell you about a little something I'm calling...
"PHASE TWO."
Oh...it's just a flash drive that looks like an olyfaunt.
I guess because it has a lot of memory.
Cute.
Peppermint Butler SET US UP, man! HE JONKED US!

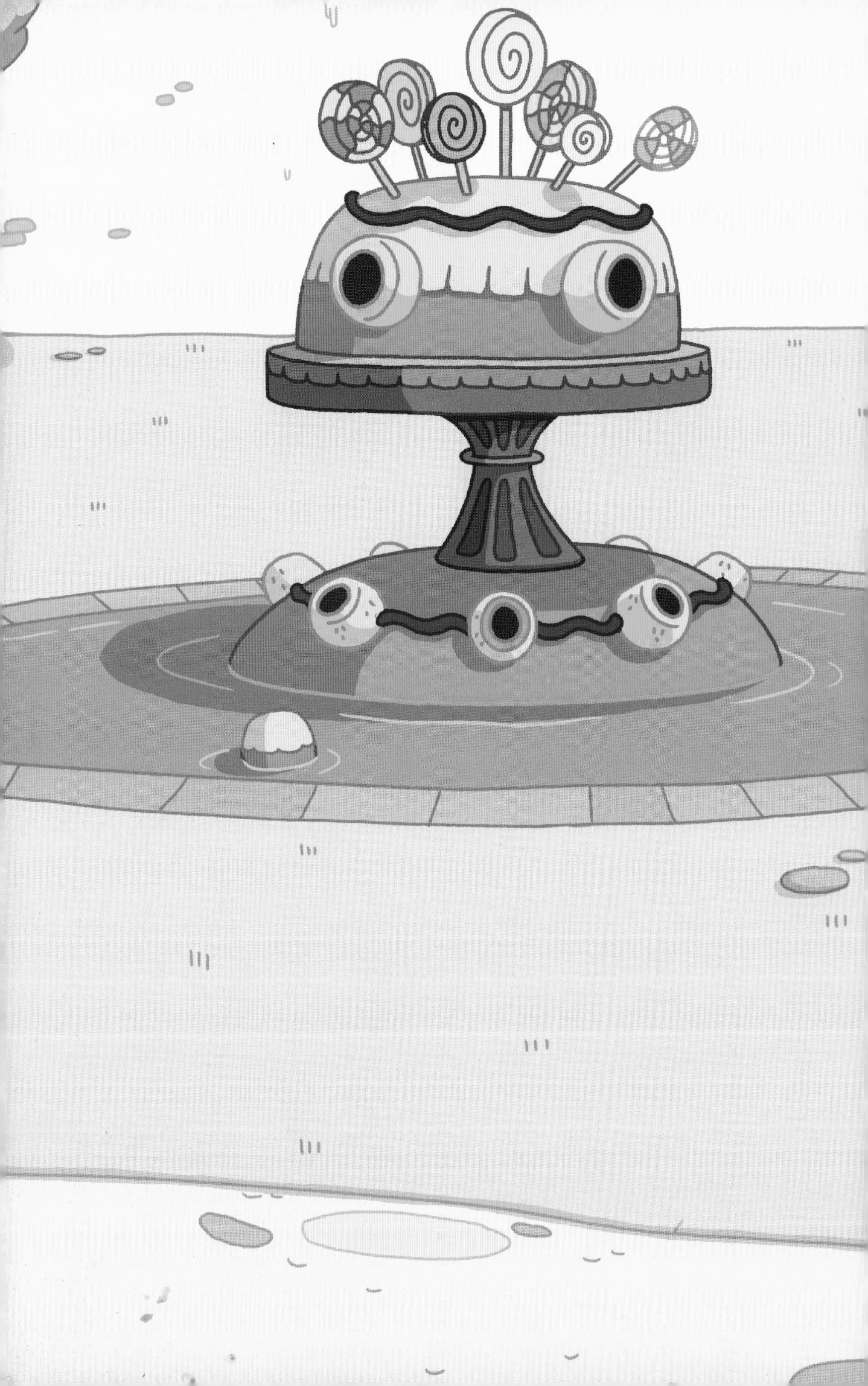

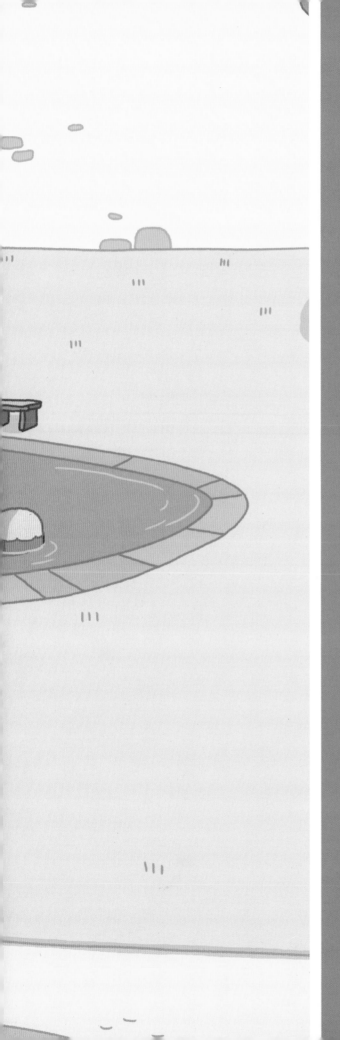

CHAPTER FIVE

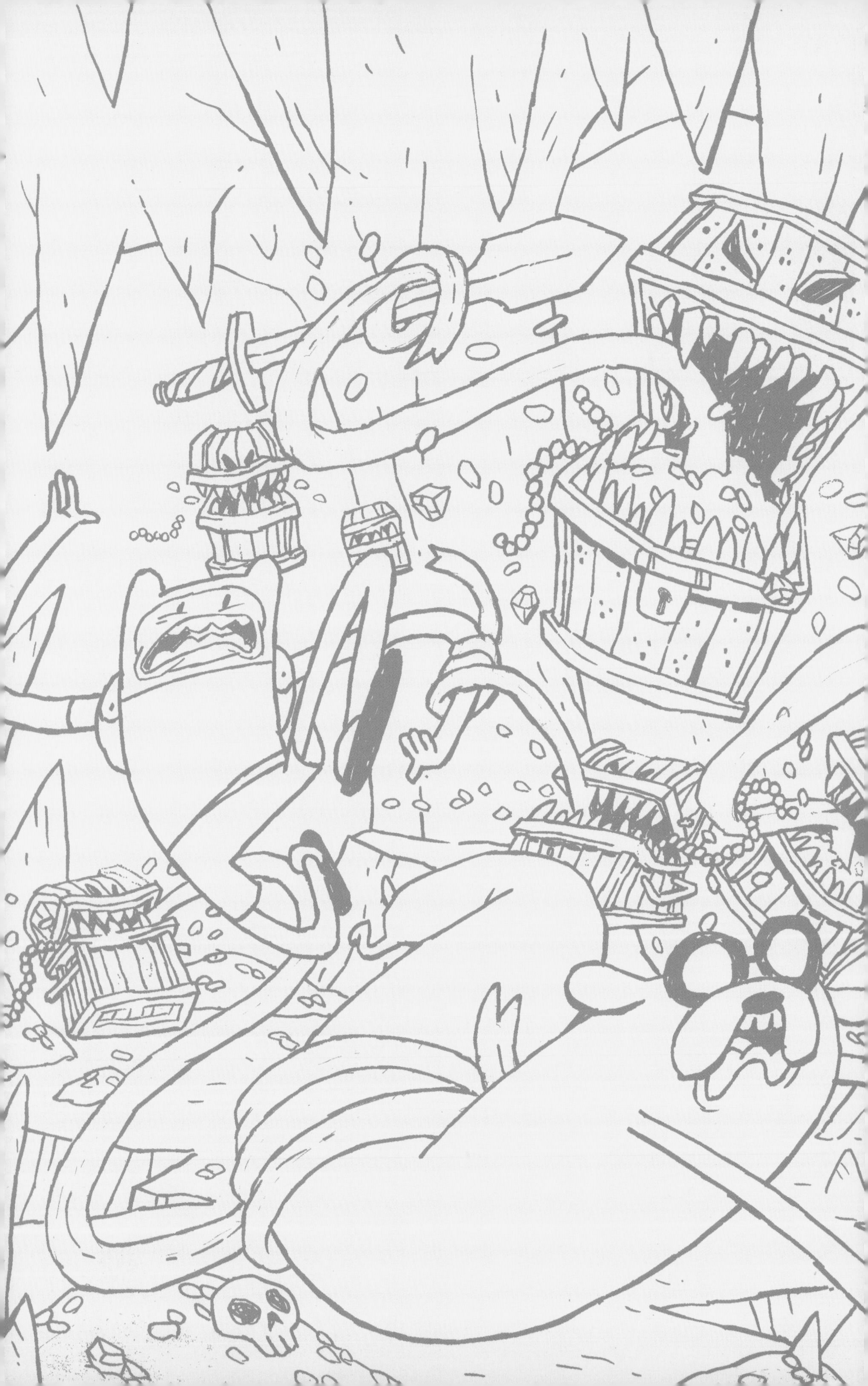

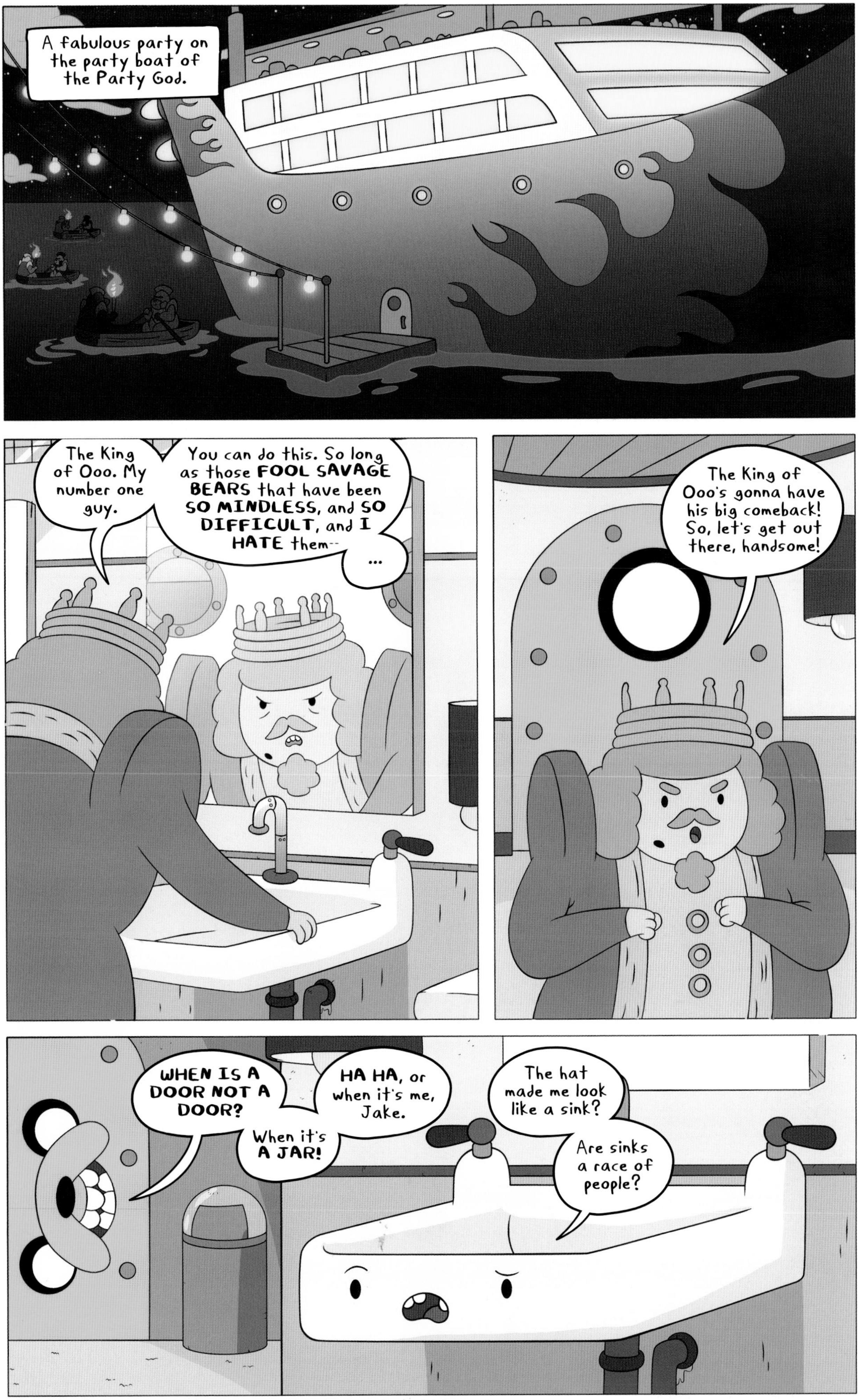
A fabulous party on the party boat of the Party God.
The King of Ooo. My number one guy.
You can do this. So long as those FOOL SAVAGE BEARS that have been SO MINDLESS, and SO DIFFICULT, and I HATE them--
...
The King of Ooo's gonna have his big comeback! So, let's get out there, handsome!
WHEN IS A DOOR NOT A DOOR?
When it's A JAR!
HA HA, or when it's me, Jake.
The hat made me look like a sink?
Are sinks a race of people?

A very thirsty people.

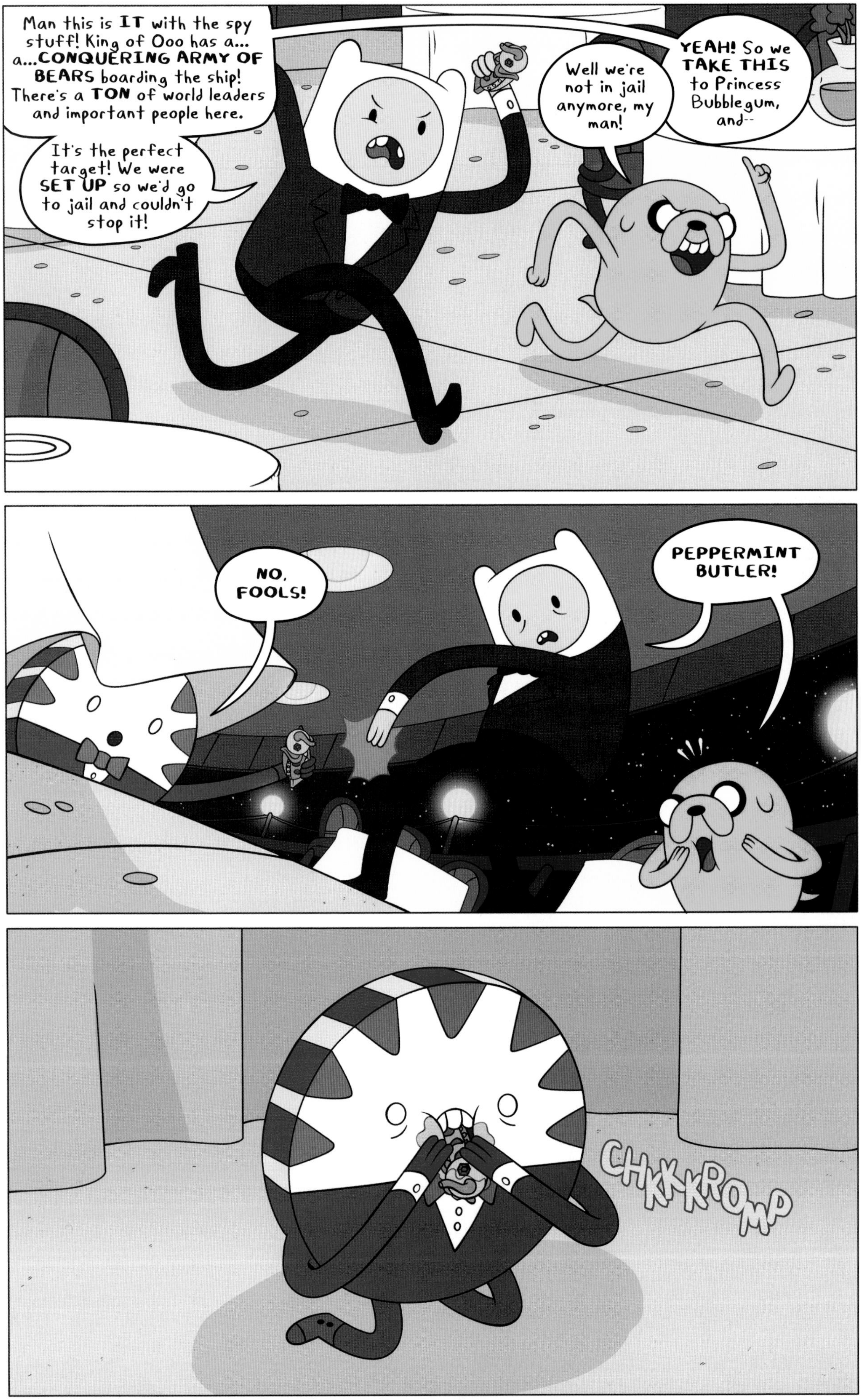
Man this is IT with the spy stuff! King of Ooo has a... a...CONQUERING ARMY OF BEARS boarding the ship! There's a TON of world leaders and important people here.
It's the perfect target! We were SET UP so we'd go to jail and couldn't stop it!
Well we're not in jail anymore, my man!
YEAH! So we TAKE THIS to Princess Bubblegum, and--
NO, FOOLS!
PEPPERMINT BUTLER!
CHKKKROMP

Dude there's like...so many snacks at this party.

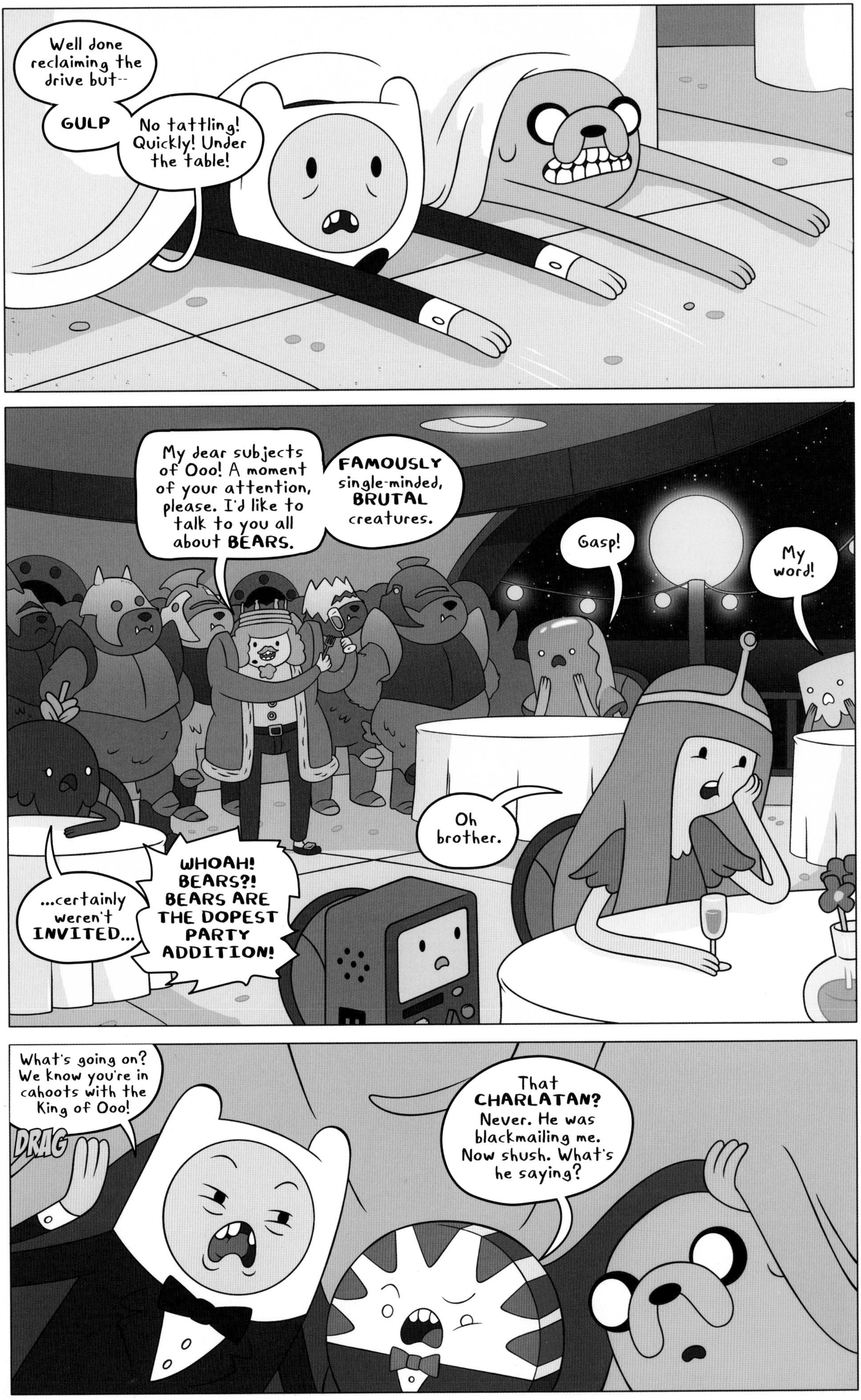
Well done reclaiming the drive but--
GULP
No tattling! Quickly! Under the table!
My dear subjects of Ooo! A moment of your attention, please. I'd like to talk to you all about BEARS.
FAMOUSLY single-minded, BRUTAL creatures.
Gasp!
My word!
Oh brother.
...certainly weren't INVITED...
WHOAH! BEARS?! BEARS ARE THE DOPEST PARTY ADDITION!
What's going on? We know you're in cahoots with the King of Ooo!
DRAG
That CHARLATAN? Never. He was blackmailing me. Now shush. What's he saying?

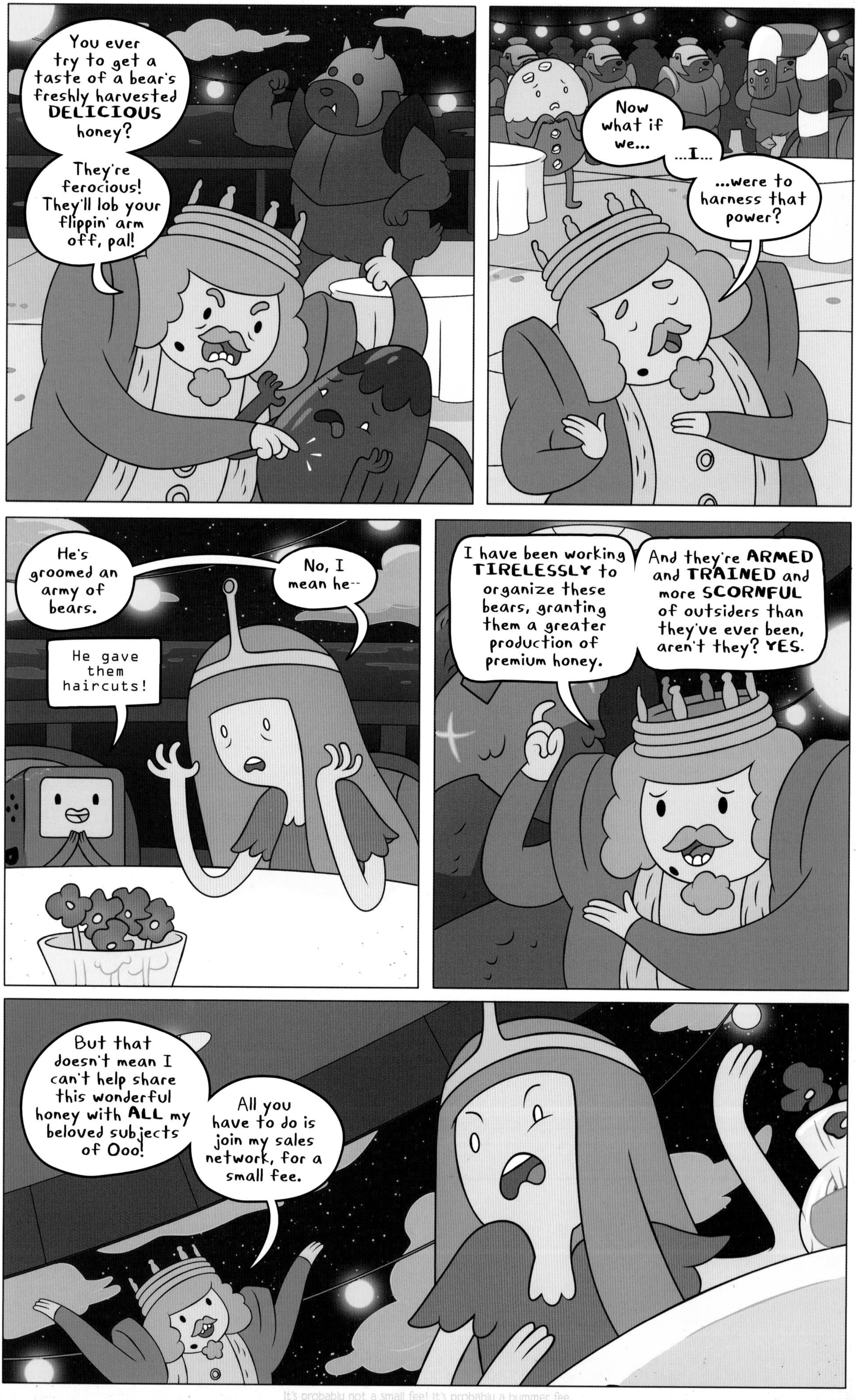
You ever try to get a taste of a bear's freshly harvested DELICIOUS honey?
They're ferocious! They'll lob your flippin' arm off, pal!
Now what if we...
...I...
...were to harness that power?
He's groomed an army of bears.
No, I mean he--
He gave them haircuts!
I have been working TIRELESSLY to organize these bears, granting them a greater production of premium honey.
And they're ARMED and TRAINED and more SCORNFUL of outsiders than they've ever been, aren't they? YES.
But that doesn't mean I can't help share this wonderful honey with ALL my beloved subjects of Ooo!
All you have to do is join my sales network, for a small fee.

It's probably not a small fee! It's probably a bummer fee.

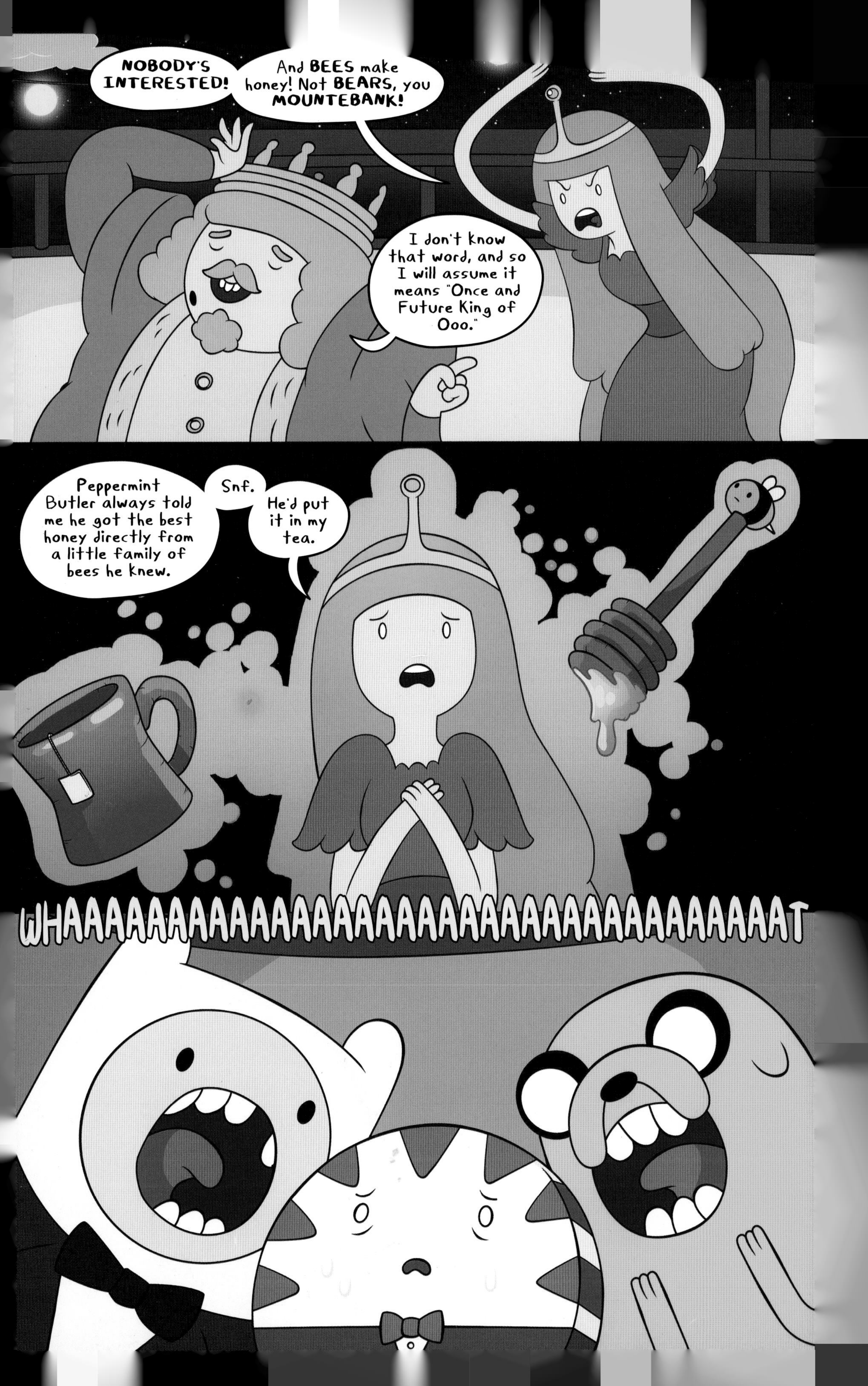
NOBODY'S INTERESTED!
And BEES make honey! Not BEARS, you MOUNTEBANK!
I don't know that word, and so I will assume it means "Once and Future King of Ooo."
Peppermint Butler always told me he got the best honey directly from a little family of bees he knew.
Snf.
He'd put it in my tea.
WHAAAAAAAAAAAAAAAAAAAAAAAAAAAAAAAAAAAT

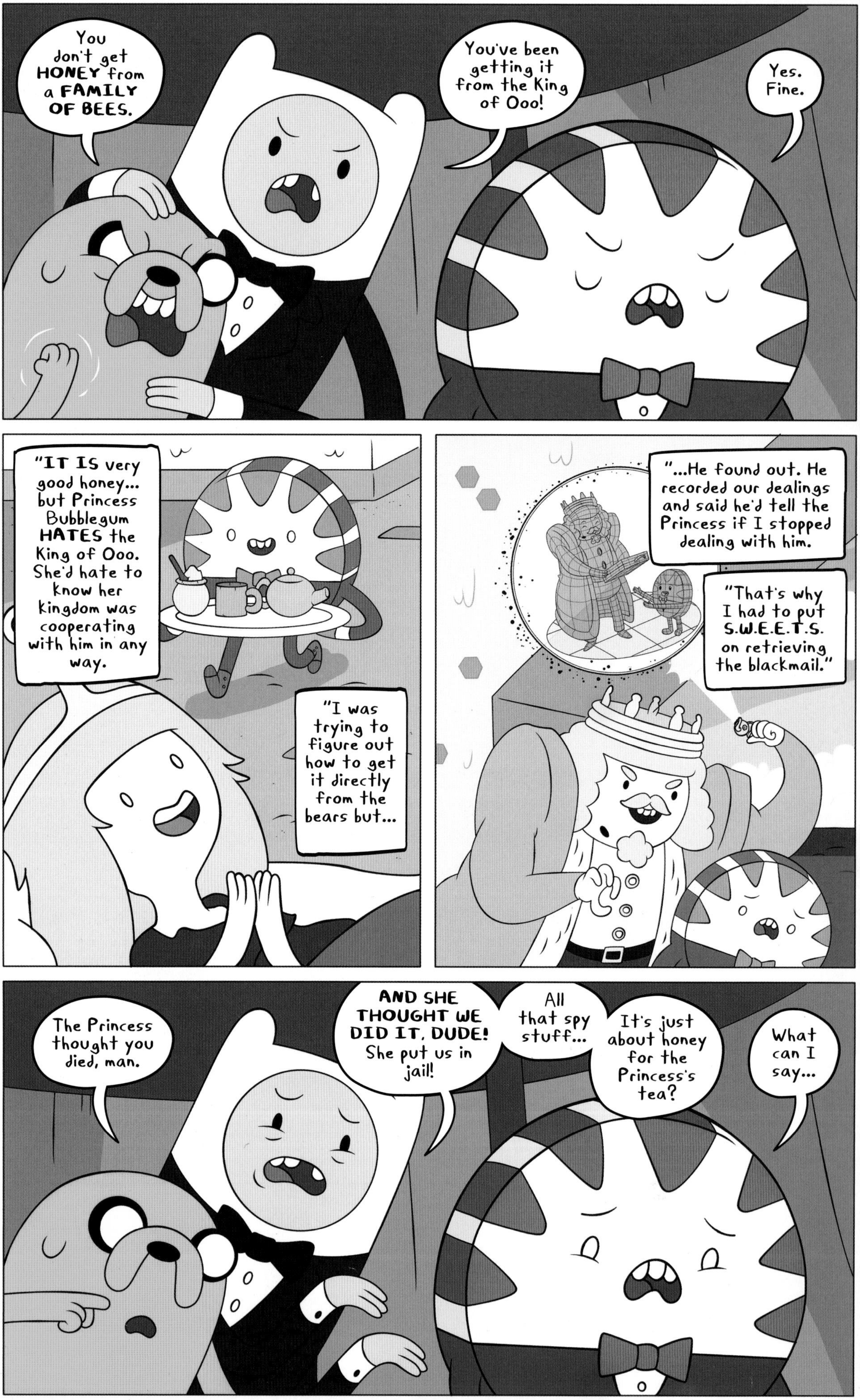
You don't get HONEY from a FAMILY OF BEES.
You've been getting it from the King of Ooo!
Yes. Fine.
"IT IS very good honey... but Princess Bubblegum HATES the King of Ooo. She'd hate to know her kingdom was cooperating with him in any way.
"I was trying to figure out how to get it directly from the bears but...
"...He found out. He recorded our dealings and said he'd tell the Princess if I stopped dealing with him.
"That's why I had to put S.W.E.E.T.S. on retrieving the blackmail."
The Princess thought you died, man.
AND SHE THOUGHT WE DID IT, DUDE! She put us in jail!
All that spy stuff...
It's just about honey for the Princess's tea?
What can I say...

I need to figure out how to stop making this comic all about food. I'M TRYING! HONESTLY!

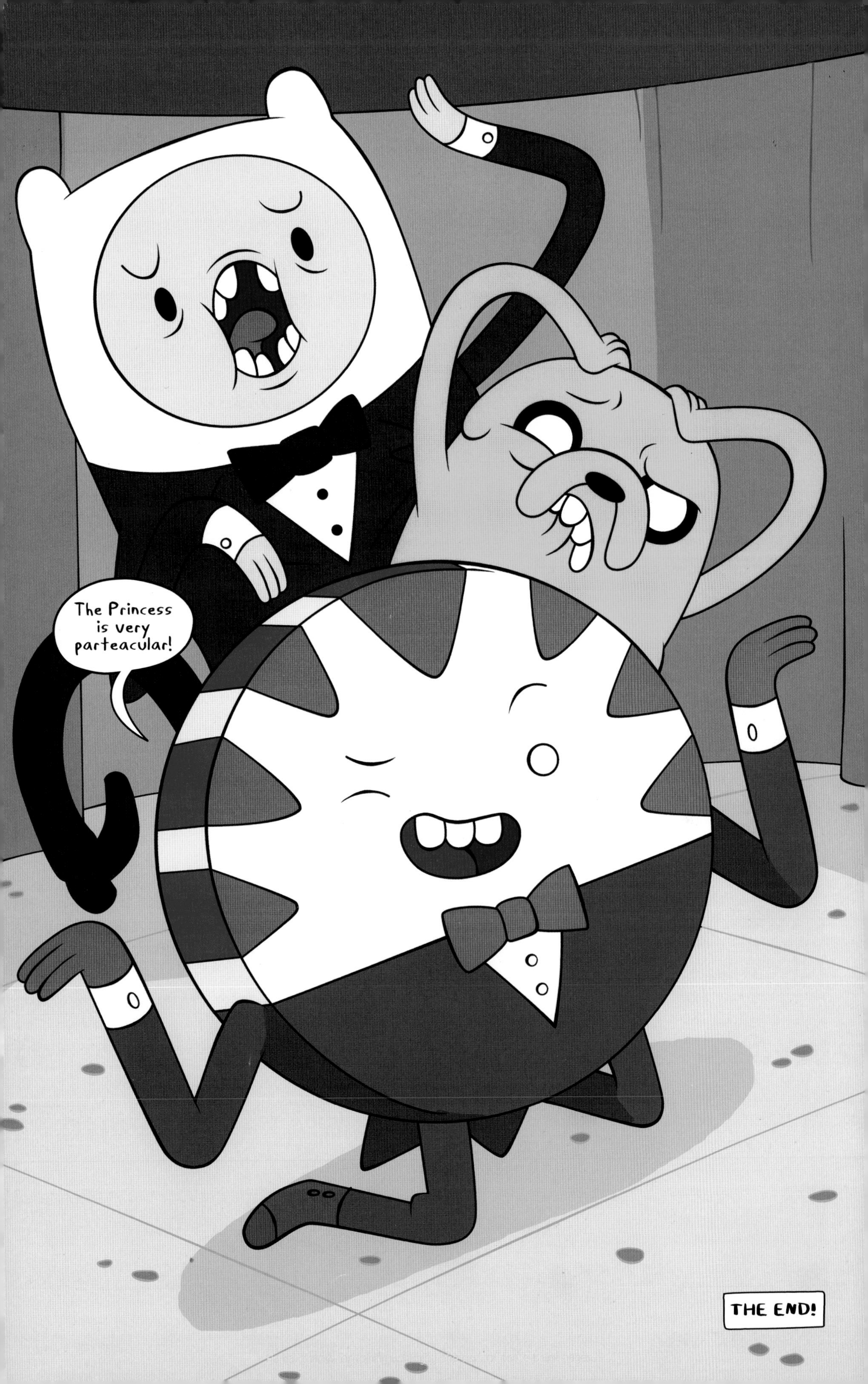
The Princess is very parteacular!
THE END!

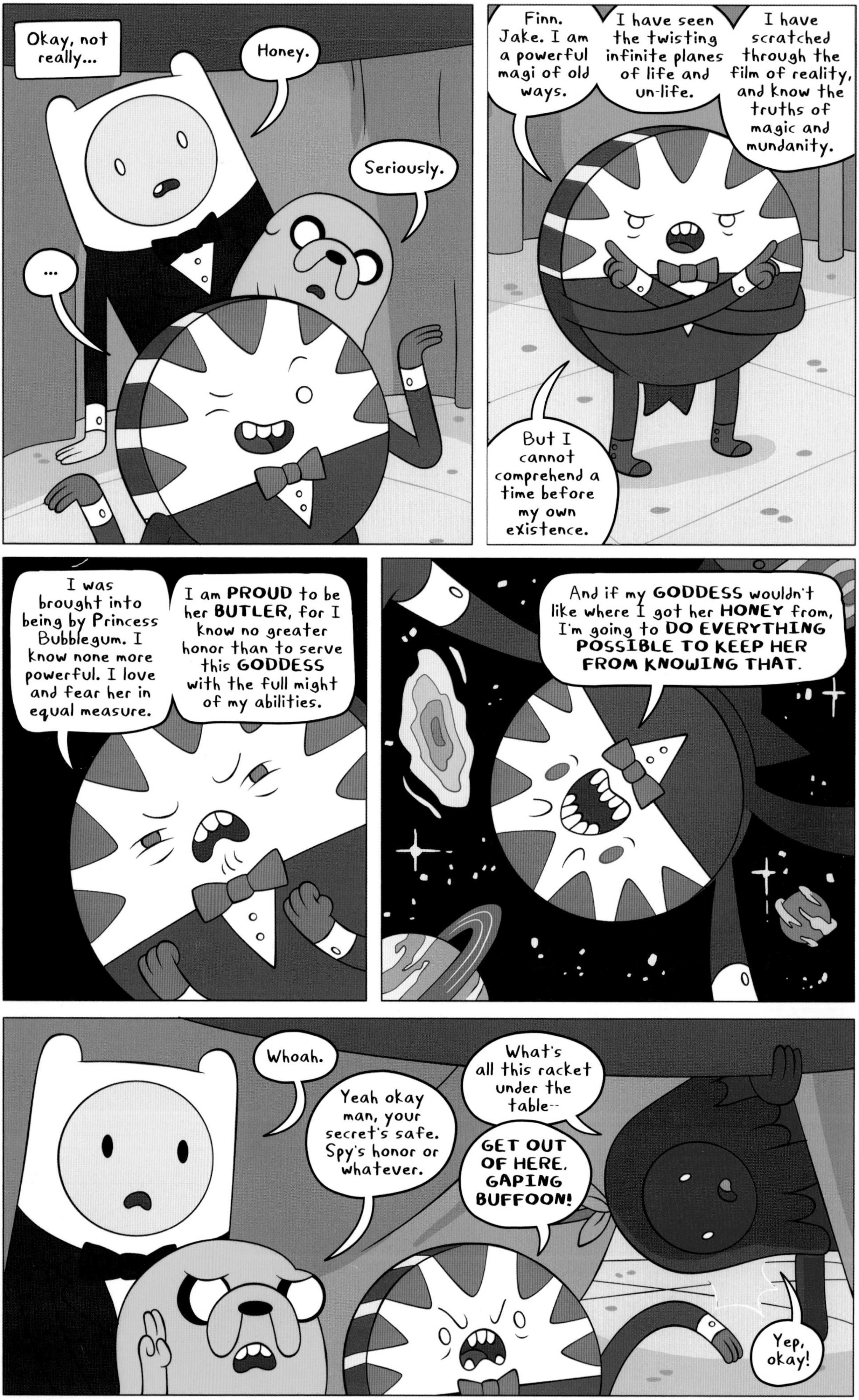
Okay, not really...
Honey.
Seriously.
...
Finn. Jake. I am a powerful magi of old ways.
I have seen the twisting infinite planes of life and un-life.
I have scratched through the film of reality, and know the truths of magic and mundanity.
But I cannot comprehend a time before my own existence.
I was brought into being by Princess Bubblegum. I know none more powerful. I love and fear her in equal measure.
I am PROUD to be her BUTLER, for I know no greater honor than to serve this GODDESS with the full might of my abilities.
And if my GODDESS wouldn't like where I got her HONEY from, I'm going to DO EVERYTHING POSSIBLE TO KEEP HER FROM KNOWING THAT.
Whoah.
Yeah okay man, your secret's safe. Spy's honor or whatever.
What's all this racket under the table--
GET OUT OF HERE, GAPING BUFFOON!
Yep, okay!
Imagine sticking your head under the table and getting yelled at by a stranger. That'd ruin my whole week!

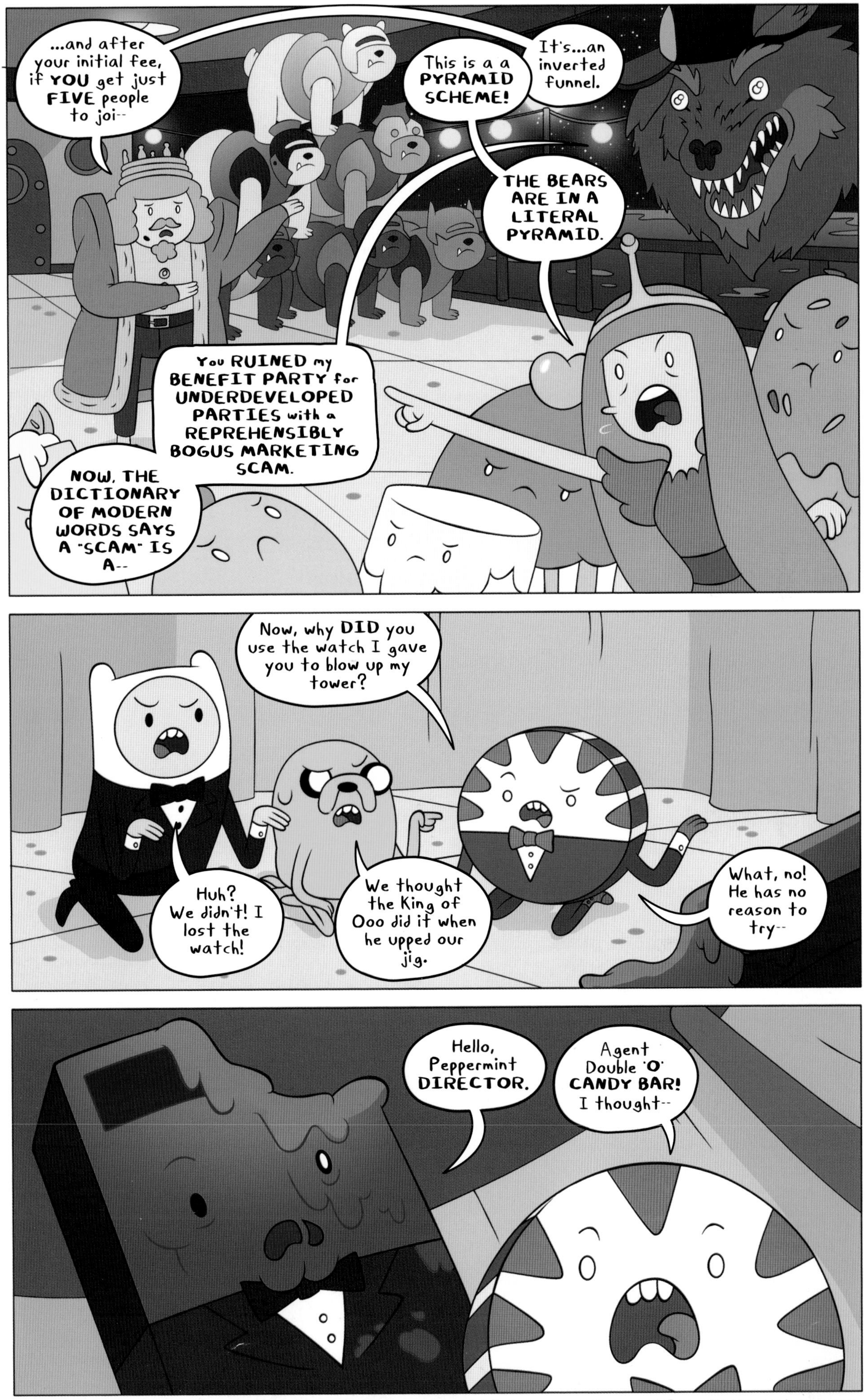
...and after your initial fee, if YOU get just FIVE people to joi--
It's...an inverted funnel.
This is a a PYRAMID SCHEME!
THE BEARS ARE IN A LITERAL PYRAMID.
You RUINED my BENEFIT PARTY for UNDERDEVELOPED PARTIES with a REPREHENSIBLY BOGUS MARKETING SCAM.
NOW, THE DICTIONARY OF MODERN WORDS SAYS A "SCAM" IS A--
Now, why DID you use the watch I gave you to blow up my tower?
Huh? We didn't! I lost the watch!
We thought the King of Ooo did it when he upped our jig.
What, no! He has no reason to try--
Hello, Peppermint DIRECTOR.
Agent Double "O" CANDY BAR! I thought--

If my budgetary requests have successfully gone through, this page should have an audible music "sting" when you read the spy reveal. If not...well I ask you to hum your own.

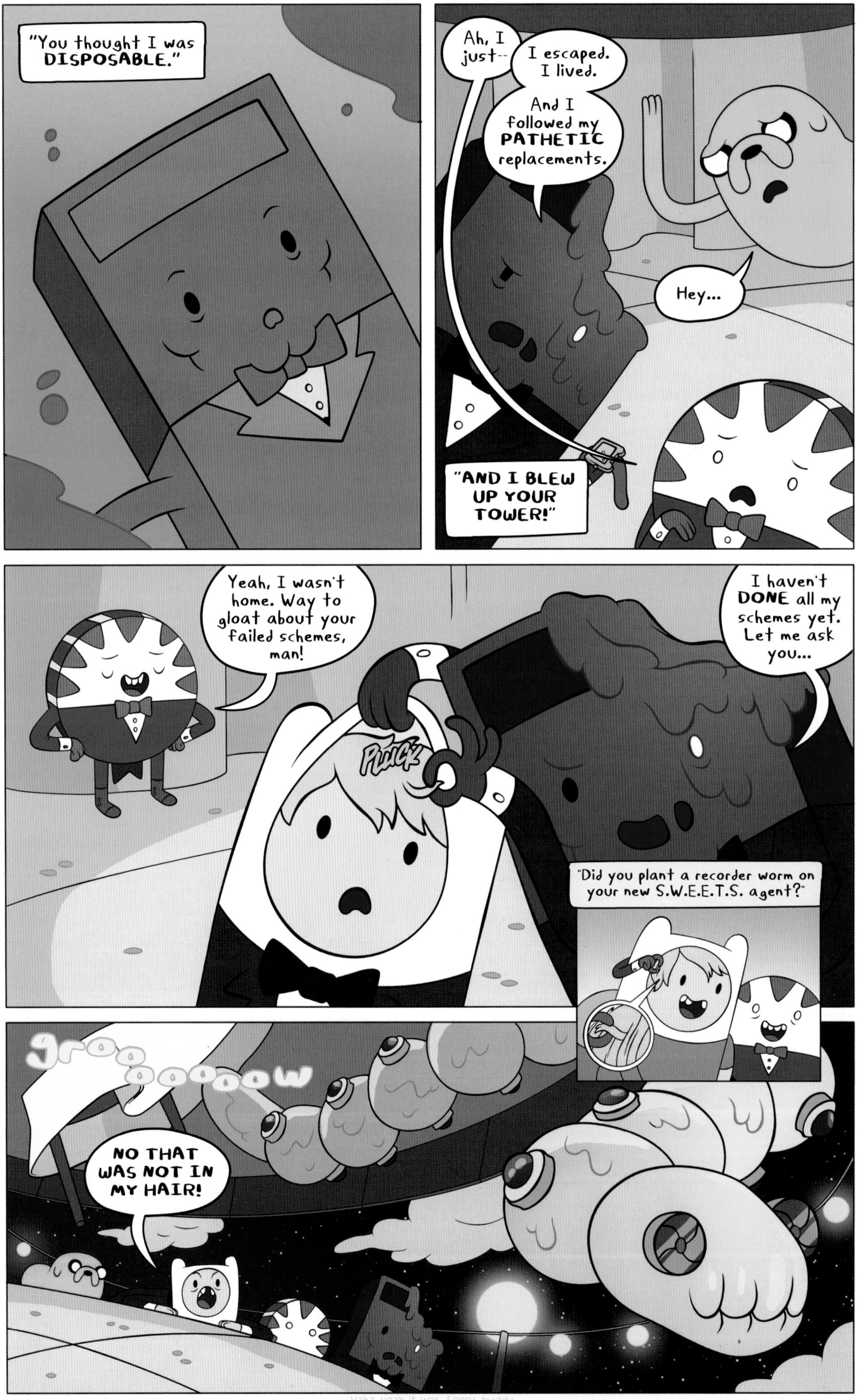
"You thought I was DISPOSABLE."
Ah, I just--
I escaped. I lived.
And I followed my PATHETIC replacements.
Hey...
"AND I BLEW UP YOUR TOWER!"
Yeah, I wasn't home. Way to gloat about your failed schemes, man!
PLUCK
I haven't DONE all my schemes yet. Let me ask you...
"Did you plant a recorder worm on your new S.W.E.E.T.S. agent?"
Groooooooow
NO THAT WAS NOT IN MY HAIR!

Haha, yeah it was. Sorry, buddy.

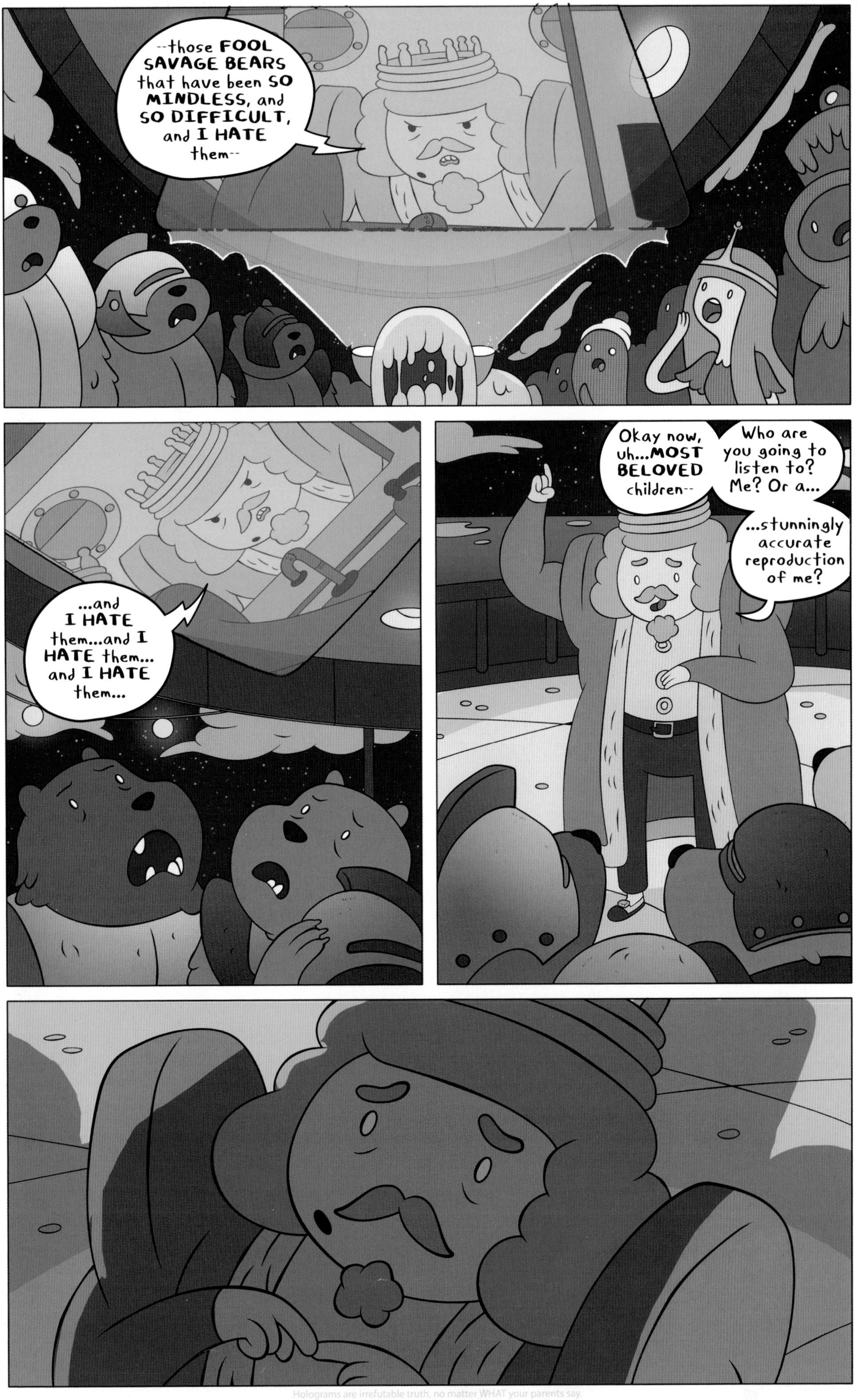
--those FOOL SAVAGE BEARS that have been SO MINDLESS, and SO DIFFICULT, and I HATE them--
...and I HATE them...and I HATE them... and I HATE them...
Okay now, uh...MOST BELOVED children--
Who are you going to listen to? Me? Or a...
...stunningly accurate reproduction of me?

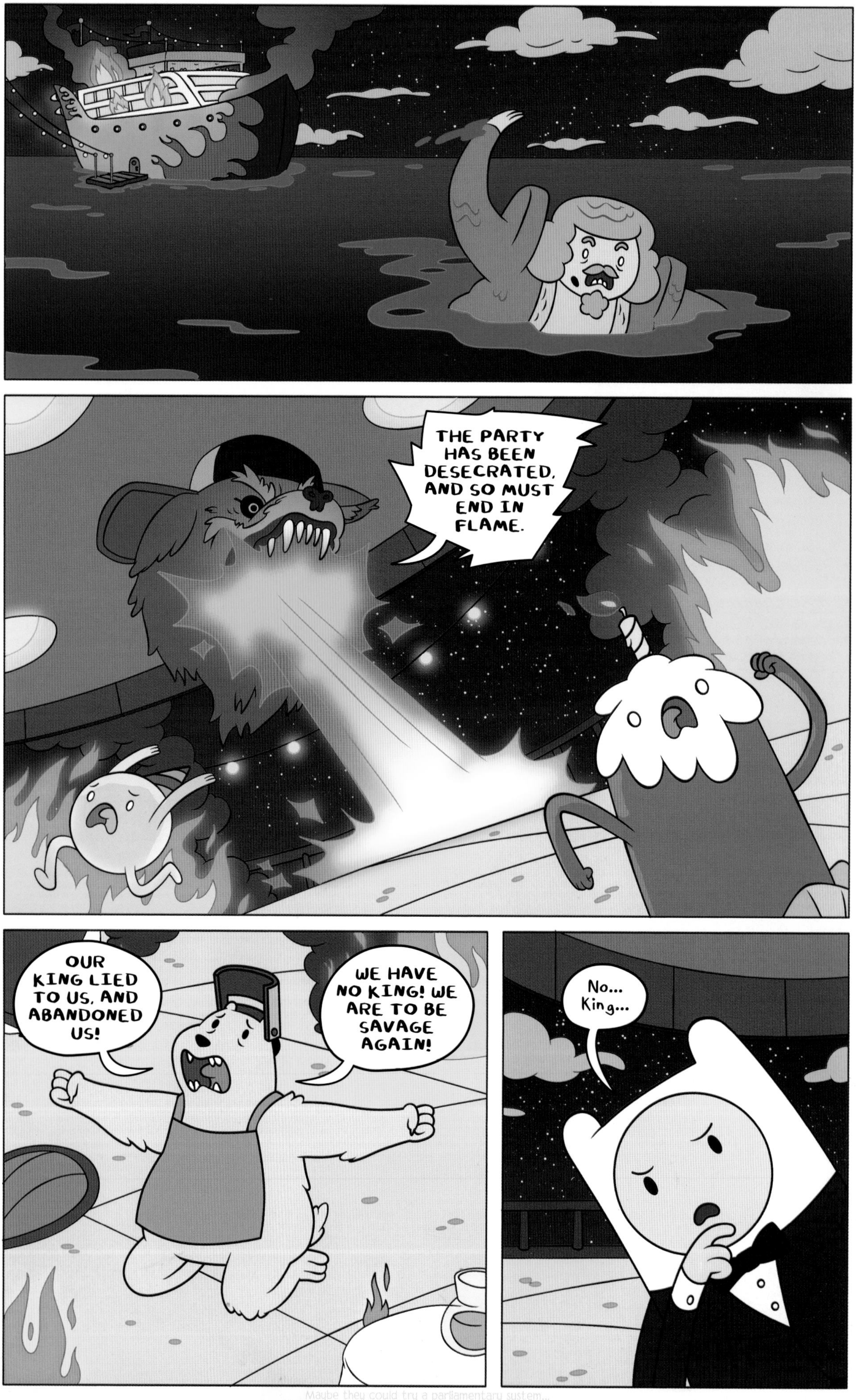
THE PARTY HAS BEEN DESECRATED, AND SO MUST END IN FLAME.
OUR KING LIED TO US, AND ABANDONED US!
WE HAVE NO KING! WE ARE TO BE SAVAGE AGAIN!
No... King...

Maybe they could try a parliamentary system...

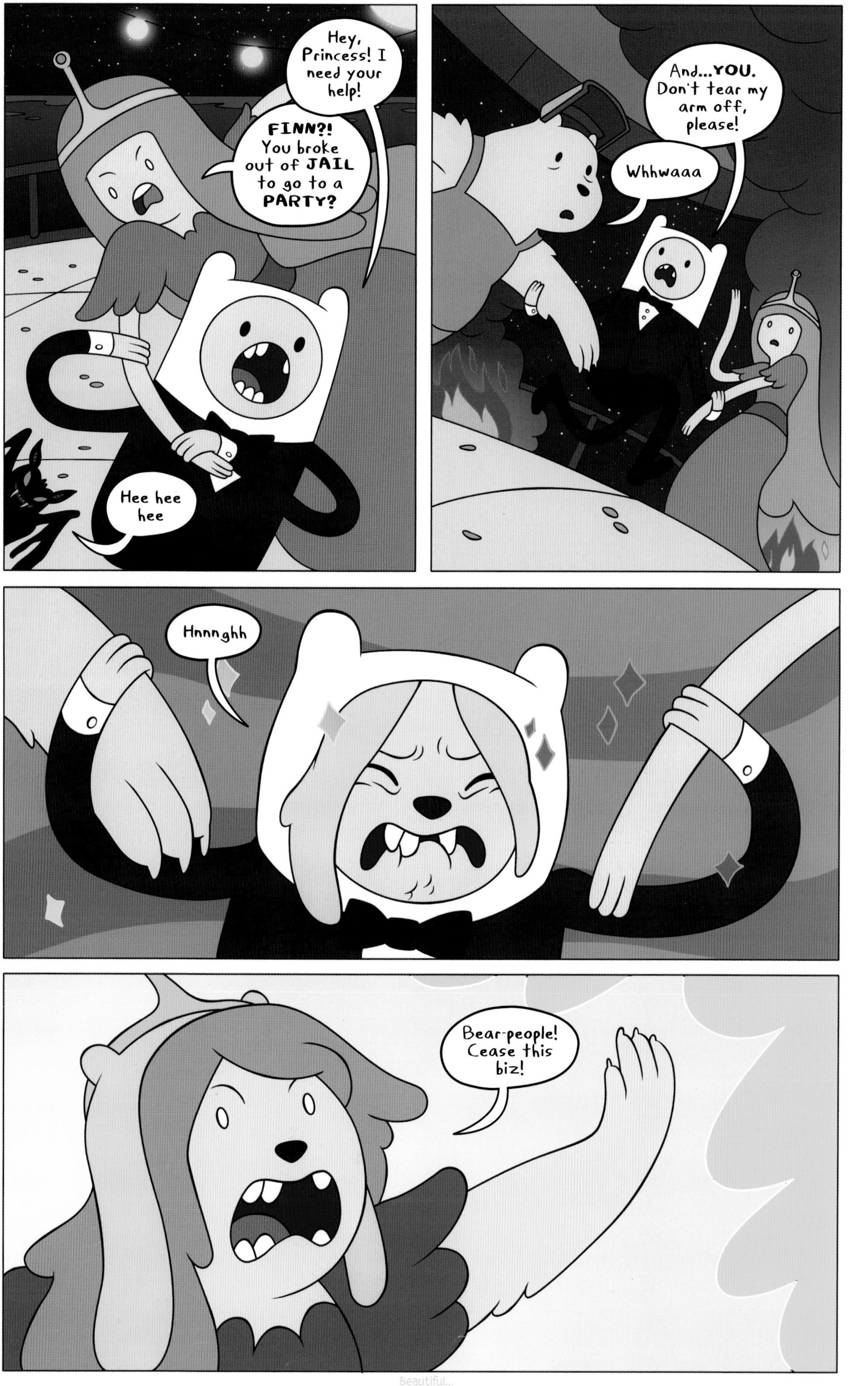
Hey, Princess! I need your help!
FINN?! You broke out of JAIL to go to a PARTY?
Hee hee hee
And...YOU. Don't tear my arm off, please!
Whhwaaa
Hnnnghh
Bear-people! Cease this biz!

Finn... what are you...

We no longer have a **SCAMMO KING**, but we still have...

ME! Your **PRINCESS!**

And I... **DO-ETH DECREE!** We should all knock it off! Get back in your boats and go home!

Sure, okay.

PHEW.

But Finn... the bears **DON'T** actually have a Princess.

Here.

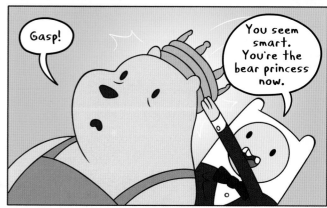

Gasp!

You seem smart. You're the bear princess now.

Politics are confusing.

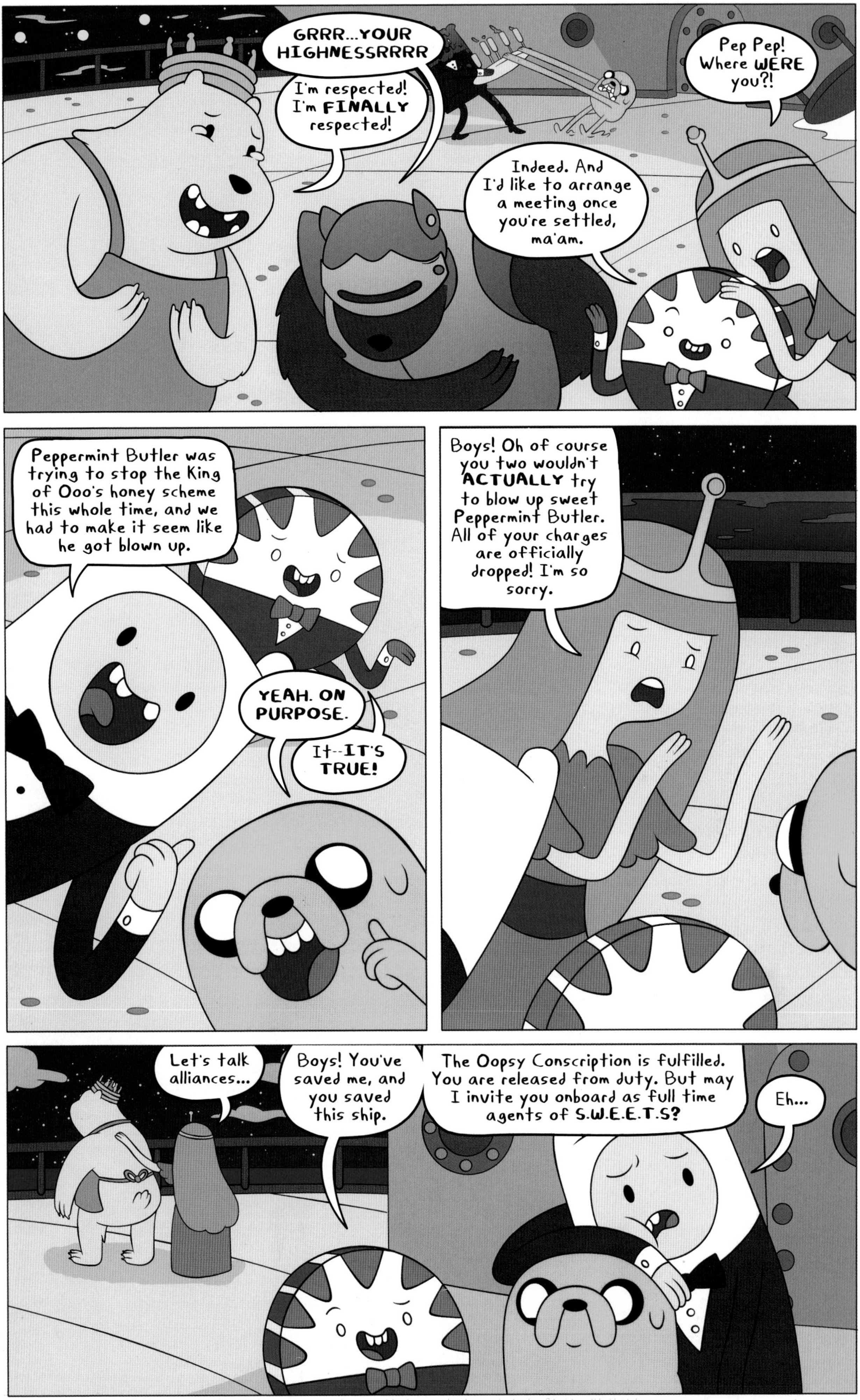
GRRR...YOUR HIGHNESSRRRR
I'm respected! I'm FINALLY respected!
Pep Pep! Where WERE you?!
Indeed. And I'd like to arrange a meeting once you're settled, ma'am.
Peppermint Butler was trying to stop the King of Ooo's honey scheme this whole time, and we had to make it seem like he got blown up.
YEAH. ON PURPOSE.
It--IT'S TRUE!
Boys! Oh of course you two wouldn't ACTUALLY try to blow up sweet Peppermint Butler. All of your charges are officially dropped! I'm so sorry.
Let's talk alliances...
Boys! You've saved me, and you saved this ship.
The Oopsy Conscription is fulfilled. You are released from duty. But may I invite you onboard as full time agents of S.W.E.E.T.S?
Eh...
You stick a crown on a bear, suddenly everybody wants to be friends with that bear.

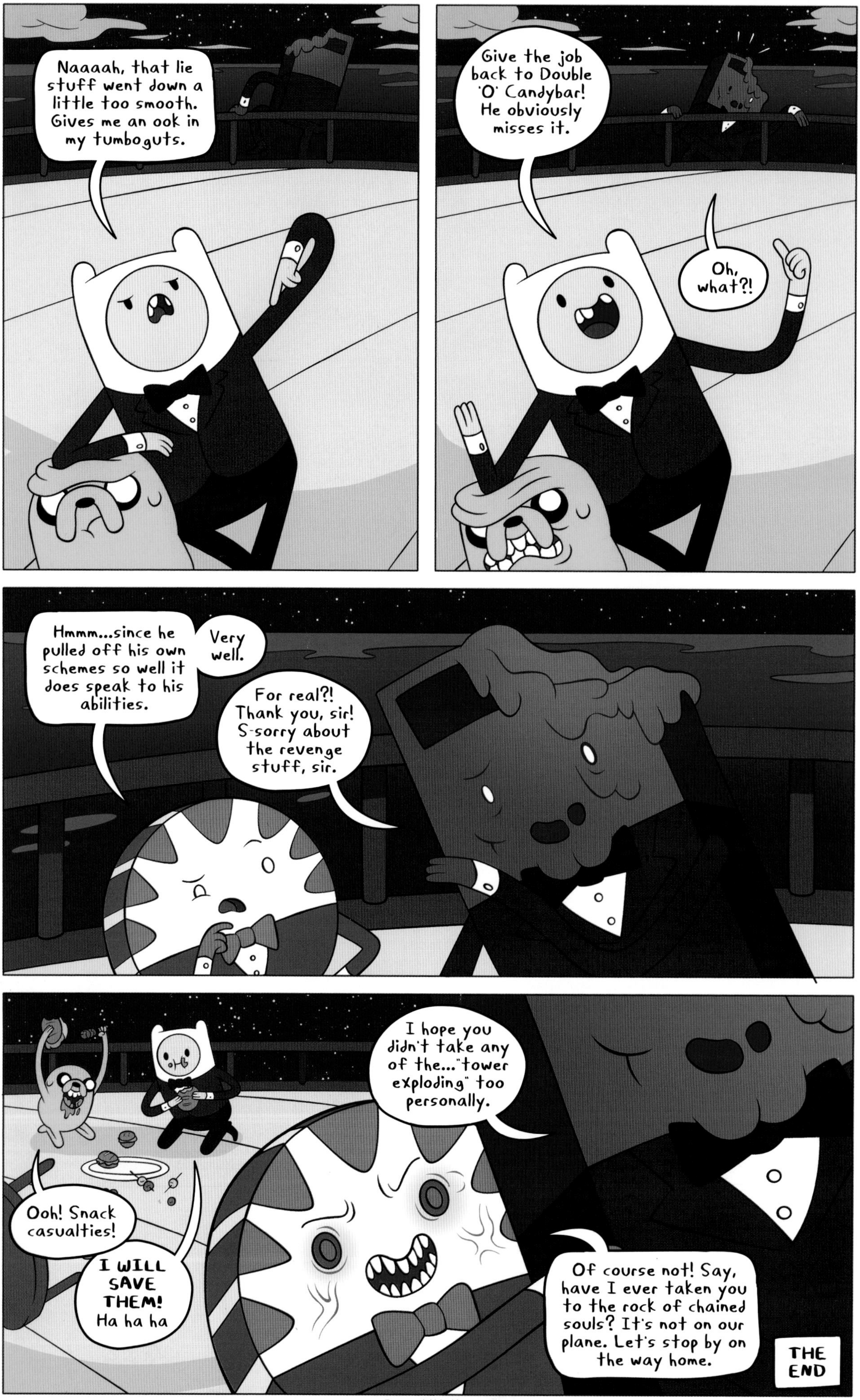
Naaaah, that lie stuff went down a little too smooth. Gives me an ook in my tumboguts.
Give the job back to Double 'O' Candybar! He obviously misses it.
Oh, what?!
Hmmm...since he pulled off his own schemes so well it does speak to his abilities.
Very well.
For real?! Thank you, sir! S-sorry about the revenge stuff, sir.
Ooh! Snack casualties!
I WILL SAVE THEM! Ha ha ha
I hope you didn't take any of the..."tower exploding" too personally.
Of course not! Say, have I ever taken you to the rock of chained souls? It's not on our plane. Let's stop by on the way home.
THE END

For real this time.

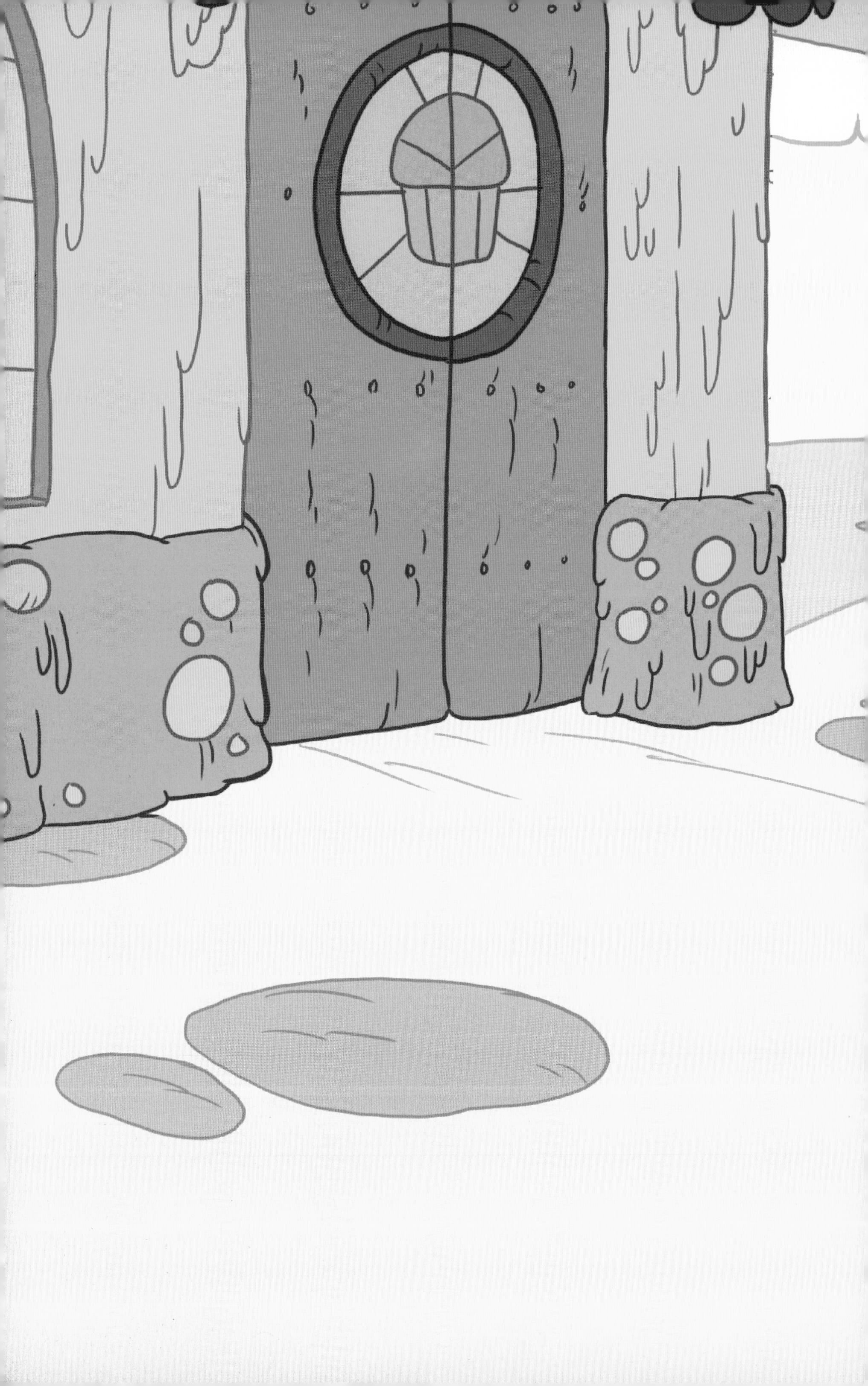

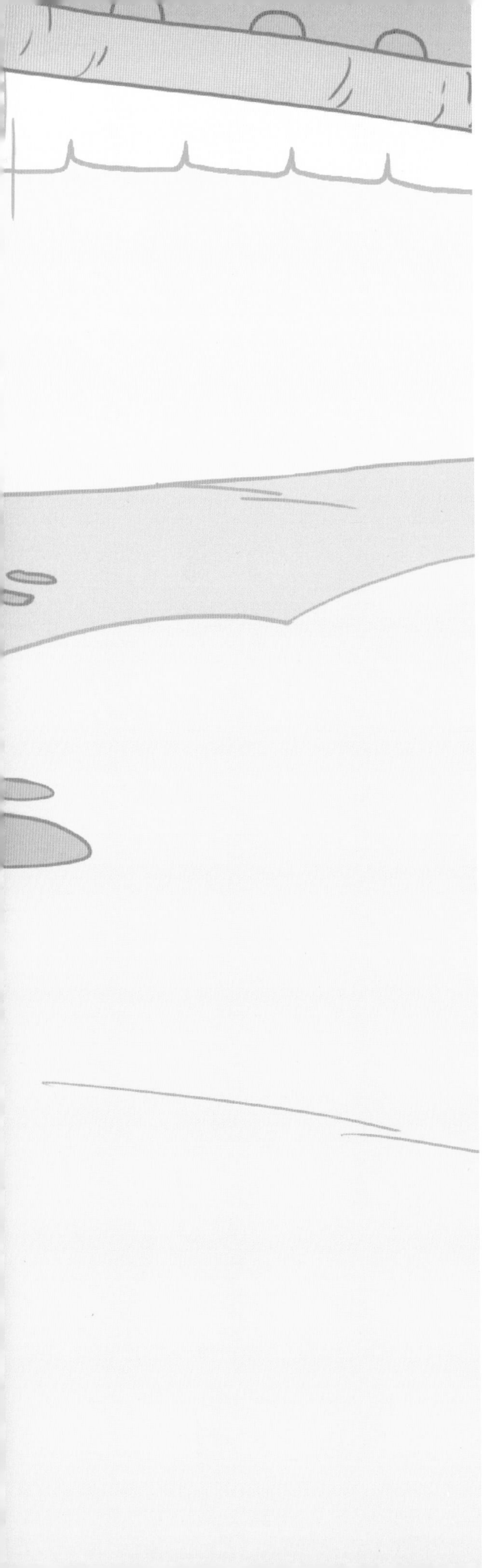

COVER GALLERY

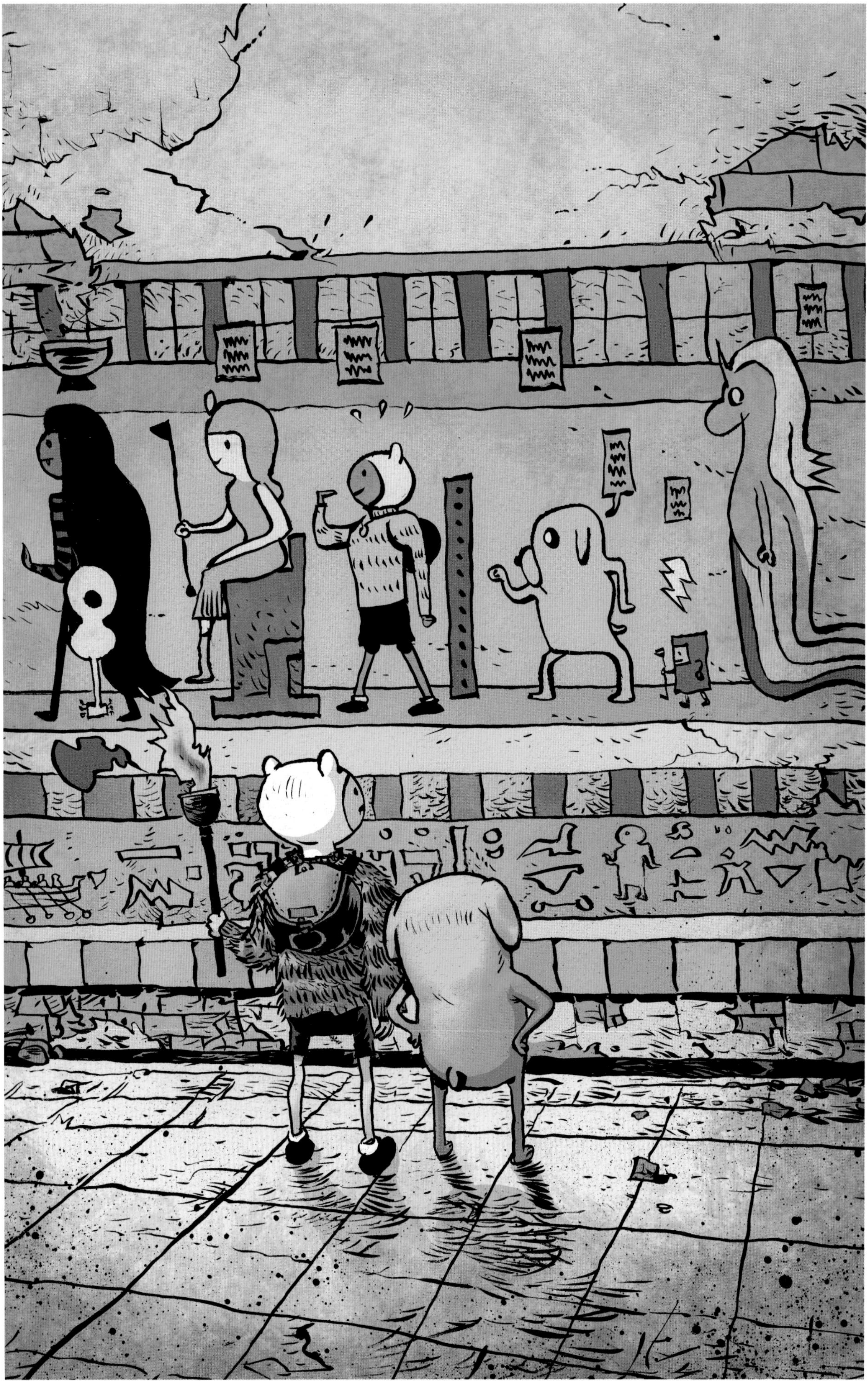

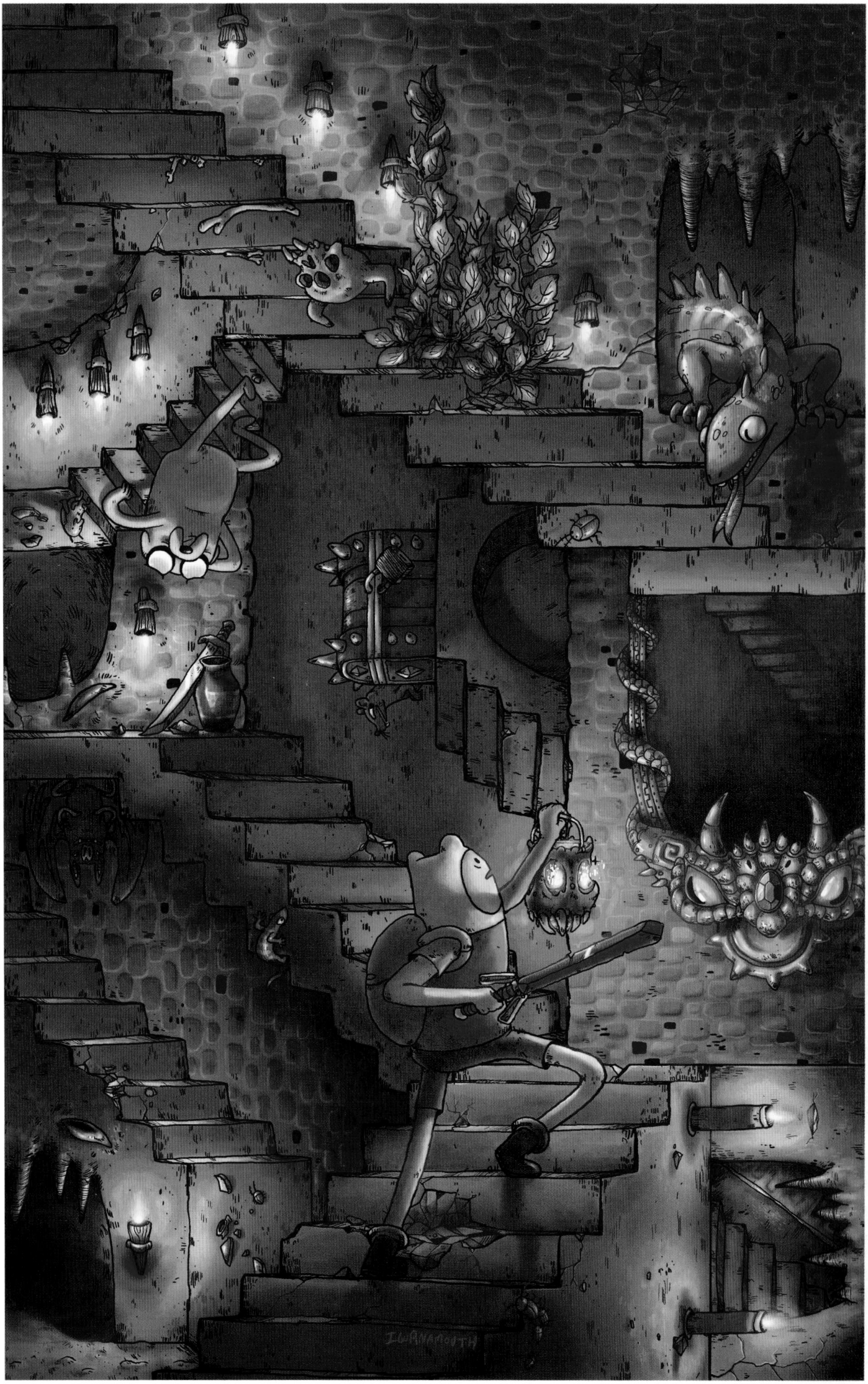

ISSUE FORTY SUBSCRIPTION | LAURA DAWSON

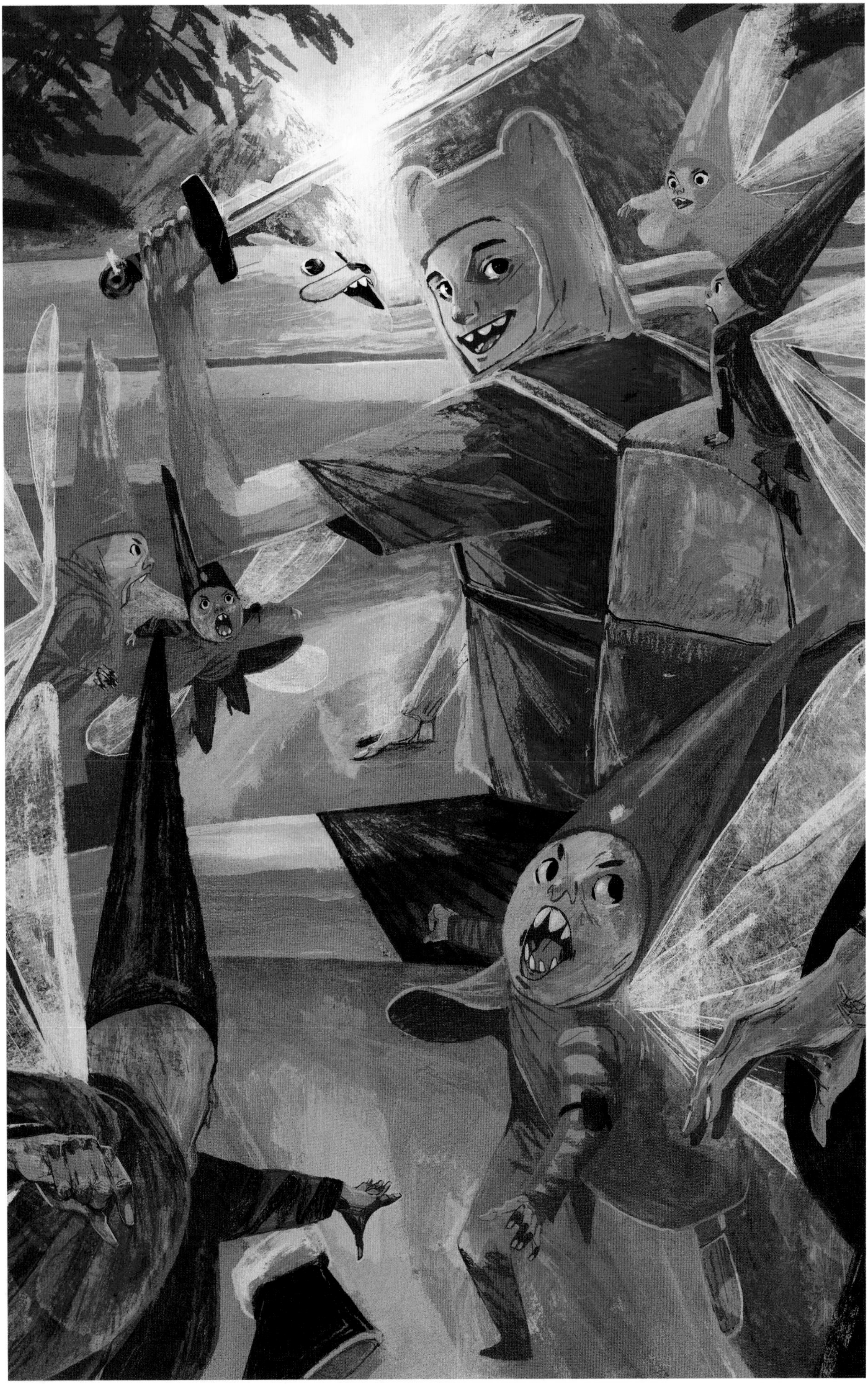

ISSUE FORTY VARIANT | SIMON LECLERC

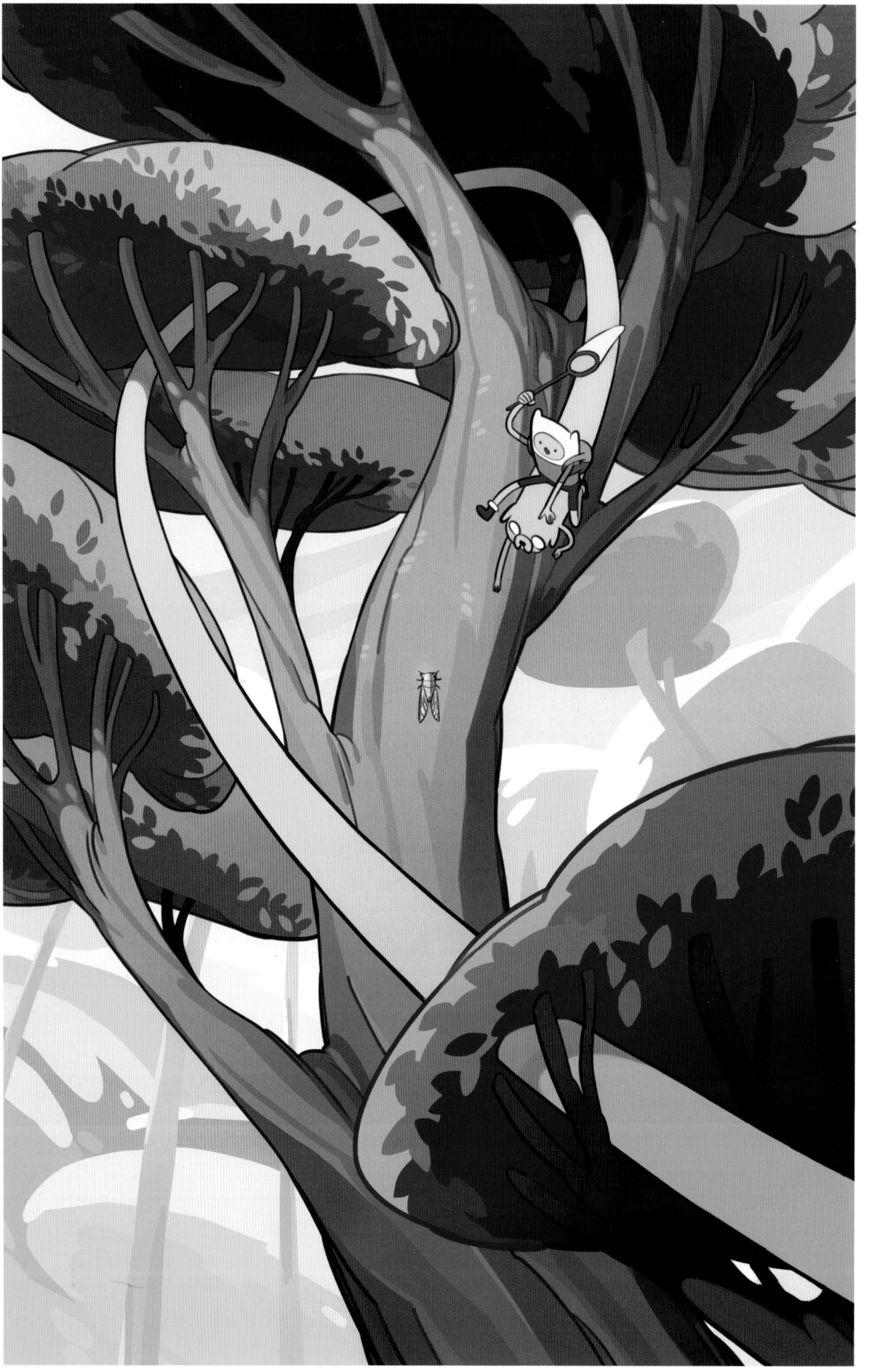

ISSUE FORTY HASTINGS EXCLUSIVE | VIVIAN NG

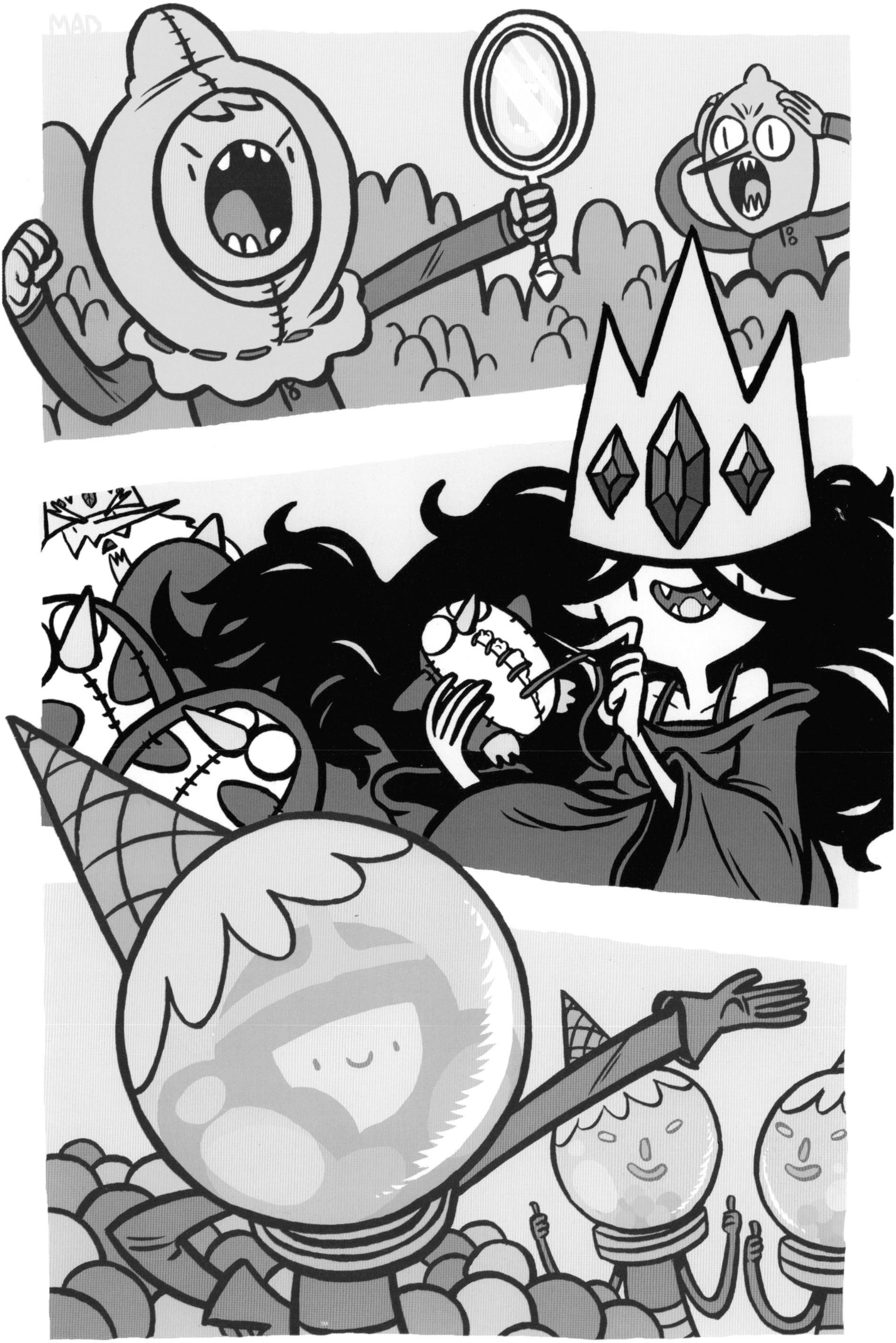
MAD

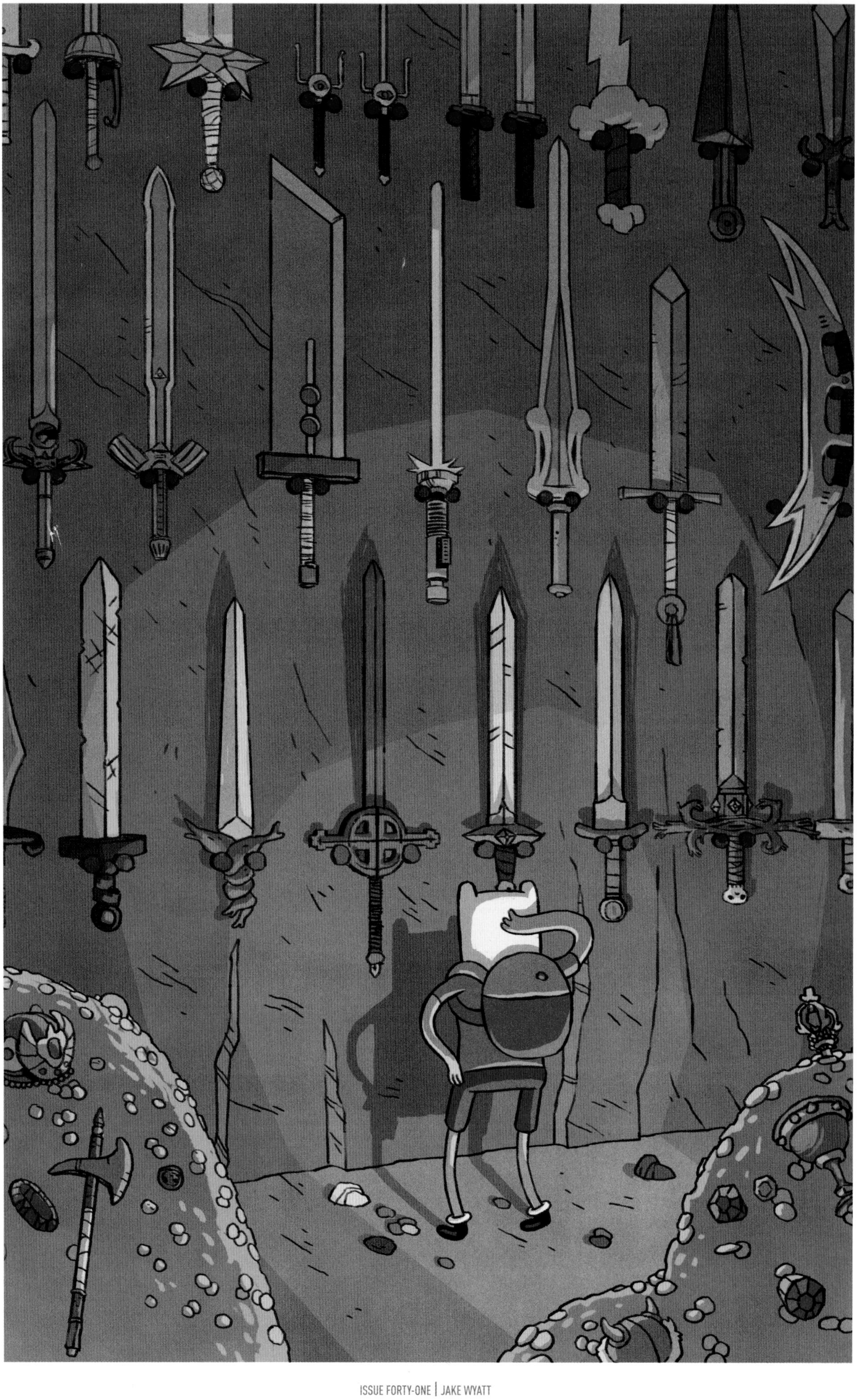

ISSUE FORTY-ONE | JAKE WYATT

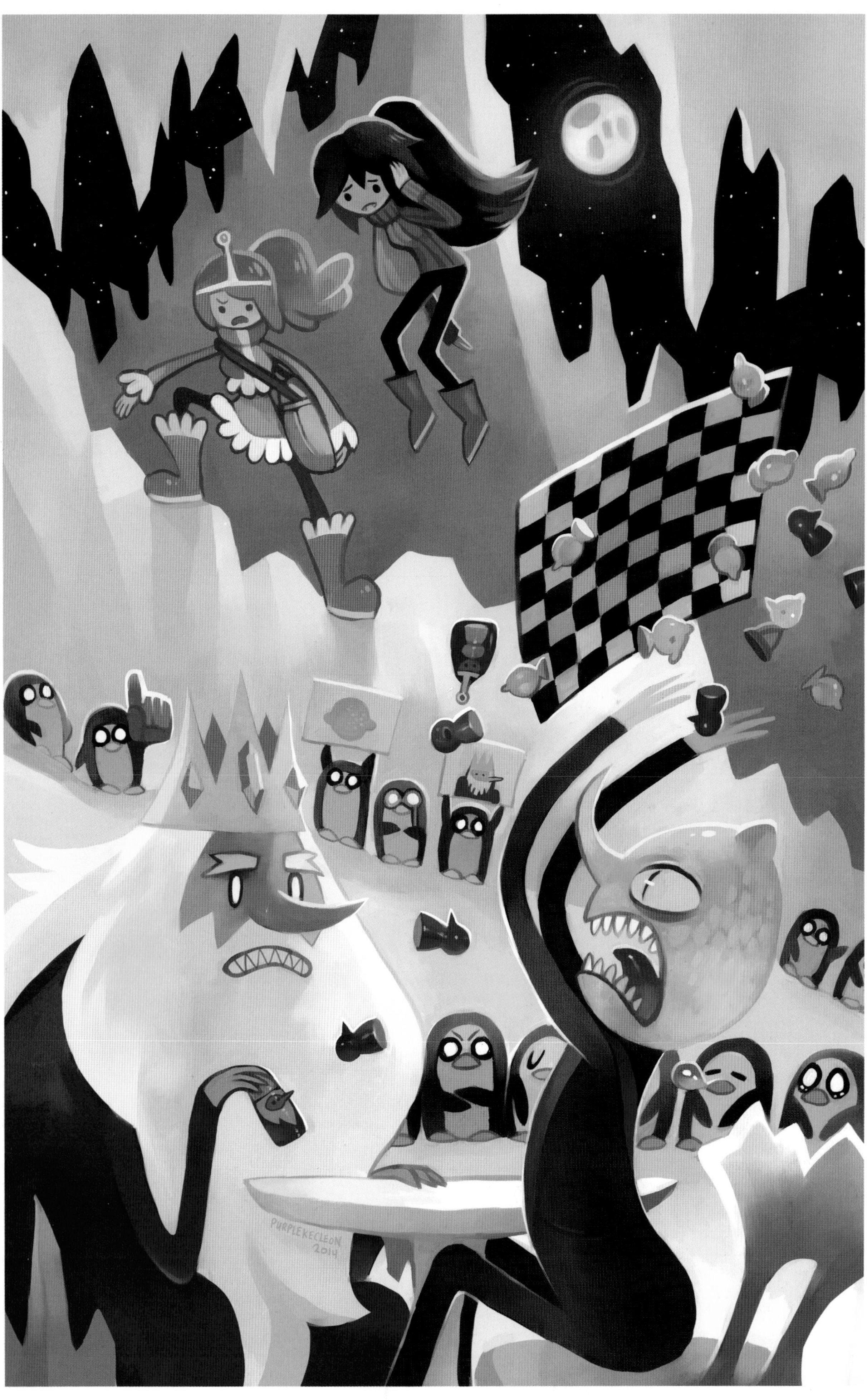
PURPLEKECLEON
2014

ISSUE FORTY-ONE SUBSCRIPTION | MELANIE HERRING

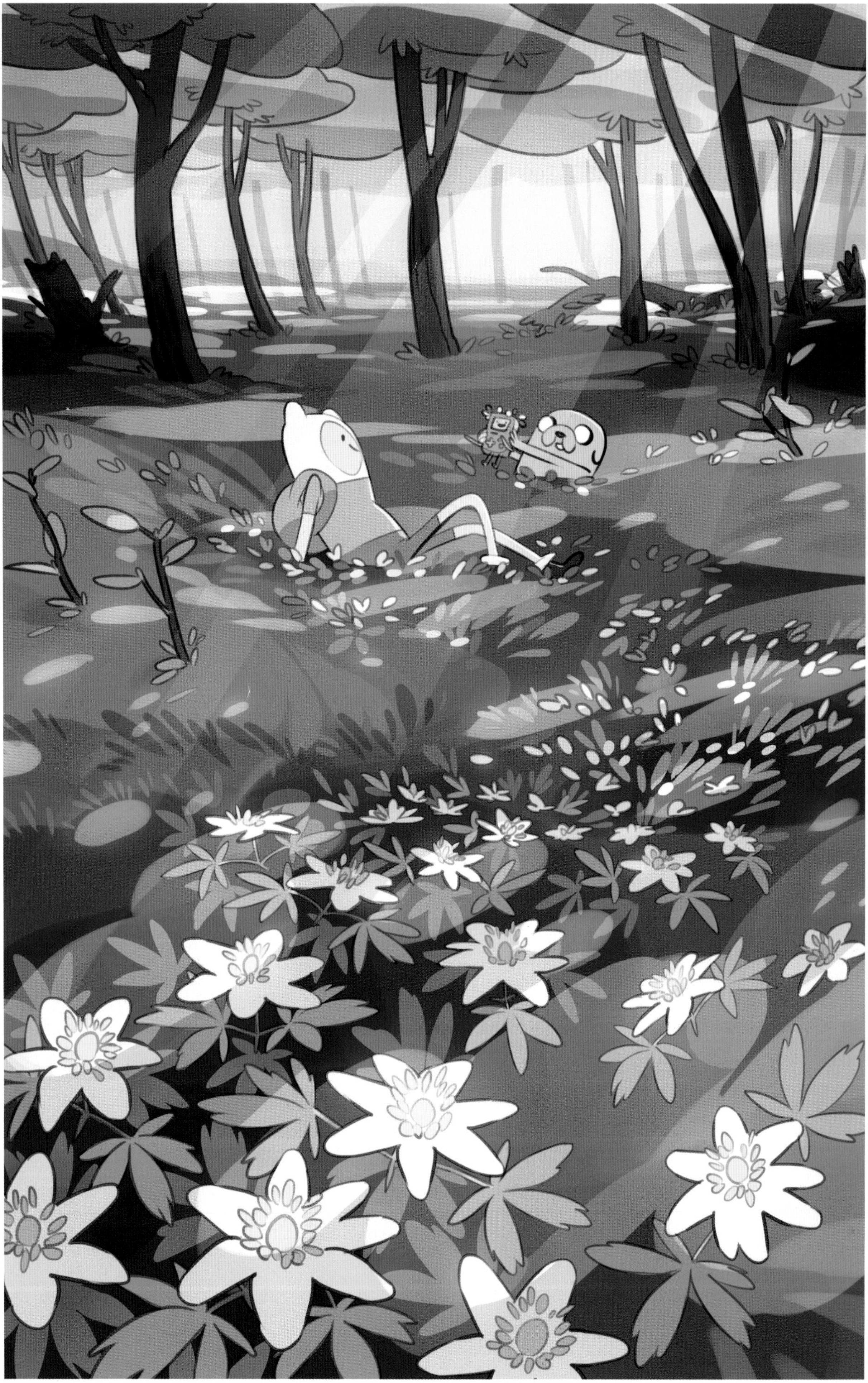

ISSUE FORTY-TWO | VIVIAN NG

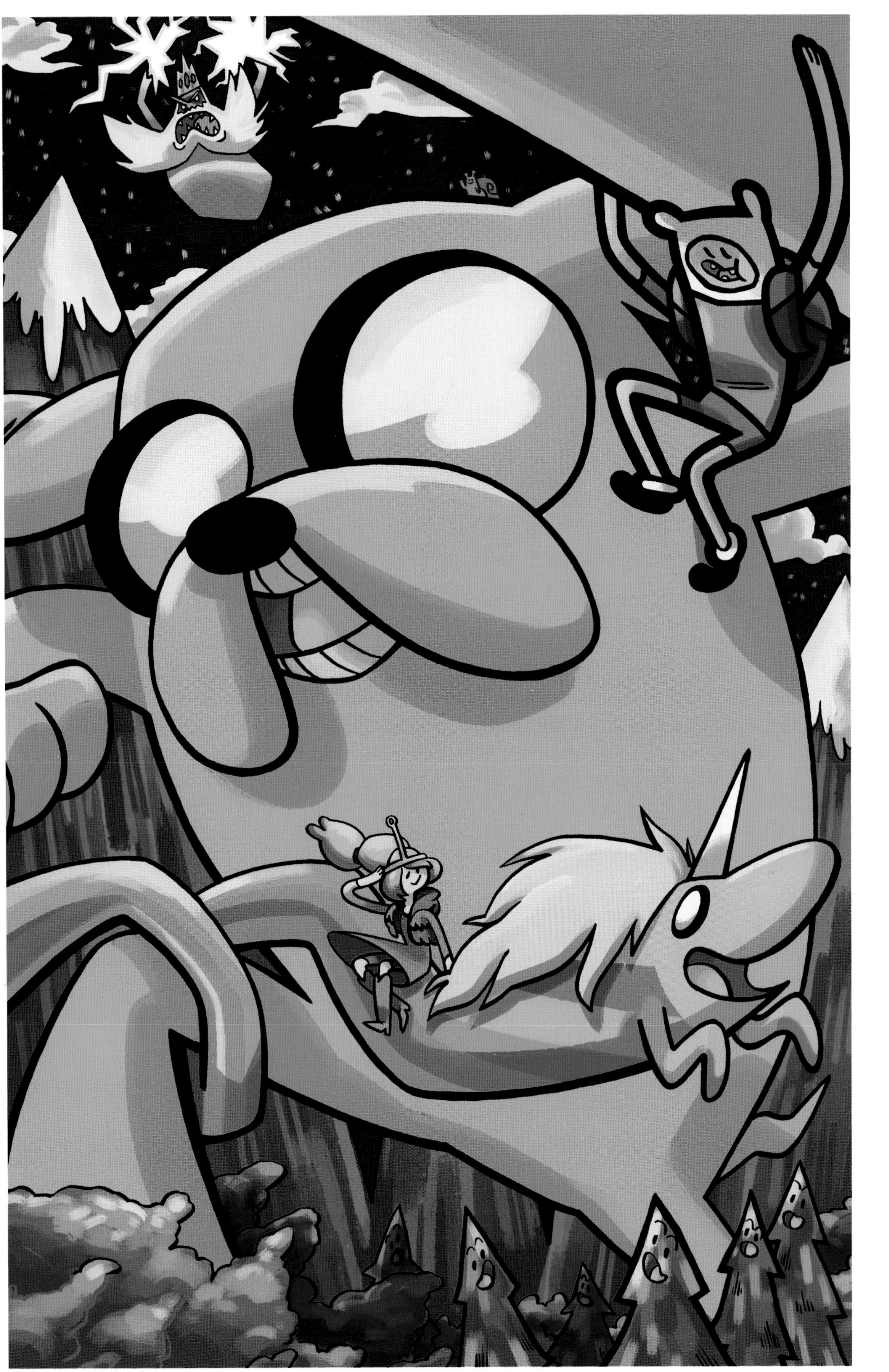

ISSUE FORTY-TWO SUBSCRIPTION | MYCHAL AMANN

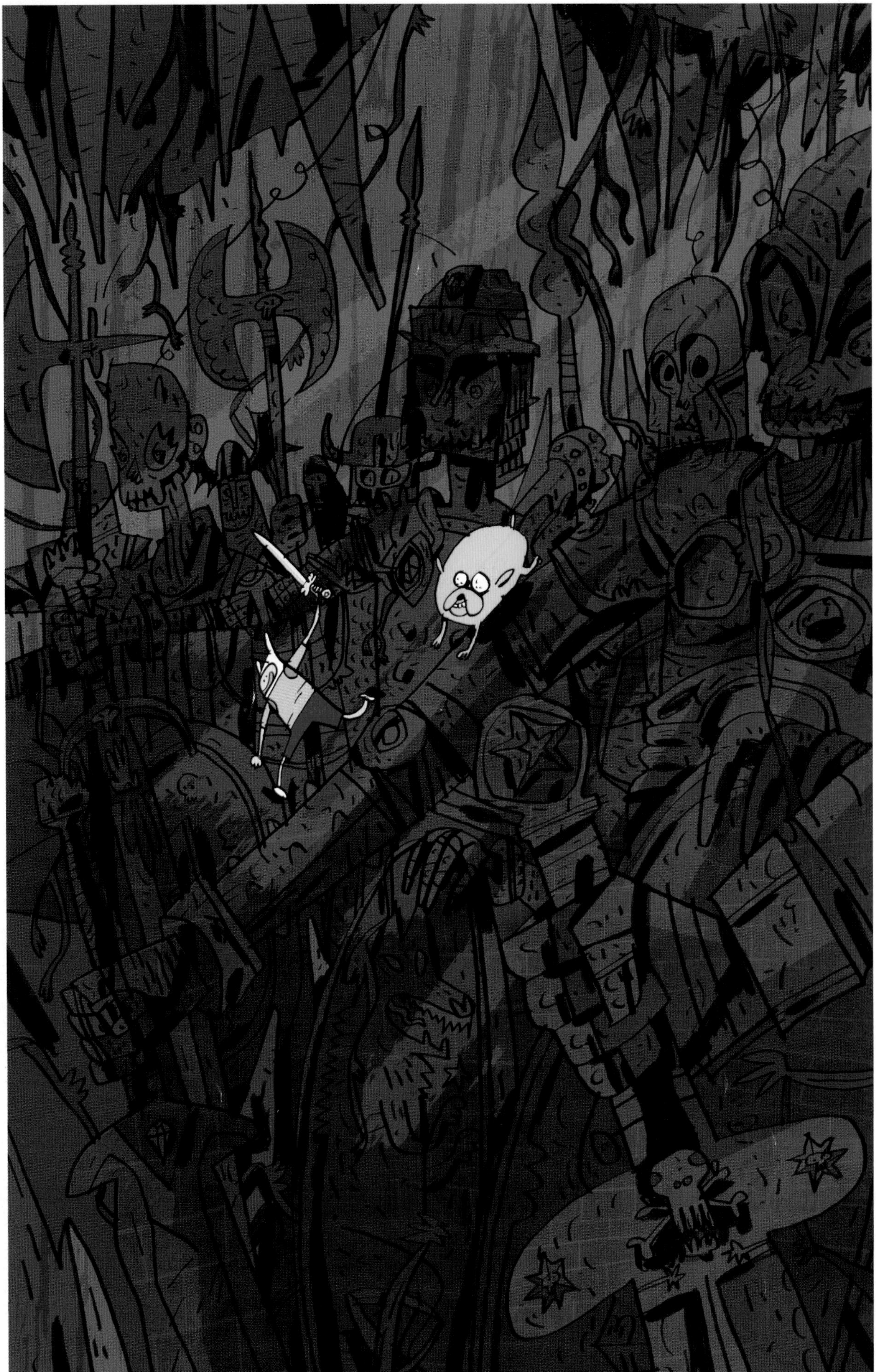

ISSUE FORTY-THREE | WARICK JOHNSON CADWELL

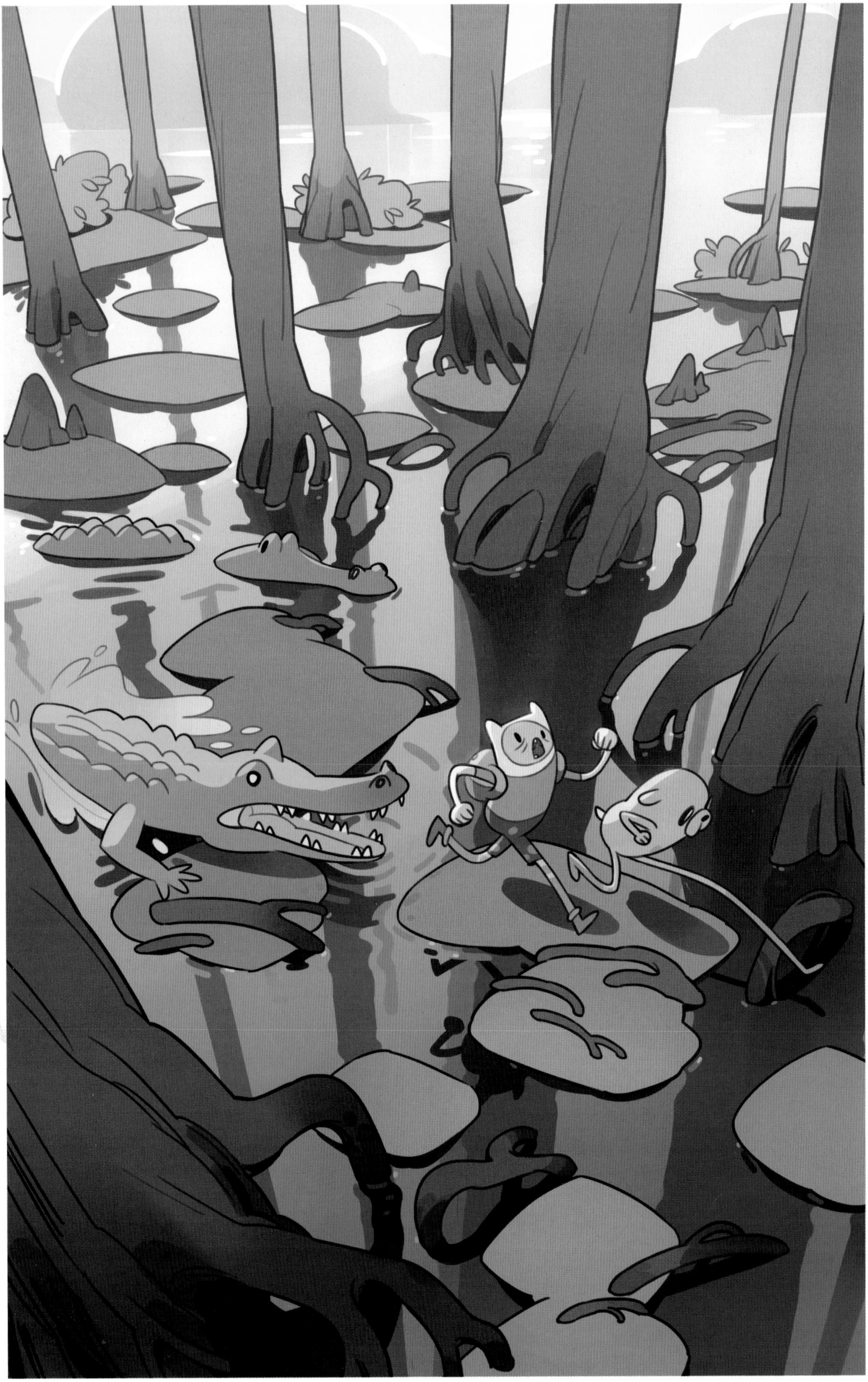

ISSUE FORTY-THREE SUBSCRIPTION | VIVIAN NG

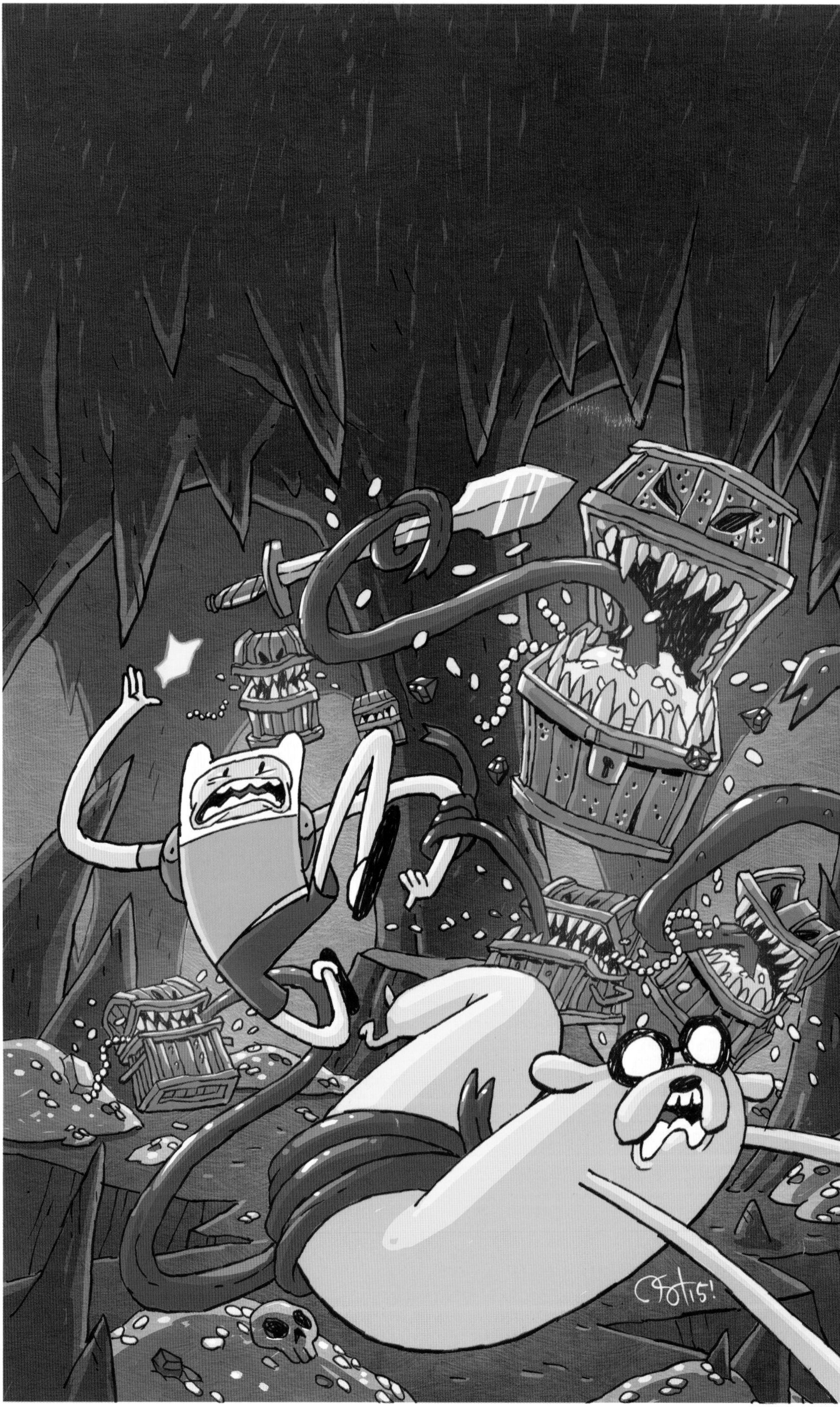

ISSUE FORTY-FOUR | DEREK HUNTER

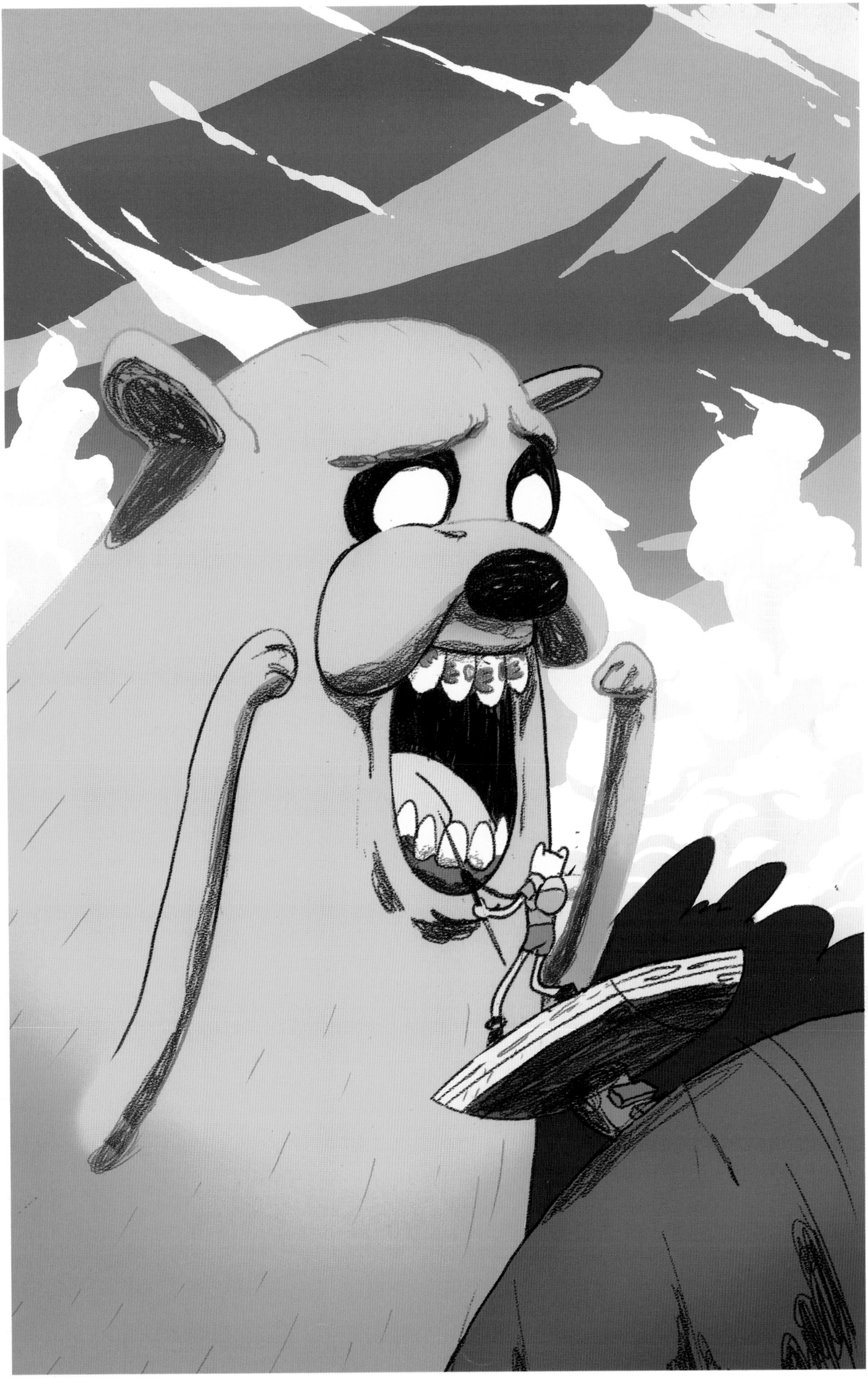

ISSUE FORTY-FOUR SUBSCRIPTION | CHRIS KINDRED

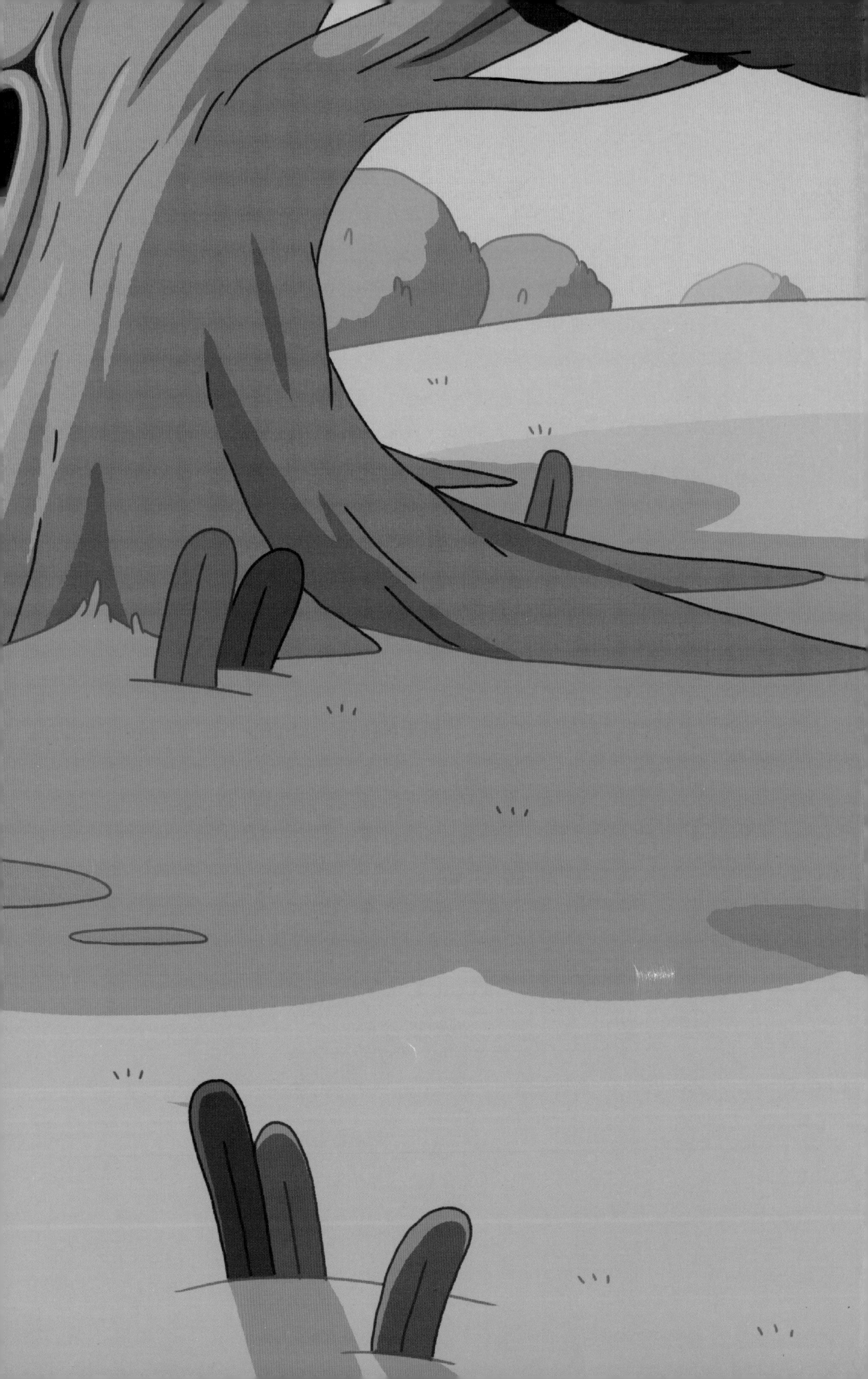

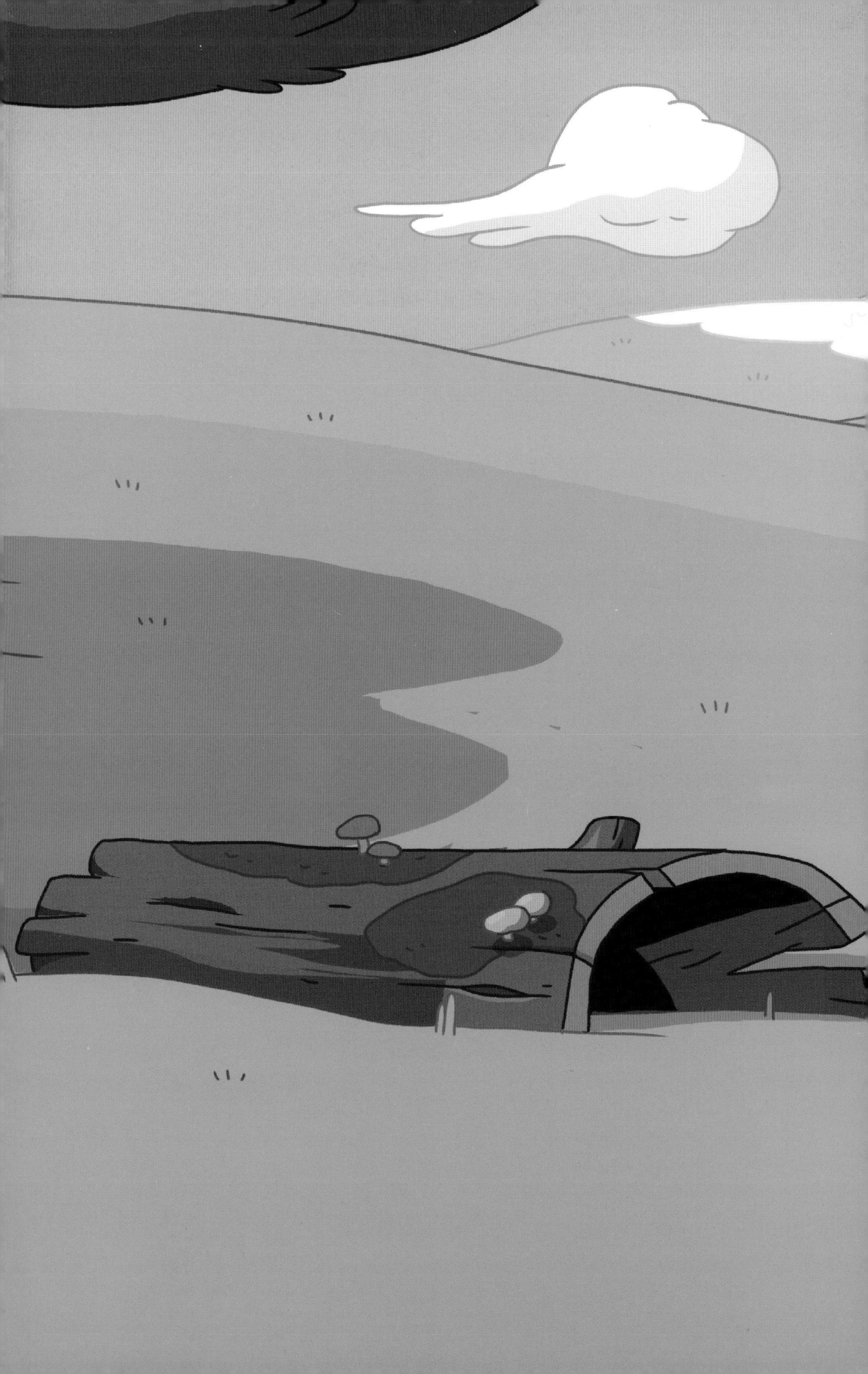

BEHIND THE SCENES

BEHIND THE SCENES

by Christopher Hastings

IT'S MAGIC MAN!

Issue 40 was a very special treat to write.

I really liked the precedent that Ryan North set with his run as writer on this title. Every fifth issue would be a special one shot, and in particular he'd try to do things that just wouldn't happen on the show. So this was my first chance to try the same, and what I decided on was a MAGIC TRIIIIICK! Courtesy of Magic Man, of course. Here is the secret to writing BMO's noir dialogue: put on the noirest possible music, and say everything you write out loud in the graveliest possible voice you can muster. If you follow these steps, you will produce insanely noir dialogue that is amazing. Use this secret well, my friends.

As you read this story, you can follow along with Magic Man speaking directly to you, the reader, through the comic. Follow his instructions, and you will find that the choices you make will actually affect the action in the story below. How can we achieve such an amazing feat in a static medium like a comic book? Easy! The weeks I would normally spend writing an issue of the comic, I instead spent gathering mystic energy from "power points" across the planet. With great focus and energy, I carefully infused every copy of the comic with reality bending arcane power.

I also watched all the episodes of Star Trek with Q in them, because Magic Man is a lot like Q.

Zachary also did an amazing job with this issue. He made sure to keep the Magic Man story going while keeping the readers engaged in everything that was happening to Finn and Jake. There was a lot of stuff happening this issue, but the most important thing was that wishes were granted.

Kind of.

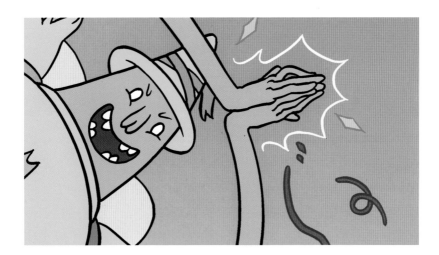

IT'S THE HUMAN, FINN THE HUMAN...

Issues 41-44 were one of those occurrences that felt like following natural paths set up by episodes of the show, and seeing what weird places you could go down with them. I love when *Adventure Time* does style or genre parodies, and I thought it high time to do a good old fashioned spy story.

So of course Finn and Jake would kind of mess things up.

It made total sense to me that Peppermint Butler, in all his princess serving ways would head a secret agency to protect the candy crown. And I love the goofy con man, the King of Ooo. He was the perfect villain for the story, and I really just wanted to see more of this character I love from the show! Beyond that, it was juggling a lot of notecards so that the twisty, backstab-y plot made sense in the end. Stuff like "Finn gets the watch HERE, but then loses it HERE, so the explosion goes off THERE, but then we have THIS GUY HERE so that later we can reveal THIS OTHER THING" and this sentence would make a lot more sense if I weren't so determined not to spoil the very story you might not have read yet, that is in THIS BOOK RIGHT HERE.

The best thing about this story was the chance to take a deep dive into the spy genre. I mean, everyone should do that at one point in their life but it was fun getting to go over some of the classics to see what elements lend themselves well to *Adventure Time*.

The truth was, a lot of them did.

I also used this as an excuse for jokes and puns. There are probably too many puns in here but I hope you enjoyed them as much as I did when they all came together.

Thanks for picking up this book and supporting this series!

Thanks!

—Chris

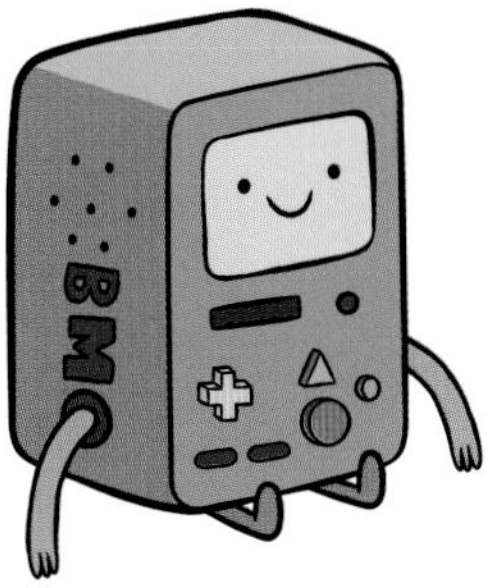
BMO

Christopher Hastings is a writer who mostly works in comic books. He is the author of *The Adventures of Dr. McNinja*, a continuing online comic series with book collections available from Dark Horse Comics. He also writes the ongoing *Adventure Time* comic series, and the *Unbelievable Gwenpool*, which he co-created. Christopher has also written *Vote Loki*, *Longshot Saves the Marvel Universe*, and a smattering of *Deadpool* comics.

Zachary Sterling is a New York Times Best-Selling illustrator, designer and sequential artist based in Portland, OR. Best known as the artist on BOOM! Studio's *Adventure Time* comic and prop designer on the *Bee & PuppyCat* cartoon. He studied at *The Pacific Northwest College of Art*, *Art Insitute of Portland* and interned at *Periscope Studio.*

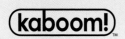

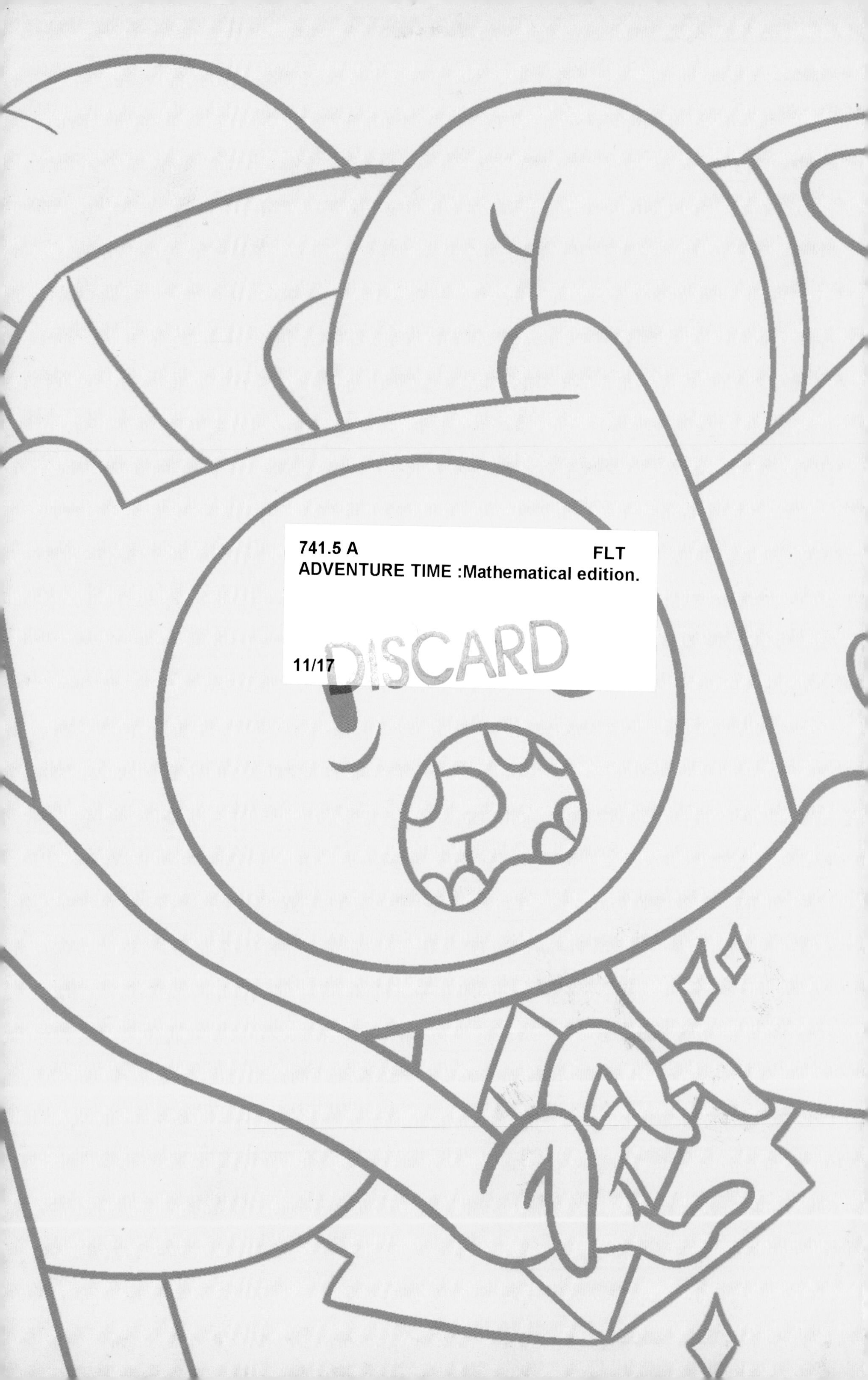